ANNE TYLER

Anne Tyler was born in Minneapolis, Minnesota, in 1941 and grew up in Raleigh, North Carolina. She is the Pulitzer Prize-winning author of *Breathing Lessons* and many other bestselling novels, including *The Accidental Tourist, Dinner at the Homesick Restaurant, Saint Maybe, Ladder of Years, A Patchwork Planet, Back When We Were Grownups, The Amateur Marriage, Digging to America* and *The Beginner's Goodbye*. In 2012 she received the *Sunday Times* Award for literary excellence, which recognises a lifetime's achievement in books. In 2015 *A Spool of Blue Thread* was a *Sunday Times* bestseller and shortlisted for both the Baileys Women's Prize for Fiction and the Man Booker Prize.

ANNE TYLER

The Accidental Tourist

VINTAGE

36
Vintage
20 Vauxhall Bridge Road,
London SW1V 2SA

Vintage is part of the Penguin Random House group of companies
whose addresses can be found at global.penguinrandomhouse.com

Penguin
Random House
UK

This edition reissued in Vintage in 2016
First published in Vintage in 1992
First published in Great Britain by Chatto & Windus in 1985

www.vintage-books.co.uk

A CIP catalogue record for this book is available
from the British Library

ISBN 9780099480013

Printed and bound in Great Britain by Clays Ltd, Elcograf S.p.A.

Penguin Random House is committed to a sustainable future
for our business, our readers and our planet. This book is made
from Forest Stewardship Council® certified paper.

MIX
Paper from
responsible sources
FSC® C018179

— They were supposed to stay at the beach a week, but neither of them had the heart for it and they decided to come back early. Macon drove. Sarah sat next to him, leaning her head against the side window. Chips of cloudy sky showed through her tangled brown curls.

Macon wore a formal summer suit, his traveling suit—much more logical for traveling than jeans, he always said. Jeans had those stiff, hard seams and those rivets. Sarah wore a strapless terry beach dress. They might have been returning from two entirely different trips. Sarah had a tan but Macon didn't. He was a tall, pale, gray-eyed man, with straight fair hair cut close to his head, and his skin was that thin kind that easily burns. He'd kept away from the sun during the middle part of every day.

Just past the start of the divided highway, the sky grew almost black and several enormous drops spattered the windshield. Sarah sat up straight. 'Let's hope it doesn't rain,' she said.

'I don't mind a little rain,' Macon said.

Sarah sat back again, but she kept her eyes on the road.

It was a Thursday morning. There wasn't much traffic. They passed a pickup truck, then a van all covered with stickers from a hundred scenic attractions. The drops on the windshield grew closer together. Macon switched his wipers on. Tick-*swoosh*, they went—a lulling sound; and there was a gentle patter on the roof. Every now and then a gust of wind blew up. Rain flattened the long, pale grass at the sides of the road. It slanted across the boat lots, lumberyards, and discount furniture outlets, which already had a darkened look as if here it might have been raining for some time.

'Can you see all right?' Sarah asked.

'Of course,' Macon said. 'This is nothing.'

They arrived behind a trailer truck whose rear wheels sent out arcs of spray. Macon swung to the left and passed. There was a moment of watery blindness till the truck had dropped behind. Sarah gripped the dashboard with one hand.

'I don't know how you can see to drive,' she said.

'Maybe you should put on your glasses.'

'Putting on my glasses would help you to see?'

'Not me; you,' Macon said. 'You're focused on the windshield instead of the road.'

Sarah continued to grip the dashboard. She had a broad, smooth face that gave an impression of calm, but if you looked closely you'd notice the tension at the corners of her eyes.

The car drew in around them like a room. Their breaths fogged the windows. Earlier the air conditioner had been running and now some artificial chill remained, quickly turning dank, carrying with it the smell of mildew. They shot through an underpass. The rain stopped completely for one blank, startling second. Sarah gave a little gasp of relief, but even before it was uttered, the hammering on the roof resumed. She turned and gazed back longingly at the underpass. Macon sped ahead, with his hands relaxed on the wheel.

'Did you notice that boy with the motorcycle?' Sarah asked. She had to raise her voice; a steady, insistent roaring sound engulfed them.

'What boy?'

'He was parked beneath the underpass.'

'It's crazy to ride a motorcycle on a day like today,' Macon said. 'Crazy to ride one any day. You're so exposed to the elements.'

'We could do that,' Sarah said. 'Stop and wait it out.'

'Sarah, if I felt we were in the slightest danger I'd have pulled over long ago.'

'Well, I don't know that you would have,' Sarah said.

They passed a field where the rain seemed to fall in sheets, layers and layers of rain beating down the cornstalks, flooding the rutted soil. Great lashings of water flung themselves at the windshield. Macon switched his wiper blades to high.

'I don't know that you really care that much,' Sarah said. 'Do you.'

Macon said, 'Care?'

'I said to you the other day, I said, "Macon, now that Ethan's dead I sometimes wonder if there's any point to life." Do you remember what you answered?'

'Well, not offhand,' Macon said.

'You said, "Honey, to tell the truth, it never seemed to me there was all that much point to begin with." Those were your exact words.'

'Um . . .'

'And you don't even know what was wrong with that.'

'No, I guess I don't,' Macon said.

He passed a line of cars that had parked at the side of the road, their windows opaque, their gleaming surfaces bouncing back the rain in shallow explosions. One car was slightly tipped, as if about to fall into the muddy torrent that churned and raced in the gully. Macon kept a steady speed.

'You're not a comfort, Macon,' Sarah said.

'Honey, I'm trying to be.'

'You just go on your same old way like before. Your little routines and rituals, depressing habits, day after day. No comfort at all.'

'Shouldn't I need comfort too?' Macon asked. 'You're not the only one, Sarah. I don't know why you feel it's your loss alone.'

'Well, I just do, sometimes,' Sarah said.

They were quiet a moment. A wide lake, it seemed, in the center of the highway crashed against the underside of the car and slammed it to the right. Macon pumped his brakes and drove on.

'This rain, for instance,' Sarah said. 'You know it makes me nervous. What harm would it do to wait it out? You'd be showing some concern. You'd be telling me we're in this together.'

Macon peered through the windshield, which was streaming so that it seemed marbled. He said, 'I've got a system, Sarah. You know I drive according to a system.'

'You and your systems!'

'Also,' he said, 'if you don't see any point to life, I can't figure why a rainstorm would make you nervous.'

Sarah slumped in her seat.

'Will you look at that!' he said. 'A mobile home's washed clear across that trailer park.'

'Macon, I want a divorce,' Sarah told him.

Macon braked and glanced over at her. 'What?' he said. The car swerved. He had to face forward again. 'What did I say?' he asked. 'What did it mean?'

'I just can't live with you anymore,' Sarah said.

Macon went on watching the road, but his nose seemed sharper and whiter, as if the skin of his face had been pulled tight. He cleared his throat. He said, 'Honey. Listen. It's been a hard year. We've had a hard time. People who lose a child often feel this way; everybody says so; everybody says it's a terrible strain on a marriage—'

'I'd like to find a place of my own as soon as we get back,' Sarah told him.

'Place of your own,' Macon echoed, but he spoke so softly, and the rain beat so loudly on the roof, it looked as if he were only moving his lips. 'Well,' he said. 'All right. If that's what you really want.'

'You can keep the house,' Sarah said. 'You never did like moving.'

For some reason, it was this that made her finally break down. She turned away sharply. Macon switched his right blinker on. He pulled into a Texaco station, parked beneath the overhang, and cut off the engine. Then he started rubbing his knees with his palms. Sarah huddled in her corner. The only sound was the drumming of rain on the overhang far above them.

2

—— After his wife left him, Macon had thought the house would seem larger. Instead, he felt more crowded. The windows shrank. The ceilings lowered. There was something insistent about the furniture, as if it were pressing in on him.

Of course Sarah's personal belongings were gone, the little things like clothes and jewelry. But it emerged that some of the big things were more personal than he'd imagined. There was the drop-leaf desk in the living room, its pigeonholes stuffed with her clutter of torn envelopes and unanswered letters. There was the radio in the kitchen, set to play 98 Rock. (She liked to keep in touch with her students, she used to say in the old days, as she hummed and jittered her way around the breakfast table.) There was the chaise out back where she had sunbathed, planted in the only spot that got any sun at all. He looked at the flowered cushions and marveled at how an empty space could be so full of a person—her faint scent of coconut oil that always made him wish for a piña colada; her wide, gleaming face inscrutable behind dark glasses; her compact body in the skirted swimsuit she had tearfully insisted on buying after her fortieth birthday. Threads of her exuberant hair showed up at the bottom of the sink. Her shelf in the medicine cabinet, stripped, was splashed with drops of liquid rouge in a particular plummy shade that brought her instantly to Macon's mind. He had always disapproved of her messiness but now those spills seemed touching, like colorful toys left on the floor after a child has gone to bed.

The house itself was medium-sized, unexceptional to look at, standing on a street of such houses in an older part of Baltimore. Heavy oak trees hung over it, shading it from the hot summer sun but also blocking breezes. The rooms inside were square and dim. All that remained in Sarah's closet was a brown silk sash hanging on a hook; in her bureau drawers, lint balls and empty perfume bottles. Their son's old room was neatly made up, as sleek as a room in a Holiday Inn. Some places, the walls gave off a kind of echo. Still, Macon noticed he had a tendency to hold his arms close to his body, to walk past furniture sideways, as if he imagined the house could barely accommodate him. He felt too tall. His long, clumsy feet seemed unusually distant. He ducked his head in doorways.

Now was his chance to reorganize, he told himself. He was struck by an incongruous little jolt of interest. The fact was that running a house required some sort of system, and Sarah had never understood that. She was the sort of woman who stored her flatware intermingled. She thought nothing of running a dishwasher with only a handful of forks stacked inside. Macon found that distressing.

He was opposed to dishwashers in general; he believed they wasted energy. Energy saving was a hobby of his, you might say.

He started keeping the kitchen sink filled at all times, adding some chlorine bleach for disinfectant. As he finished using each dish, he dropped it in. On alternate days he pulled the plug and sprayed everything with very hot water. Then he stacked the rinsed dishes in the empty dishwasher—which had become, under his new system, a gigantic storage area.

When he hunkered over the sink to let the spray attachment run, he often had the feeling that Sarah was watching. He sensed that if he slid his eyes just slightly to the left, he would find her with her arms folded across her chest, her head tipped and her full, curved lips meditatively pursed. At first glance she was simply studying his procedure; at second glance (he knew) she was laughing at him. There was a secret little gleam in her eyes that he was all too familiar with. 'I see,' she would say, nodding at some lengthy explanation of his; then he'd look up and catch the gleam and the telltale tuck at one corner of her mouth.

In this vision of her—if you could call it a vision, considering that he never did glance over at her—she was wearing a bright blue dress from the early days of their marriage. He had no idea when she had given that dress up, but certainly it was years and years ago. He almost felt that Sarah was a ghost—that she was dead. In a way (he thought, turning off the faucet), she *was* dead, that young, vivid Sarah from their first enthusiastic apartment on Cold Spring Lane. When he tried to recall those days, any image of Sarah was altered by the fact that she had left him. When he pictured their introduction—back when they were barely out of childhood—it seemed nothing more than the beginning of their parting. When she had looked up at him that first night and rattled the ice cubes in her paper cup, they were already moving toward their last edgy, miserable year together, toward those months when anything either of them said was wrong, toward that sense of narrowly missed connections. They were like people who run to meet, holding out their arms, but their aim is wrong; they pass each other and keep running. It had all amounted to nothing, in the end. He gazed down at the sink, and the warmth from the dishes drifted gently up into his face.

Well, you have to carry on. You have to carry on. He decided to switch his shower from morning to night. This showed adaptability, he felt—some freshness of spirit. While he showered he let the water collect in the tub, and he stalked around in noisy circles, sloshing the day's dirty clothes underfoot. Later he wrung out the clothes and hung them on hangers to dry. Then he dressed in tomorrow's underwear so he wouldn't have to launder any pajamas. In fact, his only real laundry was a load of towels and sheets once a week—just two towels, but quite a lot of sheets. This was because he had developed a system that enabled him to sleep in clean sheets every night without the trouble of bed changing. He'd been proposing the system to Sarah for years, but she was so set in her ways. What he did was strip the mattress of all linens, replacing them with a giant sort of envelope made from one of the seven sheets he had folded and stitched together on the sewing machine. He thought of this invention as a Macon Leary Body Bag. A body bag required no tucking in, was unmussable, easily changeable, and the perfect weight for summer nights. In winter he would have to devise something warmer, but he couldn't think of winter yet. He was barely making it from one day to the next as it was.

At moments—while he was skidding on the mangled clothes in the bathtub or struggling into his body bag on the naked, rust-stained mattress—he realized that he might be carrying things too far. He couldn't explain why, either. He'd always had a fondness for method, but not what you would call a mania. Thinking then of Sarah's lack of method, he wondered if that had got out of hand now too. Maybe all these years, they'd been keeping each other on a reasonable track. Separated, demagnetized somehow, they wandered wildly off course. He pictured Sarah's new apartment, which he had never seen, as chaotic to the point of madness, with sneakers in the oven and the sofa heaped with china. The mere thought of it upset him. He looked gratefully at his own surroundings.

Most of his work was done at home; otherwise he might not have cared so about the mechanics of the household. He had a little study in the spare room off the kitchen. Seated in a stenographer's chair, tapping away at a typewriter that had served him through four years of college, he wrote a series of guidebooks for people forced to travel on business. Ridiculous, when you thought about it: Macon hated travel. He careened through foreign territories on a desperate kind of blitz—squinching his eyes shut and holding his breath and hanging on for dear life, he sometimes imagined—and then settled back home with a sigh of relief to produce his chunky, passport-sized paperbacks. *Accidental Tourist in France. Accidental Tourist in Germany. In Belgium.* No author's name, just a logo: a winged armchair on the cover.

He covered only the cities in these guides, for people taking business trips flew into cities and out again and didn't see the countryside at all. They didn't see the cities, for that matter. Their concern was how to pretend they had never left home. What hotels in Madrid boasted king-sized Beauty-rest mattresses? What restaurants in Tokyo offered Sweet'n'-Low? Did Amsterdam have a McDonald's? Did Mexico City have a Taco Bell? Did any place in Rome serve Chef Boyardee ravioli? Other travelers hoped to discover distinctive local wines; Macon's readers searched for pasteurized and homogenized milk.

As much as he hated the travel, he loved the writing—the virtuous delights of organizing a disorganized country, stripping away the inessential and the second-rate, classifying all that remained in neat, terse paragraphs. He cribbed from other guidebooks, seizing small kernels of value and discarding the rest. He spent pleasurable hours dithering over questions of punctuation. Righteously, mercilessly, he weeded out the passive voice. The effort of typing made the corners of his mouth turn down, so that no one could have guessed how much he was enjoying himself. *I am happy to say*, he pecked out, but his face remained glum and intense. *I am happy to say that it's possible now to buy Kentucky Fried Chicken in Stockholm. Pita bread, too*, he added as an afterthought. He wasn't sure how it had happened, but lately pita had grown to seem as American as hot dogs.

'Of course you're managing,' his sister told him over the phone. 'Did I say you weren't? But at least you could have let us know. Three weeks, it's been! Sarah's been gone three weeks and I only hear about it today. And by chance, at that. If I hadn't asked to speak to her, would you ever have told us she'd left you?'

'She didn't *leave* me,' Macon said. 'I mean it's not the way you make it sound. We discussed it like adults and decided to separate, that's all. The last thing I need is my family gathered around me saying, "Oh, poor Macon, how could Sarah do this to you—"'

'Why would I say that?' Rose asked. 'Everybody knows the Leary men are difficult to live with.'

'Oh,' Macon said.

'Where is she?'

'She's got a place downtown,' he said. 'And look,' he added, 'you don't have to bend over backwards, either, and go asking her to dinner or something. She does have a family of her own. You're supposed to take my side in this.'

'I thought you didn't want us to take sides.'

'No, no, I don't. I mean you shouldn't take *her* side, is what I'm trying to say.'

'When Charles's wife got her divorce,' Rose said, 'we went on having her to dinner every Christmas, just like always. Remember?'

'I remember,' Macon said wearily. Charles was their oldest brother.

'I suppose she'd still be coming, if she hadn't got remarried to someone so far away.'

'What? If her husband had been a Baltimore man you'd have gone on inviting them both?'

'She and Porter's wife and Sarah used to sit around the kitchen—this was before Porter's wife got *her* divorce—and they'd go on and on about the Leary men. Oh, it was the Leary men this, the Leary men that: how they always had to have everything just so, always so well thought out beforehand, always clamping down on the world as if they really thought they could keep it in line. The Leary men! I can hear them still. I had to laugh: One Thanksgiving Porter and June were getting ready to leave, back when their children were small, and June was heading toward the door with the baby in her arms and Danny hanging onto her coat and this load of toys and supplies when Porter called out, "Halt!" and started reading from one of those cash-register tapes that he always writes his lists on: *blanket, bottles, diaper bag, formula out of the fridge* . . . June just looked over at the other two and rolled her eyes.'

'Well, it wasn't such a bad idea,' Macon said, 'when you consider June.'

'No, and you notice it was alphabetical, too,' Rose said. 'I do think alphabetizing helps to sort things out a little.'

Rose had a kitchen that was so completely alphabetized, you'd find the allspice next to the ant poison. She was a fine one to talk about the Leary men.

'At any rate,' she said. 'Has Sarah been in touch since she left?'

'She's come by once or twice. Once, actually,' Macon said. 'For things she needed.'

'What kind of things?'

'Well, a double boiler. Things like that.'

'It's an excuse, then,' Rose said promptly. 'She could get a double boiler at any dimestore.'

'She said she liked ours.'

'She was checking to see how you're doing. She still cares. Did you talk at all?'

'No,' Macon said, 'I just handed her the double boiler. Also that gadget that unscrews bottle tops.'

'Oh, Macon. You might have asked her in.'

'I was scared she'd say no,' he said.

There was a silence. 'Well. Anyhow,' Rose said finally.

'But I'm getting along!'

'Yes, of course you are,' she told him.

Then she said she had something in the oven and hung up.

Macon went over to his study window. It was a hot day in early July, the sky so blue it made his eyes ache. He rested his forehead against the glass and stared out at the yard, keeping his hands stuffed deep in the rear pockets of his khakis. Up in one of the oak trees, a bird sang what sounded like the first three notes of 'My Little Gypsy Sweetheart.' 'Slum . . . ber . . . on . . .' it sang. Macon wondered if even this moment would become, one day, something he looked back upon wistfully. He couldn't imagine it; he couldn't think of any period bleaker than this in all his life, but he'd noticed how time had a way of coloring things. That bird, for instance, had such a pure, sweet, piercing voice.

He turned away from the window, covered his typewriter, and left the room.

He didn't eat real meals anymore. When he was hungry he drank a glass of milk, or he spooned a bit of ice cream directly from the carton. After the smallest snack he felt overfed and heavy, but he noticed when he dressed in the mornings that he seemed to be losing weight. His shirt collar stood out around his neck. The vertical groove between his nose and mouth had deepened so that he had trouble shaving it. His hair, which Sarah used to cut for him, jutted over his forehead like a shelf. And something had caused his lower lids to droop. He used to have narrow gray slits of eyes; now they were wide and startled. Could this be a sign of malnutrition?

Breakfast: Breakfast was your most important meal. He hooked up the percolator and the electric skillet to the clock radio on his bedroom windowsill. Of course he was asking for food poisoning, letting two raw eggs wait all night at room temperature, but once he'd changed menus there was no problem. You had to be flexible about these matters. He was awakened now by the smell of fresh coffee and hot buttered popcorn, and he could partake of both without getting out of bed. Oh, he was managing fine, just fine. All things considered.

But his nights were terrible.

It wasn't that he had trouble getting to sleep in the first place. That was easy. He'd watch TV till his eyes burned; then he'd climb the stairs. He would start the shower running and spread his clothes in the tub. At times he thought of skipping this part, except there was such a danger in falling behind with your system. So he carried out each step: hanging the laundry, setting up the breakfast things, flossing his teeth. He couldn't go to bed without flossing his teeth. For some reason, Sarah had found this irritating. If Macon were condemned to death, she'd said once, and they told him he'd be executed by firing squad at dawn, he would no doubt still insist on flossing the night before. Macon, after thinking it over, had agreed. Yes, of course he would. Hadn't he flossed while in the depths of pneumonia? In the hospital with gallstones? In a motel the night his son was killed? He checked his teeth in the mirror. They were never entirely white, in spite of all his care. And now it seemed his skin was taking on a yellowish cast as well.

He turned off the lights, moved the cat over, helped the dog up onto the bed. The dog was a Welsh corgi, very short-legged, but he did love to sleep in a bed, and so every night he stood erect and propped his elbows on the mattress and gazed at Macon expectantly till Macon gave him a boost. Then they'd all three settle themselves. Macon slipped into his envelope, the cat fitted her shape to the warm spot under his arm, and the dog plopped down near his feet. Then Macon closed his eyes and drifted off.

But eventually he found himself conscious of his dreams—not borne along by them but tediously constructing them, quibbling over details. When it dawned on him that he was awake, he would open his eyes and squint at the clock radio. But it was only one a.m. At the latest, two. There were all those hours still to be survived.

His brain buzzed with little worries. Had he left the back door unlocked? Forgotten to put the milk away? Made out a check for his bank balance instead of his gas bill? He remembered all in a rush that he'd opened a can of V-8 juice and then put the can in the icebox. Oxidation of the metal seams! Resulting in lead poisoning!

The worries changed, grew deeper. He wondered what had gone wrong with his marriage. Sarah had been his first and only girlfriend; now he thought he should have practiced on someone else beforehand. During the twenty years of their marriage there'd been moments—there'd been months—when he didn't feel they had really formed a unit the way couples were supposed to. No, they'd stayed two distinct people, and not always even friends. Sometimes they'd seemed more like rivals, elbowing each other, competing over who was the better style of person. Was it Sarah, haphazard, mercurial? Was it Macon, methodical and steady?

When Ethan was born, he only brought out more of their differences. Things they had learned to ignore in each other resurfaced. Sarah never got their son on any kind of schedule at all, was lax and unconcerned. And Macon (oh, he knew it, he admitted it) had been so intent on preparing him for every eventuality that he hadn't had time to enjoy him. Ethan at two, at four floated up into his vision as clearly as a color film projected upon the bedroom ceiling. A chortling, sunny little boy, he'd been, with Macon a stooped shape above him wringing his hands. Macon had been fierce in teaching him, at age six, how to swing a bat; it would have wrenched his soul to have Ethan chosen last for any team. 'Why?' Sarah had asked. 'If he's chosen last, he's chosen last. Let it be, why don't you.' Let it be! Life was so full of things you couldn't do anything about; you had to avert what you could. She laughed when Macon spent one fall collecting Wacky Packs, which had these jokey stickers inside that Ethan liked to plaster his bedroom door with. He'd have more than anyone in the whole third grade, Macon vowed. Long after Ethan had lost interest, Macon was still doggedly bringing them home. He knew it was absurd, but still, there was this one last sticker they had not yet managed to get hold of . . .

Ethan went away to camp when he was twelve—a year ago, almost exactly. Most boys started earlier, but Macon had kept delaying it. Why have a child at all, he asked Sarah, if you were only going to ship him off to some godforsaken spot in Virginia? By the time he finally gave in, Ethan was in the top age group—a tall blond sprout of a boy with an open, friendly face and an endearing habit of bouncing on the balls of his feet when he was nervous.

Don't think about it.

He was murdered in a Burger Bonanza his second night at camp. It was one of those deaths that make no sense—the kind where the holdup man has collected his money and is free to go but decides, instead, first to shoot each and every person through the back of the skull.

Ethan wasn't even supposed to be there. He had snuck away from camp with a cabinmate, who waited outside as a lookout.

Blame the camp for not supervising. Blame Burger Bonanza for poor security. Blame the cabinmate for not going in too and altering, perhaps, what took place. (Lookout for what, for God's sake?) Blame Sarah for allowing Ethan to leave home; blame Macon for agreeing; blame even (hell, yes) Ethan. Blame Ethan for wanting to attend that camp and for sneaking off from it, and for entering Burger Bonanza like some headstrong fool while a holdup was in progress. Blame him for so meekly moving to the kitchen with the others, for placing his hands flat against the wall as he was ordered and no doubt bouncing slightly on the balls of his feet . . .

Don't think about it.

The director of the camp, not wanting to break the news on the phone, had driven to Baltimore to tell them in person. Then he'd driven them back to Virginia. Macon often recalled that director. Jim, his name was, Jim Robinson or maybe Robertson—a burly, white-whiskered man with a crew cut, wearing a suit coat, as if in respect, over a Redskins T-shirt. He'd seemed uncomfortable with silence and did his best to fill it with abrupt little fragments of chitchat. Macon hadn't listened, or he'd thought he hadn't; but now all the fragments came back to him. How Jim's mother had been a Baltimorean herself, born the year Babe Ruth was playing for the Orioles. How Jim's tomato plants had been acting queerly, producing only tiny green marbles that fell off the vines before they ripened. How Jim's wife was terrified of driving in reverse and avoided any situation that required it. Macon gave a lot of thought to that now, lying in his bed at night. Could you really drive a car without reversing? What about at intersections, where a bus driver pokes his head out his window and asks you to roll on back a few yards so he can turn? Would she refuse? Macon imagined her, staunch and defiant, glaring straight in front of her and pretending not to notice. The driver escalating into curses, horns blowing, other drivers shouting, 'Aw, lady!' It made a nice picture. He kept it firmly in mind.

Finally he would sit up and wriggle out of his sheet. The dog, sighing, roused himself and dropped off the bed to pad downstairs behind him. The floorboards were cool underfoot, the kitchen linoleum cooler still; there was a glow from the refrigerator as Macon poured himself a glass of milk. He went to the living room and turned on the TV. Generally some black-and-white movie was running—men in suits and felt hats, women with padded shoulders. He didn't try to follow the plot. He took small, steady sips of milk, feeling the calcium traveling to his bones. Hadn't he read that calcium cures insomnia? He absently stroked the cat, who had somehow crept into his lap. It was much too hot to have a cat in his lap, especially this one—a loose-strung, gray tweed female who seemed made of some unusually dense substance. And the dog, most often, would be lying on top of his feet. 'It's just you and me, old buddies,' Macon would tell them. The cat made a comma of sweat across his bare thighs.

At last he would slip out from under the animals and turn off the TV. He would put his glass in the chlorine solution in the kitchen sink. He would climb the stairs. He'd stand at the bedroom window looking over the neighborhood—black branches scrawled on a purple night sky, a glimmer of white clapboard here and there, occasionally a light. Macon always took comfort if he found a light. Someone else had trouble sleeping too, he assumed. He didn't like to consider any other possibility—a party, for instance, or a heart-to-heart talk with old friends. He preferred to believe that someone else was on his own, sitting up wide awake fending off his thoughts. That made him feel much better. He returned to his bed. He lay down. He closed his eyes and without even trying, he dropped off the edge into sleep.

3

— Sarah telephoned Macon and asked if she could come get the navy blue rug from the dining room.

'Navy blue rug,' Macon repeated. (He was stalling for time.)

'I wouldn't mention it except you never liked it,' Sarah told him. 'You said it was a mistake to have a rug where people were eating.'

Yes, he had said that. A crumb catcher, he'd said. Unsanitary. Then why did he feel this sudden, wrenching need to keep the rug for himself?

'Macon, are you there?'

'Yes, I'm here.'

'So would you mind if I came and got it?'

'No, I guess not.'

'Oh, good. My apartment has these bare floors and you've no idea how—'

She would stop by for the rug and he'd invite her in. He'd offer her a glass of sherry. They would sit on the couch with their sherry and he would say, 'Sarah, have you missed me?' Or no, he'd say, 'I've missed you, Sarah.'

She would say . . .

She said, 'I thought I'd drop over Saturday morning, if that's convenient.'

But people don't drink sherry in the morning.

And besides: He wouldn't even be here then. 'I leave for England tomorrow afternoon,' he said.

'Oh, is it time for England again?'

'Maybe you could come this evening.'

'No, my car's in the shop.'

'Your car? What's wrong with it?'

'Well, I was driving along and . . . you know that little red light on the lefthand side of the dash?'

'What, the oil pressure light?'

'Yes, and so I thought, "Well, I'll be late for the dentist if I stop and see to it now and anyway, the car does seem to be running all right, so—" '

'Wait. Are you saying the light lit up? And then you went on driving?'

'Well, nothing sounded any different and nothing *acted* any different, so I figured—'

'Jesus, Sarah.'

'What's so terrible about that?'

'You've probably ruined the engine.'

'No, I did not ruin the engine, for your information. I just need this single, simple repair job but unfortunately it's going to take a few days to do it. Well, never mind. I've got a house key; I'll just let myself in on Saturday.'

'Maybe I could bring the rug over.'

'I'll wait till Saturday.'

'That way I could see your apartment,' Macon said. 'I've never been inside, you know.'

'No, it's not fixed up yet.'

'I don't care if it's fixed up.'

'It's a disaster. Nothing's been done.'

'How could nothing be done? You've been living there over a month.'

'Well, I'm not so wonderfully perfectly efficient as you are, Macon.'

'You wouldn't have to be efficient to—'

'Some days,' Sarah said, 'I can't even make it out of my bathrobe.'

Macon was silent.

'I should have agreed to teach summer school,' Sarah said. 'Something to give some shape to things. I open my eyes in the morning and think, "Why bother getting up?" '

'Me too,' Macon said.

'Why bother eating? Why bother breathing?'

'Me too, sweetheart.'

'Macon, do you suppose that person has any idea? I want to go see him in prison, Macon. I want to sit on the other side of the grid or the screen or whatever they have and I'll say, "Look at me. Look. Look at what you did. You didn't just kill the people you shot; you killed other people besides. What you did goes on and on forever.

You didn't just kill my son; you killed me; you killed my husband. I mean I can't even manage to put up my curtains; do you understand what you did?" Then when I'm sure that he does understand, that he really does realize, that he feels just terrible, I'm going to open my purse and pull out a gun and shoot him between the eyes.'

'Oh, well, sweetheart—'

'You think I'm just raving, don't you. But Macon, I swear, I can feel that little kick against my palm when I fire the gun. I've never fired a gun in my life—Lord, I don't think I've ever *seen* a gun. Isn't it odd? Ethan's seen one; Ethan's had an experience you and I have no notion of. But sometimes I hold my hand out with the thumb cocked like when kids play cowboy, and I fold my trigger finger and feel what a satisfaction it would be.'

'Sarah, it's bad for you to talk like this.'

'Oh? How am I supposed to talk?'

'I mean if you let yourself get angry you'll be . . . consumed. You'll burn up. It's not productive.'

'Oh, productive! Well, goodness, no, let's not waste our time on anything unproductive.'

Macon massaged his forehead. He said, 'Sarah, I just feel we can't afford to have these thoughts.'

'Easy for you to say.'

'No, it is not easy for me to say, dammit—'

'Just shut the door, Macon. Just walk away. Just pretend it never happened. Go rearrange your tools, why don't you; line up your wrenches from biggest to smallest instead of from smallest to biggest; that's always fun.'

'Goddammit, Sarah—'

'Don't you curse at me, Macon Leary!'

They paused.

Macon said, 'Well.'

Sarah said, 'Well, anyhow.'

'So I guess you'll come by while I'm gone,' he said.

'If that's all right.'

'Yes, certainly,' he said.

Although he felt a curious uneasiness when he hung up, as if he were letting a stranger come. As if she might walk off with more than just the dining room rug.

For his trip to England, he dressed in his most comfortable suit. *One suit is plenty*, he counseled in his guidebooks, *if you take along some travel-size packets of spot remover*. (Macon knew every item that came in travel-size packets, from deodorant to shoe polish.) *The suit should be a medium gray. Gray not only hides the dirt; it's handy for sudden funerals and other formal events. At the same time, it isn't too somber for everyday*.

He packed a minimum of clothes and a shaving kit. A copy of his most recent guide to England. A novel to read on the plane.

Bring only what fits in a carry-on bag. Checking your luggage is asking for trouble. Add several travel-size packets of detergent so you won't fall into the hands of foreign laundries.

When he'd finished packing, he sat on the couch to rest. Or not to rest, exactly, but to collect himself—like a man taking several deep breaths before diving into a river.

The furniture was all straight lines and soothing curves. Dust motes hung in a slant of sunlight. What a peaceful life he led here!

If this were any other day he'd be making some instant coffee. He would drop the spoon in the sink and stand sipping from his mug while the cat wove between his feet. Then maybe he'd open the mail. Those acts seemed dear and gentle now. How could he have complained of boredom? At home he had everything set up around him so he hardly needed to think. On trips, even the smallest task required effort and decisions.

When it was two hours till takeoff, he stood up. The airport was a thirty-minute drive at the most, but he hated feeling rushed. He made a final tour of the house, stopping off at the downstairs bathroom—the last *real* bathroom (was how he thought of it) that he'd see for the next week. He whistled for the dog. He picked up his bag and stepped out the front door. The heat slammed into him like something solid.

The dog was going with him only as far as the vet's. If he'd known that, he never would have jumped into the car. He sat next to Macon, panting enthusiastically, his keg-shaped body alert with expectation. Macon talked to him in what he hoped was an unalarming tone. 'Hot, isn't it, Edward. You want the air conditioner on?' He adjusted the controls. 'There now. Feeling better?' He heard something unctuous in his voice. Maybe Edward did, too, for he stopped panting and gave Macon a sudden suspicious look. Macon decided to say no more.

They rolled through the neighborhood, down streets roofed over with trees. They turned into a sunnier section full of stores and service stations. As they neared Murray Avenue, Edward started whimpering. In the parking lot of the Murray Avenue Veterinary Hospital, he somehow became a much smaller animal.

Macon got out of the car and walked around to open the door. When he took hold of Edward's collar, Edward dug his toenails into the upholstery. He had to be dragged all the way to the building, scritching across the hot concrete.

The waiting room was empty. A goldfish tank bubbled in one corner, with a full-color poster above it illustrating the life cycle of the heartworm. There was a girl on a stool behind the counter, a waifish little person in a halter top.

'I've brought my dog for boarding,' Macon said. He had to raise his voice to be heard above Edward's moans.

Chewing her gum steadily, the girl handed him a printed form and a pencil. 'Ever been here before?' she asked.

'Yes, often.'

'What's the last name?'

'Leary.'

'Leary. Leary,' she said, riffling through a box of index cards. Macon started filling out the form. Edward was standing upright now and clinging to Macon's knees, like a toddler scared of nursery school.

'Whoa,' the girl said.

She frowned at the card she'd pulled.

'Edward?' she said. 'On Rayford Road?'

'That's right.'

'We can't accept him.'

'What?'

'Says here he bit an attendant. Says, "Bit Barry in the ankle, do not readmit." '

'Nobody told me that.'

'Well, they should have.'

'Nobody said a word! I left him in June when we went to the beach; I came back and they handed him over.'

The girl blinked at him, expressionless.

'Look,' Macon said. 'I'm on my way to the airport, right this minute. I've got a plane to catch.'

'I'm only following orders,' the girl said.

'And what set him off, anyhow?' Macon asked. 'Did anyone think to wonder? Maybe Edward had good reason!'

The girl blinked again. Edward had dropped to all fours by now and was gazing upward with interest, as if following the conversation.

'Ah, the hell with it,' Macon said. 'Come on, Edward.'

He didn't have to take hold of Edward's collar when they left. Edward galloped ahead of him all the way across the parking lot.

In that short time, the car had turned into an oven. Macon opened his window and sat there with the motor idling. What now? He considered going to his sister's, but she probably wouldn't want Edward either. To tell the truth, this wasn't the first time there had been complaints. Last week, for instance, Macon's brother Charles had stopped by to borrow a router, and Edward had darted in a complete circle around his feet, taking furious little nibbles of his trouser cuffs. Charles was so astonished that he just turned his head slowly, gaping down. 'What's got into him?' he asked. 'He never *used* to do this.' Then when Macon grabbed his collar, Edward had snarled. He'd curled his upper lip and snarled. Could a dog have a nervous breakdown?

Macon wasn't very familiar with dogs. He preferred cats. He liked the way cats kept their own counsel. It was only lately that he'd given Edward any thought at all. Now that he was alone so much he had taken to talking out loud to him, or sometimes he just sat studying him. He admired Edward's intelligent brown eyes and his foxy little face. He appreciated the honey-colored whorls that radiated so symmetrically from the bridge of his nose. And his walk! Ethan used to say that Edward walked as if he had sand in his bathing suit. His rear end waddled busily; his stubby legs seemed hinged by some more primitive mechanism than the legs of taller dogs.

Macon was driving toward home now, for lack of any better idea. He wondered what would happen if he left Edward in the house the way he left the cat, with plenty of food and water. No. Or could Sarah come see to him, two or three times a day? He recoiled from that; it meant asking her. It meant dialing that number he'd never used and asking her for a favor.

MEOW-BOW ANIMAL HOSPITAL, a sign across the street read. Macon braked and Edward lurched forward. 'Sorry,' Macon told him. He made a left turn into the parking lot.

The waiting room at the Meow-Bow smelled strongly of disinfectant. Behind the counter stood a thin young woman in a ruffled peasant blouse. She had aggressively frizzy black hair that burgeoned to her shoulders like an Arab headdress. 'Hi, there,' she said to Macon.

Macon said, 'Do you board dogs?'

'Sure.'

'I'd like to board Edward, here.'

She leaned over the counter to look at Edward. Edward panted up at her cheerfully. It was clear he hadn't yet realized what kind of place this was.

'You have a reservation?' the woman asked Macon.

'Reservation! No.'

'Most people reserve.'

'Well, I didn't know that.'

'Especially in the summer.'

'Couldn't you make an exception?'

She thought it over, frowning down at Edward. Her eyes were very small, like caraway seeds, and her face was sharp and colorless.

'Please,' Macon said. 'I'm about to catch a plane. I'm leaving for a week, and I don't have a soul to look after him. I'm desperate, I tell you.'

From the glance she shot at him, he sensed he had surprised her in some way. 'Can't you leave him home with your wife?' she asked.

He wondered how on earth her mind worked.

'If I could do that,' he said, 'why would I be standing here?'

'Oh,' she said. 'You're not married?'

'Well, I am, but she's . . . living elsewhere. They don't allow pets.'

'Oh.'

She came out from behind the counter. She was wearing very short red shorts; her legs were like sticks. 'I'm a divorsy myself,' she said. 'I know what you're going through.'

'And see,' Macon said, 'there's this place I usually board him but they suddenly claim he bites. Claim he bit an attendant and they can't admit him anymore.'

'Edward? Do you bite?' the woman said.

Macon realized he should not have mentioned that, but she seemed to take it in stride. 'How could you do such a thing?' she asked Edward. Edward grinned up at her and folded his ears back, inviting a pat. She bent and stroked his head.

'So will you keep him?' Macon said.

'Oh, I guess,' she said, straightening. 'If you're desperate.' She stressed the word—fixing Macon with those small brown eyes—as if giving it more weight than he had intended. 'Fill this out,' she told him, and she handed him a form from a stack on the counter. 'Your name and address and when you'll be back. Don't forget to put when you'll be back.'

Macon nodded, uncapping his fountain pen.

'I'll most likely see you again when you come to pick him up,' she said. 'I mean if you put the time of day to expect you. My name's Muriel.'

'Is this place open evenings?' Macon asked.

'Every evening but Sundays. Till eight.'

'Oh, good.'

'Muriel Pritchett,' she said.

Macon filled out the form while the woman knelt to unbuckle Edward's collar. Edward licked her cheekbone; he must have thought she was just being friendly. So when Macon had finished, he didn't say good-bye. He left the form on the counter and walked out very quickly, keeping a hand in his pocket to silence his keys.

On the flight to New York, he sat next to a foreign-looking man with a mustache. Clamped to the man's ears was a headset for one of those miniature tape recorders. Perfect: no danger of conversation. Macon leaned back in his seat contentedly.

He approved of planes. When the weather was calm, you couldn't even tell you were moving. You could pretend you were sitting safe at home. The view from the window was always the same—air and more air—and the interior of one plane was practically interchangeable with the interior of any other.

He accepted nothing from the beverage cart, but the man beside him took off his headset to order a Bloody Mary. A tinny, intricate, Middle Eastern melody came whispering out of the pink sponge earplugs. Macon stared down at the little machine and wondered if he should buy one. Not for the music, heaven knows—there was far too much noise in the world already—but for insulation. He could plug himself into it and no one would disturb him. He could play a blank tape: thirty full minutes of silence. Turn the tape over and play thirty minutes more.

They landed at Kennedy and he took a shuttle bus to his connecting flight, which wasn't due to leave till evening. Once settled in the terminal, he began filling out a crossword puzzle that he'd saved for this occasion from last Sunday's *New York Times*. He sat inside a kind of barricade—his bag on one chair, his suit coat on another. People milled around him but he kept his eyes on the page, progressing smoothly to the acrostic as soon as he'd finished the crossword. By the time he'd solved both puzzles, they were beginning to board the plane.

His seatmate was a gray-haired woman with glasses. She had brought her own knitted afghan. This was not a good sign, Macon felt, but he could handle it. First he bustled about, loosening his tie and taking off his shoes and removing a book from his bag. Then he opened the book and ostentatiously started reading.

The name of his book was *Miss MacIntosh, My Darling*, and it was 1,198 pages long. (*Always bring a book, as protection against strangers. Magazines don't last. Newspapers from home will make you homesick, and newspapers from elsewhere will remind you you don't belong. You know how alien another paper's typeface seems.*) He'd been lugging around *Miss MacIntosh* for years. It had the advantage of being plotless, as far as he could tell, but invariably interesting, so he could dip into it at random. Any time he raised his eyes, he was careful to mark a paragraph with his finger and to keep a bemused expression on his face.

There was the usual mellifluous murmur from the loudspeaker about seatbelts, emergency exits, oxygen masks. He wondered why stewardesses accented such unlikely words. '*On* our flight this evening we *will* be offering . . .' The woman next to him asked if he wanted a Lifesaver. 'No, thank you,' Macon said, and he went on with his book. She rustled some little bit of paper, and shortly afterward the smell of spearmint drifted over to him.

He refused a cocktail and he refused a supper tray, although he did accept the milk that was offered with it. He ate an apple and a little box of raisins from his bag, drank the milk, and went off to the lavatory to floss and brush his teeth. When he returned the plane was darker, dotted here and there with reading lamps. Some of the passengers were already asleep. His seatmate had rolled her hair into little O's and X-ed them over with bobby pins. Macon found it amazing that people could be so unself-conscious on airplanes. He'd seen men in whole suits of pajamas; he'd seen women slathered in face cream. You would think they felt no need to be on guard.

He angled his book beneath a slender shaft of light and turned a page. The engines had a weary, dogged sound. It was the period he thought of as the long haul—the gulf between supper and breakfast when they were suspended over the ocean, waiting for that lightening of the sky that was supposed to be morning although, of course, it was nowhere near morning back home. In Macon's opinion, morning in other time zones was like something staged—a curtain painted with a rising sun, superimposed upon the real dark.

He let his head tip back against the seat and closed his eyes. A stewardess's voice, somewhere near the front of the plane, threaded in and out of the droning of the engines. 'We just sat and sat and there wasn't a thing to do and all we had was the Wednesday paper and you know how news just never seems to happen on a Wednesday . . .'

Macon heard a man speaking levelly in his ear. 'Macon.' But he didn't even turn his head. By now he knew these tricks of sound on planes at night. He saw behind his eyelids the soap dish on the kitchen sink at home—another trick, this concreteness of vision. It was an oval china soap dish painted with yellow roses, containing a worn-down sliver of soap and Sarah's rings, her engagement ring and her wedding band, just as she had left them when she walked out. .

'I got the tickets,' he heard Ethan say. 'And they're opening the doors in five minutes.'

'All right,' Macon told him, 'let's plan our strategy.'

'Strategy?'

'Where we're going to sit.'

'Why would we need strategy for that?'

'It's you who asked to see this movie, Ethan. I would think you'd take an interest in where you're sitting. Now, here's my plan. You go around to that line on the left. Count the little kids. I'll count the line on the right.'

'Aw, Dad—'

'Do you want to sit next to some noisy little kid?'

'Well, no.'

'And which do you prefer: an aisle seat?'

'I don't care.'

'Aisle, Ethan? Or middle of the row? You must have some opinion.'

'Not really.'

'Middle of the row?'

'It doesn't make any difference.'

'Ethan. It makes a great deal of difference. Aisle, you can get out quicker. So if you plan to buy a snack or go to the restroom, you'll want to sit on the aisle. On the other hand, everyone'll be squeezing past you there. So if you don't think you'll be leaving your seat, then I suggest—'

'Aw, Dad, for Christ's sake!' Ethan said.

'Well,' Macon said. 'If that's the tone you're going to take, we'll just sit any damn place we happen to end up.'

'Fine,' Ethan said.

'Fine,' Macon said.

Now he did turn his head; he rocked it from side to side. But he kept his eyes tightly closed, and in time the voices stopped, and he found himself in that edgy twilight that passes for sleep when you're traveling.

At dawn he accepted a cup of coffee, and he swallowed a vitamin pill from his bag. The other passengers looked frowsy and pale. His seatmate dragged an entire small suitcase off to the lavatory and returned all combed, but her face was puffy. Macon believed that travel causes retention of fluids. When he put his shoes on, they felt too tight, and when he went to shave he found unfamiliar pillows of flesh beneath his eyes. He was better off than most people, though, because he hadn't touched salted food or drunk any alcohol. Alcohol was definitely retained. Drink alcohol on a plane and you'd feel befuddled for days, Macon believed.

The stewardess announced what time it was in London, and there was a stir as people reset their watches. Macon adjusted the digital alarm clock in his shaving kit. The watch on his wrist—which was not digital but real time, circular—he left as it was.

They landed abruptly. It was like being recalled to the hard facts—all that friction suddenly, the gritty runway, the roaring and braking. The loudspeaker came on, purring courteous reminders. The woman next to Macon folded her afghan. 'I'm so excited,' she said. 'I'm going to see my grandchild for the very first time.' Macon smiled and told her he hoped it went well. Now that he didn't have to fear being trapped, he found her quite pleasant. Besides, she was so American-looking.

At Heathrow, there was the usual sense of some recent disaster. People rushed about distractedly, other people stood like refugees surrounded by trunks and parcels, and uniformed authorities were trying to deal with a clamor of questions. Since he didn't have to wait for his luggage, Macon sailed through the red tape far ahead of the others. Then he exchanged his currency and boarded the Underground. *I recommend the Underground for everyone except those afraid of heights, and even for them if they will avoid the following stations, which have exceptionally steep escalators ...*

While the train racketed along, he sorted his currency into envelopes that he'd brought from home—each envelope clearly marked with a different denomination. (*No fumbling with unfamiliar coins, no peering at misleading imprints, if you separate and classify foreign money ahead of time.*) Across from him a row of faces watched. People looked different here, although he couldn't say just how. He thought they were both finer and unhealthier. A woman with a fretful baby kept saying, 'Hush now, love. Hush now, love,' in that clear, floating, effortless English voice. It was hot, and her forehead had a pallid shine. So did Macon's, no doubt. He slid the envelopes into his breast pocket. The train stopped and more people got on. They stood above him, clinging not to straps but to bulbs attached to flexible sticks, which Macon on his first visit had taken for some kind of microphone.

He was based in London, as usual. From there he would make brief forays into other cities, never listing more than a handful of hotels, a handful of restaurants within a tiny, easily accessible radius in each place; for his guidebooks were anything but all-inclusive. ('Plenty of other books say how to see as much of a city as possible,' his boss had told him. 'You should say how to see as little.') The name of Macon's hotel was the Jones Terrace. He would have preferred one of the American chain hotels, but those cost too much. The Jones Terrace was all right, though—small and well kept. He swung into action at once to make his room his own, stripping off the ugly bedspread and stuffing it into a closet, unpacking his belongings and hiding his bag. He changed clothes, rinsed the ones he'd worn and hung them in the shower stall. Then, after a wistful glance at the bed, he went out for breakfast. It was nowhere near morning back home, but breakfast was the meal that businessmen most often had to manage for themselves. He made a point of researching it thoroughly wherever he went.

He walked to the Yankee Delight, where he ordered scrambled eggs and coffee. The service here was excellent. Coffee came at once, and his cup was kept constantly filled. The eggs didn't taste like eggs at home, but then, they never did. What was it about restaurant eggs? They had no character, no backbone. Still, he opened his guidebook and put a checkmark next to the Yankee Delight. By the end of the week, these pages would be barely legible. He'd have scratched out some names, inserted others, and scrawled notes across the margins. He always revisited past entries—every hotel and restaurant. It was tedious but his boss insisted. 'Just think how it would look,' Julian said, 'if a reader walked into some café you'd recommended and found it taken over by vegetarians.'

When he'd paid his bill, he went down the street to the New America, where he ordered more eggs and more coffee. 'Decaffeinated,' he added. (He was a jangle of nerves by now.) The waiter said they didn't have decaffeinated. 'Oh, you don't,' Macon said. After the waiter had left, Macon made a note in his guidebook.

His third stop was a restaurant called the U.S. Open, where the sausages were so dry that they might have been baked on a rooftop. It figured: The U.S. Open had been recommended by a reader. Oh, the places that readers wrote in to suggest! Macon had once (before he'd grown wiser) reserved a motel room purely on the strength of such a suggestion—somewhere in Detroit or was it Pittsburgh, some city or other, for *Accidental Tourist in America*. He had checked out again at first sight of the linens and fled across the street to a Hilton, where the doorman had rushed to meet him and seized his bag with a cry of pity as if Macon had just staggered in from the desert. Never again, Macon had vowed. He left the sausages on his plate and called for his bill.

In the afternoon (so to speak), he visited hotels. He spoke with various managers and inspected sample rooms where he tested the beds, flushed the toilets, squinted at the showerheads. Most were maintaining their standards, more or less, but something had happened to the Royal Prince. The fact was that it seemed . . . well, foreign. Dark, handsome men in slim silk suits murmured in the lobby while little brown children chased each other around the spittoons. Macon had the feeling he'd got even more hopelessly lost than usual and ended up in Cairo. Cone-shaped ladies in long black veils packed the revolving doors, spinning in from the street with shopping bags full of . . . what? He tried to imagine their purchasing stone-washed denim shorts and thigh-high boots of pink mesh—the merchandise he'd seen in most shop windows. 'Er . . .' he said to the manager. How to put this? He hated to sound narrow-minded, but his readers did avoid the exotic. 'Has the hotel, ah, changed ownership?' he asked. The manager seemed unusually sensitive. He drew himself up and said the Royal Prince was owned by a corporation, always had been and always would be, always the same corporation. 'I see,' Macon said. He left feeling dislocated.

At suppertime, he should have tried someplace formal. He had to list at least one formal restaurant in every city for entertaining clients. But tonight he wasn't up to it. Instead, he went to a café he liked called My American Cousin. The diners there had American accents, and so did some of the staff, and the hostess handed out tickets at the door with numbers on them. If your number was called on the loudspeaker you could win a free TV, or at least a framed color print of the restaurant.

Macon ordered a comforting supper of plain boiled vegetables and two lamb chops in white paper bobby socks, along with a glass of milk. The man at the next table was also on his own. He was eating a nice pork pie, and when the waitress offered him dessert he said, 'Oh, now, let me see, maybe I will try some at that,' in the slow, pleased, coax-me drawl of someone whose womenfolks have all his life encouraged him to put a little meat on his bones. Macon himself had the gingerbread. It came with cream, just the way it used to at his grandmother's house.

By eight o'clock, according to his wristwatch, he was in bed. It was much too early, of course, but he could stretch the day only so far; the English thought it was midnight. Tomorrow he would start his whirlwind dashes through other cities. He'd pick out a few token hotels, sample a few token breakfasts. Coffee with caffeine and coffee without caffeine. Bacon underdone and overdone. Orange juice fresh and canned and frozen. More showerheads, more mattresses. Hairdryers supplied on request? 110-volt switches for electric shavers? When he fell asleep, he thought anonymous rooms were revolving past on a merry-go-round. He thought webbed canvas suitcase stands, ceiling sprinklers, and laminated lists of fire regulations approached and slid away and approached again, over and over all the rest of his days. He thought Ethan was riding a plaster camel and calling, 'Catch me!' and falling, but Macon couldn't get there in time and when he reached his arms out, Ethan was gone.

It was one of Macon's bad habits to start itching to go home too early. No matter how short a stay he'd planned, partway through he would decide that he ought to leave, that he'd allowed himself far too much time, that everything truly necessary had already been accomplished—or almost everything, almost accomplished. Then the rest of his visit was spent in phone calls to travel agents and fruitless trips to airline offices and standby waits that came to nothing, so that he was forced to return to the hotel he'd just checked out of. He always promised himself this wouldn't happen again, but somehow it always did. In England, it happened on his fourth afternoon. What more was there to do? he started wondering. Hadn't he got the gist of the place?

Well, be honest: It was Saturday. He chanced to notice, entering the date in his expense book, that at home it was Saturday morning. Sarah would be stopping by the house for the rug.

She would open the front door and smell home. She would pass through the rooms where she'd been so happy all these years. (Hadn't she been happy?) She would find the cat stretched out on the couch, long and lazy and languid, and she'd settle on the cushion next to her and think, *How could I have left?*

Unfortunately, it was summer, and the airlines were overbooked. He spent two days tracking down faint possibilities that evaporated the instant he drew close. 'Anything! Get me anything! I don't have to go to New York; I'll go to Dulles. I'll go to Montreal! Chicago! Shoot, I'll go to Paris or Berlin and see if they have flights. Are there ships? How long do ships take, nowadays? What if this were an emergency? I mean my mother on her deathbed or something? Are you saying there's just no way out of this place?'

The people he dealt with were unfailingly courteous and full of chirpy good humor—really, if not for the strain of travel he believed he might actually have liked the English—but they couldn't solve his problem. In the end he had to stay on. He spent the rest of the week huddled in his room watching TV, chewing a knuckle, subsisting on nonperishable groceries and lukewarm soft drinks because he couldn't face another restaurant.

So he was first in line, naturally, at the check-in counter on the day of his departure. He had his pick of seats: window, nonsmoking. Next to him was a very young couple completely absorbed in each other, so he didn't need *Miss MacIntosh* but sat staring out at the clouds all the long, dull afternoon.

Afternoon was never his favorite time; that was the worst of these homeward flights. It was afternoon for hours and hours, through drinks and lunch and drinks again—all of which he waved away. It was afternoon when they showed the movie; the passengers had to pull their shades down. An orange light filled the plane, burdensome and thick.

Once when he'd been away on an unusually difficult trip—to Japan, where you couldn't even memorize the signs in order to find your way back to a place—Sarah had met his plane in New York. It was their fifteenth anniversary and she had wanted to surprise him. She called Becky at the travel agency to ask his flight number and then she left Ethan with her mother and flew to Kennedy, bringing with her a picnic hamper of wine and cheeses which they shared in the terminal while waiting for their plane home. Every detail of that meal remained in Macon's memory: the cheeses set out on a marble slab, the wine in stemmed crystal glasses that had somehow survived the trip. He could still taste the satiny Brie. He could still see Sarah's small, shapely hand resolutely slicing the bread.

But she didn't meet him in New York today.

She didn't even meet him in Baltimore.

He collected his car from the lot and drove into the city through a glowering twilight that seemed to promise something—a thunderstorm or heat lightning, something dramatic. Could she be waiting at home? In her striped caftan that he was so fond of? With a cool summer supper laid out on the patio table?

Careful not to take anything for granted, he stopped at a Seven-Eleven for milk. He drove to the vet's to pick up Edward. He arrived at the Meow-Bow minutes before closing time; somehow, he'd managed to lose his way. There was no one at the counter. He had to ring the service bell. A girl with a ponytail poked her head through a door, letting in a jumble of animal sounds that rose at all different pitches like an orchestra tuning up. 'Yes?' she said.

'I'm here for my dog.'

She came forward to open a folder that lay on the counter. 'Your last name?'

'Leary.'

'Oh,' she said. 'Just a minute.'

Macon wondered what Edward had done wrong this time.

The girl disappeared, and a moment later the other one came out, the frizzy one. This evening she wore a V-necked black dress splashed with big pink flowers, its shoulders padded and its skirt too skimpy; and preposterously high-heeled sandals. 'Well, hi there!' she said brightly. 'How was your trip?'

'Oh, it was . . . where's Edward? Isn't he all right?'

'Sure, he's all right. He was so good and sweet and friendly!'

'Well, fine,' Macon said.

'We just got on like a house afire. Seems he took a shine to me, I couldn't say why.'

'Wonderful,' Macon said. He cleared his throat. 'So could I have him back, please?'

'Caroline will bring him.'

'Ah.'

There was a silence. The woman waited, facing him and wearing a perky smile, with her fingers laced together on the counter. She had painted her nails dark red, Macon saw, and put on a blackish lipstick that showed her mouth to be an unusually complicated shape—angular, like certain kinds of apples.

'Um,' Macon said finally. 'Maybe I could pay.'

'Oh, yes.'

She stopped smiling and peered down at the open folder. 'That'll be forty-two dollars,' she said.

Macon gave her a credit card. She had trouble working the embossing machine; everything had to be done with the flats of her hands, to spare her nails. She filled in the blanks in a jerky scrawl and then turned the bill in his direction. 'Signature and phone,' she said. She leaned over the counter to watch what he wrote. 'Is that your home phone, or your business?'

'It's both. Why? What difference does it make?' he asked.

'I was just wondering,' she told him. She tore off his copy, in that splay-fingered style of hers, and put the rest of the bill in a drawer. 'I don't know if I mentioned before that it so happens I train dogs.'

'Is that right,' Macon said.

He looked toward the door where the first girl had disappeared. It always made him nervous when they took too long bringing Edward. What were they doing back there—getting rid of some evidence?

'My speciality is dogs that bite,' the woman said.

'Specialty.'

'Pardon?'

'Webster prefers "specialty." '

She gave him a blank look.

'That must be a dangerous job,' Macon said politely.

'Oh, not for me! I'm not scared of a thing in this world.'

There was a scuffling sound at the door behind her. Edward burst through, followed by the girl with the ponytail. Edward was giving sharp yelps and flinging himself about so joyfully that when Macon bent to pat him, he couldn't really connect.

'Now, stop that,' the girl told Edward. She was trying to buckle his collar. Meanwhile, the woman behind the counter was saying,

'Biters, barkers, deaf dogs, timid dogs, dogs that haven't been treated right, dogs that have learned bad habits, dogs that grew up in pet shops and don't trust human beings . . . I can handle all of those.'

'Well, good,' Macon said.

'Not that he would bite *me*, of course,' the woman said. 'He just fell in love with me, like I think I was telling you.'

'I'm glad to hear it,' Macon said.

'But I could train him in no time not to bite other people. You think it over and call me. Muriel, remember? Muriel Pritchett. Let me give you my card.'

She handed him a salmon-pink business card that she seemed to have pulled out of nowhere. He had to fight his way around Edward to accept it. 'I studied with a man who used to train attack dogs,' she said. 'This is not some amateur you're looking at.'

'Well, I'll bear that in mind,' Macon said. 'Thank you very much.'

'Or just call for no reason! Call and talk.'

'Talk?'

'Sure! Talk about Edward, his problems, talk about . . . anything! Pick up the phone and just talk. Don't you ever get the urge to do that?'

'Not really,' Macon said.

Then Edward gave a particularly piercing yelp, and the two of them rushed home.

Well, of course she wasn't there. He knew it the instant he stepped inside the house, when he smelled that stale hot air and heard the muffled denseness of a place with every window shut. Really he'd known it all along. He'd been fooling himself. He'd been making up fairy tales.

The cat streaked past him and escaped out the door, yowling accusingly. The dog hurtled into the dining room to roll about on the rug and get rid of the scent of the kennel. But there was no rug—only bare, linty floor, and Edward stopped short, looking foolish. Macon knew just how he felt.

He put away the milk and went upstairs to unpack. He took a shower, treading the day's dirty clothes underfoot, and prepared for bed. When he turned off the light in the bathroom, the sight of his laundry dripping over the tub reminded him of travel. Where was the real difference? *Accidental Tourist at Home*, he thought, and he slid wearily into his body bag.

4

—— When the phone rang, Macon dreamed it was Ethan. He dreamed Ethan was calling from camp, wondering why they'd never come to get him. 'But we thought you were dead,' Macon said, and Ethan said—in that clear voice of his that cracked on the high notes—'Why would you think *that?*' The phone rang again and Macon woke up. There was a thud of disappointment somewhere inside his rib cage. He understood why people said hearts 'sank.'

In slow motion, he reached for the receiver. 'Yes,' he said.

'Macon! Welcome back!'

It was Julian Edge, Macon's boss, his usual loud and sprightly self even this early in the morning. 'Oh,' Macon said.

'How was the trip?'

'It was okay.'

'You just get in last night?'

'Yes.'

'Find any super new places?'

'Well, "super" would be putting it a bit strongly.'

'So now I guess you start writing it up.'

Macon said nothing.

'Just when do you figure to bring me a manuscript?' Julian asked.

'I don't know,' Macon said.

'Soon, do you figure?'

'I don't know.'

There was a pause.

'I guess I woke you,' Julian said.

'Yes.'

'Macon Leary in bed,' Julian said. He made it sound like the title of something. Julian was younger than Macon and brasher, breezier, not a serious man. He seemed to enjoy pretending that Macon was some kind of character. 'So anyway, can I expect it by the end of the month?'

'No,' Macon said.

'Why not?'

'I'm not organized.'

'Not organized! What's to organize? All you have to do is retype your old one, basically.'

'There's a lot more to it than that,' Macon said.

'Look. Fellow. Here it is—' Julian's voice grew fainter. He'd be drawing back to frown at his flashy gold calendar watch with the perforated leather racing band. 'Here it is the third of August.

I want this thing on the stands by October. That means I'd need your manuscript by August thirty-first.'

'I can't do it,' Macon said.

In fact, it amazed him he'd found the strength to carry on this conversation.

'August thirty-first, Macon. That's four full weeks away.'

'It's not enough,' Macon said.

'Not enough,' Julian said. 'Well. All right, then: mid-September. It's going to knock a good many things out of whack, but I'll give you till mid-September. How's that?'

'I don't know,' Macon said.

The dullness of his voice interested him. He felt strangely distant from himself. Julian might have sensed this, for after another pause he said, 'Hey. Pal. Are you okay?'

'I'm fine,' Macon told him.

'I know you've been through a lot, pal—'

'I'm fine! Just fine! What could be wrong? All I need is time to get organized. I'll have the manuscript in by September fifteenth. Possibly earlier. Yes, very possibly earlier. Maybe the end of August. All right?'

Then he hung up.

But his study was so dim and close, and it gave off the salty, inky smell of mental fidgeting. He walked in and felt overwhelmed by his task, as if finally chaos had triumphed. He turned around and walked out again.

Maybe he couldn't get his guidebook organized, but organizing the household was another matter entirely. There was something fulfilling about that, something consoling—or more than consoling; it gave him the sense of warding off a danger. Over the next week or so, he traveled through the rooms setting up new systems. He radically rearranged all the kitchen cupboards, tossing out the little bits of things in sticky, dusty bottles that Sarah hadn't opened in years. He plugged the vacuum cleaner into a hundred-foot extension cord originally meant for lawn mowers. He went out to the yard and weeded, trimmed, pruned, clipped—stripping down, he pictured it. Up till now Sarah had done the gardening, and certain features of it came as a surprise to him. One variety of weed shot off seeds explosively the instant he touched it, a magnificent last-ditch stand, while others gave way so easily—too easily, breaking at the topmost joint so their roots remained in the ground. Such tenacity! Such genius for survival! Why couldn't human beings do as well?

He stretched a clothesline across the basement so he wouldn't have to use the dryer. Dryers were a terrible waste of energy. Then he disconnected the dryer's wide, flexible exhaust tube, and he taught the cat to go in and out through the empty windowpane where the tube had exited. This meant no more litterbox. Several times a day the cat leapt soundlessly to the laundry sink, stood up long and sinewy on her hind legs, and sprang through the window.

It was a pity Edward couldn't do the same. Macon hated walking him; Edward had never been trained to heel and kept winding his leash around Macon's legs. Oh, dogs were so much trouble. Dogs ate mammoth amounts of food, too; Edward's kibble had to be lugged home from the supermarket, dragged out of the car trunk and up the steep front steps and through the house to the pantry.

But for that, at least, Macon finally thought of a solution. At the foot of the old coal chute in the basement he set a plastic trash can, with a square cut out of the bottom. Then he poured the remainder of a sack of kibble into the trash can, which magically became a continuous feeder like the cat's. Next time he bought dog food, he could just drive around to the side of the house and send it rattling down the coal chute.

The only hitch was, Edward turned out to be scared of the basement. Every morning he went to the pantry where his breakfast used to be served, and he sat on his fat little haunches and whimpered. Macon had to carry him bodily down the basement stairs, staggering slightly while Edward scrabbled in his arms. Since the whole idea had been to spare Macon's tricky back, he felt he'd defeated his purpose. Still, he kept trying.

Also with his back in mind, he tied the clothes basket to Ethan's old skateboard and he dropped a drawstring bag down the laundry chute at the end of a rope. This meant he never had to carry the laundry either up or down the stairs, or even across the basement. Sometimes, though—laboriously scooting the wheeled basket from the clothesline to the laundry chute, stuffing clean sheets into the bag, running upstairs to haul them in by the long, stiff rope—Macon felt a twinge of embarrassment. Was it possible that this might be sort of silly?

Well, everything was silly, when you got right down to it.

The neighborhood must have learned by now that Sarah had left him. People started telephoning on ordinary weeknights and inviting him to take 'potluck' with them. Macon thought at first they meant one of those arrangements where everybody brings a different pot of something and if you're lucky you end up with a balanced meal. He arrived at Bob and Sue Carney's with a bowl of macaroni and cheese. Since Sue was serving spaghetti, he didn't feel he'd been all that lucky. She set his macaroni at one end of the table and no one ate it but Delilah, the three-year-old. She had several helpings, though.

Macon hadn't expected to find the children at the table. He saw he was somebody different now, some kind of bachelor uncle who was assumed to need a glimpse of family life from time to time. But the fact was, he had never much liked other people's children. And gatherings of any sort depressed him. Physical contact with people not related to him—an arm around his shoulder, a hand on his sleeve—made him draw inward like a snail. 'You know, Macon,' Sue Carney said, leaning across the table to pat his wrist, 'whenever you get the urge, you're welcome to drop in on us. Don't wait for an invitation.'

'That's nice of you, Sue,' he said. He wondered why it was that outsiders' skin felt so unreal—almost waxy, as if there were an invisible extra layer between him and them. As soon as possible, he moved his wrist.

'If you could live any way you wanted,' Sarah had once told him, 'I suppose you'd end up on a desert island with no other human beings.'

'Why! That's not true at all,' he'd said. 'I'd have you, and Ethan, and my sister and brothers . . .'

'But no people. I mean, people there just by chance, people you didn't know.'

'Well, no, I guess not,' he'd said. 'Would you?'

But of course she would—back then. Back before Ethan died. She'd always been a social person. When there was nothing else to do she'd stroll happily through a shopping mall—Macon's notion of hell, with all those strangers' shoulders brushing his. Sarah thought crowds were exciting. She liked to meet new people. She was fond of parties, even cocktail parties. You'd have to be crazy to like cocktail parties, Macon thought—those scenes of confusion she used to drag him to, where he was made to feel guilty if he managed by some fluke to get involved in a conversation of any depth. 'Circulate. Circulate,' Sarah would hiss, passing behind him with her drink.

That had changed during this past year. Sarah didn't like crowds anymore. She never went near a mall, hadn't made him go to any parties. They attended only quiet little dinners and she herself had not given a dinner since Ethan died. He'd asked her once, 'Shouldn't we have the Smiths and Millards over? They've had us so often.'

Sarah said, 'Yes. You're right. Pretty soon.' And then did nothing about it.

He and she had met at a party. They'd been seventeen years old. It was one of those mixer things, combining their two schools. Even at that age Macon had disliked parties, but he was secretly longing to fall in love and so he had braved this mixer but then stood off in a corner looking unconcerned, he hoped, and sipping his ginger ale. It was 1958. The rest of the world was in button-down shirts, but Macon wore a black turtleneck sweater, black slacks, and sandals. (He was passing through his poet stage.) And Sarah, a bubbly girl with a tumble of copper-brown curls and a round face, large blue eyes, a plump lower lip—she wore something pink, he remembered, that made her skin look radiant. She was ringed by admiring boys. She was short and tidily made, and there was something plucky about the way her little tan calves were so firmly braced, as if she were determined that this looming flock of basketball stars and football stars would not bowl her over. Macon gave up on her at once. No, not even that—he didn't even consider her, not for a single second, but gazed beyond her to other, more attainable girls. So it had to be Sarah who made the first move. She came over to him and asked what he was acting so stuck-up about. 'Stuck-up!' he said. 'I'm not stuck-up.'

'You sure do look it.'

'No, I'm just . . . bored,' he told her.

'Well, so do you want to dance, or not?'

They danced. He was so unprepared that it passed in a blur. He enjoyed it only later, back home, where he could think it over in a calmer state of mind. And thinking it over, he saw that if he hadn't looked stuck-up she never would have noticed him. He was the only boy who had not openly pursued her. He would be wise not to pursue her in the future; not to seem too eager, not to show his feelings. With Sarah you had to keep your dignity, he sensed.

Lord knows, though, keeping his dignity wasn't easy. Macon lived with his grandparents, and they believed that no one under eighteen ought to have a driver's license. (Never mind if the state of Maryland felt otherwise.) So Grandfather Leary drove Macon and Sarah on their dates. His car was a long black Buick with a velvety gray backseat on which Macon sat all by himself, for his grandfather considered it unseemly for the two of them to sit there together. 'I am not your hired chauffeur,' he said, 'and besides, the backseat has connotations.' (Much of Macon's youth was ruled by connotations.) So Macon sat alone in back and Sarah sat up front with Grandfather Leary. Her cloud of hair, seen against the glare of oncoming headlights, reminded Macon of a burning bush. He would lean forward, clear his throat, and ask, 'Um, did you finish your term paper?'

Sarah would say, 'Pardon?'

'Term paper,' Grandfather Leary would tell her. 'Boy wants to know if you finished it.'

'Oh. Yes, I finished it.'

'She finished it,' Grandfather Leary relayed to Macon.

'I do have ears, Grandfather.'

'You want to get out and walk? Because I don't have to stand for any mouthing off. I could be home with my loved ones, not motoring around in the dark.'

'Sorry, Grandfather.'

Macon's only hope was silence. He sat back, still and aloof, knowing that when Sarah looked she'd see nothing but a gleam of blond hair and a blank face—the rest darkness, his black turtleneck blending into the shadows. It worked. 'What do you *think* about all the time?' she asked in his ear as they two-stepped around her school gym. He only quirked a corner of his mouth, as if amused, and didn't answer.

Things weren't much different when he got his license. Things weren't much different when he went away to college, though he did give up his black turtlenecks and turn into a Princeton man, crisply, casually attired in white shirts and khakis. Separated from

Sarah, he felt a constant hollowness, but in his letters he talked only about his studies. Sarah, home at Goucher, wrote back, *Don't you miss me a little? I can't go anywhere we've been for fear I'll see you looking so mysterious across the room.* She signed her letters *I love you* and he signed his *Fondly.* At night he dreamed she lay next to him, her curls making a whispery sound against his pillow, although all they'd done in real life was a lengthy amount of kissing. He wasn't sure, to tell the truth, that he could manage much more without . . . how did they put it in those days? Losing his cool. Sometimes, he was almost angry with Sarah. He felt he'd been backed into a false position. He was forced to present this impassive front if he wanted her to love him. Oh, so much was expected of men!

She wrote she wasn't dating other people. Neither was Macon, but of course he didn't say so. He came home in the summer and worked at his grandfather's factory; Sarah worked on a tan at the neighborhood pool. Halfway through that summer, she said she wondered why he'd never asked to sleep with her. Macon thought about that and then said, levelly, that in fact he'd like to ask her now. They went to her parents' house; her parents were vacationing in Rehoboth. They climbed the stairs to her little bedroom, all white ruffles and hot sunlight baking the smell of fresh paint. 'Did you bring a whatchamacallit?' Sarah asked, and Macon, unwilling to admit that he hardly knew what one looked like, barked, '*No, I didn't bring a whatchamacallit, who do you think I am?*'—a senseless question, if you stopped to examine it, but Sarah took it to mean that he was shocked by her, that he thought her too forward, and she said, 'Well, excuse me for living!' and ran down the stairs and out of the house. It took him half an hour to find her, and longer than that to make her stop crying. Really, he said, he'd only been thinking of her welfare: In his experience, whatchamacallits weren't all that safe. He tried to sound knowledgeable and immune to passions of the moment. He suggested she visit a doctor he knew—it happened to be the doctor who treated his grandmother's Female Complaint. Sarah dried her tears and borrowed Macon's pen to write the doctor's name on the back of a chewing gum wrapper. But wouldn't the doctor refuse her? she asked. Wouldn't he say she ought to be at least engaged? Well, all right, Macon said, they would get engaged. Sarah said that would be lovely.

Their engagement lasted three years, all through college. Grandfather Leary felt the wedding should be delayed even further, till Macon was firmly settled in his place of employment; but since his place of employment would be Leary Metals, which manufactured cork-lined caps for soft drink bottles, Macon couldn't see himself concentrating on that even briefly. Besides, the rush to and from Sarah's bedroom on her mother's Red Cross days had begun to tell on them both.

So they married the spring they graduated from college, and Macon went to work at the factory while Sarah taught English at a private school. It was seven years before Ethan was born. By that time, Sarah was no longer calling Macon 'mysterious.' When he was quiet now it seemed to annoy her. Macon sensed this, but there was nothing he could do about it. In some odd way, he was locked inside the stand-offish self he'd assumed when he and she first met. He was frozen there. It was like that old warning of his grandmother's: Don't cross your eyes, they might get stuck that way. No matter how he tried to change his manner, Sarah continued to deal with him as if he were someone unnaturally cool-headed, someone more even in temperament than she but perhaps not quite as feeling.

He had once come upon a questionnaire that she'd filled out in a ladies' magazine—one of those 'How Happy Is Your Marriage?' things—and where it said, *I believe I love my spouse more than he/she loves me*, Sarah had checked *True*. The unsettling part was that after Macon gave his automatic little snort of denial, he had wondered if it might be true after all. Somehow, his role had sunk all the way through to the heart. Even internally, by now, he was a fairly chilly man, and if you didn't count his son (who was easy, *easy*; a child is no test at all), there was not one person in his life whom he really agonized over.

When he thought about this now, it was a relief to remind himself that he did miss Sarah, after all. But then his relief seemed unfeeling too, and he groaned and shook his head and tugged his hair in great handfuls.

Some woman phoned and said, 'Macon?' He could tell at once it wasn't Sarah. Sarah's voice was light and breathy; this one was rough, tough, wiry. 'It's Muriel,' she said.

'Muriel,' he said.

'Muriel Pritchett.'

'Ah, yes,' he said, but he still had no clue who she was.

'From the vet's?' she asked. 'Who got on so good with your dog?'

'Oh, the vet's!'

He saw her, if dimly. He saw her saying her own name, the long *u* sound and the *p* drawing up her dark red mouth.

'I was just wondering how Edward was.'

Macon glanced over at Edward. The two of them were in the study, where Macon had managed to type half a page. Edward lay flat on his stomach with his legs straight out behind him—short, pudgy legs like the drumsticks of a dressed Long Island duckling. 'He looks all right to me,' Macon said.

'I mean, is he biting?'

'Well, not lately, but he's developed this new symptom. He gets angry if I leave the house. He starts barking and showing his teeth.'

'I still think he ought to be trained.'

'Oh, you know, he's four and a half and I suppose—'

'That's not too old! I could do it in no time. Tell you what, maybe I could just come around and discuss it. You and me could have a drink or something and talk about what his problems are.'

'Well, I really don't think—'

'Or you could come to *my* place. I'd fix you supper.'

Macon wondered how it would help Edward to be dragged to supper at some stranger's house.

'Macon? What do you say?' she asked.

'Oh, why, um . . . I think for now I'll just try to manage on my own.'

'Well, I can understand that,' she said. 'Believe me. I've been through that stage. So what I'll do is, I'll wait for you to get in touch. You do still have my card, don't you?'

Macon said he did, although he had no idea where it had got to.

'I don't want to be pushy!' she said.

'No, well . . .' Macon said. Then he hung up and went back to his guidebook.

He was still on the introduction, and it was already the end of August. How would he meet his deadline? The back of the desk chair hit his spine in just the wrong place. The *s* key kept sticking. The typewriter tapped out audible words. 'Inimitable,' it said. His typing sounded just like Sarah saying 'inimitable.' 'You in your inimitable way . . .' she told him. He gave a quick shake of his head. *Generally food in England is not as jarring as in other foreign countries. Nice cooked vegetables, things in white sauce, pudding for dessert . . . I don't know why some travelers complain about English food.*

In September, he decided to alter his system of dressing. If he wore sweat suits at home—the zipper-free kind, nothing to scratch or bind him—he could go from one shower to the next without changing clothes. The sweat suit would serve as both pajamas and day wear.

He bought a couple of them, medium gray. The first night he wore one to bed he enjoyed the feel of it, and he liked not having to dress the next morning. In fact, it occurred to him that he might as well wear the same outfit two days in a row; skip his shower on alternate evenings. Talk about saving energy! In the morning all he had to do was shave. He wondered if he ought to grow a beard.

Around noon of the second day, though, he started feeling a little low. He was sitting at his typewriter and something made him notice his posture—stooped and sloppy. He blamed the sweat suit. He rose and went to the full-length mirror in the hall. His reflection reminded him of a patient in a mental hospital. Part of the trouble, perhaps, was his shoes—regular black tie shoes intended for dressier clothes. Should he buy sneakers? But he would hate to be mistaken for a jogger. He noticed that without a belt around his waist, he tended to let his stomach stick out. He stood up straighter. That evening when it was time to wash the first sweat suit, he used extra-hot water to shrink out some of the bagginess.

He felt much worse in the morning. It had been a warm night and he woke up sticky and cross. He couldn't face the thought of popcorn for breakfast. He laundered a load of sheets and then, in the midst of hanging them, found himself standing motionless with his head bowed, both wrists dangling over the clothesline as if he himself had been pinned there. 'Buck up,' he said aloud. His voice sounded creaky, out of practice.

This was his day for grocery shopping—Tuesday, when the supermarket was least crowded with other human beings. But somehow, he couldn't bring himself to get going. He dreaded all that business with the address books, the three tabbed books he shopped with. (One held data from *Consumer Reports*—the top-rated brand of bread, for instance, listed under B. In another he noted prices, and in the third he filed his coupons.) He kept having to stop and riffle through them, muttering prices under his breath, comparing house brands to cents-off name brands. Oh, everything seemed so complicated. Why bother? Why eat at all, in fact?

On the other hand, he needed milk. And Edward was low on dog food, and Helen was completely out of cat food.

He did something he'd never done before. He telephoned The Market Basket, a small, expensive grocery that delivered. And he didn't order just emergency rations. No, he called in the whole week's list. 'Shall we bring this to the front or the back?' the clerk asked in her tinselly voice.

'The back,' Macon said. 'No, wait. Bring the perishables to the back, but put the dog food next to the coal chute.'

'Coal chute,' the clerk repeated, apparently writing it down.

'The coal chute at the side of the house. But not the cat food; that goes in back with the perishables.'

'Well, wait now—'

'And the upstairs items at the front of the house.'

'What upstairs items?'

'Toothpaste, Ivory soap, dog biscuits . . .'

'I thought you said the dog biscuits went to the coal chute.'

'Not the dog biscuits, the dog *food*! It's the food that goes to the coal chute, dammit.'

'Now, look here,' the clerk said. 'There's no call to be rude.'

'Well, I'm sorry,' Macon told her, 'but I just want the simplest thing, it seems to me: one puny box of Milkbone biscuits up beside my bed. If I give Edward my buttered popcorn it upsets his stomach. Otherwise I wouldn't mind; it's not as if I'm hoarding it all for myself or something, but he has this sensitivity to fats and I'm the only one in the house, it's me who has to clean up if he gets sick. I'm the only one to do it; I'm all alone; it's just me; it seems everybody's just . . . fled from me, I don't know, I've lost them, I'm left standing here saying, "Where'd they go? Where is everybody? Oh, God, what did I do that was so bad?" '

His voice was not behaving right and he hung up. He stood over the telephone rubbing his forehead. Had he given her his name? Or

not. He couldn't remember. Please, please, let him not have given
her his name.

He was falling apart; that much was obvious. He would have
to get a grip on himself. First thing: out of this sweat suit. It was
some kind of jinx. He clapped his hands together briskly, and then
he climbed the stairs. In the bathroom, he yanked off the sweat
suit and dropped it into the tub. Yesterday's hung from the shower
curtain rod, still damp. There wasn't a chance it would dry by
tonight. What a mistake! He felt like a fool. He'd come within an
inch, within a hairs-breadth of turning into one of those pathetic
creatures you see on the loose from time to time—unwashed,
unshaven, shapeless, talking to themselves, padding along in their
institutional garb.

Neatly dressed now in a white shirt and khakis, he gathered
the damp sweat suit and carried it down to the basement. It would
make good winter pajamas, at least. He put it in the dryer, wedged
the exhaust tube in the window again, and set the dials. Better to
consume a little energy than to fall into despair over a soggy sweat
suit.

At the top of the basement stairs, Edward was complaining. He
was hungry, but not brave enough to descend the stairs on his own.
When he caught sight of Macon he lay flat, with his nose poking
over the topmost step, and put on a hopeful expression. 'Coward,'
Macon told him. He scooped Edward up in both arms and turned to
lumber back down. Edward's teeth started chattering—a tickety-
tick like rice in a cup. It occurred to Macon that Edward might know
something he didn't. Was the basement haunted, or what? It had
been weeks now, and Edward was still so frightened that sometimes,

set in front of his food, he just stood there dismally and made a puddle without bothering to lift his leg. 'You're being very silly, Edward,' Macon told him.

Just then, an eerie howl rose from . . . where? From the basement's very air, it seemed. It continued steadily; it grew. Edward, who must have been expecting this all along, kicked off instantly with his sturdy, clawed hind legs against Macon's diaphragm. Macon felt the wind knocked out of him. Edward whomped into the wall of damp body bags on the clothesline, rebounded, and landed in the center of Macon's stomach. Macon set one foot blindly in the wheeled basket and his legs went out from under him. He stepped down hard into empty space.

He was lying on his back, on the clammy cement floor, with his left leg doubled beneath him. The sound that had set all this in motion paused for one split second and then resumed. It was clear now that it came from the dryer's exhaust tube. 'Shoot,' Macon said to Edward, who lay panting on top of him. 'Wouldn't you think that idiot cat would know the dryer was running?'

He could see how it must have happened. Attempting to enter from outside, she'd been met by a whistling wind, but she had stubbornly continued into the tube. He pictured her eyes pressed into slits, her ears flattened back by a lint-filled gale. Wailing and protesting, she had nonetheless clung to her course. What persistence!

Macon shook Edward off and rolled over on his stomach. Even so small a movement caused him agony. He felt a lump of nausea beginning in his throat, but he rolled once more, dragging his leg behind him. With his teeth set, he reached for the door of the dryer and pulled it open. The sweat suit slowly stopped revolving. The cat stopped howling. Macon watched her bumbling, knobby shape inching backward through the tube. Just as she reached her exit, the entire tube fell out of the window and into the laundry sink, but Helen didn't fall with it. He hoped she was all right. He watched until she scurried past the other window, looking just slightly rumpled. Then he drew a breath and began the long, hard trip up the stairs for help.

5

—— 'Oh, I've erred and I have stumbled,' Macon's sister sang in the kitchen, 'I've been sinful and unwise . . .'

She had a tremulous soprano that sounded like an old lady's, although she was younger than Macon. You could imagine such a voice in church, some country kind of church where the women still wore flat straw hats.

> *I'm just a lucky pilgrim*
> *On the road to Paradise.*

Macon was lying on the daybed in his grandparents' sun porch. His left leg, encased in plaster from mid-thigh to instep, was not painful so much as absent. There was a constant dull, cottony numbness that made him want to pinch his own shin. Not that he could, of course. He was sealed away from himself. The hardest blow felt like a knock on the wall from a neighboring room.

Still, he felt a kind of contentment. He lay listening to his sister fix breakfast, idly scratching the cat who had made herself a nest in the blankets. 'I've had trials, I've had sorrows,' Rose trilled merrily, 'I've had grief and sacrifice . . .' Once she got the coffee started, she would come help him across the living room to the downstairs bathroom. He still found it difficult to navigate, especially on polished floors. Nowadays he marveled at all those people on crutches whom he used to take for granted. He saw them as a flock of stalky wading birds, dazzlingly competent with their sprightly hops and debonaire pivots. How did they do it?

His own crutches, so new their rubber tips were not yet scuffed, leaned against the wall. His bathrobe hung over a chair. Beneath the window was a folding card table with a wood-grained cardboard top and rickety legs. His grandparents had been dead for years, but the table remained set up as if for one of their eternal bridge games. Macon knew that on its underside was a yellowed label reading ATLAS MFG. CO., with a steel engraving of six plump, humorless men in high-collared suits standing upon a board laid across the very same table. FURNISHINGS OF DECEPTIVE DELICACY, the caption said. Macon associated the phrase with his grandmother: deceptive delicacy. Lying on the sun porch floor as a boy, he had studied her fragile legs, from which her anklebones jutted out like doorknobs. Her solid, black, chunky-heeled shoes were planted squarely a foot apart, never tapping or fidgeting.

He heard his brother Porter upstairs, whistling along with Rose's song. He knew it was Porter because Charles never whistled. There was the sound of a shower running. His sister looked through the sun porch door, with Edward peering around her and panting at Macon as if he were laughing.

'Macon? Are you awake?' Rose asked.

'I've *been* awake for hours,' he told her, for there was something vague about her that caused her brothers to act put-upon and needy whenever she chanced to focus on them. She was pretty in a sober, prim way, with beige hair folded unobtrusively at the back of her neck where it wouldn't be a bother. Her figure was a very young girl's, but her clothes were spinsterly and concealing.

She wrapped him in his bathrobe and helped him stand up. Now his leg actively hurt. It seemed the pain was a matter of gravity. A throbbing ache sank slowly down the length of the bone. With Rose supporting him on one side and a crutch on the other, he hobbled out of the sun porch, through the living room with its shabby, curlicued furniture. The dog kept getting underfoot. 'Maybe I could stop and rest a moment,' Macon said when they passed the couch.

'It's only a little farther.'

They entered the pantry. Rose opened the bathroom door and helped him inside. 'Call me when you're ready,' she said, closing the door after him. Macon sagged against the sink.

At breakfast, Porter was cheerily talkative while the others ate in silence. Porter was the best-looking of all the Learys—more tightly knit than Macon, his hair a brighter shade of blond. He gave an impression of vitality and direction that his brothers lacked. 'Got a lot to do today,' he said between mouthfuls. 'That meeting with Herrin, interviews for Dave's old job, Cates flying in from Atlanta . . .'

Charles just sipped his coffee. While Porter was already dressed, Charles still wore his pajamas. He was a soft, sweet-faced man who never seemed to move; any time you looked at him he'd be watching you with his sorrowful eyes that slanted downward at the outer corners.

Rose brought the coffeepot from the stove. 'Last night, Edward woke me twice asking to go out,' she said. 'Do you think he has some sort of kidney problem?'

'It's the adjustment,' Macon said. 'Adjustment to change. I wonder how he knows not to wake *me*.'

Porter said, 'Maybe we could rig up some sort of system. One of those little round pet doors or something.'

'Edward's kind of portly for a pet door,' Macon said.

'Besides,' Rose said, 'the yard's not fenced. We can't let him out on his own if he's not fenced in.'

'A litterbox, then,' Porter suggested.

'Litterbox! For a dog?'

'Why not? If it were big enough.'

Macon said, 'Use a bathtub. The one in the basement. No one goes there anymore.'

'But who would clean it?'

'Ah.'

They all looked down at Edward, who was lying at Rose's feet. He rolled his eyes at them.

'How come you have him, anyway?' Porter asked Macon.

'He was Ethan's.'

'Oh. I see,' Porter said. He gave a little cough. 'Animals!' he said brightly. 'Ever considered what they must think of us? I mean, here we come back from the grocery store with the most amazing haul—chicken, pork, half a cow. We leave at nine and we're back at ten, evidently having caught an entire herd of beasts. They must think we're the greatest hunters on earth!'

Macon leaned back in his chair with his coffee mug cupped in both hands. The sun was warming the breakfast table, and the kitchen smelled of toast. He almost wondered whether, by some devious, subconscious means, he had engineered this injury— every elaborate step leading up to it—just so he could settle down safe among the people he'd started out with.

Charles and Porter left for the factory, and Rose went upstairs and ran the vacuum cleaner. Macon, who was supposed to be typing his guidebook, struggled back to the sun porch and collapsed. Since he'd come home he'd been sleeping too much. The urge to sleep was like a great black cannonball rolling around inside his skull, making his head heavy and droopy.

On the wall at the end of the room hung a portrait of the four Leary children: Charles, Porter, Macon, and Rose, clustered in an armchair. Their grandfather had commissioned that portrait several years before they came to live with him. They were still in California with their mother—a giddy young war widow. From time to time she sent snapshots, but Grandfather Leary found those inadequate. By their very nature, he told her in his letters, photos lied. They showed what a person looked like over a fraction of a second—not over long, slow minutes, which was what you'd take to study someone in real life. In that case, said Alicia, didn't paintings lie also? They showed hours instead of minutes. It wasn't Grandfather Leary she said this to, but the artist, an elderly Californian whose name Grandfather Leary had somehow got hold of. If the artist had had a reply, Macon couldn't remember what it was.

He could remember sitting for the portrait, though, and now when he looked at it he had a very clear picture of his mother standing just outside the gilded frame in a pink kimono, watching the painting take shape while she toweled her hair dry. She had fluffy, short, brittle hair whose color she 'helped along,' as she put it. Her face was a type no longer seen—it wasn't just unfashionable, it had vanished altogether. How did women mold their basic forms to suit the times? Were there no more of those round chins, round foreheads, and bruised, baroque little mouths so popular in the forties?

The artist, it was obvious, found her very attractive. He kept pausing in his work to say he wished she were the subject. Alicia gave a breathless laugh and shooed away his words with one hand. Probably later she had gone out with him a few times. She was always taking up with new men, and they were always the most exciting men in the world, to hear her tell it. If they were artists, why, she had to give a party and get all her friends to buy their paintings. If they flew small planes on weekends, she had to start pilot's lessons. If they were political, there she was on street corners thrusting petitions on passersby. Her children were too young to worry about the men themselves, if there was any reason to worry. No, it was her enthusiasm that disturbed them. Her enthusiasm came in spurts, a violent zigzag of hobbies, friends, boyfriends, causes. She always seemed about to fall over the brink of something. She was always going too far. Her voice had an edge to it, as if at any moment it might break. The faster she talked and the brighter her eyes grew, the more fixedly her children stared at her, as if willing her to follow their example of steadiness and dependability. 'Oh, what is it with you?' she would ask them. 'Why are you such sticks?' And she would give up on them and flounce off to meet her crowd. Rose, the baby, used to wait for her return in the hall, sucking her thumb and stroking an old fur stole that Alicia never wore anymore.

Sometimes Alicia's enthusiasm turned to her children—an unsettling experience. She took them all to the circus and bought them cotton candy that none of them enjoyed. (They liked to keep themselves tidy.) She yanked them out of school and enrolled them briefly in an experimental learning community where no one wore clothes. The four of them, chilled and miserable, sat hunched in a row in the common room with their hands pressed flat between their bare knees. She dressed as a witch and went trick-or-treating with them, the most mortifying Halloween of their lives, for she got carried away as usual and cackled, croaked, scuttled up to strangers and shook her ragged broom in their faces. She started making mother-daughter outfits for herself and Rose, in strawberry pink with puffed sleeves, but stopped when the sewing machine pierced her finger and made her cry. (She was always getting hurt. It may have been because she rushed so.) Then she turned to something else, and something else, and something else. She believed in change as if it were a religion. Feeling sad? Find a new man! Creditors after you, rent due, children running fevers? Move to a new apartment! During one year, they moved so often that every day after school, Macon had to stand deliberating a while before setting out for home.

In 1950, she decided to marry an engineer who traveled around the world building bridges. 'Portugal. Panama. Brazil,' she told the children. 'We'll finally get to see our planet.' They gazed at her stonily. If they had met this man before, they had no recollection of it. Alicia said, 'Aren't you excited?' Later—it may have been after he took them all out to dinner—she said she was sending them to live with their grandparents instead. 'Baltimore's more suitable for children, really,' she said. Did they protest? Macon couldn't remember. He recalled his childhood as a glassed-in place with grown-ups rushing past, talking at him, making changes, while he himself stayed mute. At any rate, one hot night in June Alicia put them on a plane to Baltimore. They were met by their grandparents, two thin, severe, distinguished people in dark clothes. The children approved of them at once.

After that, they saw Alicia only rarely. She would come breezing into town with an armload of flimsy gifts from tropical countries. Her print dresses struck the children as flashy; her makeup was too vivid, like a foreigner's. She seemed to find her children comical —their navy-and-white school uniforms, their perfect posture. 'My God! How stodgy you've grown!' she would cry, evidently forgetting she'd thought them stodgy all along. She said they took after their father. They sensed this wasn't meant as a compliment. (When they asked what their father had been like, she looked down at her own chin and said, 'Oh, Alicia, grow up.') Later, when her sons married, she seemed to see even more resemblance for at one time or another she'd apologized to all three daughters-in-law for what they must have to put up with. Like some naughty, gleeful fairy, Macon imagined, she darted in and out of their lives leaving a trail of irresponsible remarks, apparently never considering they might be passed on. 'I don't see how you stay married to the man,' she'd said to Sarah. She herself was now on her fourth husband, a rock-garden architect with a white goatee.

It was true the children in the portrait seemed unrelated to her. They lacked her blue-and-gold coloring; their hair had an ashy cast and their eyes were a steely gray. They all had that distinct center groove from nose to upper lip. And never in a million years would Alicia have worn an expression so guarded and suspicious.

Uncomfortably arranged-looking, they gazed out at the viewer. The two older boys, plump Charles and trim Porter, perched on either arm of the chair in white shirts with wide, flat, open collars. Rose and Macon sat on the seat in matching playsuits. Rose appeared to be in Macon's lap, although actually she'd been settled between his knees, and Macon had the indrawn tenseness of someone placed in a physically close situation he wasn't accustomed to. His hair, like the others', slanted silkily across his forehead. His mouth was thin, almost colorless, and firmed a bit, as if he'd decided to take a stand on something. The set of that mouth echoed now in Macon's mind. He glanced at it, glanced away, glanced back. It was Ethan's mouth. Macon had spent twelve years imagining Ethan as a sort of exchange student, a visitor from the outside world, and here it turned out he'd been a Leary all along. What a peculiar thing to recognize at this late date.

He sat up sharply and reached for his trousers, which Rose had cut short across the left thigh and hemmed with tiny, even stitches.

No one else in the world had the slightest idea where he was. Not Julian, not Sarah, not anyone. Macon liked knowing that. He said as much to Rose. 'It's nice to be so unconnected,' he told her. 'I wish things could stay that way a while.'

'Why can't they?'

'Oh, well, you know, someone will call here, Sarah or someone—'

'Maybe we could just not answer the phone.'

'What, let it go on ringing?'

'Why not?'

'Not answer it *any* time?'

'Most who call me are neighbors,' Rose said. 'They'll pop over in person if they don't get an answer. And you know the boys: Neither one of them likes dealing with telephones.'

'That's true,' Macon said.

Julian would come knocking on his door, planning to harangue him for letting his deadline slip past. He'd have to give up. Then Sarah would come for a soup ladle or something, and when he didn't answer she would ask the neighbors and they'd say he hadn't shown his face in some time. She would try to get in touch with his family and the telephone would ring and ring, and then she would start to worry. *What's happened?* she would wonder. *How could I have left him on his own?*

Lately, Macon had noticed he'd begun to view Sarah as a form of enemy. He'd stopped missing her and started plotting her remorsefulness. It surprised him to see how quickly he'd made the transition. Was this what two decades of marriage amounted to? He liked to imagine her self-reproaches. He composed and recomposed her apologies. He hadn't had such thoughts since he was a child, dreaming of how his mother would weep at his funeral.

In the daytime, working at the dining room table, he would hear the telephone and he'd pause, fingers at rest on the typewriter keys. One ring, two rings. Three rings. Rose would walk in with a jar of silver polish. She didn't even seem to hear. 'What if that's some kind of emergency?' he would ask. Rose would say, 'Hmm? Who would call *us* for an emergency?' and then she would take the silver from the buffet and spread it at the other end of the table.

There had always been some family member requiring Rose's care. Their grandmother had been bedridden for years before she died, and then their grandfather got so senile, and first Charles and later Porter had failed in their marriages and come back home. So she had enough right here to fill her time. Or she made it enough; for surely it couldn't be necessary to polish every piece of silver every week. Shut in the house with her all day, Macon noticed how painstakingly she planned the menus; how often she reorganized the utensil drawer; how she ironed even her brothers' socks, first separating them from the clever plastic grips she used to keep them mated in the washing machine. For Macon's lunch, she cooked a real meal and served it on regular place mats. She set out cut-glass dishes of pickles and olives that had to be returned to their bottles later on. She dolloped homemade mayonnaise into a tiny bowl.

Macon wondered if it ever occurred to her that she lived an odd sort of life—unemployed, unmarried, supported by her brothers. But what job would she be suited for? he asked himself. Although he could picture her, come to think of it, as the mainstay of some musty, antique law firm or accounting firm. Nominally a secretary, she would actually run the whole business, arranging everything just so on her employer's desk every morning and allowing no one below her or above her to overlook a single detail. Macon could use a secretary like that. Recalling the gum-chewing redhead in Julian's disastrous office, he sighed and wished the world had more Roses.

He zipped a page from his typewriter and set it face down on a stack of others. He had finished with his introduction—general instructions like *A subway is not an underground train* and *Don't say restroom, say toilet*—and he'd finished the chapter called 'Trying to Eat in England.' Rose had mailed those off for him yesterday. That was his new stratagem: sending his book piece by piece from this undisclosed location. 'There's no return address on this,' Rose told him. 'There's not meant to be,' Macon said. Rose had nodded solemnly. She was the only one in the family who viewed his guidebooks as real writing. She kept a row of them in her bedroom bookcase, alphabetized by country.

In midafternoon, Rose stopped work to watch her favorite soap opera. This was something Macon didn't understand. How could she waste her time on such trash? She said it was because there was a wonderfully evil woman in it. 'There are enough evil people in real life,' Macon told her.

'Yes, but not wonderfully evil.'

'Well, that's for sure.'

'This one, you see, is so obvious. You know exactly whom to mistrust.'

While she watched, she talked aloud to the characters. Macon could hear her in the dining room. 'It isn't *you* he's after, sweetie,' she said, and 'Just you wait. Ha!'—not at all her usual style of speech. A commercial broke in, but Rose stayed transfixed where she was. Macon, meanwhile, worked on 'Trying to Sleep in England,' typing away in a dogged, uninspired rhythm.

When the doorbell rang, Rose didn't respond. Edward went mad, barking and scratching at the door and running back to Macon and racing again to the door. 'Rose?' Macon called. She said nothing. Finally he stood up, assembled himself on his crutches, and went as quietly as possible to the hall.

Well, it wasn't Sarah. A glance through the lace curtain told him that much. He opened the door and peered out. 'Yes?' he said.

It was Garner Bolt, a neighbor from home—a scrawny little gray man who had made his fortune in cleaning supplies. When he saw Macon, every line in his pert, pointed face turned upward. 'There you are!' he said. It was hard to hear him over Edward, who went on barking frantically.

'Why, Garner,' Macon said.

'We worried you had died.'

'You did?'

Macon grabbed at Edward's collar, but missed.

'Saw the papers piling up on your lawn, mail inside your screen door, didn't know what to think.'

'Well, I meant to send my sister for those,' Macon said. 'I broke my leg, you see.'

'Now, how did you do that?'

'It's a long story.'

He gave up blocking the door. 'Come on in,' he told Garner.

Garner took off his cap, which had a Sherwin-Williams Paint sign across the front. His jacket was part of some long-ago suit, a worn shiny brown, and his overalls were faded to white at the knees. He stepped inside, skirting the dog, and shut the door behind him. Edward's barks turned to whimpers. 'My car is full of your mail,' Garner said. 'Brenda said I ought to bring it to your sister and ask if she knew of your whereabouts. Also I promised your friend.'

'What friend?'

'Lady in pedal pushers.'

'I don't know any lady in pedal pushers,' Macon said. He hadn't realized pedal pushers still existed, even.

'Saw her standing on your porch, rattling your doorknob. Calling out, "Macon? You in there?" Skinny little lady with hair. Looked to be in her twenties or so.'

'Well, I can't imagine who it was.'

'Squinching in and shading her eyes.'

'Who could it be?'

'Tripping down the porch steps in her great tall pointy high heels.'

'The dog lady,' Macon said. 'Jesus.'

'Kind of young, ain't she?'

'I don't even know her!'

'Going round the back of the house to call out, "Macon? Macon?"'

'I barely met her!'

'It was her that told me about the windle.'

'Windle?'

'Windle to the basement, all broke out. Fall sets in and it'll turn your furnace on. Waste all kinds of energy.'

'Oh. Well. Yes, I suppose it would,' Macon said.

'We thought you might've been burglarized or something.'

Macon led the way to the dining room. 'See, what happened,' he said, 'I broke my leg and I came to live at my family's till I could manage for myself again.'

'We didn't see no ambulance though or nothing.'

'Well, I called my sister.'

'Sister's a doctor?'

'Just to come and take me to the emergency room.'

'When Brenda broke her hip on the missing step,' Garner said, 'she called the ambulance.'

'Well, I called my sister.'

'Brenda called the ambulance.'

They seemed to be stuck.

'I guess I ought to notify the post office about my mail,' Macon said finally. He lowered himself into his chair.

Garner pulled out another chair and sat down with his cap in his hands. He said, 'I could just keep on bringing it.'

'No, I'll have Rose notify them. Lord, all these bills must be coming due and so forth—'

'I could bring it just as easy.'

'Thanks anyway.'

'Why don't I bring it.'

'To tell the truth,' Macon said, 'I'm not so sure I'll be going back there.'

This hadn't occurred to him before. He placed his crutches together delicately, like a pair of chopsticks, and laid them on the floor beside his chair. 'I might stay on here with my family,' he said.

'And give up that fine little house?'

'It's kind of big for just one person.'

Garner frowned down at his cap. He put it on his head, changed his mind, and took it off again. 'Look,' he said. 'Back when me and Brenda were newlyweds we were awful together. Just awful. Couldn't neither one of us stand the other, I'll never know how we lasted.'

'We aren't newlyweds, though,' Macon said. 'We've been married twenty years.'

'Brenda and me did not speak to each other for very nearly every bit of nineteen and thirty-five,' Garner said. 'January to August, nineteen and thirty-five. New Year's Day till my summer vacation. Not a single blessed word.'

Macon's attention was caught. 'What,' he said, 'not even "Pass the salt"? "Open the window"?'

'Not even that.'

'Well, how did you manage your daily life?'

'Mostly, she stayed over to her sister's.'

'Oh, then.'

'The morning my vacation began, I felt so miserable I like to died. Thought to myself, "What am I doing, anyhow?" Called long distance to Ocean City and booked a room for two. In those days long distance was some big deal, let me tell you. Took all these operators and so forth and it cost a mint. Then I packed some clothes for me and some clothes for Brenda and went on over to her sister's house. Her sister says, "What do *you* want?" She was the type that likes to see dissension. I walk right past her. Find Brenda in the living room, mending hose. Open my suitcase: "Look at here. Your sun dress for dining in a seafood restaurant," I tell her. "Two pairs of shorts. Two blouses. Your swimsuit." She don't even look at me. "Your bathrobe," I say. "Your nightgown you wore on our honeymoon." Acts like I'm not even there. "Brenda," I tell her. I say, "Brenda, I am nineteen years old and I'll never be nineteen again. I'll never be *alive* again. I mean this is the only life I get to go through, Brenda, so far as I know, and I've spent this great large chunk of it sitting alone in an empty apartment too proud to make up, too scared you'd say no, but even if you did say no it can't be worse than what I got now. I'm the loneliest man in the world, Brenda, so please come to Ocean City with me." And Brenda, she lays down her mending and says, "Well, since you ask, but it looks to me like you forgot my bathing cap." And off we went.'

He sat back triumphantly in his chair. 'So,' he said.

'So,' Macon said.

'So you get my point.'

'What point?'

'You have to let her know you need her.'

'See, Garner, I think we've gone beyond little things like letting her know I—'

'Don't take this personally, Macon, but I got to level with you: There's times when you've been sort of frustrating. I'm not talking about myself, mind; *I* understand. It's just some of the others in the neighborhood, they've been put off a little. Take during your tragedy. I mean people like to offer help at occasions like that—send flowers and visit at the viewing hour and bring casseroles for after the service. Only you didn't even have a service. Held a cremation, Lord God, somewheres off in Virginia without a word to anyone and come home directly. Peg Everett tells you she's put you in her prayers and Sarah says, "Oh, bless you, Peg," but what do *you* say? You ask Peg if her son might care to take Ethan's bike off your hands.'

Macon groaned. 'Yes,' he said, 'I never know how to behave at these times.'

'Then you mow your lawn like nothing has happened.'

'The grass did keep on growing, Garner.'

'We was all dying to do it for you.'

'Well, thanks,' Macon said, 'but I enjoyed the work.'

'See what I mean?'

Macon said, 'Now, wait. Just to insert some logic into this discussion—'

'That's *exactly* what I mean!'

'You started out talking about Sarah. You've switched to how I disappoint the neighbors.'

'What's the difference? You might not know this, Macon, but you come across as a person that charges ahead on your own somewhat. Just look at the way you walk! The way you, like, *lunge*, lope on down the street with your head running clear in front of your body. If a fellow wants to stop you and, I don't know, offer his condolences, he'd be liable to get plowed down. Now, I know you care, and you know you care, but how does it look to the others? I ask you! No wonder she up and left.'

'Garner, I appreciate your thoughts on this,' Macon said, 'but Sarah's fully aware that I care. I'm not as tongue-tied as you like to make out. And this isn't one of those open-shut, can-this-marriage-be-saved deals, either. I mean, you're just plain goddamned *wrong*, Garner.'

'Well,' Garner said. He looked down at his cap, and after a moment he jammed it abruptly on his head. 'I guess I'll fetch your mail in, then,' he said.

'Right. Thanks.'

Garner rose to his feet and shuffled out. His leaving alerted Edward, who started barking all over again. There was an empty spell during which Macon looked down at his cast and listened to the soap opera from the living room. Meanwhile Edward whined at the door and paced back and forth, clicking his toenails. Then Garner returned. 'Mostly catalogs,' he said, flinging his load on the table. He brought with him the smell of fresh air and dry leaves. 'Brenda said we might as well not bother with the newspapers; just throw them out.'

'Oh, yes, of course,' Macon said.

He stood up and they shook hands. Garner's fingers were crisp and intricately shaped, like crumpled paper. 'Thanks for stopping by,' Macon told him.

'Any time,' Garner said, looking elsewhere.

Macon said, 'I didn't mean, you know—I hope I didn't sound short-tempered.'

'Naw,' Garner said. He lifted an arm and let it drop. 'Shoot. Don't think a thing about it.' Then he turned to leave.

As soon as he did, Macon thought of a flood of other things he should have mentioned. It wasn't all his fault, he wanted to say. Sarah had a little to do with it too. What Sarah needed was a rock, he wanted to say; someone who wouldn't crumble. Otherwise, why had she picked him to marry? But he held his peace and watched Garner walk out. There was something pitiable about the two sharp cords that ran down the back of Garner's neck, cupping a little ditch of mapped brown skin between them.

When his brothers came home from work, the house took on a relaxed, relieved atmosphere. Rose drew the living room curtains and lit a few soft lamps. Charles and Porter changed into sweaters. Macon started mixing his special salad dressing. He believed that if you pulverized the spices first with a marble mortar and pestle, it made all the difference. The others agreed that no one else's dressing tasted as good as Macon's. 'Since you've been gone,' Charles told him, 'we've had to buy that bottled stuff from the grocery store.' He made it sound as if Macon had been gone a few weeks or so—as if his entire marriage had been just a brief trip elsewhere.

For supper they had Rose's pot roast, a salad with Macon's dressing, and baked potatoes. Baked potatoes had always been their favorite food. They had learned to fix them as children, and even after they were big enough to cook a balanced meal they used to exist solely on baked potatoes whenever Alicia left them to their own devices. There was something about the smell of a roasting Idaho that was so cozy, and also, well, *conservative*, was the way Macon put it to himself. He thought back on years and years of winter evenings: the kitchen windows black outside, the corners furry with gathering darkness, the four of them seated at the chipped enamel table meticulously filling scooped-out potato skins with butter. You let the butter melt in the skins while you mashed and seasoned the floury insides; the skins were saved till last. It was almost a ritual. He recalled that once, during one of their mother's longer absences, her friend Eliza had served them what she called potato boats—restuffed, not a bit like the genuine article. The children, with pinched, fastidious expressions, had emptied the stuffing and proceeded as usual with the skins, pretending to overlook her mistake. The skins should be crisp. They should not be salted. The pepper should be freshly ground. Paprika was acceptable, but only if it was American. Hungarian paprika had too distinctive a taste. Personally, Macon could do without paprika altogether.

While they ate, Porter discussed what to do with his children. Tomorrow was his weekly visitation night, when he would drive over to Washington, where his children lived with their mother. 'The thing of it is,' he said, 'eating out in restaurants is so artificial. It doesn't seem like real food. And anyway, they all three have different tastes. They always argue over where to go. Someone's on a diet, someone's turned vegetarian, someone can't stand food that crunches. And I end up shouting, "Oh, for God's sake, we're going to Such-and-Such and that's that!" So we go and everybody sulks throughout the meal.'

'Maybe you should just not visit,' Charles said reasonably. (He had never had children of his own.)

'Well, of course I want to visit, Charles. I just wish we had some different program. You know what would be ideal? If we could all do something with tools together. I mean like the old days before the divorce, when Danny helped me drain the hot water heater or Susan sat on a board I was sawing. If I could just drop by their house, say, and June and her husband could go to a movie or something, then the kids and I would clean the gutters, weatherstrip the windows, wrap the hot water pipes . . . Well, that husband of hers is no use at all, you can bet he lets his hot water pipes sit around naked. I'd bring my own tools, even. We'd have a fine time! Susan could fix us cocoa. Then at the end of the evening I'd pack up my tools and off I'd go, leaving the house in perfect repair. Why, June ought to jump at the chance.'

'Then why not suggest it,' Macon said.

'Nah. She'd never go for it. She's so impractical. I said to her last week, I said, "You know that front porch step is loose? Springing up from its nails every time you walk on it wrong." She said, "Oh, Lord, yes, it's *been* that way," as if Providence had decreed it. As if nothing could be done about it. They've got leaves in the gutter from way last winter but leaves are natural, after all; why go against nature. She's so impractical.'

Porter himself was the most practical man Macon had ever known. He was the only Leary who understood money. His talent with money was what kept the family firm solvent—if just barely. It wasn't a very wealthy business. Grandfather Leary had founded it in the early part of the century as a tinware factory, and turned to bottle caps in 1915. The Bottle Cap King, he called himself, and was called in his obituary, but in fact most bottle caps were manufactured by Crown Cork and always had been; Grandfather Leary ran a distant second or third. His only son, the Bottle Cap

Prince, had barely assumed his place in the firm before quitting to volunteer for World War II—a far more damaging enthusiasm, it turned out, than any of Alicia's. After he was killed the business limped along, never quite succeeding and never quite failing, till Porter bounced in straight from college and took over the money end. Money to Porter was something almost chemical—a volatile substance that reacted in various interesting ways when combined with other substances. He wasn't what you'd call mercenary; he didn't want the money for its own sake but for its intriguing possibilities, and in fact when his wife divorced him he handed over most of his property without a word of complaint.

It was Porter who ran the company, pumping in money and ideas. Charles, more mechanical, dealt with the production end. Macon had done a little of everything when he worked there, and had wasted away with boredom doing it, for there wasn't really enough to keep a third man busy. It was only for symmetry's sake that Porter kept urging him to return. 'Tell you what, Macon,' he said now, 'why not hitch a ride down with us tomorrow and look over your old stomping ground?'

'No, thanks,' Macon told him.

'Plenty of room for your crutches in back.'

'Maybe some other time.'

They followed Rose around while she washed the dishes. She didn't like them to help because she had her own method, she said. She moved soundlessly through the old-fashioned kitchen, replacing dishes in the high wooden cabinets. Charles took the dog out; Macon couldn't manage his crutches in the spongy backyard. And Porter pulled the kitchen shades, meanwhile lecturing Rose on how the white surfaces reflected the warmth back into the room now that the nights were cooler. Rose said, 'Yes, Porter, I know all that,' and lifted the salad bowl to the light and examined it a moment before she put it away.

They watched the news, dutifully, and then they went out to the sun porch and sat at their grandparents' card table. They played something called Vaccination—a card game they'd invented as children, which had grown so convoluted over the years that no one else had the patience to learn it. In fact, more than one outsider had accused them of altering the rules to suit the circumstances. 'Now, just a minute,' Sarah had said, back when she'd still had hopes of figuring it out. 'I thought you said aces were high.'

'They are.'

'So that means—'

'But not when they're drawn from the deck.'

'Aha! Then why was the one that Rose drew counted high?'

'Well, she did draw it after a deuce, Sarah.'

'Aces drawn after a deuce are high?'

'No, aces drawn after a number that's been drawn two times in a row just before that.'

Sarah had folded her fan of cards and laid them face down—the last of the wives to give up.

Macon was in quarantine and had to donate all his cards to Rose. Rose moved her chair over next to his and played off his points while he sat back, scratching the cat behind her ears. Opposite him, in the tiny dark windowpanes, he saw their reflections— hollow-eyed and severely cheekboned, more interesting versions of themselves.

The telephone in the living room gave a nipped squeak and then a full ring. Nobody seemed to notice. Rose laid a king on Porter's queen and Porter said, 'Stinker.' The telephone rang again and then again. In the middle of the fourth ring, it fell silent. 'Hypodermic,' Rose told Porter, and she topped the king with an ace.

'You're a real stinker, Rose.'

In the portrait on the end wall, the Leary children gazed out with their veiled eyes. It occurred to Macon that they were sitting in much the same positions here this evening: Charles and Porter on either side of him, Rose perched in the foreground. Was there any real change? He felt a jolt of something very close to panic. Here he still was! The same as ever! *What have I gone and done?* he wondered, and he swallowed thickly and looked at his own empty hands.

6

— 'Help! Help! Call off your dog!'

Macon stopped typing and lifted his head. The voice came from somewhere out front, rising above a string of sharp, excited yelps. But Edward was taking a walk with Porter. This must be some other dog.

'Call him off, dammit!'

Macon rose, propping himself on his crutches, and made his way to the window. Sure enough, it was Edward. He seemed to have treed somebody in the giant magnolia to the right of the walk. He was barking so hard that he kept popping off the ground perfectly level, all four feet at once, like one of those pull toys that bounce straight up in the air when you squeeze a rubber bulb.

'Edward! Stop that!' Macon shouted.

Edward didn't stop. He might not even have heard. Macon stubbed out to the hall, opened the front door, and said, 'Come here this instant!'

Edward barely skipped a beat.

It was a Saturday morning in early October, pale gray and cool. Macon felt the coolness creeping up his cut-off pants leg as he crossed the porch. When he dropped one crutch and took hold of the iron railing to descend the steps, he found the metal beaded with moisture.

He hopped over to the magnolia, leaned down precariously, and grabbed the leash that Edward was trailing. Without much effort, he reeled it in; Edward was already losing interest. Macon peered into the inky depths of the magnolia. 'Who *is* that?' he asked.

'This is your employer, Macon.'

'Julian?'

Julian lowered himself from one of the magnolia's weak, sprawling branches. He had a line of dirt across the front of his slacks. His white-blond hair, usually so neat it made him look like a shirt ad, stuck out at several angles. 'Macon,' he said, 'I really hate a man with an obnoxious dog. I don't hate just the dog, I hate the man who owns him.'

'Well, I'm sorry about this. I thought he was off on a walk.'

'You send him on walks by himself?'

'No, no . . .'

'A dog who takes solitary strolls,' Julian said. 'Only Macon Leary would have one.' He brushed off the sleeves of his suede blazer. Then he said, 'What happened to your leg?'

'I broke it.'

'Well, I see that, but how?'

'It's kind of hard to explain,' Macon told him.

They started toward the house, with Edward trotting docilely alongside. Julian supported Macon as they climbed the steps. He was an athletic-looking man with a casual, sauntering style—a boater. You could tell he was a boater by his nose, which was raw across the tip even this late in the year. No one so startlingly blond, so vividly flushed in the face, should expose himself to sunburn, Macon always told him. But that was Julian for you: reckless. A dashing sailor, a speedy driver, a frequenter of singles bars, he was the kind of man who would make a purchase without consulting *Consumer Reports.* He never seemed to have a moment's self-doubt and was proceeding into the house now as jauntily as if he'd been invited, first retrieving Macon's other crutch and then holding the door open and waving him ahead.

'How'd you find me, anyway?' Macon asked.

'Why, are you in hiding?'

'No, of course not.'

Julian surveyed the entrance hall, which all at once struck Macon as slightly dowdy. The satin lampshade on the table had dozens of long vertical rents; it seemed to be rotting off its frame.

'Your neighbor told me where you were,' Julian said finally.

'Oh. Garner.'

'I stopped by your house when I couldn't reach you by phone. Do you know how late you're running with this guidebook?'

'Well, you can see I've had an accident,' Macon said.

'Everybody's held up, waiting for the manuscript. I keep telling them I expect it momentarily, but—'

'Any moment,' Macon said.

'Huh?'

'You expect it any moment.'

'Yes, and all I've seen so far is two chapters mailed in with no explanation.'

Julian led the way to the living room as he spoke. He selected the most comfortable chair and sat down. 'Where's Sarah?' he asked.

'Who?'

'Your wife, Macon.'

'Oh. Um, she and I are . . .'

Macon should have practiced saying it out loud. The word 'separated' was too bald; it was something that happened to other people. He crossed to the couch and made a great business of settling himself and arranging his crutches at his side. Then he said, 'She's got this apartment downtown.'

'You've *split?*'

Macon nodded.

'Jesus.'

Edward nosed Macon's palm bossily, demanding a pat. Macon was grateful to have something to do.

'Well, Jesus, Macon, what went wrong?' Julian asked.

'Nothing!' Macon told him. His voice was a little too loud. He lowered it. 'I mean, that's not something I can answer,' he said.

'Oh. Excuse me.'

'No, I mean . . . there *is* no answer. It turns out these things can happen for no particular reason.'

'Well, you've been under a strain, you two,' Julian said. 'Shoot, with what happened and all . . . She'll be back, once she's gotten over it. Or not gotten *over* it of course but, you know . . .'

'Maybe so,' Macon said. He felt embarrassed for Julian, who kept jiggling one Docksider. He said, 'What did you think of those first two chapters?'

Julian opened his mouth to answer, but he was interrupted by the dog. Edward had flown to the hall and was barking furiously. There was a clang that Macon recognized as the sound of the front door swinging open and hitting the radiator. 'Hush, now,' he heard Rose tell Edward. She crossed the hall and looked into the living room.

Julian got to his feet. Macon said, 'Julian Edge, this is my sister Rose. And this,' he said as Charles arrived behind her, 'is my brother Charles.'

Neither Rose nor Charles could shake hands; they were carrying the groceries. They stood in the center of the room, hugging brown paper bags, while Julian went into what Macon thought of as his Macon Leary act. 'Macon Leary with a sister! And a brother, too. Who'd have guessed it? That Macon Leary had a family just never entered my mind, somehow.'

Rose gave him a polite, puzzled smile. She wasn't looking her best. She wore a long black coat that drew all the color from her face. And Charles, rumpled and out of breath, was having trouble with one of his bags. He kept trying to get a better grip on it. 'Here, let me help you,' Julian said. He took the bag and then peered into it. Macon was afraid he'd go off on some tangent about Macon Leary's groceries, but he didn't. He told Rose, 'Yes, I do see a family resemblance.'

'You're Macon's publisher,' Rose said. 'I remember from the address label.'

'Address label?'

'I'm the one who mailed you Macon's chapters.'

'Oh, yes.'

'I'm supposed to send you some more, but first I have to buy nine-by-twelve envelopes. All we've got left is ten-by-thirteen. It's terrible when things don't fit precisely. They get all out of alignment.'

'Ah,' Julian said. He looked at her for a moment.

Macon said, 'We wouldn't want to keep you, Rose.'

'Oh! No,' she said. She smiled at Julian, hoisted her groceries higher, and left the room. Charles retrieved his bag from Julian and slogged after her.

'The Macon Leary Nine-by-Twelve Envelope Crisis,' Julian said, sitting back down.

Macon said, 'Oh, Julian, drop it.'

'Sorry,' Julian said, sounding surprised.

There was a pause. Then Julian said, 'Really I had no idea, Macon. I mean, if you'd let me know what was going on in your life . . .'

He was jiggling a Docksider again. He always seemed uneasy when he couldn't do his Macon Leary act. After Ethan died he'd avoided Macon for weeks; he'd sent a tree-sized bouquet to the house but never again mentioned Ethan's name.

'Look,' he said now. 'If you want another, I don't know, another month—'

Macon said, 'Oh, nonsense, what's a missing wife or two, right? Ha, ha! Here, let me get what I've typed and you can check it.'

'Well, if you say so,' Julian said.

'After this there's only the conclusion,' Macon said. He was calling over his shoulder as he made his way to the dining room, where his latest chapter lay stacked on the buffet. 'The conclusion's nothing, a cinch. I'll crib from the old one, mostly.'

He returned with the manuscript and handed it to Julian. Then he sat on the couch again, and Julian started reading. Meanwhile, Macon heard Porter come in the back way, where he was greeted by explosive barks from Edward. 'Monster,' Porter said. 'Do you know how long I've been looking for you?' The phone rang over and over, unanswered. Julian looked at Macon and raised his eyebrows but made no comment.

Macon and Julian had met some dozen years ago, when Macon was still at the bottle-cap factory. He'd been casting about for other occupations at the time. He'd begun to believe he might like to work on a newspaper. But he'd had no training, not a single journalism course. So he started the only way he could think of: He contributed a free-lance article to a neighborhood weekly. His subject was a crafts fair over in Washington. *Getting there is difficult,* he wrote, *because the freeway is so blank you start feeling all lost and sad. And once you've arrived, it's worse. The streets are not like ours and don't even run at right angles.* He went on to evaluate some food he'd sampled at an outdoor booth, but found it contained a spice he wasn't used to, *something sort of cold and yellow I would almost describe as foreign,* and settled instead for a hot dog from a vendor across the street who wasn't even part of the fair. *The hot dog I can recommend,* he wrote, *though it made me a little regretful because*

Sarah, my wife, uses the same kind of chili sauce and I thought of home the minute I smelled it. He also recommended the patchwork quilts, one of which had a starburst pattern like the quilt in his grandmother's room. He suggested that his readers leave the fair no later than three thirty, *since you'll be driving into Baltimore right past Lexington Market and will want to pick up your crabs before it closes.*

His article was published beneath a headline reading CRAFTS FAIR DELIGHTS, INSTRUCTS. There was a subhead under that. *Or,* it read, *I Feel So Break-Up, I Want to Go Home.* Until he saw the subhead, Macon hadn't realized what tone he'd given his piece. Then he felt silly.

But Julian Edge thought it was perfect. Julian phoned him. 'You the fellow who wrote that hot dog thing in the *Watchbird*?'

'Well, yes.'

'Ha!'

'Well, I don't see what's so funny,' Macon said stiffly.

'Who said it was funny? It's perfect. I've got a proposition for you.'

They met at the Old Bay Restaurant, where Macon's grandparents used to take the four children on their birthdays. 'I can personally guarantee the crab soup,' Macon said. 'They haven't done a thing to it since I was nine.' Julian said, 'Ha!' again and rocked back in his chair. He was wearing a polo shirt and white duck trousers, and his nose was a bright shade of pink. It was summer, or maybe spring. At any rate, his boat was in the water.

'Now, here's my plan,' he said over the soup. 'I own this little company called the Businessman's Press. Well, little: I say little.

Actually we sell coast to coast. Nothing fancy, but useful, you know? Appointment pads, expense account booklets, compound interest charts, currency conversion wheels . . . And now I want to put out a guidebook for commercial travelers. Just the U.S., to begin with; maybe other countries later. We'd call it something catchy, I don't know: *Reluctant Tourist* . . . And you're the fellow to write it.'

'Me?'

'I knew the minute I read your hot dog piece.'

'But I hate to travel.'

'I kind of guessed that,' Julian said. 'So do businessmen. I mean, these folks are not running around the country for the hell of it, Macon. They'd rather be home in their living rooms. So you'll be helping them pretend that's where they are.'

Then he pulled a square of paper from his breast pocket and said, 'What do you think?'

It was a steel engraving of an overstuffed chair. Attached to the chair's back were giant, feathered wings such as you would see on seraphim in antique Bibles. Macon blinked.

'Your logo,' Julian explained. 'Get it?'

'Um . . .'

'While armchair travelers dream of going places,' Julian said, 'traveling armchairs dream of staying put. I thought we'd use this on the cover.'

'Ah!' Macon said brightly. Then he said, 'But would I actually have to travel myself?'

'Well, yes.'

'Oh.'

'But just briefly. I'm not looking for anything encyclopedic, I'm looking for the opposite of encyclopedic. And think of the pay.'

'It pays?'

'It pays a bundle.'

Well, not a bundle, exactly. Still, it did make a comfortable living. It sold briskly at airport newsstands, train stations, and office supply shops. His guide to France did even better. That was part of a major promotion by an international car-rental agency—slipcased with *The Businessman's Foreign Phrase Book*, which gave the German, French, and Spanish for 'We anticipate an upswing in cross-border funds.' Macon, of course, was not the author of the phrase book. His only foreign language was Latin.

Now Julian restacked the pages he'd been reading. 'Fine,' he said. 'I think we can send this through as is. What's left of the conclusion?'

'Not much.'

'After this I want to start on the U.S. again.'

'So soon?'

'It's been three years, Macon.'

'Well, but . . .' Macon said. He gestured toward his leg. 'You can see I'd have trouble traveling.'

'When does your cast come off?'

'Not till the first of November at the earliest.'

'So? A few weeks!'

'But it really seems to me I just did the U.S.,' Macon said. A kind of fatigue fell over him. These endlessly recurring trips, Boston and Atlanta and Chicago . . . He let his head drop back on the couch.

Julian said, 'Things are changing every minute, Macon. Change!

It's what keeps us in the black. How far do you think we'd get selling out-of-date guidebooks?'

Macon thought of the crumbling old *Tips for the Continent* in his grandfather's library. Travelers were advised to invert a wineglass on their hotel beds, testing the sheets for damp. Ladies should seal the corks of their perfume bottles with melted candlewax before packing. Something about that book implied that tourists were all in it together, equally anxious and defenseless. Macon might almost have enjoyed a trip in those days.

Julian was preparing to go now. He stood up, and with some difficulty Macon did too. Then Edward, getting wind of a leavetaking, rushed into the living room and started barking. 'Sorry!' Macon shouted above the racket. 'Edward, stop it! I figure that's his sheep-herding instinct,' he explained to Julian. 'He hates to see anyone straying from the flock.'

They moved toward the front hall, wading through a blur of dancing, yelping dog. When they reached the door, Edward blocked it. Luckily, he was still trailing his leash, so Macon gave one crutch to Julian and bent to grasp it. The instant Edward felt the tug, he turned and snarled at Macon. 'Whoa!' Julian said, for Edward when he snarled was truly ugly. His fangs seemed to lengthen. He snapped at his leash with an audible click. Then he snapped at Macon's hand. Macon felt Edward's hot breath and the oddly intimate dampness of his teeth. His hand was not so much bitten as struck—slammed into with a jolt such as you'd get from an electric fence. He stepped back and dropped the leash. His other crutch clattered to the floor. The front hall seemed to be full of crutches; there was some splintery, spiky feeling to the air.

'Whoa, there!' Julian said. He spoke into a sudden silence. The dog sat back now, panting and shamefaced. 'Macon? Did he get you?' Julian asked.

Macon looked down at his hand. There were four red puncture marks in the fleshy part—two in front, two in back—but no blood at all and very little pain. 'I'm all right,' he said.

Julian gave him his crutches, keeping one eye on Edward. 'I wouldn't have a dog like that,' he said. 'I'd shoot him.'

'He was just trying to protect me,' Macon said.

'I'd call the S.P.C.A.'

'Why don't you go now, Julian, while he's calm.'

'Or the what's-it, dogcatcher. Tell them you want him done away with.'

'Just *go*, Julian.'

Julian said, 'Well, fine.' He opened the door and slid through it sideways, glancing back at Edward. 'That is not a well dog,' he said before he vanished.

Macon hobbled to the rear of the house and Edward followed, snuffling a bit and staying close to the ground. In the kitchen, Rose stood on a stepstool in front of a towering glass-fronted cupboard, accepting the groceries that Charles and Porter handed up to her. 'Now I need the *n*'s, anything starting with *n*,' she was saying.

'How about these noodles?' Porter asked. '*N* for noodles? *P* for pasta?'

'*E* for elbow macaroni. You might have passed those up earlier, Porter.'

'Rose?' Macon said. 'It seems Edward's given me a little sort of nip.'

She turned, and Charles and Porter stopped work to examine the hand he held out. It was hurting him by now—a deep, stinging pain. 'Oh, Macon!' Rose cried. She came down off the stepstool. 'How did it happen?'

'It was an accident, that's all. But I think I need an antiseptic.'

'You need a tetanus shot, too,' Charles told him.

'You need to get rid of that dog,' Porter said.

They looked at Edward. He grinned up at them nervously.

'He didn't mean any harm,' Macon said.

'Takes off your hand at the elbow and he means no harm? You should get rid of him, I tell you.'

'See, I can't,' Macon said.

'Why not?'

'Well, see . . .'

They waited.

'You know I don't mind the cat,' Rose said. 'But Edward is so disruptive, Macon. Every day he gets more and more out of control.'

'Maybe you could give him to someone who wants a guard dog,' Charles said.

'A service station,' Rose suggested. She took a roll of gauze from a drawer.

'Oh, never,' Macon said. He sat where she pointed, in a chair at the kitchen table. He propped his crutches in the corner. 'Edward alone in some Exxon? He'd be wretched.'

Rose swabbed Mercurochrome on his hand. It looked bruised; each puncture mark was puffing and turning blue.

'He's used to sleeping with me,' Macon told her. 'He's never been alone in his life.'

Besides, Edward wasn't a bad dog at heart—only a little unruly. He was sympathetic and he cared about Macon and plodded after him wherever he went. There was a furrowed W on his forehead that gave him a look of concern. His large, pointed, velvety ears seemed more expressive than other dogs' ears; when he was happy they stuck straight out at either side of his head like airplane wings. His smell was unexpectedly pleasant—the sweetish smell a favorite sweater takes on when it's been folded away in a drawer unwashed.

And he'd been Ethan's.

Once upon a time Ethan had brushed him, bathed him, wrestled on the floor with him; and when Edward stopped to paw at one ear Ethan would ask, with the soberest courtesy, 'Oh, may I scratch that for you?' The two of them watched daily at the window for the afternoon paper, and the instant it arrived Ethan sent Edward bounding out to fetch it—hind legs meeting front legs, heels kicking up joyfully. Edward would pause after he got the paper in his mouth and look around him, as if hoping to be noticed, and then he'd swagger back all bustling and self-important and pause again at the front hall mirror to admire the figure he cut. 'Conceited,' Ethan would say fondly. Ethan picked up a tennis ball to throw and Edward grew so excited that he wagged his whole hind end. Ethan took Edward outside with a soccer ball and when Edward got carried away—tearing about and shouldering the ball into a hedge and growling ferociously—Ethan's laugh rang out so high and clear, such a buoyant sound floating through the air on a summer evening.

'I just can't,' Macon said.

There was a silence.

Rose wrapped gauze around his hand, so gently he hardly felt it. She tucked the end under and reached for a roll of adhesive tape. Then she said, 'Maybe we could send him to obedience school.'

'Obedience school is for minor things—walking to heel and things,' Porter told her. 'What we have here is major.'

'It is not!' Macon said. 'It's really nothing at all. Why, the woman at the Meow-Bow got on wonderfully with him.'

'Meow-Bow?'

'Where I boarded him when I went to England. She was just crazy about him. She wanted me to let her train him.'

'So call her, why don't you.'

'Maybe I will,' Macon said.

He wouldn't, of course. The woman had struck him as bizarre. But there was no sense going into that now.

On Sunday morning Edward tore the screen door, trying to get at an elderly neighbor who'd stopped by to borrow a wrench. On Sunday afternoon he sprang at Porter to keep him from leaving on an errand. Porter had to creep out the rear when Edward wasn't watching. 'This is undignified,' Porter told Macon. 'When are you going to call the Kit-Kat or whatever it is?'

Macon explained that on Sundays the Meow-Bow would surely be closed.

Monday morning, when Edward went for a walk with Rose, he lunged at a passing jogger and yanked Rose off her feet. She came home with a scraped knee. She said, 'Have you called the Meow-Bow yet?'

'Not quite,' Macon said.

'Macon,' Rose said. Her voice was very quiet. 'Tell me something.'

'What's that, Rose?'

'Can you explain why you're letting things go on this way?'

No, he couldn't, and that was the truth. It was getting so he was baffling even to himself. He felt infuriated by Edward's misdeeds, but somehow he viewed them as visitations of fate. There was nothing he could do about them. When Edward approached him later with a mangled belt of Porter's trailing from his mouth, all Macon said was, 'Oh, Edward . . .'

He was sitting on the couch at the time, having been snagged by an especially outrageous moment in Rose's soap opera. Rose looked over at him. Her expression was odd. It wasn't disapproving; it was more like . . . He cast about for the word. Resigned. That was it. She looked at him the way she would look at, say, some hopeless wreck of a man wandering drugged on a downtown street. After all, she seemed to be thinking, there was probably not much that you could do for such a person.

'Meow-Bow Animal Hospital.'

'Is, ah, Muriel there, please?'

'Hold on a minute.'

He waited, braced against a cabinet. (He was using the pantry telephone.) He heard two women discussing Fluffball Cohen's rabies shot. Then Muriel picked up the receiver. 'Hello?'

'Yes, this is Macon Leary. I don't know if you remember me or—'

'Oh, Macon! Hi there! How's Edward doing?'

'Well, he's getting worse.'

She tsk-tsked.

'He's been attacking right and left. Snarling, biting, chewing things—'

'Did your neighbor tell you I came looking for you?'

'What? Yes, he did.'

'I was right on your street, running an errand. I make a little extra money running errands. George, it's called. Don't you think that's cute?'

'Excuse me?'

'George. It's the name of my company. I stuck a flyer under your door. *Let George do it*, it says, and then it lists all the prices: meeting planes, chauffeuring, courier service, shopping . . . Gift shopping's most expensive because for that I have to use my own taste. Didn't you get my flyer? I really stopped by just to visit, though. But your neighbor said you hadn't been around.'

'No, I broke my leg,' Macon said.

'Oh, that's too bad.'

'And I couldn't manage alone of course, so—'

'You should have called George.'

'George who?'

'George my company! The one I was just telling you about.'

'Oh, yes.'

'Then you wouldn't have had to leave that nice house. I liked your house. Is that where you lived when you were married, too?'

'Well, yes.'

'I'm surprised she agreed to give it up.'

'The point is,' Macon said, 'I'm really at the end of my rope with Edward here, and I was wondering if you might be able to help me.'

'Sure I can help!'

'Oh, that's wonderful,' Macon said.

'I can do anything,' Muriel told him. 'Search and alert, search and rescue, bombs, narcotics——'

'Narcotics?'

'Guard training, attack training, poison-proofing, kennelosis——'

'Wait, I don't even know what some of those things are,' Macon said.

'I can even teach split personality.'

'What's split personality?'

'Where your dog is, like, nice to you but kills all others.'

'You know, I think I may be over my head here,' Macon said.

'No, no! Don't say that!'

'But this is just the simplest problem. His only fault is, he wants to protect me.'

'You can take protection too far,' Muriel told him.

Macon tried a little joke. ' "It's a jungle out there," he's saying. That's what he's trying to say. "I know better than you do, Macon." '

'Oh?' Muriel said. 'You let him call you by your first name?'

'Well——'

'He needs to learn respect,' she said. 'Five or six times a week I'll come out, for however long it takes. I'll start with the basics; you always do that: sitting, heeling . . . My charge is five dollars a lesson. You're getting a bargain. Most I charge ten.'

Macon tightened his hold on the receiver. 'Then why not ten for me?' he asked.

'Oh, no! You're a friend.'

He felt confused. He gave her his address and arranged a time with the nagging sense that something was slipping out of his control. 'But look,' he said, 'about the fee, now—'

'See you tomorrow!' she said. She hung up.

At supper that night when he told the others, he thought they did a kind of double take. Porter said, 'You actually called?' Macon said, 'Yes, why not?'—acting very offhand—and so the others took their cue and dropped the subject at once.

— 'When I was a little girl,' Muriel said, 'I didn't like dogs at all or any other kinds of animals either. I thought they could read my mind. My folks gave me a puppy for my birthday and he would, like, cock his head, you know how they do? Cock his head and fix me with these bright round eyes and I said, "Ooh! Get him away from me! You know I can't stand to be stared at." '

She had a voice that wandered too far in all directions. It screeched upward; then it dropped to a raspy growl. 'They had to take him back. Had to give him to a neighbor boy and buy me a whole different present, a beauty-parlor permanent which is what I'd set my heart on all along.'

She and Macon were standing in the entrance hall. She still had her coat on—a bulky-shouldered, three-quarter length, nubby black affair of a type last seen in the 1940s. Edward sat in front of her as he'd been ordered. He had met her at the door with his usual display, leaping and snarling, but she'd more or less walked right through him and pointed at his rump and told him to sit. He'd gaped at her. She had reached over and poked his rear end down with a long, sharp index finger.

'Now you kind of cluck your tongue,' she'd told Macon, demonstrating. 'They get to know a cluck means praise. And when I hold my hand out—see? That means he has to stay.'

Edward stayed, but a yelp erupted from him every few seconds, reminding Macon of the periodic bloops from a percolator. Muriel hadn't seemed to hear. She'd started discussing her lesson plan and then for no apparent reason had veered to her autobiography. But shouldn't Edward be allowed to get up now? How long did she expect him to sit there?

'I guess you're wondering why I'd want a permanent when this hair of mine is so frizzy,' she said. 'Old mop! But I'll be honest, this is not natural. My natural hair is real straight and lanky. Times I've just despaired of it. It was blond when I was a baby, can you believe that? Blond as a fairy-tale princess. People told my mother I'd look like Shirley Temple if she would just curl my hair, and so she did, she rolled my hair on orange juice tins. I had blue eyes, too, and they stayed that way for a long long time, a whole lot longer than most babies' do. People thought I'd look that way forever and they talked about me going into the movies. Seriously! My mother arranged for tap-dance school when I wasn't much more than a toddler. No one ever dreamed my hair would turn on me.'

Edward moaned. Muriel looked past Macon, into the glass of a picture that hung behind him. She cupped a hand beneath the ends of her hair, as if testing its weight. 'Think what it must feel like,' she said, 'waking up one morning and finding you've gone dark. It near about killed my mother, I can tell you. Ordinary dull old Muriel, muddy brown eyes and hair as black as dirt.'

Macon sensed he was supposed to offer some argument, but he was too anxious about Edward. 'Oh, well . . .' he said. Then he said, 'Shouldn't we be letting him up now?'

'Up? Oh, the dog. In a minute,' she said. 'So anyway. The reason it's so frizzy is, I got this thing called a body perm. You ever heard of those? They're supposed to just add body, but something went wrong. You think *this* is bad! If I was to take a brush to it, my hair would spring straight out from my head. I mean absolutely straight out. Kind of like a fright wig, isn't that what you call it? So I can't even brush it. I get up in the morning and there I am, ready to go. Lord, I hate to think of the tangles.'

'Maybe you could just comb it,' Macon suggested.

'Hard to drag a comb *through* it. All the little teeth would break off.'

'Maybe one of those thick-toothed combs that black people use.'

'I know what you mean but I'd feel silly buying one.'

'What for?' Macon asked. 'They're just hanging there in supermarkets. It wouldn't have to be a big deal. Buy milk and bread or something and an Afro comb, no one will even think twice.'

'Well, I suppose you're right,' she said, but now that she'd got him involved it seemed she'd lost interest in the problem herself. She snapped her fingers over Edward's head. 'Okay!' she said. Edward jumped up, barking. 'That was very good,' she told him.

In fact, it was so good that Macon felt a little cross. Things couldn't be that easy, he wanted to say. Edward had improved too quickly, the way a toothache will improve the moment you step into a dentist's waiting room.

Muriel slipped her purse off her shoulder and set it on the hall table. Out came a long blue leash attached to a choke chain. 'He's supposed to wear this all the time,' she said. 'Every minute till he's trained. That way you can yank him back whenever he does something wrong. The leash is six dollars even, and the chain is two ninety-five. With tax it comes to, let's see, nine forty. You can pay me at the end of the lesson.'

She slipped the choke chain over Edward's head. Then she paused to examine a fingernail. 'If I break another nail I'm going to scream,' she said. She took a step back and pointed to Edward's rump. After a brief hesitation, he sat. Seated, he looked noble, Macon thought—chesty and solemn, nothing like his usual self. But when Muriel snapped her fingers, he jumped up as unruly as ever.

'Now you try,' Muriel told Macon.

Macon accepted the leash and pointed to Edward's rump. Edward stood fast. Macon frowned and pointed more sternly. He felt foolish. Edward knew, if this woman didn't, how little authority Macon had.

'Poke him down,' Muriel said.

This was going to be awkward. He propped a crutch against the radiator and bent stiffly to jab Edward with one finger. Edward sat. Macon clucked. Then he straightened and backed away, holding out his palm, but instead of staying, Edward rose and followed him.

Muriel hissed between her teeth. Edward shrank down again. 'He doesn't take you seriously,' Muriel said.

'Well, I know that,' Macon snapped.

His broken leg was starting to ache.

'In fact I didn't have so much as a kitten the whole entire time I was growing up,' Muriel said. Was she just going to leave Edward sitting there? 'Then a couple of years ago I saw this ad in the paper, *Make extra money in your off hours. Work as little or as much as you like.* Place was a dog-training firm that went around to people's houses. Doggie, Do, it was called. Don't you just hate that name? Reminds me of dog-do. But anyhow, I answered the ad. "To be honest I don't like animals," I said, but Mr Quarles, the owner, he told me that was just as well. He told me it was people who got all mushy about them that had the most trouble.'

'Well, that makes sense,' Macon said, glancing at Edward. He had heard that dogs developed backaches if they were made to sit too long.

'I was just about his best pupil, it turns out. Seems I had a way with animals. So then I got a job at the Meow-Bow. Before that I worked at the Rapid-Eze Copy Center and believe me, I was looking for a change. Who's the lady?'

'Lady?'

'The lady I just saw walking through the dining room.'

'That's Rose.'

'Is she your ex-wife? Or what.'

'She's my sister.'

'Oh, your sister!'

'This house belongs to her,' Macon said.

'I don't live with anybody either,' Muriel told him.

Macon blinked. Hadn't he just said he lived with his sister?

'Sometimes late at night when I get desperate for someone to talk to I call the time signal,' Muriel said. ' "At the tone the time will be eleven . . . forty-eight. And fifty seconds." ' Her voice took on a fruity fullness. ' "At the tone the time will be eleven . . . forty-nine. Exactly." You can release him now.'

'Pardon?'

'Release your dog.'

Macon snapped his fingers and Edward jumped up, yapping.

'How about you?' Muriel asked. 'What do you do for a living?'

Macon said, 'I write tour guides.'

'Tour guides! Lucky.'

'What's lucky about it?'

'Why, you must get to travel all kinds of places!'

'Oh, well, travel,' Macon said.

'I'd love to travel.'

'It's just red tape, mostly,' Macon said.

'I've never even been on an airplane, you realize that?'

'It's red tape in motion. Ticket lines, customs lines . . . Should Edward be barking that way?'

Muriel gave Edward a slit-eyed look and he quieted.

'If I could go anywhere I'd go to Paris,' she said.

'Paris is terrible. Everybody's impolite.'

'I'd walk along the Seine, like they say in the song. "You will find your love in Paris," ' she sang scratchily, ' "if you walk along the—" I just think it sounds so romantic.'

'Well, it's not,' Macon said.

'I bet you don't know where to look, is all. Take me with you next time! I could show you the good parts.'

Macon cleared his throat. 'Actually, I have a very limited expense account,' he told her. 'I never even took my wife, or, um, my . . . wife.'

'I was only teasing,' she told him.

'Oh.'

'You think I meant it?'

'Oh, no.'

She grew suddenly brisk. 'That will be fourteen forty, including the leash and the choke chain.' Then while Macon was fumbling through his wallet she said, 'You have to practice what he's learned, and no one else can practice for you. I'll come back tomorrow for the second lesson. Will eight in the morning be too early? I've got to be at the Meow-Bow at nine.'

'Eight will be fine,' Macon told her. He counted out fourteen dollars and all the change he had loose in his pocket—thirty-six cents.

'You can pay me the other four cents tomorrow,' she said.

Then she made Edward sit and she handed the leash to Macon. 'Release him when I'm gone,' she said.

Macon held out his palm and stared hard into Edward's eyes, begging him to stay. Edward stayed, but he moaned when he saw Muriel leave. When Macon snapped his fingers, Edward jumped up and attacked the front door.

All that afternoon and evening, Macon and Edward practiced. Edward learned to plop his rump down at the slightest motion of a finger. He stayed there, complaining and rolling his eyes, while Macon clucked approvingly. By suppertime, a cluck was part of the family language. Charles clucked over Rose's pork chops. Porter clucked when Macon dealt him a good hand of cards.

'Imagine a flamenco dancer with galloping consumption,' Rose told Charles and Porter. 'That's Edward's trainer. She talks nonstop, I don't know when she comes up for air. When she talked about her lesson plan she kept saying "simplistic" for "simple." '

'I thought you were going to stay out of sight,' Macon told Rose.

'Well? Did you ever see me?'

'Muriel did.'

'I guess so! The way she was always peering around your back and snooping.'

There were constant slamming sounds from the living room, because Edward's new leash kept catching on the rocking chair and dragging it behind him. During the course of the evening he chewed a pencil to splinters, stole a pork-chop bone from the garbage bin, and threw up on the sun porch rug; but now that he could sit on command, everyone felt more hopeful.

'When I was in high school I made nothing but A's,' Muriel said. 'You're surprised at that, aren't you. You think I'm kind of like, not an intellect. I know what you're thinking! You're surprised.'

'No, I'm not,' Macon said, although he was, actually.

'I made A's because I caught on to the trick,' Muriel told him. 'You think it's not a trick? There's a trick to everything; that's how you get through life.'

They were in front of the house—both of them in raincoats, for it was a damp, drippy morning. Muriel wore truncated black suede boots with witchy toes and needle heels. Her legs rose out of them like toothpicks. The leash trailed from her fingers. Supposedly, she was teaching Edward to walk right. Instead she went on talking about her schooldays.

'Some of my teachers told me I should go to college,' she said. 'This one in particular, well she wasn't a teacher but a librarian, I worked in the library for her, shelving books and things; she said, "Muriel, why don't you go on to Towson State?" But I don't know . . . and now I tell my sister, "You be thinking of college, hear? Don't drop out like I dropped out." I've got this little sister? Claire? *Her* hair never turned. She's blond as an angel. Here's what's funny, though: she couldn't care less. Braids her hair back any old how to keep it out of her eyes. Wears raggy jeans and forgets to shave her legs. Doesn't it always work that way? My folks believe she's wonderful. She's the good one and I'm the bad one. It's not her fault, though; I don't blame Claire. People just get fixed in these certain frames of other people's opinions, don't you find that's true? Claire was always Mary in the Nativity Scene at Christmas. Boys in her grade school were always proposing, but there I was in high school and no one proposed to *me*, I can tell you. Aren't high school boys just so frustrating? I mean they'd invite me out and all, like to drive-in movies and things, and they'd act so tense and secret, sneaking one arm around my shoulder inch by inch like they thought I wouldn't notice and then dropping a hand down, you know how they do, lower and lower while all the time staring straight ahead at the movie like it was the most fascinating spectacle they'd ever seen in their lives. You just had to feel sorry for them. But then Monday morning there they were like nothing had taken place, real boisterous and horsing around with their friends and nudging each other when I walked past but not so much as saying hello to me. You think that didn't hurt my feelings? Not one boy in all that time treated me like a steady girlfriend. They'd ask me out on Saturday night and expect me to be so nice to them, but you think they ever ate lunch with me next Monday in the school cafeteria, or walked me from class to class?'

She glanced down at Edward. Abruptly, she slapped her hip; her black vinyl raincoat made a buckling sound. 'That's the "heel" command,' she told Macon. She started walking. Edward followed uncertainly. Macon stayed behind. It had been hard enough getting down the front porch steps.

'He's supposed to match his pace to anything,' she called back. 'Slow, fast, anything I do.' She speeded up. When Edward crossed in front of her, she walked right into him. When he dawdled, she yanked his leash. She tip-tapped briskly eastward, her coat a stiff, swaying triangle beneath the smaller triangle of her hair blowing back. Macon waited, ankle-deep in wet leaves.

On the return trip, Edward kept close to Muriel's left side. 'I think he's got the hang of it,' she called. She arrived in front of Macon and offered him the leash. 'Now you.'

He attempted to slap his hip—which was difficult, on crutches. Then he set off. He was agonizingly slow and Edward kept pulling ahead. 'Yank that leash!' Muriel said, clicking along behind. 'He knows what he's supposed to do. Contrary thing.'

Edward fell into step, finally, although he gazed off in a bored, lofty way. 'Don't forget to cluck,' Muriel said. 'Every little minute, you have to praise him.' Her heels made a scraping sound behind them. 'Once I worked with this dog that had never in her life been housebroken. Two years old and not one bit housebroken and the owners were losing their minds. First I can't figure it out; then it comes to me. That dog thought she wasn't supposed to piddle *any*place, not indoors or outdoors, either one. See, no one had ever praised her when she did it right. Did you ever hear of such a thing? I had to catch her peeing outdoors which wasn't easy, believe me, because she was all the time ashamed and trying to hide it, and then I praised her to bits and after a while she caught on.'

They reached the corner. 'Now, when you stop, he has to sit,' she said.

'But how will I practice?' Macon asked.

'What do you mean?'

'I'm on these crutches.'

'So? It's good exercise for your leg,' she said. She didn't ask how the leg had been broken. Come to think of it, there was something impervious about her, in spite of all her interest in his private life. She said, 'Practice lots, ten minutes a session.'

'Ten minutes!'

'Now let's start back.'

She led the way, her angular, sashaying walk broken by the jolt of her sharp heels. Macon and Edward followed. When they reached the house, she asked what time it was. 'Eight fifty,' Macon said severely. He mistrusted women who wore no watches.

'I have to get going. That will be five dollars, please, and the four cents you owe me from yesterday.'

He gave her the money and she stuffed it in her raincoat pocket. 'Next time, I'll stay longer and talk,' she said. 'That's a promise.' She trilled her fingers at him, and then she clicked off toward a car that was parked down the street—an aged, gray, boatlike sedan polished to a high shine. When she slid in and slammed the door behind her, there was a sound like falling beer cans. The engine twanged and rattled before it took hold. Macon shook his head, and he and Edward returned to the house.

Between Wednesday and Thursday, Macon spent what seemed a lifetime struggling up and down Dempsey Road beside Edward. His armpits developed a permanent ache. There was a vertical seam of pain in his thigh. This made no sense; it should have been in the shin. He wondered if something had gone wrong—if the break had been set improperly, for instance, so that some unusual strain was being placed upon the thighbone. Maybe he'd have to go back to the hospital and get his leg rebroken, probably under general anesthesia with all its horrifying complications; and then he'd spend months in traction and perhaps walk the rest of his life with a limp. He imagined himself tilting across intersections with a grotesque, lopsided gait. Sarah, driving past, would screech to a halt. 'Macon?' She would roll down her window. 'Macon, what *happened*?'

He would raise one arm and let it flop and totter away from her.

Or tell her, 'I'm surprised you care enough to inquire.'

No, just totter away.

Most likely these little spells of self-pity (an emotion he despised ordinarily) were caused by sheer physical exhaustion. How had he got himself into this? Slapping his haunch was the first problem; then summoning his balance to jerk the leash when Edward fell out of step, and staying constantly alert for any squirrel or pedestrian. 'Sss!' he kept saying, and 'Cluck-cluck!' and 'Sss!' again. He supposed passersby must think he was crazy. Edward loped beside him, occasionally yawning, looking everywhere for bikers. Bikers were his special delight. Whenever he saw one, the hair between his shoulders stood on end and he lunged forward. Macon felt like a man on a tightrope that was suddenly set swinging.

At this uneven, lurching pace, he saw much more than he would have otherwise. He had a lengthy view of every bush and desiccated flower bed. He memorized eruptions in the sidewalk that might trip him. It was an old people's street, and not in the best of repair. The neighbors spent their days telephoning back and forth amongst themselves, checking to see that no one had suffered a stroke alone on the stairs or a heart attack in the bathroom, a broken hip, blocked windpipe, dizzy spell over the stove with every burner alight. Some would set out for a walk and find themselves hours later in the middle of the street, wondering where they'd been headed. Some would start fixing a bite to eat at noon, a soft-boiled egg or a cup of tea, and by sundown would still be puttering in their kitchen, fumbling for the salt and forgetting how the toaster worked. Macon knew all this through his sister, who was called upon by neighbors in distress. 'Rose, dear! Rose, dear!' they would quaver, and they'd stumble into her yard waving an overdue bill, an alarming letter, a bottle of pills with a childproof top.

In the evening, taking Edward for his last walk, Macon glanced in windows and saw people slumped in flowered armchairs, lit blue and shivery by their TV sets. The Orioles were winning the second game of the World Series, but these people seemed to be staring at their own thoughts instead. Macon imagined they were somehow dragging him down, causing him to walk heavily, to slouch, to grow short of breath. Even the dog seemed plodding and discouraged.

And when he returned to the house, the others were suffering one of their fits of indecisiveness. Was it better to lower the thermostat at night, or not? Wouldn't the furnace have to work harder if it were lowered? Hadn't Porter read that someplace? They debated back and forth, settling it and then beginning again. Why! Macon thought. They were not so very different from their neighbors. They were growing old themselves. He'd been putting in his own two bits (by all means, lower the thermostat), but now his voice trailed off, and he said no more.

That night, he dreamed he was parked near Lake Roland in his grandfather's '57 Buick. He was sitting in the dark and some girl was sitting next to him. He didn't know her, but the bitter smell of her perfume seemed familiar, and the rustle of her skirt when she moved closer. He turned and looked at her. It was Muriel. He drew a breath to ask what she was doing here, but she put a finger to his lips and stopped him. She moved closer still. She took his keys from him and set them on the dashboard. Gazing steadily into his face, she unbuckled his belt and slipped a cool, knowing hand down inside his trousers.

He woke astonished and embarrassed, and sat bolt upright in his bed.

'Everybody always asks me, "What is *your* dog like?" ' Muriel said. ' "I bet he's a model of good behavior," they tell me. But you want to hear something funny? I don't own a dog. In fact, the one time I had one around, he ran off. That was Norman's dog, Spook. My ex-husband's. First night we were married, Spook ran off to Norman's mom's. I think he hated me.'

'Oh, surely not,' Macon said.

'He hated me. I could tell.'

They were outdoors again, preparing to put Edward through his paces. By now, Macon had adjusted to the rhythm of these lessons. He waited, gripping Edward's leash. Muriel said, 'It was just like one of those Walt Disney movies. You know: where the dog walks all the way to the Yukon or something. Except Spook only walked to Timonium. Me and Norman had him downtown in our apartment, and Spook took off and traveled the whole however many miles it was back to Norman's mom's house in Timonium. His mom calls up: "When did you drop Spook off?" "What're you talking about?" Norman asks her.'

She changed her voice to match each character. Macon heard the thin whine of Norman's mother, the stammering boyishness of Norman himself. He remembered last night's dream and felt embarrassed all over again. He looked at her directly, hoping for flaws, and found them in abundance—a long, narrow nose, and sallow skin, and two freckled knobs of collarbone that promised an unluxurious body.

'Seems his mom woke up in the morning,' she was saying, 'and there was Spook, sitting on the doorstep. But that was the first we realized he was missing. Norman goes, "I don't know what got into him. He never ran off before." And gives me this doubtful kind of look. I could tell he wondered if it might be my fault. Maybe he thought it was a omen or something. We were awful young to get married. I can see that now. I was seventeen. He was eighteen—an only child. His mother's pet. Widowed mother. He had this fresh pink face like a girl's and the shortest hair of any boy in my school and he buttoned his shirt collars all the way to the neck. Moved in from Parkville the end of junior year. Caught sight of me in my strapless sun dress and goggled at me all through every class; other boys teased him but he didn't pay any mind. He was just so . . . innocent, you know? He made me feel like I had powers. There he was following me around the halls with his arms full of books and I'd say, "Norman? You want to eat lunch with me?" and he'd blush and say, "Oh, why, uh, you serious?" He didn't even know how to drive, but I told him if he got his license I'd go out with him. "We could ride to someplace quiet and talk and be alone," I'd say, "you know what I mean?" Oh, I was bad. I don't know what was wrong with me, back then. He got his license in no time flat and came for me in his mother's Chevy, which incidentally she happened to have purchased from my father, who was a salesman for Ruggles Chevrolet. We found that out at the wedding. Got married the fall of senior year, he was just dying to marry me so what could I say? and at the wedding my daddy goes to Norman's mom, "Why, I believe I sold you a car not long ago," but she was too busy crying to take much notice. That woman carried on like marriage was a fate worse than death. Then when Spook runs off to her house she tells us, "I suppose I'd best keep him, it's clear as day he don't like it there with you-all." With *me*, is what she meant. She held it against me I took her son away. She claimed I ruined his chances; she wanted him to get his diploma. But I never kept him from getting his diploma. He was the one who said he might as well drop out; said why bother staying in school when he could make a fine living on floors.'

'On what?' Macon asked.

'Floors. Sanding floors. His uncle was Pritchett Refinishing. Norman went into the business as soon as we got married and his mom was always talking about the waste. She said he could have been an accountant or something, but I don't know who she thought she was kidding. He never mentioned accounting to *me*.'

She pulled a dog hair off her coat sleeve, examined it, and flicked it away. 'So let's see him,' she said.

'Pardon?'

'Let's see him heel.'

Macon slapped his hip and started off, with Edward lagging just a bit behind. When Macon stopped, Edward stopped too and sat down. Macon was pleasantly surprised, but Muriel said, 'He's not sitting.'

'What? What do you call it, then?'

'He's keeping his rear end about two inches off the ground. Trying to see what he can get away with.'

'Oh, Edward,' Macon said sadly.

He pivoted and returned. 'Well, you'll have to work on that,' Muriel said. 'But meantime, we'll go on to the down-stay. Let's try it in the house.'

Macon worried they'd meet up with Rose, but she was nowhere to be seen. The front hall smelled of radiator dust. The clock in the living room was striking the half hour.

'This is where we start on Edward's real problem,' Muriel said. 'Getting him to lie down and stay, so he won't all the time be jumping at the door.'

She showed him the command: two taps of the foot. Her boot made a crisp sound. When Edward didn't respond, she bent and pulled his forepaws out from under him. Then she let him up and went through it again, several times over. Edward made no progress. When she tapped her foot, he panted and looked elsewhere. 'Stubborn,' Muriel told him. 'You're just as stubborn as they come.' She said to Macon, 'A lot of dogs will act like this. They hate to lie down; I don't know why. Now you.'

Macon tapped his foot. Edward seemed fascinated by something off to his left.

'Grab his paws,' Muriel said.

'On crutches?'

'Sure.'

Macon sighed and propped his crutches in the corner. He lowered himself to the floor with his cast in front of him, took Edward's paws and forced him down. Edward rumbled threateningly, but in the end he submitted. To get up again, Macon had to hold onto the lamp table. 'This is really very difficult,' he said, but Muriel said, 'Listen, I've taught a man with no legs at all.'

'You have?' Macon said. He pictured a legless man dragging along the sidewalk with some vicious breed of dog, Muriel standing by unconcerned and checking her manicure. 'I don't suppose *you* ever broke a leg,' he accused her. 'Getting around is harder than it looks.'

'I broke an arm once,' Muriel said.

'An arm is no comparison.'

'I did it training dogs, in fact. Got knocked off a porch by a Doberman pinscher.'

'A Doberman!'

'Came to to find him standing over me, showing all his teeth. Well, I thought of what they said at Doggie, Do: Only one of you can be boss. So I tell him, "Absolutely not." Those were the first words that came to me—what my mother used to say when she wasn't going to let me get away with something. "Absolutely not," I tell him, and my right arm is broken so I hold out my left, hold out my palm and stare into his eyes—they can't stand for you to meet their eyes—and get to my feet real slow. And durned if that dog doesn't settle right back on his haunches.'

'Good Lord,' Macon said.

'I've had a cocker spaniel fly directly at my throat. Meanest thing you ever saw. Had a German shepherd take my ankle in his teeth. Then he let it go.'

She lifted a foot and rotated it. Her ankle was about the thickness of a pencil.

'Have you ever met with a failure?' Macon asked her. 'Some dog you just gave up on?'

'Not a one,' she said. 'And Edward's not about to be the first.'

But Edward seemed to think otherwise. Muriel worked with him another half hour, and although he would stay once he was down, he flatly refused to lie down on his own. Each time, he had to be forced. 'Never mind,' Muriel said. 'This is the way most of them do. I bet tomorrow he'll be just as stubborn, so I'm going to skip a day. You keep practicing, and I'll be back this same time Saturday.'

Then she told Edward to stay, and she accepted her money and slipped out the door. Observing Edward's erect, resisting posture, Macon felt discouraged. Why hire a trainer at all, if she left him to do the training? 'Oh, I don't know, I don't know,' he said. Edward gave a sigh and walked off, although he hadn't been released.

All that afternoon and evening, Edward refused to lie down. Macon wheedled, threatened, cajoled; Edward muttered ominously and stood firm. Rose and the boys edged around the two of them, politely averting their eyes as if they'd stumbled on some private quarrel.

Then the next morning, Edward charged the mailman. Macon managed to grab the leash, but it raised some doubts in his mind. What did all this sitting and heeling have to do with Edward's real problem? 'I should just ship you off to the pound,' he told Edward. He tapped his foot twice. Edward did not lie down.

In the afternoon, Macon called the Meow-Bow. 'May I speak to Muriel, please?' he asked. He couldn't think of her last name.

'Muriel's not working today,' a girl told him.

'Oh, I see.'

'Her little boy is sick.'

He hadn't known she had a little boy. He felt some inner click of adjustment; she was a slightly different person from the one he'd imagined. 'Well,' he said, 'this is Macon Leary. I guess I'll talk to her tomorrow.'

'Oh, Mr Leary. You want to call her at home?'

'No, that's all right.'

'I can give you her number if you want to call her at home.'

'I'll just talk to her tomorrow. Thank you.'

Rose had an errand downtown, so she agreed to drop him off at the Businessman's Press. He wanted to deliver the rest of his guidebook. Stretched across the backseat with his crutches, he gazed at the passing scenery: antique office buildings, tasteful restaurants, health food stores and florists' shops, all peculiarly hard-edged and vivid in the light of a brilliant October afternoon. Rose perched behind the wheel and drove at a steady, slow pace that was almost hypnotic. She wore a little round basin-shaped hat with ribbons down the back. It made her look prim and Sunday schoolish.

One of the qualities that all four Leary children shared was a total inability to find their way around. It was a kind of dyslexia, Macon believed—a geographic dyslexia. None of them ever stepped outside without obsessively noting all available landmarks, clinging to a fixed and desperate mental map of the neighborhood. Back home, Macon had kept a stack of index cards giving detailed directions to the houses of his friends—even friends he'd known for decades. And it used to be that whenever Ethan met a new boy, Macon's first anxious question was, 'Where exactly does he live, do you know?' Ethan had had a tendency to form inconvenient alliances. He couldn't just hang out with the boy next door; oh, no, it had to be someone who lived way beyond the Beltway. What did Ethan care? *He* had no trouble navigating. This was because he'd lived all his life in one house, was Macon's theory; while a person who'd been moved around a great deal never acquired a fixed point of reference but wandered forever in a fog—adrift upon the planet, helpless, praying that just by luck he might stumble across his destination.

At any rate, Rose and Macon got lost. Rose knew where she wanted to go—a shop that sold a special furniture oil—and Macon had visited Julian's office a hundred times; but even so, they drove in circles till Macon noticed a familiar steeple. 'Stop! Turn left,' he said. Rose pulled up where he directed. Macon struggled out. 'Will you be all right?' he asked Rose. 'Do you think you can find your way back to pick me up?'

'I hope so.'

'Look for the steeple, remember.'

She nodded and drove away.

Macon swung up three granite steps to the brick mansion that housed the Businessman's Press. The door was made of polished, golden wood. The floor inside was tiled with tiny black and white hexagons, just uneven enough to give purchase to Macon's crutches.

This wasn't an ordinary office. The secretary typed in a back room while Julian, who couldn't stand being alone, sat out front. He was talking on a red telephone, lounging behind a desk that was laden with a clutter of advertisements, pamphlets, unpaid bills, unanswered letters, empty Chinese carry-out cartons, and Perrier bottles. The walls were covered with sailing charts. The bookshelves held few books but a great many antique brass mariners' instruments that probably didn't even work anymore. Anybody with eyes could see that Julian's heart was not in the Businessman's Press but out on the Chesapeake Bay someplace. This was to Macon's advantage, he figured. Surely no one else would have continued backing his series, with its staggering expenses and its constant need for updating.

'Rita's bringing croissants,' Julian said into the phone. 'Joe is making his quiche.' Then he caught sight of Macon. 'Macon!' he said. 'Stefanie, I'll get back to you.' He hung up. 'How's the leg? Here, have a seat.'

He dumped a stack of yachting magazines off a chair. Macon sat down and handed over his folder. 'Here's the rest of the material on England,' he said.

'Well, finally!'

'This edition as I see it is going to run about ten or twelve pages longer than the last one,' Macon said. 'It's adding the business *women* that does it—listing which hotels offer elevator escorts, which ones serve drinks in the lobbies . . . I think I ought to be paid more.'

'I'll talk it over with Marvin,' Julian said, flipping through the manuscript.

Macon sighed. Julian spent money like water but Marvin was more cautious.

'So now you're on the U.S. again,' Julian said.

'Well, if you say so.'

'I hope it's not going to take you long.'

'I can only go so fast,' Macon said. 'The U.S. has more cities.'

'Yes, I realize that. In fact I might print this edition in sections: northeast, mid-Atlantic, and so forth; I don't know . . .' But then he changed the subject. (He had a rather skittery mind.) 'Did I tell you my new idea? Doctor friend of mine is looking into it: *Accidental*

Tourist in Poor Health. A list of American-trained doctors and dentists in every foreign capital, plus maybe some suggestions for basic medical supplies: aspirin, Merck Manual—'

'Oh, not a Merck Manual away from home!' Macon said. 'Every hangnail could be cancer, when you're reading a Merck Manual.'

'Well, I'll make a note of that,' Julian said (without so much as lifting a pencil). 'Aren't you going to ask me to autograph your cast? It's so white.'

'I like it white,' Macon said. 'I polish it with shoe polish.'

'I didn't realize you could do that.'

'I use the liquid kind. It's the brand with a nurse's face on the label, if you ever need to know.'

'*Accidental Tourist on Crutches,*' Julian said, and he rocked back happily in his chair.

Macon could tell he was about to start his Macon Leary act. He got hastily to his feet and said, 'Well, I guess I'll be going.'

'So soon? Why don't we have a drink?'

'No, thanks, I can't. My sister's picking me up as soon as she gets done with her errand.'

'Ah,' Julian said. 'What kind of errand?'

Macon looked at him suspiciously.

'Well? Dry cleaner's? Shoe repair?'

'Just an ordinary errand, Julian. Nothing special.'

'Hardware store? Pharmacy?'

'No.'

'So what is it?'

'Uh . . . she had to buy Furniture Food.'

Julian's chair rocked so far back, Macon thought he was going to tip over. He wished he would, in fact. 'Macon, do me a favor,' Julian said. 'Couldn't you just once invite me to a family dinner?'

'We're really not much for socializing,' Macon told him.

'It wouldn't have to be fancy. Just whatever you eat normally. What *do* you eat normally? Or I'll bring the meal myself. You could lock the dog up . . . what's his name again?'

'Edward.'

'Edward. Ha! And I'll come spend the evening.'

'Oh, well,' Macon said vaguely. He arranged himself on his crutches.

'Why don't I step outside and wait with you.'

'I'd really rather you didn't,' Macon said.

He couldn't bear for Julian to see his sister's little basin hat.

He pegged out to the curb and stood there, gazing in the direction Rose should be coming from. He supposed she was lost again. The cold was already creeping through the stretched-out sock he wore over his cast.

The trouble was, he decided, Julian had never had anything happen to him. His ruddy, cheerful face was unscarred by anything but sunburn; his only interest was a ridiculously inefficient form of transportation. His brief marriage had ended amicably. He had no children. Macon didn't want to sound prejudiced, but he couldn't help feeling that people who had no children had never truly grown up. They weren't entirely . . . real, he felt.

Unexpectedly, he pictured Muriel after the Doberman had knocked her off the porch. Her arm hung lifeless; he knew the leaden look a broken limb takes on. But Muriel ignored it; she didn't even glance at it. Smudged and disheveled and battered, she held her other hand up. 'Absolutely not,' she said.

She arrived the next morning with a gauzy bouffant scarf swelling over her hair, her hands thrust deep in her coat pockets. Edward danced around her. She pointed to his rump. He sat, and she bent to pick up his leash.

'How's your little boy?' Macon asked her.

She looked over at him. 'What?' she said.

'Wasn't he sick?'

'Who told you that?'

'Someone at the vet's, when I phoned.'

She went on looking at him.

'What was it? The flu?' he asked.

'Oh, yes, probably,' she said after a moment. 'Some little stomach thing.'

'It's that time of year, I guess.'

'How come you phoned?' she asked him.

'I wanted to know why Edward wouldn't lie down.'

She turned her gaze toward Edward. She wound the leash around her hand and considered him.

'I tap my foot but he never obeys me,' Macon said. 'Something's wrong.'

'I told you he'd be stubborn about it.'

'Yes, but I've been practicing two days now and he's not making any—'

'What do you expect? You think I'm magical or something? Why blame me?'

'Oh, I'm not blaming—'

'You most certainly are. You tell me something's wrong, you call me on the phone—'

'I just wanted to—'

'You think it's weird I didn't mention Alexander, don't you?'

'Alexander?'

'You think I'm some kind of unnatural mother.'

'What? No, wait a minute—'

'You're not going to give me another thought, are you, now you know I've got a kid. You're like, "Oh, forget it, no point getting involved in *that*," and then you wonder why I didn't tell you about him right off. Well, isn't it obvious? Don't you see what happens when I do?'

Macon wasn't quite following her logic, perhaps because he was distracted by Edward. The shriller Muriel's voice grew, the stiffer Edward's hair stood up on the back of his neck. A bad sign. A very bad sign. Edward's lip was slowly curling. Gradually, at first almost soundlessly, he began a low growl.

Muriel glanced at him and stopped speaking. She didn't seem alarmed. She merely tapped her foot twice. But Edward not only failed to lie down; he rose from his sitting position. Now he had a distinct, electrified hump between his shoulders. He seemed to have altered his basic shape. His ears were flattened against his skull.

'Down,' Muriel said levelly.

With a bellow, Edward sprang straight at her face. Every tooth was bare and gleaming. His lips were drawn back in a horrible grimace and flecks of white foam flew from his mouth. Muriel instantly raised the leash. She jerked it upward with both fists and lifted Edward completely off the floor. He stopped barking. He started making gargling sounds.

'He's choking,' Macon said.

Edward's throat gave an odd sort of click.

'Stop it. It's enough! You're choking him!'

Still, she let him hang. Now Edward's eyes rolled back in their sockets. Macon grabbed at Muriel's shoulder but found himself with a handful of coat, bobbled and irregular like something alive. He shook it, anyhow. Muriel lowered Edward to the floor. He landed in a boneless heap, his legs crumpling beneath him and his head flopping over. Macon crouched at his side. 'Edward? Edward? Oh, God, he's dead!'

Edward raised his head and feebly licked his lips.

'See that? When they lick their lips it's a sign they're giving in,' Muriel said cheerfully. 'Doggie, Do taught me that.'

Macon stood up. He was shaking.

'When they lick their lips it's good but when they put a foot on top of your foot it's bad,' Muriel said. 'Sounds like a secret language, just about, doesn't it?'

'Don't you ever, ever do that again,' Macon told her.

'Huh?'

'In fact, don't even bother coming again.'

There was a startled silence.

'Well, fine,' Muriel said, tightening her scarf. 'If that's the way you feel, just fine and dandy.' She stepped neatly around Edward and opened the front door. 'You want a dog you can't handle? Fine with me.'

'I'd rather a barking dog than a damaged, timid dog,' Macon said.

'You want a dog that bites all your friends? Scars neighbor kids for life? Gets you into lawsuits? You want a dog that hates the whole world? Evil, nasty, *angry* dog? That kills the whole world?'

She slipped out the screen door and closed it behind her. Then she looked through the screen directly into Macon's eyes. 'Why, yes, I guess you do,' she said.

From the hall floor, Edward gave a moan and watched her walk away.

8

— Now the days were shorter and colder, and the trees emptied oceans of leaves on the lawn but remained, somehow, as full as ever, so you'd finish raking and look upward to see a great wash of orange and yellow just waiting to cover the grass again the minute your back was turned. Charles and Porter drove over to Macon's house and raked there as well, and lit the pilot light in the furnace and repaired the basement window. They reported that everything seemed fine. Macon heard the news without much interest. Next week he'd be out of his cast, but no one asked when he was moving back home.

Each morning he and Edward practiced heeling. They would trudge the length of the block, with Edward matching Macon's gait so perfectly that he looked crippled himself. When they met passersby now he muttered but he didn't attack. 'See there?' Macon wanted to tell someone. Bikers were another issue, but Macon had confidence they would solve that problem too, eventually.

He would make Edward sit and then he'd draw back, holding out a palm. Edward waited. Oh, he wasn't such a bad dog! Macon wished he could change the gestures of command—the palm, the pointed finger, all vestiges of that heartless trainer—but he supposed it was too late. He tapped his foot. Edward growled. 'Dear one,' Macon said, dropping heavily beside him. 'Won't you please consider lying down?' Edward looked away. Macon stroked the soft wide space between his ears. 'Ah, well, maybe tomorrow,' he said.

His family was not so hopeful. 'What about when you start traveling again?' Rose asked. 'You're not leaving him with me. I wouldn't know how to handle him.'

Macon told her they would get to that when they got to it.

It was hard for him to imagine resuming his travels. Sometimes he wished he could stay in his cast forever. In fact, he wished it covered him from head to foot. People would thump faintly on his chest. They'd peer through his eyeholes. 'Macon? You in there?' Maybe he was, maybe he wasn't. No one would ever know.

One evening just after supper, Julian stopped by with a stack of papers. Macon had to slam Edward into the pantry before he opened the door. 'Here you are!' Julian said, strolling past him. He wore corduroys and looked rugged and healthy. 'I've been phoning you for three days straight. That dog sounds awfully close by, don't you think?'

'He's in the pantry,' Macon said.

'Well, I've brought you some materials, Macon—mostly on New York. We've got a lot of suggestions for New York.'

Macon groaned. Julian set his papers on the couch and looked around him. 'Where are the others?' he asked.

'Oh, here and there,' Macon said vaguely, but just then Rose appeared, and Charles was close behind.

'I hope I'm not interfering with supper,' Julian told them.

'No, no,' Rose said.

'We've finished,' Macon said triumphantly.

Julian's face fell. 'Really?' he said. 'What time do you eat, anyhow?'

Macon didn't answer that. (They ate at five thirty. Julian would laugh.)

Rose said, 'But we haven't had our coffee. Wouldn't you like some coffee?'

'I'd love some.'

'It seems a little silly,' Macon said, 'if you haven't eaten.'

'Well, yes,' Julian said, 'I suppose it does, Macon, to someone like you. But for me, home-brewed coffee is a real treat. All the people in my apartment building eat out, and there's nothing in any of the kitchens but a couple cans of peanuts and some diet soda.'

'What kind of place *is* that?' Rose asked.

'It's the Calvert Arms—a singles building. Everybody's single.'

'Oh! What an interesting idea.'

'Well, not really,' Julian said gloomily. 'Not after a while. I started out enjoying it but now I think it's getting me down. Sometimes I wish for the good old-fashioned way of doing things, with children and families and old people like normal buildings have.'

'Well, of course you do,' Rose told him. 'I'm going to get you some nice hot coffee.'

She left, and the others sat down. 'So. Are you three all there is?' Julian asked.

Macon refused to answer, but Charles said, 'Oh, no, there's Porter too.'

'Porter? Where is Porter?'

'Um, we're not too sure.'

'Missing?'

'He went to a hardware store and we think he got lost.'

'Good grief, when did this happen?'

'A little while before supper.'

'Supper. You mean today.'

'He's just running an errand,' Macon said. 'Not lost in any permanent sense.'

'Where was the store?'

'Someplace on Howard Street,' Charles said. 'Rose needed hinges.'

'He got lost on Howard Street?'

Macon stood up. 'I'll go help Rose,' he said.

Rose was setting their grandmother's clear glass coffee mugs on a silver tray. 'I hope he doesn't take sugar,' she said. 'The sugarbowl is empty and Edward's in the pantry where I keep the bag.'

'I wouldn't worry about it.'

'Maybe you could go to the pantry and get it for me.'

'Oh, just give him his coffee straight and tell him to take it or leave it.'

'Why, Macon! This is your employer!'

'He's only here because he hopes we'll do something eccentric,' Macon told her. 'He has this one-sided notion of us. I just pray none of us says anything unconventional around him, are you listening?'

'What would we say?' Rose asked. 'We're the most conventional people I know.'

This was perfectly true, and yet in some odd way it wasn't. Macon couldn't explain it. He sighed and followed her out of the kitchen.

In the living room, Charles was doggedly debating whether they should answer the phone in case it rang, in case it might be Porter, in case he needed them to consult a map. 'Chances are, though, he wouldn't bother calling,' he decided, 'because he knows we wouldn't answer. Or he thinks we wouldn't answer. Or I don't know, maybe he figures we would answer even so, because we're worried.'

'Do you always give this much thought to your phone calls?' Julian asked.

Macon said, 'Have some coffee, Julian. Try it black.'

'Why, thank you,' Julian said. He accepted a mug and studied the inscription that arched across it. 'CENTURY OF PROGRESS 1933,' he read off. He grinned and raised the mug in a toast. 'To progress,' he said.

'Progress,' Rose and Charles echoed. Macon scowled.

Julian said, 'What do you do for a living, Charles?'

'I make bottle caps.'

'Bottle caps! Is that a fact!'

'Oh, well, it's no big thing,' Charles said. 'I mean it's not half as exciting as it sounds, really.'

'And Rose? Do you work?'

'Yes, I do,' Rose said, in the brave, forthright style of someone being interviewed. 'I work at home; I keep house for the boys. Also I take care of a lot of the neighbors. They're mostly old and they need me to read their prescriptions and repair their plumbing and such.'

'You repair their plumbing?' Julian asked.

The telephone rang. The others stiffened.

'What do you think?' Rose asked Macon.

'Um . . .'

'But he knows we wouldn't answer,' Charles told them.

'Yes, he'd surely call a neighbor instead.'

'On the other hand . . .' Charles said.

'On the other hand,' Macon said.

It was Julian's face that decided him—Julian's pleased, perked expression. Macon reached over to the end table and picked up the receiver. 'Leary,' he said.

'Macon?'

It was Sarah.

Macon shot a glance at the others and turned his back to them. 'Yes,' he said.

'Well, finally,' she said. Her voice seemed oddly flat and concrete. All at once he saw her clearly: She wore one of his cast-off shirts and she sat hugging her bare knees. 'I've been trying to get in touch with you at home,' she said. 'Then it occurred to me you might be having supper with your family.'

'Is something wrong?' he asked.

He was nearly whispering. Maybe Rose understood, from that,

who it was, for she suddenly began an animated conversation with the others. Sarah said, 'What? I can't hear you.'

'Is everything all right?'

'Who's that talking?'

'Julian's here.'

'Oh, Julian! Give him my love. How's Sukie?'

'Sukie?'

'His boat, Macon.'

'It's fine,' he said. Or should he have said 'she'? For all he knew, *Sukie* was at the bottom of the Chesapeake.

'I called because I thought we should talk,' Sarah said. 'I was hoping we could meet for supper some night.'

'Oh. Well. Yes, we could do that,' Macon said.

'Would tomorrow be all right?'

'Certainly.'

'What restaurant?'

'Well, why not the Old Bay,' Macon said.

'The Old Bay. Of course,' Sarah said. She either sighed or laughed, he wasn't sure which.

'It's only because you could walk there,' he told her. 'That's the only reason I suggested it.'

'Yes, well, let's see. You like to eat early; shall we say six o'clock?'

'Six will be fine,' he said.

When he hung up, he found Rose embarked on a discussion of the English language. She pretended not to notice he had rejoined them. It was shocking, she was saying, how sloppy everyday speech had become. How the world seemed bound and determined to say '*the* hoi polloi,' a clear redundancy in view of the fact that 'hoi' was an article. How 'chauvinist' had come to be a shorthand term for 'male chauvinist,' its original meaning sadly lost to common knowledge. It was incredible, Charles chimed in, that a female movie star traveled 'incognito' when any fool should know she was 'incognita' instead. Julian appeared to share their indignation. It was more incredible still, he said, how everyone slung around the word 'incredible' when really there was very little on earth that truly defied credibility. 'Credence,' Macon corrected him, but Rose rushed in as if Macon hadn't spoken. 'Oh, I know just what you mean,' she told Julian. 'Words are getting devalued, isn't that right?' She tugged handfuls of her gray tube skirt over her knees in a childlike gesture. You would think she had never been warned that outsiders were not to be trusted.

To enter the Old Bay Restaurant, Macon had to climb a set of steps. Before he broke his leg he hadn't even noticed those steps existed—let alone that they were made of smooth, unblemished marble, so that his crutches kept threatening to slide out from under him. Then he had to fight the heavy front door, hurrying a bit because Rose had taken a wrong turn driving him down and it was already five after six.

The foyer was dark as night. The dining room beyond was only slightly brighter, lit by netted candles on the tables. Macon peered into the gloom. 'I'm meeting someone,' he told the hostess. 'Is she here yet?'

'Not as I know of, hon.'

She led him past a tankful of sluggish lobsters, past two old ladies in churchy hats sipping pale pink drinks, past a whole field of empty tables. It was too early for anyone else to be eating; all the other customers were still in the bar. The tables stood very close together, their linens brushing the floor, and Macon had visions of catching a crutch on a tablecloth and dragging the whole thing after him, candle included. The maroon floral carpet would burst into flames. His grandfather's favorite restaurant—his great-grandfather's too, quite possibly—would be reduced to a heap of charred metal crab pots. 'Miss! Slow down!' he called, but the hostess strode on, muscular and athletic in her off-the-shoulder square-dance dress and sturdy white crepe-soled shoes.

She put him in a corner, which was lucky because it gave him a place to lean his crutches. But just as he was matching them up and preparing to set them aside, she said, 'I'll take those for you, darlin'.'

'Oh, they'll be fine here.'

'I need to check them up front, sweetheart. It's a rule.'

'You have a rule about crutches?'

'They might trip the other customers, honeybunch.'

This was unlikely, since the two other customers were clear across the room, but Macon handed his crutches over. Come to think of it, he might be better off without them. Then Sarah wouldn't get the impression (at least at first glance) that he'd fallen apart in her absence.

As soon as he was alone he tugged each shirt cuff till a quarter-inch of white showed. He was wearing his gray tweed suit coat with gray flannel trousers—an old pair of trousers, so it hadn't mattered if he cut one leg off. Charles had fetched them from home and Rose had hemmed them, and she'd also trimmed his hair. Porter had lent him his best striped tie. They had all been so discreetly helpful that Macon had felt sad, for some reason.

The hostess reappeared in the doorway, followed by Sarah. Macon had an instant of stunned recognition; it was something like accidentally glimpsing his own reflection in a mirror. Her halo of curls, the way her coat fell around her in soft folds, her firm, springy walk in trim pumps with wineglass heels—how had he forgotten all that?

He half stood. Would she kiss him? Or just, God forbid, coolly shake hands. But no, she did neither; she did something much worse. She came around the table and pressed her cheek to his briefly, as if they were mere acquaintances meeting at a cocktail party.

'Hello, Macon,' she said.

He waved her speechlessly into the chair across from his. He sat again, with some effort.

'What happened to your leg?' she asked.

'I had a kind of . . . fall.'

'Is it broken?'

He nodded.

'And what did you do to your hand?'

He held it up to examine it. 'Well, it's a sort of dog bite. But it's nearly healed by now.'

'I meant the other one.'

The other one had a band of gauze around the knuckles. 'Oh, that,' he said. 'It's just a scrape. I've been helping Rose build a cat door.'

She studied him.

'But I'm all right!' he told her. 'In fact the cast is almost comfortable. Almost familiar! I'm wondering if I broke a leg once before in some previous incarnation.'

Their waitress asked, 'Can I bring you something from the bar?'

She was standing over them, pad and pencil poised. Sarah started flipping hastily through the menu, so Macon said, 'A dry sherry, please.' Then he and the waitress turned back to Sarah. 'Oh, my,' Sarah said. 'Let me see. Well, how about a Rob Roy. Yes, a Rob Roy would be nice, with extra cherries.'

That was something else he'd forgotten—how she loved to order complicated drinks in restaurants. He felt the corners of his mouth twitching upward.

'So,' Sarah said when the waitress had gone. 'Why would Rose be building a cat door? I thought they didn't have any pets.'

'No, this is for our cat. Helen. Helen and I have been staying there.'

'What for?'

'Well, because of my leg.'

Sarah said nothing.

'I mean, can you see me managing those steps at home?' Macon asked her. 'Taking Edward for walks? Lugging the trash cans out?'

But she was busy shucking off her coat. Beneath it she wore a gathered wool dress in an indeterminate color. (The candlelight turned everything to shades of sepia, like an old-fashioned photograph.) Macon had time to wonder if he'd given her the wrong idea. It sounded, perhaps, as if he were complaining—as if he were reproaching her for leaving him alone.

'But really,' he said, 'I've been getting along wonderfully.'

'Good,' Sarah said, and she smiled at him and went back to her menu.

Their drinks were set before them on little cardboard disks embossed with crabs. The waitress said, 'Ready to order, dearies?'

'Well,' Sarah said, 'I think I'll have the hot antipasto and the beef Pierre.'

The waitress, looking startled, peered over Sarah's shoulder at the menu. (Sarah had never seemed to realize what the Old Bay Restaurant was all about.) 'Here,' Sarah said, pointing, 'and here.'

'If you say so,' the waitress said, writing it down.

'I'll just have the, you know,' Macon said. 'Crab soup, shrimp salad platter . . .' He handed back his menu. 'Sarah, do you want wine?'

'No, thank you.'

When they were alone again, she said, 'How long have you been at your family's?'

'Since September,' Macon said.

'September! Your leg's been broken all that time?'

He nodded and took a sip of his drink. 'Tomorrow I get the cast off,' he said.

'And is Edward over there too?'

He nodded again.

'Was it Edward who bit your hand?'

'Well, yes.'

He wondered if she'd act like the others, urge him to call the S.P.C.A.; but instead she meditatively plucked a cherry off the plastic sword from her drink. 'I guess he's been upset,' she said.

'Yes, he has, in fact,' Macon said. 'He's not himself at all.'

'Poor Edward.'

'He's getting kind of out of control, to tell the truth.'

'He always did have a sensitivity to change,' Sarah said.

Macon took heart. 'Actually, he's been attacking right and left,' he told her. 'I had to hire a special trainer. But she was too harsh; let's face it, she was brutal. She nearly strangled him when he tried to bite her.'

'Ridiculous,' Sarah said. 'He was only frightened. When Edward's frightened he attacks; that's just the way he is. There's no point scaring him more.'

Macon felt a sudden rush of love.

Oh, he'd raged at her and hated her and entirely forgotten her, at different times. He'd had moments when he imagined he'd never cared for her to begin with; only went after her because everybody else had. But the fact was, she was his oldest friend. The two of them had been through things that no one else in the world knew of. She was embedded in his life. It was much too late to root her out.

'What he wants,' she was saying, 'is a sense of routine. That's all he needs: reassurance.'

'Sarah,' he said, 'it's been awful living apart.'

She looked at him. Some trick of light made her eyes appear a darker blue, almost black.

'Hasn't it?' he said.

She lowered her glass. She said, 'I asked you here for a reason, Macon.'

He could tell it was something he didn't want to hear.

She said, 'We need to spell out the details of our separation.'

'We've been separated; what's to spell out?' he asked.

'I meant in a legal way.'

'Legal. I see.'

'Now, according to the state of Maryland—'

'I think you ought to come home.'

Their first course arrived, placed before them by a hand that, as far as Macon was concerned, was not attached to a body. Condiment bottles were shifted needlessly; a metal stand full of sugar packets was moved a half-inch over. 'Anything else?' the waitress asked.

'No!' Macon said. 'Thank you.'

She left.

He said, 'Sarah?'

'It's not possible,' she told him.

She was sliding a single pearl up and down the chain at her throat. He had given her that pearl when they were courting. Was there any significance in her wearing it this evening? Or maybe she cared so little now, it hadn't even occurred to her to leave it off. Yes, that was more likely.

'Listen,' he said. 'Don't say no before you hear me out. Have you ever considered we might have another baby?'

He had shocked her, he saw; she drew in a breath. (He had shocked himself.)

'Why not?' he asked her. 'We're not too old.'

'Oh, Macon.'

'This time, it would be easy,' he said. 'It wouldn't take us seven years again; I bet you'd get pregnant in no time!' He leaned toward her, straining to make her see it: Sarah blossoming in that luscious pink maternity smock she used to wear. But oddly enough, what flashed across his mind instead was the memory of those first seven years—their disappointment each month. It had seemed to Macon back then (though of course it was pure superstition) that their failures were a sign of something deeper, some essential incompatibility. They had missed connections in the most basic and literal sense. When she finally got pregnant, he had felt not only relieved but guilty, as if they had succeeded in putting something over on someone.

He pushed these thoughts back down. 'I realize,' he said, 'that it wouldn't be Ethan. I realize we can't replace him. But—'

'No,' Sarah said.

Her eyes were very steady. He knew that look. She'd never change her mind.

Macon started on his soup. It was the best crab soup in Baltimore, but unfortunately the spices had a tendency to make his nose run. He hoped Sarah wouldn't think he was crying.

'I'm sorry,' she said more gently. 'But it would never work.'

He said, 'All right, forget that. It was crazy, right? Crazy notion. By the time that baby was twenty we'd be . . . Aren't you going to eat?'

She glanced down at her plate. Then she picked up a fork.

'Suppose I did this,' Macon said. 'Suppose I packed a suitcase with your clothes and knocked on your door and said, "Come on, we're going to Ocean City. We've wasted long enough." '

She stared, an artichoke heart raised halfway to her mouth.

'Ocean City?' she said. 'You hate Ocean City!'

'Yes, but I meant—'

'You always said it was way too crowded.'

'Yes, but—'

'And what clothes could you be talking about? They're all in my apartment.'

'It was only a manner of speaking,' Macon said.

'Really, Macon,' she told him. 'You don't even communicate when you communicate.'

'Oh, *communicate*,' he said. (His least favorite word.) 'All I'm saying is, I think we ought to start over.'

'I am starting over,' she said. She returned the artichoke heart to her plate. 'I'm doing everything I can to start over,' she said, 'but that doesn't mean I want to live the same life twice. I'm trying to branch off in new directions. I'm taking some courses. I'm even dating, a little.'

'Dating?'

'I've been going out with this physician.'

There was a pause.

Macon said, 'Why not just call him a doctor.'

Sarah briefly closed her eyes.

'Look,' she said. 'I know this is hard for you. It's hard for both of us. But we really didn't have much left, don't you see? Look who you turned to when you broke your leg: your sister Rose! You didn't even let me know, and you do have my telephone number.'

'If I'd turned to you instead,' he said, 'would you have come?'

'Well . . . but at least you could have asked. But no, you called on your family. You're closer to them than you ever were to me.'

'That's not true,' Macon said. 'Or rather, it's true but it's not the point. I mean, in one sense, of course we're closer; we're blood relations.'

'Playing that ridiculous card game no one else can fathom,' Sarah said. 'Plotting your little household projects, Rose with her crescent wrench and her soldering gun. Cruising hardware stores like other people cruise boutiques.'

'*As* other people cruise boutiques,' Macon said. And then regretted it.

'Picking apart people's English,' Sarah said. 'Hauling forth the dictionary at every opportunity. Quibbling over *method*. The kind of family that always fastens their seatbelts.'

'For God's sake, Sarah, what's wrong with fastening your seatbelt?'

'They always go to one restaurant, the one their grandparents went to before them, and even there they have to rearrange the silver and set things up so they're sitting around the table the same way they sit at home. They dither and deliberate, can't so much as close a curtain without this group discussion back and forth, to and fro, all the pros and cons. "Well if we leave it open it will be so hot but if we close it things will get musty . . ." They have to have their six glasses of water every day. Their precious baked potatoes every night. They don't believe in ballpoint pens or electric typewriters or automatic transmissions. They don't believe in hello and good-bye.'

'Hello? Good-bye?' Macon said.

'Just watch yourself some time! People walk in and you just, oh, register it with your eyes; people leave and you just look away quickly. You don't admit to comings and goings. And the best house in the world might come on the market, but you can't buy it because you've ordered these address labels for the old house, a thousand five hundred gummed labels, and you have to use them up before you move.'

'That wasn't me, it was Charles,' Macon said.

'Yes, but it could have been you. And his wife divorced him for it, and I don't blame her.'

'And now you're about to do the same damn thing,' Macon said. 'Ruin twenty years of marriage over whether I fasten my seatbelt.'

'They were ruined long ago, believe me,' Sarah said.

Macon laid down his spoon. He forced himself to take a deep breath.

'Sarah,' he said. 'We're getting away from the point.'

After a silence, Sarah said, 'Yes, I guess we are.'

'It's what happened to Ethan that ruined us,' Macon told her.

She set an elbow on the table and covered her eyes.

'But it wouldn't have to,' he said. 'Why, some people, a thing like this brings them closer together. How come we're letting it part us?'

The waitress said, 'Is everything all right?'

Sarah sat up straighter and started rummaging through her purse.

'Yes, certainly,' Macon said.

The waitress was carrying a tray with their main dishes. She cast a doubtful look at Sarah's antipasto. 'Isn't she going to eat that, or what?' she asked Macon.

'No, I guess, um, maybe not.'

'Didn't she like it?'

'She liked it fine. Take it away.'

The waitress bustled around the table in an offended silence. Sarah put aside her purse. She looked down at her meal, which was something brown and gluey.

'You're welcome to half my shrimp salad,' Macon told her when the waitress had gone.

She shook her head. Her eyes were deep with tears, but they hadn't spilled over.

'Macon,' she said, 'ever since Ethan died I've had to admit that people are basically bad. Evil, Macon. So evil they would take a twelve-year-old boy and shoot him through the skull for no reason. I read a paper now and I despair; I've given up watching the news on TV. There's so much wickedness, children setting other children on fire and grown men throwing babies out second-story windows, rape and torture and terrorism, old people beaten and robbed, men in our very own government willing to blow up the world, indifference and greed and instant anger on every street corner. I look at my students and they're so ordinary, but they're exactly like the boy who killed Ethan. If it hadn't said beneath that boy's picture what he'd been arrested for, wouldn't you think he was just anyone? Someone who'd made the basketball team or won a college scholarship? You can't believe in a soul. Last spring, Macon, I didn't tell you this, I was cutting back our hedge and I saw the bird feeder had been stolen out of the crape myrtle tree. Someone will even steal food from little birds! And I just, I don't know, went kind of crazy and attacked the crape myrtle. Cut it all up, ripped off branches, slashed it with my pruning shears . . .'

Tears were running down her face now. She leaned across the table and said, 'There are times when I haven't been sure I could—I don't want to sound melodramatic but—Macon, I haven't been sure I could live in this kind of a world anymore.'

Macon felt he had to be terribly careful. He had to choose exactly the right words. He cleared his throat and said, 'Yes, um, I see what you mean but . . . ' He cleared his throat again. 'It's true,' he said, 'what you say about human beings. I'm not trying to argue. But tell me this, Sarah: Why would that cause you to leave me?'

She crumpled up her napkin and dabbed at her nose. She said, 'Because I *knew* you wouldn't try to argue. You've believed all along they were evil.'

'Well, so—'

'This whole last year I felt myself retreating. Withdrawing. I could feel myself shrinking. I stayed away from crowds, I didn't go to parties, I didn't ask our friends in. When you and I went to the beach in the summer I lay on my blanket with all those people around me, their squawking radios and their gossip and their quarrels, and I thought, "Ugh, they're so depressing. They're so unlikable. So vile, really." I felt myself shrinking away from them. Just like you do, Macon—just *as* you do; sorry. Just as you have always done. I felt I was turning into a Leary.'

Macon tried for a lighter tone. He said, 'Well, there are worse disasters than that, I guess.'

She didn't smile. She said, 'I can't afford it.'

'Afford?'

'I'm forty-two years old. I don't have enough time left to waste it holing up in my shell. So I've taken action. I've cut myself loose. I live in this apartment you'd hate, all clutter. I've made a whole bunch of new friends, and you wouldn't like them much either, I guess. I'm studying with a sculptor. I always did want to be an artist, only teaching seemed more sensible. That's how you would think: sensible. You're so quick to be sensible, Macon, that you've given up on just about everything.'

'What have I given up on?'

She refolded the napkin and blotted her eyes. An appealing blur of mascara shadowed the skin beneath them. She said, 'Remember Betty Grand?'

'No.'

'Betty Grand, she went to my school. You used to like her before you met me.'

'I never liked anyone on earth before I met you,' Macon said.

'You liked Betty Grand, Macon. You told me so when we first went out. You asked me if I knew her. You said you used to think she was pretty and you'd invited her to a ball game but she turned you down. You told me you'd changed your mind about her being pretty. Her gums showed any time she smiled, you said.'

Macon still didn't remember, but he said, 'Well? So?'

'Everything that might touch you or upset you or disrupt you, you've given up without a murmur and done without, said you never wanted it anyhow.'

'I suppose I would have done better if I'd gone on pining for Betty Grand all my life.'

'Well, you would have shown some feeling, at least.'

'I do show feeling, Sarah. I'm sitting here with you, am I not? You don't see me giving up on *you*.'

She chose not to hear this. 'And when Ethan died,' she said, 'you peeled every single Wacky Pack sticker off his bedroom door. You emptied his closet and his bureau as if you couldn't be rid of him soon enough. You kept offering people his junk in the basement, stilts and sleds and skateboards, and you couldn't understand why they didn't accept them. "I hate to see stuff sitting there useless," you said. Macon, I know you loved him but I can't help thinking you didn't love him as much as I did, you're not so torn apart by his going. I know you mourned him but there's something so what-do-you-call, so muffled about the way you experience things, I mean love or grief or anything; it's like you're trying to slip through life unchanged. Don't you see why I had to get out?'

'Sarah, I'm not muffled. I . . . endure. I'm trying to endure, I'm standing fast, I'm holding steady.'

'If you really think that,' Sarah said, 'then you're fooling yourself. You're not holding steady; you're ossified. You're encased. You're like something in a capsule. You're a dried-up kernel of a man that nothing really penetrates. Oh, Macon, it's not by chance you write those silly books telling people how to take trips without a jolt. That traveling armchair isn't just your logo; it's you.'

'No, it's not,' Macon said. 'It's not!'

Sarah pulled her coat on, making a sloppy job of it. One corner of her collar was tucked inside. 'So anyway,' she said. 'This is what I wanted to tell you: I'm having John Albright send you a letter.'

'Who's John Albright?'

'He's an attorney.'

'Oh,' Macon said.

It was at least a full minute before he thought to say, 'I guess you must mean a lawyer.'

Sarah collected her purse, stood up, and walked out.

*

Macon made his way conscientiously through his shrimp salad. He ate his cole slaw for the vitamin C. Then he finished every last one of his potato chips, although he knew his tongue would feel shriveled the following morning.

Once when Ethan was little, not more than two or three, he had run out into the street after a ball. Macon had been too far away to stop him. All he could do was shout, 'No!' and then watch, frozen with horror, as a pickup truck came barreling around the curve. In that instant, he released his claim. In one split second he adjusted to a future that held no Ethan—an immeasurably bleaker place but also, by way of compensation, plainer and simpler, free of the problems a small child trails along with him, the endless demands and the mess and the contests for his mother's attention. Then the truck stopped short and Ethan retrieved his ball, and Macon's knees went weak with relief. But he remembered forever after how quickly he had adjusted. He wondered, sometimes, if that first adjustment had somehow stuck, making what happened to Ethan later less of a shock than it might have been. But if people didn't adjust, how could they bear to go on?

He called for his bill and paid it. 'Was there something wrong?' the waitress asked. 'Did your friend not like her meal? She could always have sent it back, hon. We always let you send it back.'

'I know that,' Macon said.

'Maybe it was too spicy for her.'

'It was fine,' he said. 'Could I have my crutches, please?'

She went off to get them, shaking her head.

He would have to locate a taxi. He'd made no arrangements for Rose to pick him up. Secretly, he'd been hoping to go home with Sarah. Now that hope seemed pathetic. He looked around the dining room and saw that most of the tables were filled, and that every person had someone else to eat with. Only Macon sat alone. He kept very erect and dignified but inside, he knew, he was crumbling. And when the waitress brought him his crutches and he stood to leave, it seemed appropriate that he had to walk nearly doubled, his chin sunk low on his chest and his elbows jutting out awkwardly like the wings of a baby bird. People stared at him as he passed. Some snickered. Was his foolishness so obvious? He passed the two churchy old ladies and one of them tugged at his sleeve. 'Sir? Sir?'

He came to a stop.

'I suspect they may have given you my crutches,' she said.

He looked down at the crutches. They were, of course, not his. They were diminutive—hardly more than child-sized. Any other time he would have grasped the situation right off, but today it had somehow escaped him. Any other time he would have swung into action—called for the manager, pointed out the restaurant's lack of concern for the handicapped. Today he only stood hanging his head, waiting for someone to help him.

9

—— Back when Grandfather Leary's mind first began to wander, no one had guessed what was happening. He was such an upright, firm old man. He was all sharp edges. Definite. 'Listen,' he told Macon, 'by June the twelfth I'll need my passport from the safe deposit box. I'm setting sail for Lassaque.'

'Lassaque, Grandfather?'

'If I like it I may just stay there.'

'But where is Lassaque?'

'It's an island off the coast of Bolivia.'

'Ah,' Macon said. And then, 'Well, wait a minute . . .'

'It interests me because the Lassaquans have no written language. In fact if you bring any reading matter they confiscate it. They say it's black magic.'

'But I don't think Bolivia _has_ a coast,' Macon said.

'They don't even allow, say, a checkbook with your name on it. Before you go ashore you have to soak the label off your deodorant. You have to get your money changed into little colored wafers.'

'Grandfather, is this a joke?'

'A joke! Look it up if you don't believe me.' Grandfather Leary checked his steel pocket watch, then wound it with an assured, back-and-forth motion. 'An intriguing effect of their illiteracy,' he said, 'is their reverence for the elderly. This is because the Lassaquans' knowledge doesn't come from books but from living; so they hang on every word from those who have lived the longest.'

'I see,' Macon said, for now he thought he did see. '*We* hang on *your* words, too,' he said.

'That may be so,' his grandfather told him, 'but I still intend to see Lassaque before it's corrupted.'

Macon was silent a moment. Then he went over to the bookcase and selected a volume from his grandfather's set of faded brown encyclopedias. 'Give it here,' his grandfather said, holding out both hands. He took the book greedily and started riffling through the pages. A smell of mold floated up. 'Laski,' he muttered, 'Lassalle, Lassaw . . .' He lowered the book and frowned. 'I don't . . .' he said. He returned to the book. 'Lassalle, Lassaw . . .'

He looked confused, almost frightened. His face all at once collapsed—a phenomenon that had startled Macon on several occasions lately. 'I don't understand,' he whispered to Macon. 'I don't understand.'

'Well,' Macon said, 'maybe it was a dream. Maybe it was one of those dreams that seem real.'

'Macon, this was no dream. I *know* the place. I've bought my ticket. I'm sailing June the twelfth.'

Macon felt a strange coldness creeping down his back.

Then his grandfather became an inventor—spoke of various projects he was tinkering with, he said, in his basement. He would sit in his red leather armchair, his suit and white shirt immaculate, his black dress shoes polished to a glare, his carefully kept hands folded in his lap, and he would announce that he'd just finished welding together a motorcycle that would pull a plow. He would earnestly discuss crankshafts and cotter pins, while Macon—though terribly distressed—had to fight down a bubble of laughter at the thought of some leather-booted Hell's Angel grinding away at a wheatfield. 'If I could just get the kinks ironed out,' his grandfather said, 'I'd have my fortune made. We'll all be rich.' For he seemed to believe he was poor again, struggling to earn his way in the world. His motorized radio that followed you from room to room, his floating telephone, his car that came when you called it—wouldn't there be some application for those? Wouldn't the right person pay an arm and a leg?

Having sat out on the porch for one entire June morning, studiously pinching the creases of his trousers, he announced that he had perfected a new type of hybrid: flowers that closed in the presence of tears. 'Florists will be mobbing me,' he said. 'Think of the dramatic effect at funerals!' He was working next on a cross between basil and tomatoes. He said the spaghetti-sauce companies would make him a wealthy man.

By then, all three of his grandsons had left home and his wife had died; so Rose alone took care of him. Her brothers began to worry about her. They took to dropping by more and more often. Then Rose said, 'You don't have to do this, you know.'

They said, 'What? Do what? What are you talking about?' And other such things.

'If you're coming so often on account of Grandfather, it's not necessary. I'm managing fine, and so is he. He's very happy.'

'Happy!'

'I honestly believe,' Rose said, 'that he's having the richest and most . . . colorful, really, time of his life. I'll bet even when he was young, he never enjoyed himself this much.'

They saw what she meant. Macon felt almost envious, once he thought about it. And later, when that period was over, he was sorry it had been so short. For their grandfather soon passed to pointless, disconnected mumbles, and then to a staring silence, and at last he died.

Early Wednesday morning, Macon dreamed Grandfather Leary woke him and asked where the center punch was. 'What are you talking about?' Macon said. 'I never had your center punch.'

'Oh, Macon,' his grandfather said sadly, 'can't you tell that I'm not saying what I mean?'

'What do you mean, then?'

'You've lost the center of your *life*, Macon.'

'Yes, I know that,' Macon said, and it seemed that Ethan stood just slightly to the left, his bright head nearly level with the old man's.

But his grandfather said, 'No, no,' and made an impatient, shaking-off gesture and went over to the bureau. (In this dream, Macon was not in the sun porch but upstairs in his boyhood bedroom, with the bureau whose cut-glass knobs Rose had stolen long ago to use as dishes for her dolls.) 'It's Sarah I mean,' his grandfather said, picking up a hairbrush. 'Where is Sarah?'

'She's left me, Grandfather.'

'Why, Sarah's the best of all of us!' his grandfather said. 'You want to sit in this old house and rot, boy? It's time we started digging out! How long are we going to stay fixed here?'

Macon opened his eyes. It wasn't morning yet. The sun porch was fuzzy as blotting paper.

There was still a sense of his grandfather in the air. His little shaking-off gesture was one that Macon had forgotten entirely; it had reappeared on its own. But Grandfather Leary would never have said in real life what he'd said in the dream. He had liked Sarah well enough, but he seemed to view wives as extraneous, and he'd attended each of his grandsons' weddings with a resigned and tolerant expression. He wouldn't have thought of any woman as a 'center.' Except, perhaps, Macon thought suddenly, his own wife, Grandmother Leary. After whose death—why, yes, immediately after—his mind had first begun to wander.

Macon lay awake till dawn. It was a relief to hear the first stirrings overhead. Then he got up and shaved and dressed and sent Edward out for the paper. By the time Rose came downstairs, he had started the coffee perking. This seemed to make her anxious. 'Did you use the morning beans or the evening beans?' she asked.

'The morning beans,' he assured her. 'Everything's under control.'

She moved around the kitchen raising shades, setting the table, opening a carton of eggs. 'So today's the day you get your cast off,' she said.

'Looks that way.'

'And this afternoon's your New York trip.'

'Oh, well . . .' he said vaguely, and then he asked if she wanted a bacon coupon he'd spotted in the paper.

She persisted: 'Isn't it this afternoon you're going?'

'Well, yes.'

The fact of the matter was, he was leaving for New York without having made any arrangements for Edward. The old place wouldn't accept him, the new place had that Muriel woman . . . and in Macon's opinion, Edward was best off at home with the family. Rose, no doubt, would disagree. He held his breath, but Rose started humming 'Clementine' and breaking eggs into a skillet.

At nine o'clock, in an office down on St Paul Street, the doctor removed Macon's cast with a tiny, purring electric saw. Macon's leg emerged dead-white and wrinkled and ugly. When he stood up, his ankle wobbled. He still had a limp. Also, he'd forgotten to bring different trousers and he was forced to parade back through the other patients in his one-legged summer khakis, exposing his repulsive-looking shin. He wondered if he'd ever return to his old, unbroken self.

Driving him home, Rose finally thought to ask where he planned to board Edward. 'Why, I'm leaving him with you,' Macon said, acting surprised.

'With me? Oh, Macon, you know how out of hand he gets.'

'What could happen in such a short time? I'll be home by tomorrow night. If worst comes to worst you could lock him in the pantry; toss him some kibble now and then till I get back.'

'I don't like this at all,' Rose said.

'It's visitors that set him off. It's not as if you're expecting any visitors.'

'Oh, no,' she said, and then she let the subject drop, thank heaven. He'd been fearing more of a battle.

He took a shower, and he dressed in his traveling suit. Then he had an early lunch. Just before noon Rose drove him down to the railroad station, since he didn't yet trust his clutch foot. When he stepped from the car, his leg threatened to buckle. 'Wait!' he said to Rose, who was handing his bag out after him. 'Do you suppose I'm up to this?'

'I'm sure you are,' she said, without giving it anywhere near enough thought. She pulled the passenger door shut, waved at him, and drove off.

In the period since Macon's last train trip, something wonderful had happened to the railroad station. A skylight in shades of watery blue arched gently overhead. Pale globe lamps hung from brass hooks. The carpenters' partitions that had divided the waiting room for so long had disappeared, revealing polished wooden benches. Macon stood bewildered at the brand-new, gleaming ticket window. Maybe, he thought, travel was not so bad. Maybe he'd got it all wrong. He felt a little sprig of hopefulness beginning.

But immediately afterward, limping toward his gate, he was overcome by the lost feeling that always plagued him on these trips. He envisioned himself as a stark Figure 1 in a throng of 2's and 3's. Look at that group at the Information counter, those confident young people with their knapsacks and sleeping bags. Look at the family occupying one entire bench, their four little daughters so dressed up, so stiff in new plaid coats and ribboned hats, you just knew they'd be met by grandparents at the other end of the line. Even those sitting alone—the old woman with the corsage, the blonde with her expensive leather luggage—gave the impression of belonging to someone.

He sat down on a bench. A southbound train was announced and half the crowd went off to catch it, followed by the inevitable breathless, disheveled woman galloping through some time later with far too many bags and parcels. Arriving passengers began to straggle up the stairs. They wore the dazed expressions of people who had been elsewhere till just this instant. A woman was greeted by a man holding a baby; he kissed her and passed her the baby at once, as if it were a package he'd been finding unusually heavy. A young girl in jeans, reaching the top of the stairs, caught sight of another girl in jeans and threw her arms around her and started crying. Macon watched, pretending not to, inventing explanations. (She was home for their mother's funeral? Her elopement hadn't worked out?)

Now his own train was called, so he picked up his bag and limped behind the family with all the daughters. At the bottom of the stairs a gust of cold, fresh air hit him. Wind always seemed to be howling down these platforms, no matter what the weather elsewhere. The smallest of the daughters had to have her coat buttoned. The train came into view, slowly assembling itself around a pinpoint of yellow light.

Most of the cars were full, it turned out. Macon gave up trying to find a completely empty seat and settled next to a plump young man with a briefcase. Just to be on the safe side, he unpacked *Miss MacIntosh*.

The train lurched forward and then changed its mind and then lurched forward again and took off. Macon imagined he could feel little scabs of rust on the tracks; it wasn't a very smooth ride. He watched the sights of home rush toward him and disappear—a tumble of row houses, faded vacant lots, laundry hanging rigid in the cold.

'Gum?' his seatmate asked.

Macon said, 'No, thanks,' and quickly opened his book.

When they'd been traveling an hour or so, he felt his lids grow heavy. He let his head fall back. He thought he was only resting his eyes, but he must have gone to sleep. The next thing he knew, the conductor was announcing Philadelphia. Macon jerked and sat up straight and caught his book just before it slid off his lap.

His seatmate was doing some kind of paperwork, using his briefcase as a desk. A businessman, obviously—one of the people Macon wrote his guides for. Funny, Macon never pictured his readers. What did businessmen do, exactly? This one was jotting notes on index cards, referring now and then to a booklet full of graphs. One graph showed little black trucks marching across the page—four trucks, seven trucks, three and a half trucks. Macon thought the half-truck looked deformed and pitiable.

Just before they arrived, he used the restroom at the rear of the car—not ideal, but more homey than anything he'd find in New York. He went back to his seat and packed *Miss MacIntosh*. 'Going to be cold there,' his seatmate told him.

'I imagine so,' Macon said.

'Weather report says cold and windy.'

Macon didn't answer.

He believed in traveling without an overcoat—just one more thing to carry—but he wore a thermal undershirt and long johns. Cold was the least of his worries.

In New York the passengers scattered instantly. Macon thought of a seed pod bursting open. He refused to be rushed and made his way methodically through the crowd, up a set of clanking, dark stairs, and through another crowd that seemed more extreme than the one he had left down below. Goodness, where did these women get their clothes? One wore a bushy fur tepee and leopardskin boots. One wore an olive-drab coverall exactly like an auto mechanic's except that it was made of leather. Macon took a firmer grip on his bag and pushed through the door to the street, where car horns blasted insistently and the air smelled gray and sharp, like the interior of a dead chimney. In his opinion, New York was a foreign city. He was forever taken aback by its pervasive atmosphere of purposefulness—the tight focus of its drivers, the brisk intensity of its pedestrians drilling their way through all obstacles without a glance to either side.

He hailed a cab, slid across the worn, slippery seat, and gave the address of his hotel. The driver started talking at once about his daughter. 'I mean she's thirteen years old,' he said, nosing out into traffic, 'and got three sets of holes in her ears and an earring in each hole, and now she wants to get another set punched up toward the top. Thirteen years old!' He either had or had not heard the address. At any rate, he was driving along. 'I wasn't even in favor of the first set of holes,' he said. 'I told her, "What; you don't read Ann Landers?" Ann Landers says piercing your ears is mutilating your body. Was it Ann Landers? I think it was Ann Landers. You might as well wear a ring through your nose like the Africans, right? I told my daughter that. She says, "So? What's wrong with a ring through my nose? Maybe that's what I'll get next." I wouldn't put it past her, either. I would not put it past her. Now this fourth set goes through cartilage and most of these ear-piercing places won't do that; so you see how crazy it is. Cartilage is a whole different ball game. It's not like your earlobe, all spongy.'

Macon had the feeling he wasn't fully visible. He was listening to a man who was talking to himself, who may have been talking before he got in and might possibly go on talking after he got out. Or was he present in this cab at all? Such thoughts often attacked while he was traveling. In desperation, he said, 'Um—'

The driver stopped speaking, surprisingly enough. The back of his neck took on an alert look. Macon had to continue. He said, 'Tell her something scary.'

'Like what?'

'Like . . . tell her you know a girl whose ears dropped off.'

'She'd never go for that.'

'Make it scientific. Say if you puncture cartilage, it will wither right away.'

'Hmm,' the driver said. He honked his horn at a produce truck.

' "Imagine how you'd feel," tell her, "having to wear the same hairstyle forever. Covering up your withered ears." '

'Think she'd believe me?'

'Why not?' Macon asked. And then, after a pause, 'In fact, it may be true. Do you suppose I could have read it someplace?'

'Well, now, maybe you did,' the driver said. 'There's this sort of familiar ring to it.'

'I might even have seen a photograph,' Macon said. 'Somebody's ears, shriveled. All shrunken.'

'Wrinkly, like,' the driver agreed.

Macon said, 'Like two dried apricots.'

'Christ! I'll tell her.'

The taxi stopped in front of Macon's hotel. Macon paid the fare and said, as he slid out, 'I hope it works.'

'Sure it will,' the driver said, 'till next time. Till she wants a nose ring or something.'

'Noses are cartilage too, remember! Noses can wither too!'

The driver waved and pulled into traffic again.

After Macon had claimed his room, he took a subway to the Buford Hotel. An electronics salesman had written to suggest it; the Buford rented small apartments, by the day or the week, to businessmen. The manager, a Mr Aggers, turned out to be a short, round man who walked with a limp exactly like Macon's. Macon thought they must look very odd together, crossing the lobby to the elevators. 'Most of our apartments are owned by corporations,' Mr Aggers said. He pressed the 'Up' button. 'Companies who send their men to the city regularly will often find it cheaper to buy their own places. Then those weeks the apartments are empty, they look to me to find other tenants, help defray the costs.'

Macon made a note of this in the margin of his guidebook. Using an infinitesimal script, he also noted the decor of the lobby, which reminded him of some old-fashioned men's club. On the massive, claw-footed table between the two elevators stood a yard-high naked lady in brass, trailing brass draperies and standing on brass clouds, holding aloft a small, dusty light bulb with a frayed electric cord dangling from it. The elevator, when it arrived, had dim floral carpeting and paneled walls.

'May I ask,' Mr Aggers said, 'whether you personally write the Accidental Tourist series?'

'Yes, I do,' Macon told him.

'Well!' Mr Aggers said. 'This is a real honor, then. We keep your books in the lobby for our guests. But I don't know, I somehow pictured you looking a little different.'

'How did you think I would look?' Macon asked.

'Well, maybe not quite so tall. Maybe a bit, well, heavier. More . . . upholstered.'

'I see,' Macon said.

The elevator had stopped by now but it took its time sliding open. Then Mr Aggers led Macon down a hall. A woman with a laundry cart stood aside to let them pass. 'Here we are,' Mr Aggers said. He unlocked a door and turned on a light.

Macon walked into an apartment that could have come straight from the 1950s. There was a square sofa with metallic threads in its fabric, a chrome-trimmed dinette set, and in the bedroom a double bed whose headboard was quilted in cream-colored vinyl. He tested the mattress. He took off his shoes, lay down, and thought a while. Mr Aggers stood above him with his fingers laced. 'Hmm,' Macon said. He sat up and put his shoes back on. Then he went into the bathroom, where the toilet bore a white strip reading SANITIZED. 'I've never understood these things,' he said. 'Why should it reassure me to know they've glued a paper band across my toilet seat?' Mr Aggers made a helpless gesture with both hands. Macon drew aside a shower curtain printed with pink and blue fish, and he inspected the tub. It looked clean enough, although there was a rust stain leading down from the faucet.

In the kitchenette he found a single saucepan, two faded plastic plates and mugs, and an entire shelf of highball glasses. 'Usually our guests don't cook much,' Mr Aggers explained, 'but they might have their associates in for drinks.' Macon nodded. He was faced with a familiar problem, here: the narrow line between 'comfortable' and 'tacky.' In fact, sometimes comfortable *was* tacky. He opened the refrigerator, a little undercounter affair. The ice trays in the freezing compartment were exactly the same kind of trays—scummy aqua plastic, heavily scratched—that Rose had back in Baltimore.

'You have to admit it's well stocked,' Mr Aggers said. 'See? An apron in the kitchen drawer. My wife's idea. Protects their suits.'

'Yes, very nice,' Macon said.

'It's just like home away from home; that's how I like to think of it.'

'Oh, well, home,' Macon said. 'Nothing's *home*, really.'

'Why? What's missing?' Mr Aggers asked. He had very pale, fine-grained skin that took on a shine when he was anxious. 'What more would you like to see added?'

'To tell the truth,' Macon said, 'I've always thought a hotel ought to offer optional small animals.'

'Animals?'

'I mean a cat to sleep on your bed at night, or a dog of some kind to act pleased when you come in. You ever notice how a hotel room feels so lifeless?'

'Yes, but—well, I don't see how I could—there are surely health regulations or something . . . complications, paperwork, feeding all those different . . . and allergies, of course, many guests have—'

'Oh, I understand, I understand,' Macon said. In the margin of his guidebook he was noting the number of wastebaskets: four. Excellent. 'No,' he said, 'it doesn't seem that people ever take me up on that.'

'Will you recommend us anyway?'

'Certainly,' Macon said, and he closed his guidebook and asked for a list of the rates.

The rest of the afternoon he spent in hotels that he'd covered before. He visited managers in their offices, took brief guided tours to see that nothing had slid into ruin, and listened to talk of rising costs and remodeling plans and new, improved conference settings. Then he returned to his room and switched on the evening news. The world was doing poorly; but watching this unfamiliar TV set, propping his aching leg and braced in this chair that seemed designed for someone else's body, Macon had the feeling that none of the wars and famines he saw were real. They were more like, oh, staged. He turned off the set and went downstairs to hail a cab.

At Julian's suggestion, he was dining on the very top of an impossibly tall building. (Julian had a fondness for restaurants with gimmicks, Macon had noticed. He wasn't happy unless a place revolved, or floated, or could be reached only by catwalk.) 'Imagine,' Julian had said, 'the effect on your out-of-town client. Yes, he'd have to be from out of town; I don't suppose a native

New Yorker . . .' Macon had snorted. Now the cabdriver snorted, too. 'Cup of coffee there will cost you five bucks,' he told Macon.

'It figures.'

'You're better off at one of those little Frenchy places.'

'That's for tomorrow. *In*-town clients.'

The taxi coasted down streets that grew darker and more silent, leading away from the crowds. Macon peered out of his window. He saw a lone man huddled in a doorway, wrapped in a long coat. Wisps of steam drifted up from manhole covers. All the shops were locked behind iron grilles.

At the end of the darkest street of all, the taxi stopped. The driver gave another snort, and Macon paid his fare and stepped out. He wasn't prepared for the wind, which rushed up against him like a great flat sheet of something. He hurried across the sidewalk, or was propelled, while his trousers twisted and flapped about his legs. Just before entering the building, he thought to look up. He looked up and up and up, and finally he saw a faint white pinnacle dwindling into a deep, black, starless sky eerily far away. He thought of once long ago when Ethan, visiting the zoo as a toddler, had paused in front of an elephant and raised his face in astonishment and fallen over backwards.

Inside, everything was streaky pink marble and acres of textureless carpeting. An elevator the size of a room stood open, half filled with people, and Macon stepped in and took his place between two women in silks and diamonds. Their perfume was almost visible. He imagined he could see it rippling the air.

Have chewing gum handy, he wrote in his guidebook as the elevator shot upward. His ears were popping. There was a dense, unresonant stillness that made the women's voices sound tinny. He tucked his guidebook in his pocket and glanced at the numbers flashing overhead. They progressed by tens: forty, fifty, sixty . . . One of the men said they'd have to bring Harold sometime— remember Harold when he got so scared on the ski lift?—and everyone laughed.

The elevator gave a sort of lilt and the door slid open without a sound. A girl in a white trouser suit directed them down a corridor, into a spacious darkness flickering with candles. Great black windows encircled the room from floor to ceiling, but Macon was taken to a table without a view. Lone diners, he supposed, were an embarrassment here. He might be the first they'd ever had. The array of silver at his single place could easily serve a family of four.

His waiter, far better dressed than Macon, handed him a menu and asked what he wanted to drink. 'Dry sherry, please,' Macon said. The minute the waiter left, Macon folded his menu in two and sat on it. Then he looked around at his neighbors. Everyone seemed to be celebrating something. A man and a pregnant woman held hands and smiled across the moony glow of their candle. A boisterous group to his left toasted the same man over and over.

The waiter returned, balancing a sherry neatly on a tray. 'Very good,' Macon said. 'And now perhaps a menu.'

'Menu? Didn't I give you one?'

'There could have been an oversight,' he said, not exactly lying.

A second menu was brought and opened with a flourish before him. Macon sipped his sherry and considered the prices. Astronomical. He decided, as usual, to eat what he thought his readers might eat—not the quenelles or the sweetbreads but the steak, medium rare. After he'd given his order, he rose and slid his chair in and took his sherry over to a window.

All of a sudden, he thought he had died.

He saw the city spread far below like a glittering golden ocean, the streets tiny ribbons of light, the planet curving away at the edges, the sky a purple hollow extending to infinity. It wasn't the height; it was the distance. It was his vast, lonely distance from everyone who mattered. Ethan, with his bouncy walk—how would he ever know that his father had come to be trapped in this spire in the heavens? How would Sarah know, lazily tanning herself in the sunshine? For he did believe the sun could be shining wherever she was at this moment; she was so removed from him. He thought of his sister and brothers going about their business, playing their evening card game, unaware of how far behind he'd left them. He was too far gone to return. He would never, ever get back. He had somehow traveled to a point completely isolated from everyone else in the universe, and nothing was real but his own angular hand clenched around the sherry glass.

He dropped the glass, causing a meaningless little flurry of voices, and he spun around and ran lopsidedly across the room and out the door. But there was that endless corridor, and he couldn't manage the trip. He took a right turn instead. He passed a telephone alcove and stumbled into a restroom—yes, a men's room, luckily. More marble, mirrors, white enamel. He thought he was going to throw up, but when he entered one of the cubicles the sick feeling left his stomach and floated to his head. He noticed how light his brain felt. He stood above the toilet pressing his temples. It occurred to him to wonder how many feet of pipe a toilet at this altitude required.

He heard someone else come in, coughing. A cubicle door slammed shut. He opened his own door a crack and looked out. The impersonal lushness of the room made him think of science-fiction movies.

Well, this difficulty probably happened here often, didn't it? Or maybe not this difficulty exactly but others like it—people with a fear of heights, say, going into a panic, having to call upon . . . whom? The waiter? The girl who met the elevator?

He ventured cautiously out of the cubicle, then out of the restroom altogether, and he nearly bumped into a woman in the telephone alcove. She wore yards and yards of pale chiffon. She was just hanging up the phone, and she gathered her skirts around her and moved languidly, gracefully toward the dining room. *Excuse me, ma'am, I wonder if you would be so kind as to, um* . . . But the only request that came to mind rose up from his earliest childhood: *Carry me!*

The woman's little sequined evening purse was the last of her to go, trailed behind her in one white hand as she disappeared into the darkness of the restaurant.

He stepped over to the telephone and lifted the receiver. It was cool to the touch; she hadn't talked long. He fumbled through his pockets, found coins and dropped them in. But there was no one he could contact. He didn't know a soul in all New York. Instead he called home, miraculously summoning up his credit card number. He worried his family would let the phone ring—it was a habit, by now—but Charles answered. 'Leary.'

'Charles?'

'Macon!' Charles said, unusually animated.

'Charles, I'm up on top of this building and a sort of . . . silly thing has happened. Listen: You've got to get me out of here.'

'*You* out! What are you talking about? You've got to get *me* out!'

'Pardon?'

'I'm shut in the pantry; your dog has me cornered.'

'Oh. Well, I'm sorry, but . . . Charles, it's like some kind of illness. I don't think I can manage the elevator and I doubt I could manage a stairway either and—'

'Macon, do you hear that barking? That's Edward. Edward has me treed, I tell you, and you have to come home this instant.'

'But I'm in New York! I'm up on top of this building and I can't get down!'

'Every time I open the door he comes roaring over and I slam the door and he attacks it, he must have clawed halfway through it by now.'

Macon made himself take a deep breath. He said, 'Charles, could I speak to Rose?'

'She's out.'

'Oh.'

'How do you think I got into this?' Charles asked. 'Julian came to take her to dinner and—'

'Julian?'

'Isn't that his name?'

'Julian my *boss*?'

'Yes, and Edward went into one of his fits; so Rose said, "Quick, shut him in the pantry." So I grabbed his leash and he turned on me and nearly took my hand off. So I shut myself in the pantry instead and Rose must have left by then so—'

'Isn't Porter there?'

'It's his visitation night.'

Macon imagined how safe the pantry must feel, with Rose's jams lined up in alphabetical order and the black dial telephone so ancient that the number on its face was still the old Tuxedo exchange. What he wouldn't give to be there!

Now he had a new symptom. His chest had developed a flutter that bore no resemblance to a normal heartbeat.

'If you don't get me out of this I'm going to call for the police to come shoot him,' Charles said.

'No! Don't do that!'

'I can't just sit here waiting for him to break through.'

'He won't break through. You could open the door and walk right past him. Believe me, Charles. Please: I'm up on top of this building and—'

'Maybe you don't know that I'm prone to claustrophobia,' Charles said.

One possibility, Macon decided, was to tell the restaurant people he was having a coronary. A coronary was so respectable. They would send for an ambulance and he would be, yes, carried— just what he needed. Or he wouldn't have to be carried but only touched, a mere human touch upon his arm, a hand on his shoulder, something to put him back in connection with the rest of the world. He hadn't felt another person's touch in so long.

'I'll tell them about the key in the mailbox so they won't have to break down the door,' Charles said.

'What? Who?'

'The police, and I'll tell them to—Macon, I'm sorry but you knew that dog would have to be done away with sooner or later.'

'Don't do it!' Macon shouted.

A man emerging from the restroom glanced in his direction. Macon lowered his voice and said, 'He was Ethan's.'

'Does that mean he's allowed to tear my throat out?'

'Listen. Let's not be hasty. Let's think this through. Now, I'm going to . . . I'm going to telephone Sarah. I'm going to ask her to come over and take charge of Edward. Are you listening, Charles?'

'But what if he attacks her too?' Charles asked.

'He won't, believe me. Now, don't do anything till she comes, you understand? Don't do anything hasty.'

'Well . . .' Charles said doubtfully.

Macon hung up and took his wallet from his pocket. He rummaged through the business cards and torn-off snippets of paper, some of them yellow with age, that he kept in the secret compartment. When he found Sarah's number he punched it in with a trembling finger and held his breath. *Sarah*, he would say, *I'm up on top of this building and—*

She didn't answer.

That possibility hadn't occurred to him. He listened to her phone ring. What now? What on earth now?

Finally he hung up. He sifted despairingly through the other numbers in his wallet—dentist, pharmacist, animal trainer . . .

Animal trainer?

He thought at first of someone from a circus—a brawny man in satin tights. Then he saw the name: Muriel Pritchett. The card was handwritten, even hand-cut, crookedly snipped from a larger piece of paper.

He called her. She answered at once. '*Hel*-lo,' roughly, like a weary barmaid.

'Muriel? It's Macon Leary,' he told her.

'Oh! How you doing?'

'I'm fine. Or, rather . . . See, the trouble is, Edward's got my brother cornered in the pantry, overreacting, Charles I mean, he always overreacts, and here I am on top of this building in New York and I'm having this kind of, um, disturbance, you know? I was looking down at the city and it was miles away, miles, I can't describe to you how—'

'Let's make sure I've got this right,' Muriel said. 'Edward's in your pantry—'

Macon collected himself. He said, 'Edward's *outside* the pantry, barking. My brother's inside. He says he's going to call the police and tell them to come shoot Edward.'

'Well, what a dumb fool idea.'

'Yes!' Macon said. 'So I thought if you could go over and get the key from the mailbox, it's lying on the bottom of the mailbox—'

'I'll go right away.'

'Oh, wonderful.'

'So good-bye for now, Macon.'

'Well, but also—' he said.

She waited.

'See, I'm up on top of this building,' he said, 'and I don't know what it is but something has scared the hell out of me.'

'Oh, Lord, I'd be scared too after I went and saw *Towering Inferno.*'

'No, no, it's nothing like that, fire or heights—'

'Did you see *Towering Inferno?* Boy, after that you couldn't get me past jumping level in any building. I think people who go up in skyscrapers are just plain brave. I mean if you think about it, Macon, you *have* to be brave to be standing where you are right now.'

'Oh, well, not so brave as all that,' Macon said.

'No, I'm serious.'

'You're making too much out of it. It's nothing, really.'

'You just say that because you don't realize what you went through before you stepped into the elevator. See, underneath you said, "Okay. I'll trust it." That's what everyone does; I bet it's what they do on airplanes, too. "This is dangerous as all get-out but what the hay," they say, "let's fling ourselves out on thin air and trust it." Why, you ought to be walking around that building so amazed and proud of yourself!'

Macon gave a small, dry laugh and gripped the receiver more tightly.

'Now, here's what I'm going to do,' she said. 'I'm going to go get Edward and take him to the Meow-Bow. It doesn't sound to me like your brother is much use with him. Then when you get back from your trip, we need to talk about his training. I mean, things just can't go on this way, Macon.'

'No, they can't. You're right. They can't,' Macon said.

'I mean this is ridiculous.'

'You're absolutely right.'

'See you, then. Bye.'

'Well, wait!' he said.

But she was gone.

After he hung up, he turned and saw the latest arrivals just heading toward him from the elevator. First came three men, and then three women in long gowns. Behind them was a couple who couldn't be past their teens. The boy's wrist bones stuck out of the sleeves of his suit. The girl's dress was clumsy and touching, her small chin obscured by a monstrous orchid.

Halfway down the corridor, the boy and girl stopped to gaze around them. They looked at the ceiling, and then at the floor. Then they looked at each other. The boy said, 'Hoo!' and grabbed both the girl's hands, and they stood there a moment, laughing, before they went into the restaurant.

Macon followed them. He felt soothed and tired and terribly hungry. It was good to find the waiter just setting his food in place when he sank back into his seat.

10

—— 'I'll be honest,' Muriel said, 'my baby was not exactly planned for. I mean we weren't exactly even married yet, if you want to know the truth. If you want to know the truth the baby was the reason we got married in the first place, but I did tell Norman he didn't have to go through with it if he didn't want to. It's not like I pushed him into it or anything.'

She looked past Macon at Edward, who lay prone on the front hall rug. He'd had to be forced into position, but at least he was staying put.

'Notice I let him move around some, as long as he stays down,' she said. 'Now I'm going to turn my back, and you watch how he does.'

She wandered into the living room. She lifted a vase from a table and examined its underside. 'So anyhow,' she said, 'we went ahead and got married, with everybody acting like it was the world's biggest tragedy. My folks really never got over it. My mom said, "Well, I always knew this was going to happen. Back when you were hanging out with Dana Scully and them, one or another of them no-count boys always honking out front for you, didn't I tell you this was going to happen?" We had a little bitty wedding at my folks' church, and we didn't take a honeymoon trip but went straight to our apartment and next day Norman started work at his uncle's. He just settled right into being married—shopping with me for groceries and picking out curtains and such. Oh, you know, sometimes I get to thinking what kids we were. It was almost like playing house! It was pretend! The candles I lit at suppertime, flowers on the table, Norman calling me "hon" and bringing his plate to the sink for me to wash. And then all at once it turned serious. Here I've got this little boy now, this great big seven-year-old boy with his clumpy leather shoes, and it wasn't playing house after all. It was for real, all along, and we just didn't know it.'

She sat on the couch and raised one foot in front of her. She turned it admiringly this way and that. Her stocking bagged at the ankle.

'What is Edward up to?' she asked.

Macon said, 'He's still lying down.'

'Pretty soon he'll do that for three hours straight.'

'Three *hours?*'

'Easy.'

'Isn't that sort of cruel?'

'I thought you promised not to talk like that,' she told him.

'Right. Sorry,' Macon said.

'Maybe tomorrow he'll lie down on his own.'

'You think so?'

'If you practice. If you don't give in. If you don't go all softhearted.'

Then she stood up and came over to Macon. She patted his arm. 'But never mind,' she told him. '*I* think softhearted men are sweet.'

Macon backed away. He just missed stepping on Edward.

It was getting close to Thanksgiving, and the Learys were debating as usual about Thanksgiving dinner. The fact was, none of them cared for turkey. Still, Rose said, it didn't seem right to serve anything else. It would just feel wrong. Her brothers pointed out that she'd have to wake up at five a.m. to put a turkey in the oven. But it was she who'd be doing it, Rose said. It wouldn't be troubling *them* any.

Then it began to seem she had had an ulterior motive, for as soon as they settled on turkey she announced that she might just invite Julian Edge. Poor Julian, she said, had no close family living nearby, and he and his neighbors gathered forlornly at holidays, each bringing his or her specialty. Thanksgiving dinner last year had been a vegetarian pasta casserole and goat cheese on grape leaves and kiwi tarts. The least she could do was offer him a normal family dinner.

'What!' Macon said, acting surprised and disapproving, but unfortunately, it wasn't that much of a surprise. Oh, Julian was up to something, all right. But what could it be? Whenever Rose came down the stairs in her best dress and two spots of rouge, whenever she asked Macon to shut Edward in the pantry because Julian would be stopping by to take her this place or that—well, Macon had a very strong urge to let Edward accidentally break loose. He made a point of meeting Julian at the door, eyeing him for a long, silent moment before calling Rose. But Julian behaved; no glint of irony betrayed him. He was respectful with Rose, almost shy, and hovered clumsily when he ushered her out the door. Or was that the irony? His Rose Leary act. Macon didn't like the looks of this.

Then it turned out that Porter's children would be coming for Thanksgiving too. They usually came at Christmas instead, but wanted to trade off this year due to some complication with their grandparents on their stepfather's side. So really, Rose said, wasn't it good they were having turkey? Children were such traditionalists. She set to work baking pumpkin pies. 'We gather together,' she sang, 'to ask the Lord's blessing...' Macon looked up from the sheaf of stolen menus he was spreading across the kitchen table. There was a note of gaiety in her voice that made him uneasy. He wondered if she had any mistaken ideas about Julian—if, for instance, she hoped for some kind of romance. But Rose was so plain and sensible in her long white apron. She reminded him of Emily Dickinson; hadn't Emily Dickinson also baked for her nieces and nephews? Surely there was no need for concern.

'My son's name is Alexander,' Muriel said. 'Did I tell you that? I named him Alexander because I thought it sounded high-class. He was never an easy baby. For starters something went wrong while I was carrying him and they had to do a Caesarean and take him out early and I got all these complications and can't ever have any more children. And then Alexander was so teeny he didn't even look like a human, more like a big-headed newborn kitten, and he had to stay in an incubator forever, just about, and nearly died. Norman said, "When's it going to look like other babies?" He always called Alexander "it." I adjusted better; I mean pretty soon it seemed to me that that was what a baby *ought* to look like, and I hung around the hospital nursery but Norman wouldn't go near him, he said it made him too nervous.'

Edward whimpered. He was just barely lying down—his haunches braced, his claws digging into the carpet. But Muriel gave no sign she had noticed.

'Maybe you and Alexander should get together some time,' she told Macon.

'Oh, I, ah . . . ' Macon said.

'He doesn't have enough men in his life.'

'Well, but—'

'He's supposed to see men a lot; it's supposed to show him how to act. Maybe the three of us could go to a movie. Don't you ever go to movies?'

'No, I don't,' Macon said truthfully. 'I haven't been to a movie in months. I really don't care for movies. They make everything seem so close up.'

'Or just out to a McDonald's, maybe.'

'I don't think so,' Macon said.

Porter's children arrived the evening before Thanksgiving, traveling by car because Danny, the oldest, had just got his driver's license. That worried Porter considerably. He paced the floor from the first moment they could be expected. 'I don't know where

June's brain is,' he said. 'Letting a sixteen-year-old boy drive all the way from Washington the first week he has his license! With his two little sisters in the car! I don't know how her mind works.'

To make it worse, the children were almost an hour late. When Porter finally saw their headlights, he rushed out the door and down the steps well ahead of the others. 'What kept you?' he cried.

Danny unfurled himself from the car with exaggerated nonchalance, yawning and stretching, and shook Porter's hand as a kind of afterthought while turning to study his tires. He was as tall as Porter now but very thin, with his mother's dark coloring. Behind him came Susan, fourteen—just a few months older than Ethan would have been. It was lucky she was so different from Ethan, with her cap of black curls and her rosy cheeks. This evening she wore jeans and hiking boots and one of those thick down jackets that made young people look so bulky and graceless. Then last came Liberty. What a name, Macon always thought. It was an invention of her mother's—a flighty woman who had run away from Porter with a hippie stereo salesman eight and a half years ago and discovered immediately afterward that she was two months pregnant. Ironically, Liberty was the one who looked most like Porter. She had fair, straight hair and a chiseled face and she was dressed in a little tailored coat. 'Danny got lost,' she said severely. 'What a dummy.' She kissed Porter and her aunt and uncles, but Susan wandered past them in a way that let everyone know she had outgrown all that.

'Oh, isn't this nice?' Rose said. 'Aren't we going to have a wonderful Thanksgiving?' She stood on the sidewalk wrapping her hands in her apron, perhaps to stop herself from reaching out to

Danny as he slouched toward the house. It was dusk, and Macon, happening to glance around, saw the grown-ups as pale gray wraiths—four middle-aged unmarried relatives yearning after the young folks.

For supper they had carry-out pizza, intended to please the children, but Macon kept smelling turkey. He thought at first it was his imagination. Then he noticed Danny sniffing the air. 'Turkey? Already?' Danny asked his aunt.

'I'm trying this new method,' she said. 'It's supposed to save energy. You set your oven extremely low and cook your meat all night.'

'Weird.'

After supper they watched TV—the children had never seemed to warm to cards—and then they went to bed. But in the middle of the night, Macon woke with a start and gave serious thought to that turkey. She was cooking it till tomorrow? At an extremely low temperature? What temperature was that, exactly?

He was sleeping in his old room, now that his leg had mended. Eventually he nudged the cat off his chest and got up. He made his way downstairs in the dark, and he crossed the icy kitchen linoleum and turned on the little light above the stove. One hundred and forty degrees, the oven dial read. 'Certain death,' he told Edward, who had tagged along behind him. Then Charles walked in, wearing large, floppy pajamas. He peered at the dial and sighed. 'Not only that,' he said, 'but this is a *stuffed* turkey.'

'Wonderful.'

'Two quarts of stuffing. I heard her say so.'

'Two quarts of teeming, swarming bacteria.'

'Unless there's something more to this method we don't understand.'

'We'll ask her in the morning,' Macon said, and they went back to bed.

In the morning, Macon came down to find Rose serving pancakes to the children. He said, 'Rose, what exactly is it you're doing to this turkey?'

'I told you: slow heat. Jam, Danny, or syrup?'

'Is that *it*?' Macon asked.

'You're dripping,' Rose said to Liberty. 'What, Macon? See, I read an article about slow-cooked beef and I thought, well, if it works with beef it must work with turkey too so I—'

'It might work with beef but it will murder us with turkey,' Macon told her.

'But at the end I'm going to raise the temperature!'

'You'd have to raise it mighty high. You'd have to autoclave the thing.'

'You'd have to expose it to a nuclear flash,' Danny said cheerfully.

Rose said, 'Well, you're both just plain wrong. Who's the cook here, anyhow? I say it's going to be delicious.'

Maybe it was, but it certainly didn't look it. By dinnertime the breast had caved in and the skin was all dry and dull. Rose entered the dining room holding the turkey high as if in triumph, but the only people who looked impressed were those who didn't know its history—Julian and Mrs Barrett, one of Rose's old people. Julian said, 'Ah!' and Mrs Barrett beamed. 'I just wish my neighbors could see this,' Julian said. He wore a brass-buttoned navy blazer, and he seemed to have polished his face.

'Well, there may be a little problem here,' Macon said.

Rose set the turkey down and glared at him.

'Of course, the rest of the meal is excellent,' he said. 'Why, we could fill up on the vegetables alone! In fact I think I'll do that. But the turkey . . .'

'It's pure poison,' Danny finished for him.

Julian said, 'Come again?' but Mrs Barrett just smiled harder.

'We think it may have been cooked at a slightly inadequate temperature,' Macon explained.

'It was not!' Rose said. 'It's perfectly good.'

'Maybe you'd rather just stick to the side dishes,' Macon told Mrs Barrett. He was worried she might be deaf.

But she must have heard, for she said, 'Why, perhaps I will,' never losing her smile. 'I don't have much of an appetite anyhow,' she said.

'And I'm a vegetarian,' Susan said.

'So am I,' Danny said suddenly.

'Oh, Macon, how could you do this?' Rose asked. 'My lovely turkey! All that work!'

'I think it looks delicious,' Julian said.

'Yes,' Porter told him, 'but you don't know about the other times.'

'Other times?'

'Those were just bad luck,' Rose said.

'Why, of course!' Porter said. 'Or economy. You don't like to throw things away; I can understand that! Pork that's been sitting too long, or chicken salad left out all night . . .'

Rose sat down. Tears were glazing her eyes. 'Oh,' she said, 'you're all so mean! You don't fool me for an instant; I know why you're doing this. You want to make me look bad in front of Julian.'

'Julian?'

Julian seemed distressed. He took a handkerchief from his breast pocket but then went on holding it.

'You want to drive him off! You three wasted your chances and now you want me to waste mine, but I won't do it. I can see what's what! Just listen to any song on the radio; look at any soap opera. *Love* is what it's all about. On soap operas everything revolves around love. A new person comes to town and right away the question is, who's he going to love? Who's going to love him back? Who'll lose her mind with jealousy? Who's going to ruin her life? And you want to make me miss it!'

'Well, goodness,' Macon said, trying to sort this out.

'You know perfectly well there's nothing wrong with that turkey. You just don't want me to stop cooking for you and taking care of this house, you don't want Julian to fall in love with me.'

'Do what?'

But she scraped her chair back and ran from the room. Julian sat there with his mouth open.

'Don't you dare laugh,' Macon told him.

Julian just went on gaping.

'Don't even consider it.'

Julian swallowed. He said, 'Do you think I ought to go after her?'

'No,' Macon said.

'But she seems so—'

'She's fine! She's perfectly fine.'

'Oh.'

'Now, who wants a baked potato?'

There was a kind of murmur around the table; everyone looked unhappy. 'That poor, dear girl,' Mrs Barrett said. 'I feel just awful.'

'Me too,' Susan said.

'Julian?' Macon asked, clanging a spoon. 'Potato?'

'I'll take the turkey,' Julian said firmly.

At that moment, Macon almost liked the man.

'It was having the baby that broke our marriage up,' Muriel said. 'When you think about it, that's funny. First we got married on account of the baby and then we got divorced on account of the baby, and in between, the baby was what we argued about. Norman couldn't understand why I was all the time at the hospital visiting Alexander. "It doesn't know you're there, so why go?" he said. I'd go early in the morning and just hang around, the nurses were as nice as could be about it, and I'd stay till night. Norman said, "Muriel, won't we ever get our ordinary life back?" Well, you can see his point, I guess. It's like I only had room in my mind for Alexander. And he was in the hospital for months, for really months; there was everything in this world wrong with him. You should have seen our medical bills. We only had partial insurance and there were these bills running up, thousands and thousands of dollars. Finally I took a job at the hospital. I asked if I could work in the nursery but they said no, so I got a kind of, more like a maid's job, cleaning patients' rooms and so forth. Emptying trash cans, wet-mopping floors . . .'

She and Macon were walking along Dempsey Road with Edward, hoping to run into a biker. Muriel held the leash. If a biker came, she said, and Edward lunged or gave so much as the smallest yip, she was going to yank him so hard he wouldn't know what hit him. She warned Macon of that before they started out. She said he'd better not object because this was for Edward's own good. Macon hoped he'd be able to remember that when the time came.

It was the Friday after Thanksgiving and there'd been a light snow earlier, but the air didn't have a real bite to it yet and the sidewalks were merely damp. The sky seemed to begin about two feet above their heads.

'This one patient, Mrs Brimm, she took a liking to me,' Muriel said. 'She said I was the only person who ever bothered talking to her. I'd come in and tell her about Alexander. I'd tell her what the doctors said, how they didn't give him much of a chance and some had even wondered if we *wanted* a chance, what with all that might be wrong with him. I'd tell her about me and Norman and the way he was acting, and she said it sounded exactly like a story in a magazine. When they let her go home she wanted me to come with her, take a job looking out for her, but I couldn't on account of Alexander.'

A biker appeared at the end of the street, a girl with a Baskin-Robbins uniform bunching below her jacket. Edward perked his ears up. 'Now, act like we expect no trouble,' Muriel told Macon. 'Just go along, go along, don't even look in Edward's direction.'

The girl skimmed toward them—a little slip of a person with a tiny, serious face. When she passed, she gave off a definite smell of chocolate ice cream. Edward sniffed the breeze but marched on.

'Oh, Edward, that was wonderful!' Macon told him.

Muriel just clucked. She seemed to take his good behavior for granted.

'So anyhow,' she said. 'They finally did let Alexander come home. But he was still no bigger than a minute. All wrinkles like a little old man. Cried like a kitten would cry. Struggled for every breath. And *Norman* was no help. I think he was jealous. He got this kind of stubborn look whenever I had to do something, go warm a bottle or something. He'd say, "Where you off to? Don't you want to watch the end of this program?" I'd be hanging over the crib watching Alexander fight for air, and Norman would call, "Muriel? Commercial's just about over!" Then next thing I knew, there was his mother standing on my doorstep saying it wasn't his baby anyhow.'

'What? Well, of all things!' Macon said.

'Can you believe it? Standing on my doorstep looking so pleased with herself. "Not his baby!" I said. "Whose, then?" "Well, that I couldn't say," she said, "and I doubt if you could either. But I can tell you this much: If you don't give my son a divorce and release all financial claims on him, I will personally produce Dana Scully and his friends in a court of law and they will swear you're a known tramp and that baby could be any one of theirs. Clearly it's not Norman's; Norman was a *darling* baby." Well. I waited till Norman got home from work and I said, "Do you know what your mother told me?" Then I saw by his face that he did. I saw she must have been talking behind my back for who knows how long, putting these suspicions in his head. I said, "Norman?" He just stuttered around. I said, "Norman, she's lying, it's not true, I wasn't going with those boys when I met you! That's all in the past!" He said, "I don't know what to think." I said, "Please!" He said, "I don't know." He went out to the kitchen and started fixing this screen I'd been nagging him about, window screen halfway out of its frame, even though supper was already on the table. I'd made him this special supper. I followed after him. I said, "Norman. Dana and them are from way, way back. That baby couldn't be theirs." He pushed up on one side of the screen and it wouldn't go, and he pushed up on the other side and it cut his hand, and all at once he started crying and wrenched the whole thing out of the window and threw it as far as he could. And next day his mother came to help him pack his clothes and he left me.'

'Good Lord,' Macon said. He felt shocked, as if he'd known Norman personally.

'So I thought about what to do. I knew I couldn't go back to my folks. Finally I phoned Mrs Brimm and asked if she still wanted me to come take care of her, and she said yes, she did; the woman she had wasn't any use at all. So I said I would do it for room and board if I could bring the baby and she said yes, that would be fine. She had this little row house downtown and there was an extra bedroom where me and Alexander could sleep. And that's how I managed to keep us going.'

They were several blocks from home now, but she didn't suggest turning back. She held the leash loosely and Edward strutted next to her, matching her pace. 'I was lucky, wasn't I,' she said. 'If it wasn't for Mrs Brimm I don't know what I'd have done. And it's not like it was all that much work. Just keeping the house straight, fixing her a bite to eat, helping her get around. She was crippled up with arthritis but just as spunky! It's not like I really had to nurse her.'

She slowed and then came to a stop. Edward, with a martyred sigh, sat down at her left heel. 'When you think about it, it's funny,' she said. 'All that time Alexander was in the hospital seemed so awful, seemed it would go on forever, but now when I look back, I almost miss it. I mean there was something cozy about it, now that I recall. I think about those nurses gossiping at the nurses' station and those rows of little babies sleeping. It was winter and sometimes I'd stand at a window and look out and I'd feel happy to be warm and safe. I'd look down at the emergency room entrance and watch the ambulances coming in. You ever wonder what a Martian might think if he happened to land near an emergency room? He'd see an ambulance whizzing in and everybody running out to meet it, tearing the doors open, grabbing up the stretcher, scurrying along with it. "Why," he'd say, "what a helpful planet, what kind and helpful creatures." He'd never guess we're not always that way; that we had to, oh, put aside our natural selves to do it. "What a helpful race of beings," a Martian would say. Don't you think so?'

She looked up at Macon then. Macon experienced a sudden twist in his chest. He felt there was something he needed to do, some kind of connection he wanted to make, and when she raised her face he bent and kissed her chapped, harsh lips even though that wasn't the connection he'd intended. Her fist with the leash in it was caught between them like a stone. There was something insistent about her—pressing. Macon drew back. 'Well . . .' he said.

She went on looking up at him.

'Sorry,' he said.

Then they turned around and walked Edward home.

Danny spent the holiday practicing his parallel parking, tirelessly wheeling his mother's car back and forth in front of the house. And Liberty baked cookies with Rose. But Susan had nothing to do, Rose said, and since Macon was planning a trip to Philadelphia, wouldn't he consider taking her along? 'It's only hotels and restaurants,' Macon said. 'And I'm cramming it into one day, leaving at crack of dawn and coming back late at night—'

'She'll be company for you,' Rose told him.

However, Susan went to sleep when the train was hardly out of Baltimore, and she stayed asleep for the entire ride, sunk into her jacket like a little puffed-up bird roosting on a branch. Macon sat next to her with a rock magazine he'd found rolled up in one of her pockets. He saw that the Police were experiencing personality conflicts, that David Bowie worried about mental illness, that Billy Idol's black shirt appeared to have been ripped halfway off his body. Evidently these people led very difficult lives; he had no idea who they were. He rolled the magazine up again and replaced it in Susan's pocket.

If Ethan were alive, would he be sitting where Susan was? He hadn't traveled with Macon as a rule. The overseas trips were too expensive, the domestic trips too dull. Once he'd gone with Macon to New York, and he'd developed stomach pains that resembled appendicitis. Macon could still recall his frantic search for a doctor, his own stomach clenching in sympathy, and his relief when they were told it was nothing but too many breakfasts. He hadn't taken

Ethan anywhere else after that. Only to Bethany Beach every summer, and that was not so much a trip as a kind of relocation of home base, with Sarah sunbathing and Ethan joining other Baltimore boys, also relocated, and Macon happily tightening all the doorknobs in their rented cottage or unsticking the windows or—one blissful year—solving a knotty problem he'd discovered in the plumbing.

In Philadelphia, Susan came grumpily awake and staggered off the train ahead of him. She complained about the railroad station. 'It's way too big,' she said. 'The loudspeakers echo so you can't hear what they're saying. Baltimore's station is better.'

'Yes, you're absolutely right,' Macon said.

They went for breakfast to a café he knew well, which unfortunately seemed to have fallen upon hard times. Little chips of ceiling plaster kept dropping into his coffee. He crossed the name out of his guidebook. Next they went to a place that a reader had suggested, and Susan had walnut waffles. She said they were excellent. 'Are you going to quote me on this?' she asked. 'Will you put my name in your book and say I recommended the waffles?'

'It's not that kind of a book,' he told her.

'Call me your companion. That's what restaurant critics do. "My companion, Susan Leary, pronounced the waffles remarkable." '

Macon laughed and signaled for their bill.

After their fourth breakfast, they started on hotels. Susan found these less enjoyable, though Macon kept trying to involve her. He told a manager, 'My companion here is the expert on bathrooms.' But Susan just opened a medicine cabinet, yawned, and said, 'All they have is Camay.'

'What's wrong with that?'

'When Mama came back from her honeymoon she brought us perfumed designer soap from her hotel. One bar for me and one for Danny, in little plastic boxes with drainage racks.'

'*I* think Camay is fine,' Macon told the manager, who was looking worried.

Late in the afternoon Susan started feeling peckish again; so they had two more breakfasts. Then they went to Independence Hall. (Macon felt they should do something educational.) 'You can tell your civics teacher,' he said. She rolled her eyes and said, 'Social studies.'

'Whatever.'

The weather was cold, and the interior of the hall was chilly and bleak. Macon noticed Susan gaping vacantly at the guide, who wasn't making his spiel very exciting; so he leaned over and whispered, 'Imagine. George Washington sat in that very chair.'

'I'm not really into George Washington, Uncle Macon.'

'Human beings can only go "into" houses, cars, and coffins, Susan.'

'Huh?'

'Never mind.'

They followed the crowd upstairs, through other rooms, but Susan had plainly exhausted her supply of good humor. 'If it weren't for what was decided in this building,' Macon told her, 'you and I might very well be living under a dictatorship.'

'We are anyhow,' she said.

'Pardon?'

'You really think that you and me have any power?'

'You and I, honey.'

'It's just free speech, that's all we've got. We can say whatever we like, then the government goes on and does exactly what it pleases. You call that democracy? It's like we're on a ship, headed someplace terrible, and somebody else is steering and the passengers can't jump off.'

'Why don't we go get some supper,' Macon said. He was feeling a little depressed.

He took her to an old-fashioned inn a few streets over. It wasn't even dark yet, and they were the first customers. A woman in a Colonial gown told them they'd have to wait a few minutes. She led them into a small, snug room with a fireplace, and a waitress offered them their choice of buttered rum or hot spiked cider. 'I'll have buttered rum,' Susan said, shucking off her jacket.

Macon said, 'Uh, Susan.'

She glared at him.

'Oh, well, make that two,' he told the waitress. He supposed a little toddy couldn't do much harm.

But it must have been an exceptionally strong toddy—either that, or Susan had an exceptionally weak head for alcohol. At any rate, after two small sips she leaned toward him in an unbalanced way. 'This is sort of fun!' she said. 'You know, Uncle Macon, I like you much better than I thought I did.'

'Why, thank you.'

'I used to think you were kind of finicky. Ethan used to make us laugh, pointing to your artichoke plate.'

'My artichoke plate.'

She pressed her fingertips to her mouth. 'I'm sorry,' she said.

'For what?'

'I didn't mean to talk about him.'

'You can talk about him.'

'I don't want to,' she said.

She gazed off across the room. Macon, following her eyes, found only a harpsichord. He looked back at her and saw her chin trembling.

It had never occurred to him that Ethan's cousins missed him too.

After a minute, Susan picked her mug up and took several large swallows. She wiped her nose with the back of her hand. 'Hot,' she explained. It was true she seemed to have recovered herself.

Macon said, 'What was funny about my artichoke plate?'

'Oh, nothing.'

'I won't be hurt. What was funny?'

'Well, it looked like geometry class. Every leaf laid out in such a perfect circle when you'd finished.'

'I see.'

'He was laughing *with* you, not at you,' Susan said, peering anxiously into his face.

'Well, since I wasn't laughing myself, that statement seems inaccurate. But if you mean he wasn't laughing unkindly, I believe you.'

She sighed and drank some more of her rum.

'Nobody talks about him,' Macon said. 'None of you mentions his name.'

'We do when you're not around,' Susan said.

'You do?'

'We talk about what he'd think, you know. Like when Danny got his license, or when I had a date for the Halloween Ball. I mean we used to make so much fun of the grown-ups. And Ethan was the funniest one; he could always get us to laugh. Then here we are, growing up ourselves. We wonder what Ethan would think of us, if he could come back and see us. We wonder if he'd laugh at *us*. Or if he'd feel . . . left out. Like we had moved on and left him behind.'

The woman in the Colonial gown came to show them to their table. Macon brought his drink; Susan had already finished hers. She was a bit unsteady on her feet. When their waitress asked them if they'd like a wine list, Susan gave Macon a bright-eyed look but Macon said, 'No,' very firmly. 'I think we ought to start with soup,' he said. He had some idea soup was sobering.

But Susan talked in a reckless, headlong way all through the soup course, and the main course, and the two desserts she hadn't been able to decide between, and the strong black coffee that he pressed upon her afterward. She talked about a boy she liked who either liked her back or else preferred someone named Sissy Pace. She talked about the Halloween Ball where this really juvenile eighth-grader had thrown up all over the stereo. She said that when Danny was eighteen, the three of them were moving to their own apartment because now that their mother was expecting (which Macon hadn't known), she wouldn't even realize they were gone. 'That's not true,' Macon told her. 'Your mother would feel terrible if you left.' Susan propped her cheek on her fist in a sort of slipshod manner and said that she wasn't born yesterday. Her hair had grown wilder through the evening, giving her an electrified appearance.

Macon found it difficult to stuff her into her jacket, and he had to hold her up more or less by the back of her collar while they were waiting for a taxi.

In the railroad station she got a confused, squinty look, and once they were on the train she fell asleep with her head against the window. In Baltimore, when he woke her, she said, 'You don't think he's mad at us, do you, Uncle Macon?'

'Who's that?'

'You think he's mad we're starting to forget him?'

'Oh, no, honey. I'm sure he's not.'

She slept in the car all the way from the station, and he drove very gently so as not to wake her. When they got home, Rose said it looked as if he'd worn the poor child right down to a frazzle.

'You want your dog to mind you in every situation,' Muriel said. 'Even out in public. You want to leave him outside a public place and come back to find him waiting. That's what we'll work on this morning. We'll start with him waiting right on your own front porch. Then next lesson we'll go on to shops and things.'

She picked up the leash and they stepped out the door. It was raining, but the porch roof kept them dry. Macon said, 'Hold on a minute, I want to show you something.'

'What's that?'

He tapped his foot twice. Edward looked uncomfortable; he gazed off toward the street and gave a sort of cough. Then slowly, slowly, one forepaw crumpled. Then the other. He lowered himself by degrees until he was lying down.

'Well! Good dog!' Muriel said. She clucked her tongue.

Edward flattened his ears back for a pat.

'I worked on him most of yesterday,' Macon said. 'It was Sunday and I had nothing to do. And then my brother's kids were getting ready to leave and Edward was growling the way he usually does; so I tapped my foot and down he went.'

'I'm proud of both of you.'

She told Edward, 'Stay,' holding out a hand. She backed into the house again. 'Now, Macon, you come in too.'

They closed the front door. Muriel tweaked the lace curtain and peered out. 'Well, he's staying so far,' she announced.

She turned her back to the door. She checked her fingernails and said, 'Tsk!' Tiny beads of rain trickled down her raincoat, and her hair—reacting to the damp—stood out in corkscrews. 'Someday I'm going to get me a professional manicure,' she said.

Macon tried to see around her; he wasn't sure that Edward would stay put.

'Have you ever been to a manicurist?' she asked.

'Me? Goodness, no.'

'Well, some men go.'

'Not me.'

'I'd like just once to get everything done professional. Nails, skin . . . My girlfriend goes to this place where they vacuum your skin. They just vacuum all your pores, she says. I'd like to go there sometime. And I'd like to have my colors done. What colors look good on me? What don't? What brings out the best in me?'

She looked up at him. All at once, Macon got the feeling she had not been talking about colors at all but something else. It seemed she used words as a sort of background music. He took a step away from her. She said, 'You didn't have to apologize, the other day.'

'Apologize?'

Although he knew exactly what she was referring to.

She seemed to guess that. She didn't explain herself.

'Um, I don't remember if I ever made this clear,' Macon said, 'but I'm not even legally divorced yet.'

'So?'

'I'm just, what do you call. Separated.'

'Well? So?'

He wanted to say, *Muriel, forgive me, but since my son died, sex has . . . turned.* (As milk turns; that was how he thought of it. As milk will alter its basic nature and turn sour.) *I really don't think of it anymore. I honestly don't. I can't imagine anymore what all that fuss was about. Now it seems pathetic.*

But what he said was, 'I'm worried the mailman's going to come.'

She looked at him for a moment longer, and then she opened the door for Edward.

Rose was knitting Julian a pullover sweater for Christmas. 'Already?' Macon asked. 'We've barely got past Thanksgiving.'

'Yes, but this is a really hard pattern and I want to do it right.'

Macon watched her needles flashing. 'Actually,' he said, 'have you ever noticed that Julian wears cardigans?'

'Yes, I guess he does,' she said.

But she went on knitting her pullover.

It was a heathery gray wool, what he believed they called Ragg wool. Macon and both his brothers had sweaters that color. But

Julian wore crayon colors or navy blue. Julian dressed like a golfer. 'He tends toward the V-necked look,' Macon said to Rose.

'That doesn't mean he wouldn't wear a crew neck if he had one.'

'Look,' Macon said. 'I guess what I'm getting at—'

Rose's needles clicked serenely.

'He's really kind of a playboy,' he said. 'I don't know if you realize that. And besides, he's younger.'

'Two years,' she said.

'But he's got a younger, I don't know, style of living. Singles apartments and so on.'

'He says he's tired of all that.'

'Oh, Lord.'

'He says he likes homeyness. He appreciates my cooking. He can't believe I'm knitting him a sweater.'

'No, I guess not,' Macon said grimly.

'Don't try to spoil this, Macon.'

'Sweetheart, I only want to protect you. It's wrong, you know, what you said at Thanksgiving. Love is *not* what it's all about. There are other things to consider besides, all kinds of other issues.'

'He ate my turkey and did not get sick. Two big helpings,' Rose said.

Macon groaned and tore at a handful of his hair.

'First we try him on a real quiet street,' Muriel said. 'Someplace public, but not too busy. Some out-of-the-way little store or something.'

She was driving her long gray boat of a car. Macon sat in front beside her, and Edward sat in back, his ears out horizontal with joy.

Edward was always happy to be invited for a car ride, though very soon he'd turn cranky. ('How much *longer?*' you could almost hear him whine.) It was lucky they weren't going far.

'I got this car on account of its big old trunk,' Muriel said. She slung it dashingly around a corner. 'I needed it for my errand business. Guess how much it cost?'

'Um . . .'

'Only two hundred dollars. That's because it needed work, but I took it to this boy down the street from where I live. I said, "Here's the deal. You fix my car up, I let you have the use of it three nights a week and all day Sunday." Wasn't that a good idea?'

'Very inventive,' Macon said.

'I've *had* to be inventive. It's been scrape and scrounge, nail and knuckle, ever since Norman left me,' she said. She had pulled into a space in front of a little shopping center, but she made no move to get out of the car. 'I've lain awake, oh, many a night, thinking up ways to earn money. It was bad enough when room and board came free, but after Mrs Brimm died it was worse; her house passed on to her son and I had to pay him rent. Her son's an old skinflint. Always wanting to jack up the price. I said, "How's about this? You leave the rent where it is and I won't trouble you with maintenance. I'll tend to it all myself," I said. "Think of the headaches you'll save." So he agreed and now you should see what I have to deal with, things go wrong and *I* can't fix them and so we just live with them. Leaky roof, stopped-up sink, faucet dripping hot water so my gas bill's out of this world, but at least I've kept the rent down. And I've got about fifty jobs, if you count them all up. You could say I'm lucky; I'm good at spotting a chance. Like those lessons at Doggie, Do, or another time a course in massage at the Y. The massage turned out to be a dud, seems you have to have a license and all like that, but I will say Doggie, Do paid off. And also I'm trying to start this research service; that's on account of all I picked up helping the school librarian. Wrote out these little pink cards I passed around at Towson State: We-Search Research. Xeroxed these flyers and mailed them to every Maryland name in the *Writer's Directory. Men and Women of Letters!* I said. *Do you want a long slow illness that will effectively kill off a character without unsightly disfigurement?* So far no one's answered but I'm still hoping. Twice now I've paid for an entire Ocean City vacation just by going up and down the beach offering folks these box lunches me and Alexander fixed in our motel room every morning. We lug them in Alexander's red wagon; I call out, "Cold drinks! Sandwiches! Step right up!" And this is not even counting the regular jobs, like the Meow-Bow or before that the Rapid-Eze. Tiresome old Rapid-Eze; they did let me bring Alexander but it was nothing but copying documents and tedious things like that, canceled checks and invoices, little chits of things. I've never been so disinterested.'

Macon stirred and said, 'Don't you mean uninterested?'

'Exactly. Wouldn't you be? Copies of letters, copies of exams, copies of articles on how to shop for a mortgage. Knitting instructions, crochet instructions, all rolling out of the machine real slow and stately like they're such a big deal. Finally I quit. When I got my training at Doggie, Do I said, "I quit. I've had it!" Why don't we try the grocery.'

Macon felt confused for a second. Then he said, 'Oh. All right.'

'You go into the grocery, put Edward on a down-stay outside. I'll wait here in the car and see if he behaves.'

'All right.'

He climbed from the car and opened the back door for Edward. He led him over to the grocery. He tapped his foot twice. Edward looked distressed, but he lay down. Was this humane, when the sidewalk was still so wet? Reluctantly, Macon stepped into the store. It had the old-fashioned smell of brown paper bags. When he looked back out, Edward's expression was heartbreaking. He wore a puzzled, anxious smile and he was watching the door intently.

Macon cruised an aisle full of fruits and vegetables. He picked up an apple and considered it and set it down again. Then he went back outside. Edward was still in place. Muriel had emerged from her car and was leaning against the fender, making faces into a brown plastic compact. 'Give him lots of praise!' she called, snapping the compact shut. Macon clucked and patted Edward's head.

They went next door to the drugstore. 'This time we'll both go in,' Muriel said.

'Is that safe?'

'We'll have to try it sooner or later.'

They strolled the length of the hair care aisle, all the way back to cosmetics, where Muriel stopped to try on a lipstick. Macon imagined Edward yawning and getting up and leaving. Muriel said, 'Too pink.' She took a tissue from her purse and rubbed the pink off. Her own lipstick stayed on, as if it were not merely a 1940s color but a 1940s formula—that glossless, cakey substance that used to cling to pillowcases, napkins, and the rims of coffee cups. She said, 'What are you doing for dinner tomorrow night?'

'For——?'

'Come and eat at my house.'

He blinked.

'Come on. We'll have fun.'

'Um . . .'

'Just for dinner, you and me and Alexander. Say six o'clock. Number Sixteen Singleton Street. Know where that is?'

'Oh, well, I don't believe I'm free then,' Macon said.

'Think it over a while,' she told him.

They went outside. Edward was still there but he was standing up, bristling in the direction of a Chesapeake Bay retriever almost a full block away. 'Shoot,' Muriel said. 'Just when I thought we were getting someplace.' She made him lie down again. Then she released him and the three of them walked on. Macon was wondering how soon he could decently say that he had thought it over now and remembered he definitely had an invitation elsewhere. They rounded a corner. 'Oh, look, a thrift shop!' Muriel said. 'My biggest weakness.' She tapped her foot at Edward. 'This time, I'll go in,' she said. 'I want to see what they have. You step back a bit and watch he doesn't stand up like before.'

She went inside the thrift shop while Macon waited, skulking around the parking meters. Edward knew he was there, though. He kept turning his head and giving Macon beseeching looks.

Macon saw Muriel at the front of the shop, picking up and setting down little gilded cups without saucers, chipped green glass florists' vases, ugly tin brooches as big as ashtrays. Then he saw her dimly in the back where the clothes were. She drifted into sight and out again like a fish in dark water. She appeared all at once in the doorway, holding up a hat. 'Macon? What do you think?' she called. It was a dusty beige turban with a jewel pinned to its center, a great false topaz like an eye.

'Very interesting,' Macon said. He was starting to feel the cold.

Muriel vanished again, and Edward sighed and settled his chin on his paws.

A teenaged girl walked past—a gypsy kind of girl with layers of flouncy skirts and a purple satin knapsack plastered all over with Grateful Dead emblems. Edward tensed. He watched every step she took; he rearranged his position to watch after her as she left. But he said nothing, and Macon—tensed himself—felt relieved but also a little let down. He'd been prepared to leap into action. All at once the silence seemed unusually deep; no other people passed. He experienced one of those hallucinations of sound that he sometimes got on planes or trains. He heard Muriel's voice, gritty and thin, rattling along. 'At the tone the time will be . . .' she said, and then she sang, 'You will find your love in . . .' and then she shouted, 'Cold drinks! Sandwiches! Step right up!' It seemed she had webbed his mind with her stories, wound him in slender steely threads from her life—her Shirley Temple childhood, unsavory girlhood, Norman flinging the screen out the window, Alexander mewing like a newborn kitten, Muriel wheeling on Doberman pinschers and scattering her salmon-pink business cards and galloping down the beach, all spiky limbs and flying hair, hauling a little red wagon full of lunches.

Then she stepped out of the thrift shop. 'It was way too expensive,' she told Macon. 'Good dog,' she said, and she snapped her fingers to let Edward up. 'Now one more test.' She was heading back toward her car. 'We want to try both of us going in again. We'll do it down at the doctor's.'

'What doctor's?'

'Dr Snell's. I've got to pick up Alexander; I want to return him to school after I drop you off.'

'Will that take long?'

'Oh, no.'

They drove south, with the engine knocking in a way that Macon hadn't noticed the first time. In front of a building on Cold Spring Lane, Muriel parked and got out. Macon and Edward followed her. 'Now, I don't know if he's ready or not,' she said. 'But all the better if he's not; gives Edward practice.'

'I thought you said this wouldn't take long.'

She didn't seem to hear him.

They left Edward on the stoop and went into the waiting room. The receptionist was a gray-haired woman with sequined glasses dangling from a chain of fake scarabs. Muriel asked her, 'Is Alexander through yet?'

'Any minute, hon.'

Muriel found a magazine and sat down but Macon remained standing. He raised one of the slats of the venetian blind to check on Edward. A man in a nearby chair glanced over at him suspiciously. Macon felt like someone from a gangster movie—one of those shady characters who twitches back a curtain to make sure the coast is clear. He dropped the blind. Muriel was reading an article called 'Put on the New Sultry, Shadowed Eyes!' There were pictures of different models looking malevolent.

'How old did you say Alexander was?' Macon asked.

She glanced up. Her own eyes, untouched by cosmetics, were disquietingly naked compared to those in the magazine.

'He's seven,' she said.

Seven.

Seven was when Ethan had learned to ride a bicycle.

Macon was visited by one of those memories that dent the skin, that strain the muscles. He felt the seat of Ethan's bike pressing into his hand—the curled-under edge at the rear that you hold onto when you're trying to keep a bicycle upright. He felt the sidewalk slapping against his soles as he ran. He felt himself let go, slow to a walk, stop with his hands on his hips to call out, 'You've got her now! You've got her!' And Ethan rode away from him, strong and proud and straight-backed, his hair picking up the light till he passed beneath an oak tree.

Macon sat down next to Muriel. She looked over and said, 'Have you thought?'

'Hmm?'

'Have you given any thought to coming to dinner?'

'Oh,' he said. And then he said, 'Well, I could come. If it's only for dinner.'

'What else would it be for?' she asked. She smiled at him and tossed her hair back.

The receptionist said, '_Here_ he is.'

She was talking about a small, white, sickly boy with a shaved-looking skull. He didn't appear to have quite enough skin for his face; his skin was stretched, his mouth was stretched to an unattractive width, and every bone and blade of cartilage made its presence known. His eyes were light blue and lashless, bulging slightly, rimmed with pink, magnified behind large, watery spectacles whose clear frames had an unfortunate pinkish cast themselves. He wore a carefully coordinated shirt-and-slacks set such as only a mother would choose.

'How'd it go?' Muriel asked him.

'Okay.'

'Sweetie, this is Macon. Can you say hi? I've been training his dog.'

Macon stood up and held out his hand. After a moment, Alexander responded. His fingers felt like a collection of wilted stringbeans. He took his hand away again and told his mother, 'You have to make another appointment.'

'Sure thing.'

She went over to the receptionist, leaving Macon and Alexander standing there. Macon felt there was nothing on earth he could talk about with this child. He brushed a leaf off his sleeve. He pulled his cuffs down. He said, 'You're pretty young to be at the doctor's without your mother.'

Alexander didn't answer, but Muriel—waiting for the receptionist to flip through her calendar—turned and answered for him. 'He's used to it,' she said, 'because he's had to go so often. He's got these allergies.'

'I see,' Macon said.

Yes, he was just the type for allergies.

'He's allergic to shellfish, milk, fruits of all kinds, wheat, eggs, and most vegetables,' Muriel said. She accepted a card from the receptionist and dropped it into her purse. She said as they were walking out, 'He's allergic to dust and pollen and paint, and there's some belief he's allergic to air. Whenever he's outside a long time he gets these bumps on any uncovered parts of his body.'

She clucked at Edward and snapped her fingers. Edward jumped up, barking. 'Don't pat him,' she told Alexander. 'You don't know what dog fur will do to you.'

They got into her car. Macon sat in back so Alexander could take the front seat, as far from Edward as possible. They had to drive with all the windows down so Alexander wouldn't start wheezing. Over the rush of wind, Muriel called, 'He's subject to asthma, eczema, and nosebleeds. He has to get these shots all the time. If a bee ever stings him and he hasn't had his shots he could be dead in half an hour.'

Alexander turned his head slowly and gazed at Macon. His expression was prim and censorious.

When they drew up in front of the house, Muriel said, 'Well, let's see now. I'm on full time at the Meow-Bow tomorrow . . .' She ran a hand through her hair, which was scratchy, rough, disorganized. 'So I guess I won't see you till dinner,' she said.

Macon couldn't think of any way to tell her this, but the fact was that he would never be able to make that dinner. He missed his wife. He missed his son. They were the only people who seemed real to him. There was no point looking for substitutes.

11

Muriel Pritchett, was how she was listed. Brave and cocky: no timorous initials for Muriel. Macon circled the number. He figured now was the time to call. It was nine in the evening. Alexander would have gone to bed. He lifted the receiver.

But what would he say?

Best to be straightforward, of course, much less hurtful; hadn't Grandmother Leary always told them so? *Muriel, last year my son died and I don't seem to . . . Muriel, this has nothing to do with you personally but really I have no . . .*

Muriel, I can't. I just can't.

It seemed his voice had rusted over. He held the receiver to his ear but great, sharp clots of rust were sticking in his throat.

He had never actually said out loud that Ethan was dead. He hadn't needed to; it was in the papers (page three, page five), and

then friends had told other friends, and Sarah got on the phone . . .
So somehow, he had never spoken the words. How would he do it
now? Or maybe he could make Muriel do it. *Finish this sentence,*
please: I did have a son but he ——. 'He what?' she would ask. 'He
went to live with your wife? He ran away? He died?' Macon would
nod. 'But *how* did he die? Was it cancer? Was it a car wreck? Was it
a nineteen-year-old with a pistol in a Burger Bonanza restaurant?'

He hung up.

He went to ask Rose for notepaper and she gave him some
from her desk. He took it to the dining room table, sat down, and
uncapped his fountain pen. *Dear Muriel,* he wrote. And stared at
the page a while.

Funny sort of name.

Who would think of calling a little newborn baby Muriel?

He examined his pen. It was a Parker, a swirly tortoiseshell
lacquer with a complicated gold nib that he liked the looks of. He
examined Rose's stationery. Cream colored. Deckle edged. Deckle!
What an odd word.

Well.

Dear Muriel.

I am very sorry, he wrote, *but I won't be able to have dinner with you*
after all. Something has come up. He signed it, *Regretfully, Macon.*

Grandmother Leary would not have approved.

He sealed the envelope and tucked it in his shirt pocket. Then he
went to the kitchen where Rose kept a giant city map thumbtacked
to the wall.

Driving through the labyrinth of littered, cracked, dark streets
in the south of the city, Macon wondered how Muriel could feel

safe living here. There were too many murky alleys and stairwells full of rubbish and doorways lined with tattered shreds of posters. The gridded shops with their ineptly lettered signs offered services that had a sleazy ring to them: CHECKS CASHED NO QUESTIONS, TINY BUBBA'S INCOME TAX, SAME DAY AUTO RECOLORING. Even this late on a cold November night, clusters of people lurked in the shadows— young men drinking out of brown paper bags, middle-aged women arguing under a movie marquee that read CLOSED.

He turned onto Singleton and found a block of row houses that gave a sense of having been skimped on. The roofs were flat, the windows flush and lacking depth. There was nothing to spare, no excess material for overhangs or decorative moldings, no generosity. Most were covered in formstone, but the bricks of Number 16 had been painted a rubbery maroon. An orange bugproof bulb glowed dimly above the front stoop.

He got out of the car and climbed the steps. He opened the screen door, which was made of pitted aluminum. It clattered in a cheap way and the hinges shrieked. He winced. He took the letter from his pocket and bent down.

'I've got a double-barreled shotgun,' Muriel said from inside the house, 'and I'm aiming it exactly where your head is.'

He straightened sharply. His heart started pounding. (Her voice sounded level and accurate—like her shotgun, he imagined.) He said, 'It's Macon.'

'Macon?'

The latch clicked and the inner door opened several inches. He saw a sliver of Muriel in a dark-colored robe. She said, 'Macon! What are you doing here?'

He gave her the letter.

She took it and opened it, using both hands. (There wasn't a trace of a shotgun.) She read it and looked up at him.

He saw he had done it all wrong.

'Last year,' he said, 'I lost . . . I experienced a . . . loss, yes, I lost my . . .'

She went on looking into his face.

'I lost my son,' Macon said. 'He was just . . . he went to a hamburger joint and then . . . someone came, a holdup man, and shot him. I can't go to dinner with people! I can't talk to their little boys! You have to stop asking me. I don't mean to hurt your feelings but I'm just not up to this, do you hear?'

She took one of his wrists very gently and she drew him into the house, still not fully opening the door, so that he had a sense of slipping through something, of narrowly evading something. She closed the door behind him. She put her arms around him and hugged him.

'Every day I tell myself it's time to be getting over this,' he said into the space above her head. 'I know that people expect it of me. They used to offer their sympathy but now they don't; they don't even mention his name. They think it's time my life moved on. But if anything, I'm getting worse. The first year was like a bad dream—I was clear to his bedroom door in the morning before I remembered he wasn't there to be wakened. But this second year is real. I've stopped going to his door. I've sometimes let a whole day pass by without thinking about him. That absence is more terrible than the first, in a way. And you'd suppose I would turn to Sarah but no, we only do each other harm. I believe that Sarah thinks I could have prevented what happened, somehow—she's so used to my arranging her life. I wonder if all this has only brought out the truth about us—how far apart we are. I'm afraid we got married *because* we were far apart. And now I'm far from everyone; I don't have any friends anymore and everyone looks trivial and foolish and not related to me.'

She drew him through a living room where shadows loomed above a single beaded lamp, and a magazine lay face down on a lumpy couch. She led him up a stairway and across a hall and into a bedroom with an iron bedstead and a varnished orange bureau.

'No,' he said, 'wait. This is not what I want.'

'Just sleep,' she told him. 'Lie down and sleep.'

That seemed reasonable.

She removed his duffel coat and hung it on a hook in a closet curtained with a length of flowered sheeting. She knelt and untied his shoes. He stepped out of them obediently. She rose to unbutton his shirt and he stood passive with his hands at his sides. She hung his trousers over a chair back. He dropped onto the bed in his underwear and she covered him with a thin, withered quilt that smelled of bacon grease.

Next he heard her moving through the rest of the house, snapping off lights, running water, murmuring something in another room. She returned to the bedroom and stood in front of the bureau. Earrings clinked into a dish. Her robe was old, shattered silk, the color of sherry. It tied at the waist with a twisted cord and the elbows were clumsily darned. She switched off the lamp. Then she came over to the bed and lifted the quilt and slid under it. He wasn't surprised when she pressed against him. 'I just want to sleep,' he told her. But there were those folds of silk. He felt how cool and fluid the silk was. He put a hand on her hip and felt the two layers of her, cool over warm. He said, 'Will you take this off?'

She shook her head. 'I'm bashful,' she whispered, but immediately afterward, as if to deny that, she put her mouth on his mouth and wound herself around him.

In the night he heard a child cough, and he swam up protestingly through layers of dreams to answer. But he was in a room with one tall blue window, and the child was not Ethan. He turned over and found Muriel. She sighed in her sleep and lifted his hand and placed it upon her stomach. The robe had fallen open; he felt smooth skin, and then a corrugated ridge of flesh jutting across her abdomen. The Caesarean, he thought. And it seemed to him, as he sank back into his dreams, that she had as good as spoken aloud. *About your son*, she seemed to be saying: *Just put your hand here. I'm scarred, too. We're all scarred. You are not the only one.*

12

—— 'I don't understand you,' Rose told Macon. 'First you say yes, you'll be here all afternoon, and then you say you won't. How can I plan when you're so disorganized?'

She was folding linen napkins and stacking them on the table, preparing her annual tea for the old people. Macon said, 'Sorry, Rose, I didn't think it would matter that much.'

'Last night you said you'd want supper and then you weren't here to eat it. Three separate mornings these past two weeks I go to call you for breakfast and I find you haven't slept in your bed. Don't you think I worry? Anything might have happened.'

'Well, I said I was sorry.'

Rose smoothed the stack of napkins.

'Time creeps up on me,' he told her. 'You know how it is. I mean I don't intend to go out at all, to begin with, but then I think, "Oh, maybe for a little while," and next thing I know it's so late, much too late to be driving, and I think to myself, "Well . . ." '

Rose turned away quickly and went over to the buffet. She started counting spoons. 'I'm not asking about your private life,' she said.

'I thought in a sense you were.'

'I just need to know how much food to cook, that's all.'

'I wouldn't blame you for being curious,' he said.

'I just need to know how many breakfasts to fix.'

'You think I don't notice you three? Whenever she's here giving Edward his lesson, everyone starts coming out of the woodwork. Edging through the living room—"Just looking for the pliers! Don't mind me!" Sweeping the entire front porch the minute we take Edward out for a walk.'

'Could I help it if the porch was dirty?'

'Well, I'll tell you what,' he said. 'Tomorrow night I'll definitely be here for supper. That's a promise. You can count on it.'

'I'm not asking you to stay if you don't want to,' she told him.

'Of course I want to! It's just this evening I'll be out,' he said, 'but not late, I'm sure of that. Why, I bet I'll be home before ten!'

Although even as he spoke, he heard how false and shallow he sounded, and he saw how Rose lowered her eyes.

He bought a large combination pizza and drove downtown with it. The smell made him so hungry that he kept snitching bits off the top at every stoplight—coins of pepperoni, crescents of mushroom. His fingers got all sticky and he couldn't find his handkerchief.

Pretty soon the steering wheel was sticky too. Humming to himself, he drove past tire stores, liquor stores, discount shoe stores, the Hot-Tonight Novelty Company. He took a shortcut through an alley and jounced between a double row of backyards—tiny rectangles crammed with swing sets and rusted auto parts and stunted, frozen bushes. He turned onto Singleton and drew up behind a pickup truck full of moldy rolls of carpet.

The next-door neighbor's twin daughters were perched on their front stoop—flashy sixteen-year-olds in jeans as tight as sausage casings. It was too cold to sit outside, but that never stopped them. 'Hey there, Macon,' they singsonged.

'How are you, girls.'

'You going to see Muriel?'

'I thought I might.'

He climbed Muriel's steps, holding the pizza level, and knocked on the door. Debbie and Dorrie continued to watch him. He flashed them a broad smile. They sometimes baby-sat with Alexander; he had to be nice to them. Half the neighborhood sat with Alexander, it seemed. He still felt confused by Muriel's network of arrangements.

It was Alexander who opened the door. 'Pizza man!' Macon told him.

'Mama's on the phone,' Alexander said flatly. He turned away and wandered back to the couch, adjusting his glasses on his nose. Evidently he was watching TV.

'Extra-large combination, no anchovies,' Macon said.

'I'm allergic to pizza.'

'What part of it?'

'Huh?'

'What part are you allergic to? The pepperoni? Sausage? Mushrooms? We could take those off.'

'All of it,' Alexander said.

'You can't be allergic to all of it.'

'Well, I am.'

Macon went on into the kitchen. Muriel stood with her back to him, talking on the phone with her mother. He could tell it was her mother because of Muriel's high, sad, querulous tone. 'Aren't you going to ask how Alexander is? Don't you want to know about his rash? I ask after *your* health, why don't you ask about ours?'

He stepped up behind her soundlessly. 'You didn't even ask what happened with his eye doctor,' she said, 'and here I was so worried about it. I swear sometimes you'd think he wasn't your grandson! That time I sprained my ankle falling off my shoes and called to see if you'd look after him, what did you say? Said, "Now let me get this straight. You want me to come all the way down to your house." You'd think Alexander was nothing to do with you!'

Macon presented himself in front of her, holding out the pizza. 'Ta-da!' he whispered. She looked up at him and gave that perky smile of hers—an ornate, Victorian V.

'Ma,' she said, 'I'm going now! Macon's here!'

It had been a long, long time since anyone made such an event of his arrival.

He went to Julian's office on a Monday afternoon and handed over what he'd done on the U.S. guidebook. 'That wraps up the Northeast,' he said. 'I guess next I'll start on the South.'

'Well, good,' Julian told him. He was bent over behind his desk, rummaging through a drawer. 'Excellent. Like to show you something, Macon. Now, where in hell—ah.'

He straightened, with his face flushed. He gave Macon a tiny blue velvet box. 'Your sister's Christmas present,' he said.

Macon raised the lid. Inside, on a bed of white satin, was a diamond ring. He looked at Julian.

'What is it?' he asked.

'What *is* it?'

'I mean, is this a . . . what you would call, dinner ring? Or is it meant to be, rather . . .'

'It's an engagement ring, Macon.'

'Engagement?'

'I want to marry her.'

'You want to marry Rose?'

'What's so odd about that?'

'Well, I—' Macon said.

'If she'll agree to it, that is.'

'What, you haven't asked her yet?'

'I'll ask her at Christmas, when I give her the ring. I want to do this properly. Old-fashioned. Do you think she'll have me?'

'Well, I really couldn't say,' Macon said. Unfortunately, he was sure she would, but he'd be damned if he'd tell Julian that.

'She's got to,' Julian said. 'I am thirty-six years old, Macon, but I tell you, I feel like a schoolboy about that woman. She's everything those girls in my apartment building are not. She's so . . . true. Want to know something? I've never even slept with her.'

'Well, I don't care to hear about that,' Macon said hastily.

'I want us to have a real wedding night,' Julian told him. 'I want to do everything right. I want to join a real family. God, Macon, isn't it amazing how two separate lives can link up together? I mean two *differentnesses*? What do you think of the ring?'

Macon said, 'It's okay.' He looked down at it. Then he said, 'It's very nice, Julian,' and he closed the box gently and handed it back.

'Now, this is not your ordinary airplane,' Macon told Muriel. 'I wouldn't want you to get the wrong idea. This is what they call a commuter plane. It's something a businessman would take, say, to hop to the nearest city for a day and make a few sales and hop back again.'

The plane he was referring to—a little fifteen-seater that resembled a mosquito or a gnat—stood just outside the door of the commuters' waiting room. A girl in a parka was loading it with baggage. A boy was checking something on the wings. This appeared to be an airline run by teenagers. Even the pilot was a teenager, it seemed to Macon. He entered the waiting room, carrying a clipboard. He read off a list of names. 'Marshall? Noble? Albright?' One by one the passengers stepped forward—just eight or ten of them. To each the pilot said, 'Hey, how you doing.' He let his eyes rest longest on Muriel. Either he found her the most attractive or else he was struck by her outfit. She wore her highest heels, black stockings spattered with black net roses, and a flippy little fuchsia dress under a short fat coat that she referred to as her 'fun fur.' Her hair was caught all to one side in a great bloom of frizz, and there was a silvery dust of some kind on her eyelids.

Macon knew she'd overdone it, but at the same time he liked her considering this such an occasion.

The pilot propped open the door and they followed him outside, across a stretch of concrete, and up two rickety steps into the plane. Macon had to bend almost double as he walked down the aisle. They threaded between two rows of single seats, each seat as spindly as a folding chair. They found spaces across from each other and settled in. Other passengers struggled through, puffing and bumping into things. Last came the copilot, who had round, soft, baby cheeks and carried a can of Diet Pepsi. He slammed the door shut behind him and went up front to the controls. Not so much as a curtain hid the cockpit. Macon could lean out into the aisle and see the banks of knobs and gauges, the pilot positioning his headset, the copilot taking a final swig and setting his empty can on the floor.

'Now, on a bigger plane,' Macon called to Muriel as the engines roared up, 'you'd hardly feel the takeoff. But here you'd better brace yourself.'

Muriel nodded, wide-eyed, gripping the seat ahead of her. 'What's that light that's blinking in front of the pilot?' she asked.

'I don't know.'

'What's that little needle that keeps sweeping round and round?'

'I don't know.'

He felt he'd disappointed her. 'I'm used to jets, not these toys,' he told her. She nodded again, accepting that. It occurred to Macon that he was really a very worldly and well-traveled man.

The plane started taxiing. Every pebble on the runway jolted it; every jolt sent a series of creaks through the framework. They gathered speed. The crew, suddenly grave and professional, made complicated adjustments to their instruments. The wheels left the ground. 'Oh!' Muriel said, and she turned to Macon with her face all lit up.

'We're off,' he told her.

'I'm flying!'

They rose—with some effort, Macon felt—over the fields surrounding the airport, over a stand of trees and a grid of houses. Above-ground swimming pools dotted backyards here and there like pale blue thumbtacks. Muriel pressed so close to her window that she left a circle of mist on the glass. 'Oh, look!' she said to Macon, and then she said something else that he couldn't hear. The engines on this plane were loud and harsh, and the Pepsi can was rolling around with a clattering sound, and also the pilot was bellowing to the copilot, saying something about his refrigerator. 'So I wake up in the middle of the night,' he was shouting, 'damn thing's thudding and thumping—'

Muriel said, 'Wouldn't Alexander enjoy this!'

Macon hadn't seen Alexander enjoying anything yet, but he said dutifully, 'We'll have to bring him sometime.'

'We'll have to take just lots of trips! France and Spain and Switzerland . . .'

'Well,' Macon said, 'there's the little matter of money.'

'Just America, then. California, Florida . . .'

California and Florida took money too, Macon should have said (and Florida wasn't even given space in his guidebook), but for the moment, he was borne along by her vision of things. 'Look!' she said, and she pointed to something. Macon leaned across the aisle to see what she meant. This airplane flew so low that it might have been following road signs; he had an intimate view of farmlands, woodlands, roofs of houses. It came to him very suddenly that every little roof concealed actual lives. Well, of course he'd known that, but all at once it took his breath away. He saw how real those lives were to the people who lived them—how intense and private and absorbing. He stared past Muriel with his mouth open. Whatever she had wanted him to look at must be long past by now, but still he went on gazing out her window.

Porter and the others were talking money. Or Porter was talking money and the others were half listening. Porter was planning ahead for income taxes. He was interested in something called a chicken straddle. 'The way it works,' he said, 'you invest in baby chicks right now, before the end of the year. Deduct the cost of feed and such. Then sell the grown hens in January and collect the profit.'

Rose wrinkled her forehead. She said, 'But chickens are so prone to colds. Or would you call it distemper. And December and January aren't usually all that warm here.'

'They wouldn't be here in Baltimore, Rose. God knows where they'd be. I mean these are not chickens you actually see; they're a way to manage our taxes.'

'Well, I don't know,' Charles said. 'I hate to get involved in things someone else would be handling. It's someone else's word those chickens even exist.'

'You people have no imagination,' Porter said.

The four of them stood around the card table in the sun porch, helping Rose with her Christmas present for Liberty. She had constructed an addition to Liberty's dollhouse—a garage with a guest apartment above it. The garage was convincingly untidy. Miniature wood chips littered the floor around a stack of twig-sized fire logs, and a coil of green wire made a perfect garden hose. Now they were working on the upstairs. Rose was stuffing an armchair cushion no bigger than an aspirin. Charles was cutting a sheet of wallpaper from a sample book. Porter was drilling holes for the curtain rods. There was hardly elbow room; so Macon, who had just come in with Edward, stood back and merely watched.

'Besides,' Charles said, 'chickens are really not, I don't know, very classy animals. I would hate to go round saying I'm a chicken magnate.'

'You don't even have to mention the fact,' Porter said.

'*Beef* magnate, now; that I wouldn't mind. Beef has more of a ring to it.'

'They're not offering a straddle for beef, Charles.'

Macon picked up some color photos that sat beside the wallpaper book. The top photo showed a window in a room he didn't recognize—a white-framed window with louvered shutters closed across its lower half. The next was a group portrait. Four people—blurry, out of focus—stood in a line in front of a couch. The woman wore an apron, the men wore black suits. There was something artificial about their posture. They were lined up too precisely; none of them touched the others. 'Who *are* these people?' Macon asked.

Rose glanced over. 'That's the family from Liberty's doll-house,' she said.

'Oh.'

'Her mother sent me those pictures.'

'It's a family with nothing but grown-ups?' he asked.

'One's a boy; you just can't tell. And one's a grandpa or a butler; June says Liberty switches him back and forth.'

Macon laid the photos aside without looking at the rest of them. He knelt to pat Edward. 'A cattle straddle,' Charles was saying thoughtfully. Macon suddenly wished he were at Muriel's. He wrapped his arms around Edward and imagined he smelled her sharp perfume deep in Edward's fur.

Oh, above all else he was an orderly man. He was happiest with a regular scheme of things. He tended to eat the same meals over and over and to wear the same clothes; to drop off his cleaning on a certain set day and to pay all his bills on another. The teller who helped him on his first trip to a bank was the teller he went to forever after, even if she proved not to be efficient, even if the next teller's line was shorter. There was no room in his life for anyone as unpredictable as Muriel. Or as extreme. Or as . . . well, unlikable, sometimes.

Her youthfulness was not appealing but unsettling. She barely remembered Vietnam and had no idea where she'd been when Kennedy was shot. She made him anxious about his own age, which had not previously troubled him. He realized how stiffly he walked after he had been sitting in one position too long; how he favored his back, always expecting it to go out on him again; how once was plenty whenever they made love.

And she talked so much—almost ceaselessly; while Macon was the kind of man to whom silence was better than music. ('Listen!

They're playing my song,' he used to say when Sarah switched the radio off.) She talked about blushers, straighteners, cellulite, hemlines, winter skin. She was interested in the appearance of things, only the appearance: in lipstick shades and nail wrapping and facial masques and split ends. Once, on one of her more attractive days, he told her she was looking very nice, and she grew so flustered that she stumbled over a curb. She asked if that was because she had tied her hair back; and was it the hair itself or the ribbon; or rather the color of the ribbon, which she'd feared might be just a little too bright and set off the tone of her complexion wrong. And didn't he think her hair was hopeless, kerblamming out the way it did in the slightest bit of humidity? Till he was sorry he had ever brought it up. Well, not sorry, exactly, but tired. Exhausted.

Yet she could raise her chin sometimes and pierce his mind like a blade. Certain images of her at certain random, insignificant moments would flash before him: Muriel at her kitchen table, ankles twined around her chair rungs, filling out a contest form for an all-expense-paid tour of Hollywood. Muriel telling her mirror, 'I look like the wrath of God'—a kind of ritual of leavetaking. Muriel doing the dishes in her big pink rubber gloves with the crimson fingernails, raising a soapy plate and trailing it airily over to the rinse water and belting out one of her favorite songs—'War Is Hell on the Home Front Too' or 'I Wonder If God Likes Country Music.' (Certainly *she* liked country music—long, complaining ballads about the rocky road of life, the cold gray walls of prison, the sleazy, greasy heart of a two-faced man.) And Muriel at the hospital window, as he'd never actually seen her, holding a mop and gazing down at the injured coming in.

Then he knew that what mattered was the pattern of her life; that although he did not love her he loved the surprise of her, and also the surprise of himself when he was with her. In the foreign country that was Singleton Street he was an entirely different person. This person had never been suspected of narrowness, never been accused of chilliness; in fact, was mocked for his soft heart. And was anything but orderly.

'Why don't you come to my folks' house for Christmas dinner?' she asked him.

Macon was in her kitchen at the time. He was crouched beneath the sink, turning off a valve. For a moment he didn't answer; then he emerged and said, 'Your folks?'

'For Christmas dinner.'

'Oh, well, I don't know,' he said.

'Come on, Macon, please say yes! I want you to meet them. Ma thinks I'm making you up. "You made him up," she says. You know how she is.'

Yes, Macon did know, at least from second hand, and he could just imagine what that dinner would be like. Booby-trapped. Full of hidden digs and hurt feelings. The fact was, he just didn't want to get involved.

So instead of answering, he turned his attention to Alexander. He was trying to teach Alexander how to fix a faucet. 'Now,' he said, 'you see I shut the valve off. What did I do that for?'

All he got was a glassy pale stare. This was Macon's idea, not Alexander's. Alexander had been hauled away from the TV like a sack of stones, plunked on a kitchen chair, and instructed to watch closely. 'Oh,' Muriel said, 'I'm not so sure about this. He's not so very strong.'

'You don't have to be Tarzan to fix a kitchen faucet, Muriel.'

'Well, no, but I don't know . . .'

Sometimes Macon wondered if Alexander's ailments were all in Muriel's head.

'Why did I shut off the valve, Alexander?' he asked.

Alexander said, 'Why.'

'You tell me.'

'You tell *me*.'

'No, you,' Macon said firmly.

There was a bad moment or two in which it seemed that Alexander might keep up that stare of his forever. He sat C-shaped in his chair, chin on one hand, eyes expressionless. The shins emerging from his trousers were thin as Tinkertoys, and his brown school shoes seemed very large and heavy. Finally he said, 'So the water won't whoosh all over.'

'Right.'

Macon was careful not to make too much of his victory.

'Now, this leak is not from the spout, but from the handle,' he said. 'So you want to take the handle apart and replace the packing. First you unscrew the top screw. Let's see you do it.'

'Me?'

Macon nodded and offered him the screwdriver.

'I don't want to,' Alexander said.

'Let him just watch,' Muriel suggested.

'If he just watches he won't know how to fix the one in the bathtub, and I'm going to ask him to manage that without me.'

Alexander took the screwdriver, in one of those small, stingy gestures of his that occupied a minimum of space. He inched off the chair and came over to the sink. Macon pulled another chair up close and Alexander climbed onto it. Then there was the problem of fitting the screwdriver into the slot of the screw. It took him forever. He had tiny fingers, each tipped with a little pink pad above painfully bitten nails. He concentrated, his glasses slipping down on his nose. Always a mouth-breather, he was biting his tongue now and panting slightly.

'Wonderful,' Macon said when the screwdriver finally connected.

At each infinitesimal turn, though, it slipped and had to be repositioned. Macon's stomach muscles felt tight. Muriel, for once, was silent, and her silence was strained and anxious.

Then, 'Ah!' Macon said. The screw had loosened enough so that Alexander could twist it by hand. He managed that part fairly easily. He even removed the faucet without being told. 'Very good,' Macon said. 'I believe you may have natural talents.'

Muriel relaxed. Leaning back against the counter, she said, 'My folks have their Christmas dinner in the daytime. I mean it's not at noon but it's not at night either, it's more like mid-afternoon, or this year it's really late afternoon because I've got the morning shift at the Meow-Bow and—'

'Look at this,' Macon told Alexander. 'See that gunk? That's old, rotted packing. So take it away. Right. Now here's the new packing. You wind it around, wind even a little more than you need. Let's see you wind it around.'

Alexander wrapped the thread. His fingers turned white with the effort. Muriel said, 'Usually we have a goose. My daddy brings a goose from the Eastern Shore. Or don't you care for goose. Would you rather just a turkey? A duck? What are you used to eating, Macon?'

Macon said, 'Oh, well . . .' and was saved by Alexander. Alexander turned, having reassembled the faucet without any help, and said, 'Now what?'

'Now make sure the screw is well in.'

Alexander resumed his struggles with the screwdriver. Muriel said, 'Maybe you'd rather a good hunk of beef. I know some men are like that. They think poultry is kind of pansy. Is that how you think too? You can tell me! I won't mind! My folks won't mind!'

'Oh, um, Muriel . . .'

'Now what,' Alexander ordered.

'Why, now we turn the water back on and see what kind of job you've done.'

Macon crouched beneath the sink and showed him where the valve was. Alexander reached past him and twisted it, grunting. Wasn't it odd, Macon thought, how little boys all had that same slightly green smell, like a cedar closet. He rose and turned on the faucet. No leak. 'Look at that!' he told Alexander. 'You've solved the problem.'

Alexander fought to hold a grin back.

'Will you know how to do it the next time?'

He nodded.

'Now when you're grown,' Macon said, 'you can fix the faucets for your wife.'

Alexander's face squinched up with amusement at the thought.

' "Step back, dearie," you can say. "Just let me see to this." '

Alexander said, 'Tssh!'—his face like a little drawstring purse.

' "Let a real *man* take care of this," you can tell her.'

'Tssh! Tssh!'

'Macon? Are you coming to my folks', or aren't you?' Muriel asked.

It seemed unreasonable to say he wasn't. Somehow or other, he had got himself involved already.

13

— Muriel's parents lived out in Timonium, in a development called Foxhunt Acres. Muriel had to show Macon the way. It was the coldest Christmas Day either of them could remember, but they drove with the windows slightly open so that Alexander, riding in back, would not be bothered by the dog hair. The radio was tuned to Muriel's favorite station. Connie Francis was singing 'Baby's First Christmas.'

'You warm enough?' Muriel asked Alexander. 'You doing okay?'

Alexander must have nodded.

'You feel like you're wheezing at all?'

'Nope.'

'No, ma'am,' she corrected him.

Sarah used to do that, too, Macon remembered—give their son a crash course in manners any time they set out to visit her mother.

Muriel said, 'Once I was riding Alexander uptown on some errands for George? My company? And I'd had these two cats in the car just the day before? And I didn't think a thing about it, clean forgot to vacuum like I usually do, and all at once I turn around and Alexander's stretched across the seat, flat out.'

'I wasn't flat *out*,' Alexander said.

'You were just as good as.'

'I was only laying down so I wouldn't need so much air.'

'See there?' Muriel said to Macon.

They were traveling up York Road now, past body shops and fast food outlets all closed and bleak. Macon had never seen this road so empty. He overtook a van and then a taxicab; nothing else. Swags of Christmas greens hung stiffly above a used car lot.

'He can get shots, though,' Muriel said.

'Shots?'

'He can get shots to keep him from wheezing.'

'Then why doesn't he?'

'Well, if Edward was to move in I guess that's what we'd do.'

'Edward?'

'I mean if, you know. If you moved in on a permanent basis and Edward came too.'

'Oh,' Macon said.

Brenda Lee was singing 'I'm Gonna Lasso Santa Claus.' Muriel hummed along, tipping her head perkily left and right to keep time.

'Would you ever think of doing that?' she asked him finally.

'Doing what?' he said, pretending not to know.

'Would you ever think of moving in with us?'

'Oh, um . . .'

'Or we could move in with you,' she said. 'Either way you preferred.'

'With me? But my sister and my—'

'I'm talking about *your* house.'

'Oh. My house.'

His house swam up before him—small and dim and abandoned, hunkered beneath the oak trees like a woodchopper's cottage in a fairy tale. Muriel glanced at his face and then said, quickly, 'I could understand if you didn't want to go back there.'

'It's not that,' he said. He cleared his throat. He said, 'It's just that I haven't given it much thought.'

'Oh, I understand!'

'Not yet, at least.'

'You don't have to explain!'

She pointed out where to turn, and they started down a winding road. The eating places grew sparser and shabbier. There were scratchy little trees, frozen fields, a whole village of different-sized mailboxes bristling at the end of a driveway.

Every time the car jounced, something rattled on the backseat. That was Macon's Christmas present to Alexander—a kit full of tools that were undersized but real, with solid wooden handles. Macon had hunted those tools down one by one. He had rearranged them in their compartments a dozen times at least, like a miser counting his money.

They passed a segment of rickrack fence that was dissolving back into the ground. Muriel said, 'What is *your* family doing today?'

'Oh, nothing much.'

'Having a big Christmas dinner?'

'No, Rose has gone to Julian's. Charles and Porter are, I don't know, I think they said something about caulking the second-floor bathtub.'

'Oh, the poor things! They should have come with us to my folks'.'

Macon smiled, picturing that.

He turned where she directed, into a meadow dotted with houses. All were built to the same general plan—brick with half-stories of aluminum siding above. The streets were named for trees that weren't there, Birch Lane and Elm Court and Apple Blossom Way. Muriel had him make a right onto Apple Blossom Way. He pulled up behind a station wagon. A girl burst out of the house—a chunky, pretty teenager in blue jeans and a long yellow ponytail. 'Claire!' Alexander shouted, bouncing in his seat.

'That's my sister,' Muriel told Macon.

'Ah.'

'Do you think she's good-looking?'

'Yes, she's very good-looking.'

Claire had the car door open by now and was hoisting Alexander into her arms. 'How's my fellow?' she was asking. 'What did Santa Claus bring you?' She was so unlike Muriel that you'd never guess they were sisters. Her face was almost square, and her skin was golden, and by present-day standards she was probably ten pounds overweight. After she'd set Alexander down, she stuffed her hands awkwardly into the back pockets of her jeans. 'So anyhow,' she told Macon and Muriel. 'Merry Christmas, and all that.'

'Look,' Muriel said, flashing a wristwatch. 'See what Macon gave me.'

'What'd you give him?'

'A key tag from a thrift shop. Antique.'

'Oh.'

With her house key attached, Muriel had neglected to say.

Macon unloaded things from the trunk—Muriel's presents for her family, along with his hostess gift—and Alexander took his toolbox from the backseat. They followed Claire across the yard. Muriel was anxiously feeling her hair as she walked. 'You ought to see what Daddy gave Ma,' Claire told her. 'Gave her a microwave oven. Ma says she's scared to death of it. "I just know I'll get radiation," she says. We're worried she won't use it.'

The door was held open for them by a small, skinny, gray woman in an aqua pantsuit. 'Ma, this is Macon,' Muriel said. 'Macon, this is my mother.'

Mrs Dugan studied him, pursing her lips. Lines radiated from the corners of her mouth like cat whiskers. 'Pleased to meet you,' she said finally.

'Merry Christmas, Mrs Dugan,' Macon said. He handed her his gift—a bottle of cranberry liqueur with a ribbon tied around it. She studied that, too.

'Just put the rest of those things under the tree,' Muriel told Macon. 'Ma, aren't you going to say hello to your grandson?'

Mrs Dugan glanced briefly at Alexander. He must not have expected anything more; he was already wandering over to the Christmas tree. Unrelated objects sat beneath it—a smoke detector, an electric drill, a makeup mirror encircled with light bulbs. Macon laid Muriel's packages next to them, and then he removed his coat and draped it across the arm of a white satin couch. Fully a third of the couch was occupied by the microwave oven, still jauntily decorated with a large red bow. 'Look at my new microwave,' Mrs Dugan said. 'If that's not just the weirdest durn thing I ever laid eyes on.' She cleared a crumple of gift wrap off an armchair and waved Macon into it.

'Something certainly smells good,' he said.

'Goose,' she told him. 'Boyd went and shot me a goose.'

She sat down next to the oven. Claire was on the floor with Alexander, helping him open a package. Muriel, still in her coat, scanned a row of books on a shelf. 'Ma—' she said. 'No, never mind, I found it.' She came over to Macon with a photo album, the modern kind with clear plastic pages. 'Look here,' she said, perching on the arm of his chair. 'Pictures of me when I was little.'

'Why not take off your coat and stay a while,' Mrs Dugan told her.

'Me at six months. Me in my stroller. Me and my first birthday cake.'

They were color photos, shiny, the reds a little too blue. (Macon's own baby pictures were black-and-white, which was all that was generally available back then.) Each showed her to be a chubby, giggling blonde, usually with her hair fixed in some coquettish style—tied in a sprig at the top of her head, or in double ponytails so highly placed they looked like puppy ears. At first the stages of her life passed slowly—it took her three full pages to learn to walk—but then they speeded up. 'Me at two. Me at five. Me when I was seven and a half.' The chubby blonde turned thin and dark and sober and then vanished altogether, replaced by the infant Claire. Muriel said, 'Oh, well,' and snapped the album shut just midway through. 'Wait,' Macon told her. He had an urge to see her at her worst, at her most outlandish, hanging out with motorcycle gangs. But when he took the album away from her and flipped to the very last pages, they were blank.

Mr Dugan wandered in—a fair, freckled man in a plaid flannel shirt—and gave Macon a callused hand to shake and then wandered out again, mumbling something about the basement. 'He's fretting over the pipes,' Mrs Dugan explained. 'Last night it got down below zero, did you know that? He's worried the pipes'll freeze.'

'Oh, could I help?' Macon asked, perking up.

'Now, you just sit right where you are, Mr Leary.'

'Macon,' he said.

'Macon. And you can call me Mother Dugan.'

'Um . . .'

'Muriel tells me you're separated, Macon.'

'Well, yes, I am.'

'Do you think it's going to take?'

'Pardon?'

'I mean you're not just leading this child around Robin Hood's barn now, are you?'

'Ma, quit that,' Muriel said.

'Well, I wouldn't have to ask, Muriel, if you had ever showed the least bit of common sense on your own. I mean face it, you don't have such a great track record.'

'She's just worried for me,' Muriel told Macon.

'Well, of course,' he said.

'This girl was not but thirteen years old,' Mrs Dugan said, 'when all at once it seemed boys of the very slipperiest character just came crawling out of the woodwork. I haven't had a good night's sleep since.'

'Well, I don't know why not,' Muriel told her. 'That was years and years ago.'

'Seemed every time we turned around, off she'd gone to the Surf 'n' Turf or the Torch Club or the Hi-Times Lounge on Highway Forty.'

'Ma, will you please open up you and Daddy's Christmas present?'

'Oh, did you bring us a present?'

Muriel rose to fetch it from under the tree, where Claire sat with Alexander. She was helping him set up some little cardboard figures. 'This one goes on the green. This one goes on the blue,' she said. Alexander jittered next to her, impatient to take over.

'Claire was the one who picked that game for him,' Mrs Dugan said, accepting the package Muriel handed her. 'I thought it was too advanced, myself.'

'It is not,' Muriel said (although she hadn't even glanced at it). She returned to Macon's chair. 'Alexander's just as smart as a tack. He'll catch on in no time.'

'Nobody said he wasn't smart, Muriel. You don't have to take offense at every little thing a person says.'

'Will you just open your present?'

But Mrs Dugan proceeded at her own pace. She took off the ribbon and laid it in a box on the coffee table. 'Your daddy has a bit of cash for your Christmas,' she told Muriel. 'Remind him before you go.' She examined the wrapping. 'Will you look at that! Teeny little Rudolph the Red-nosed Reindeers all over it. Real aluminum foil for their noses. I don't know why you couldn't just use tissue like I do.'

'I wanted it to be special,' Muriel told her.

Mrs Dugan took off the paper, folded it, and laid it aside. Her gift was something in a gilded frame. 'Well, isn't that nice,' she said finally. She turned it toward Macon. It was a picture of Muriel and Alexander—a studio portrait in dreamy pastels, the lighting so even that it seemed to be coming from no particular place at all. Muriel was seated and Alexander stood beside her, one hand resting delicately upon her shoulder. Neither of them smiled. They looked wary and uncertain, and very much alone.

Macon said, 'It's beautiful.'

Mrs Dugan only grunted and leaned forward to lay the photo beside the box of ribbons.

Dinner was an industrious affair, with everyone working away at the food—goose, cranberry relish, two kinds of potatoes, and three kinds of vegetables. Mr Dugan remained spookily quiet, although Macon offered him several openers about the basement plumbing. Muriel devoted herself to Alexander. 'There's bread in that stuffing, Alexander. Put it back this instant. You want your allergy to start up? I wouldn't trust that relish, either.'

'Oh, for Lord's sake, let him be,' Mrs Dugan said.

'You wouldn't say that if it was you he kept awake at night with itchy rashes.'

'Half the time I believe you bring on those rashes yourself with all your talk,' Mrs Dugan said.

'That just shows how much you know about it.'

Macon had a sudden feeling of dislocation. What would Sarah say if she could see him here? He imagined her amused, ironic expression. Rose and his brothers would just look baffled. Julian would say, 'Ha! *Accidental Tourist in Timonium.*'

Mrs Dugan brought out three different pies, and Claire scurried around with the coffeepot. Over her jeans now she wore an embroidered dirndl skirt—her gift from Muriel, purchased last week at Value Village. Her layers of clothing reminded Macon of some native costume. 'What about the liqueur?' she asked her mother. 'Shall I set out Macon's liqueur?'

'Maybe he wants you to call him Mr Leary, hon.'

'No, please, Macon's fine,' he said.

He supposed there'd been a lot of discussion about his age. Oh, no doubt about it: He was too old, he was too tall, he was too dressed up in his suit and tie.

Mrs Dugan said the liqueur was just about the best thing she'd ever drunk. Macon himself found it similar to the fluoride mixture his dentist coated his teeth with; he'd envisioned something different. Mr Dugan said, 'Well, these sweet-tasting, pretty-colored drinks are all very well for the ladies, but personally I favor a little sipping whiskey, don't you, Macon?' and he rose and brought back a fifth of Jack Daniel's and two shot glasses. The mere weight of the bottle in his hand seemed to loosen his tongue. 'So!' he said, sitting down. 'What you driving these days, Macon?'

'Driving? Oh, um, a Toyota.'

Mr Dugan frowned. Claire giggled. 'Daddy hates and despises foreign cars,' she told Macon.

'What is it, you don't believe in buying American?' Mr Dugan asked him.

'Well, as a matter of fact—'

As a matter of fact his wife drove a Ford, he'd been going to say, but he changed his mind. He took the glass that Mr Dugan held out to him. 'I did once have a Rambler,' he said.

'You want to try a Chevy, Macon. Want to come to the showroom sometime and let me show you a Chevy. What's your preference? Family-size? Compact?'

'Well, compact, I guess, but—'

'I'll tell you one thing: There is no way on earth you're going to get me to sell you a *sub*compact. No sir, you can beg and you can whine, you can get down on bended knee, I won't sell you one of those deathtraps folks are so set on buying nowadays. I tell my customers, I say, "You think I got no principles? You're looking here before you at a man of principle," I tell them, and I say, "You want a subcompact you better go to Ed Mackenzie there. He'll sell you one without a thought. What does he care? But I'm a man of principle." Why, Muriel here near about lost her life in one of them things.'

'Oh, Daddy, I did not,' Muriel said.

'Came a lot closer than *I'd* like to get.'

'I walked away without a scratch.'

'Car looked like a little stove-in sardine can.'

'Worst thing I got was a run in my stocking.'

'Muriel was taking a lift from Dr Kane at the Meow-Bow,' Mr Dugan told Macon, 'one day when her car was out of whack, and some durn fool woman driver swung directly into their path. See, she was hanging a left when——'

'Let me tell it,' Mrs Dugan said. She leaned toward Macon, gripping the wineglass that held her liqueur. 'I was just coming in from the grocery store, carrying these few odds and ends I needed for Claire's school lunches. That child eats more than some grown men I know. Phone rings. I drop everything and go to answer. Man says, "Mrs Dugan?" I say, "Yes." Man says, "Mrs Dugan, this is the Baltimore City Police and I'm calling about your daughter Muriel." I think, "Oh, my God." Right away my heart starts up and I have to find someplace to sit. Still have my coat on, rain scarf tied around my head so I couldn't even hear all that good but I never thought to take it off, that's how flustered I was. It was one of those hard rainy days like someone is purposely heaving buckets of water at you. I think, "Oh, my God, now what has Muriel gone and——" '

'Lillian, you are getting way off the subject here,' Mr Dugan said.

'How can you say that? I'm telling him about Muriel's accident.'

'He don't want to hear every little oh-my-God, he wants to know why he can't have a subcompact. Lady hangs a left smack in front of Dr Kane's little car,' Mr Dugan told Macon, 'and he has no choice but to ram her. He had the right of way. Want to know what happened? His little car is totaled. Little bitty Pinto. Lady's big old Chrysler barely dents its fender. Now tell me you still want a subcompact.'

'But I didn't——'

'And the other thing is that Dr Kane never, ever offered her another ride home, even after he got a new car,' Mrs Dugan said.

'Well, I don't exactly live in his neighborhood, Ma.'

'He's a bachelor,' Mrs Dugan told Macon. 'Have you met him? Real good-looking, Muriel says. First day on the job she says, "Guess what, Ma." Calls me on the phone. "Guess what, my boss is single and he's real good-looking, a professional man, the other girls tell me he isn't even engaged." Then he offers her that one lift home and they go and have an accident and he never offers again. Even when she lets him know she don't have her car some days, he never offers again.'

'He does live clear up in Towson,' Muriel said.

'I believe he thinks you're bad luck.'

'He lives up in Towson and I live down on Singleton Street! What do you expect?'

'Next he got a Mercedes sports car,' Claire put in.

'Well, sports cars,' Mr Dugan said. 'We don't even talk about those.'

Alexander said, 'Can I be excused now?'

'I really had high hopes for Dr Kane,' Mrs Dugan said sadly.

'Oh, quit it, Ma.'

'You did, too! You said you did!'

'Why don't you just hush up and drink your drink.'

Mrs Dugan shook her head, but she took another sip of liqueur.

They left in the early evening, when the last light had faded and the air seemed crystallized with cold. Claire stood in the doorway singing out, 'Come back soon! Thanks for the skirt! Merry Christmas!' Mrs Dugan shivered next to her, a sweater draped over her shoulders. Mr Dugan merely lifted an arm and disappeared—presumably to check on the basement again.

Traffic was heavier now. Headlights glowed like little white smudges. The radio—having given up on Christmas for another year—played 'I Cut My Fingers on the Pieces of Your Broken Heart,' and the toolbox rattled companionably in the backseat.

'Macon? Are you mad?' Muriel asked.

'Mad?'

'Are you mad at me?'

'Why, no.'

She glanced back at Alexander and said no more.

It was night when they reached Singleton Street. The Butler twins, bundled into identical lavender jackets, stood talking with two boys on the curb. Macon parked and opened the back door for Alexander, who had fallen asleep with his chin on his chest. He gathered him up and carried him into the house. In the living room, Muriel set down her own burdens—the toolbox, Alexander's new game, and a pie Mrs Dugan had pressed on them—and followed Macon up the stairs. Macon walked sideways to keep Alexander's feet from banging into the wall. They went into the smaller of the bedrooms and he laid Alexander on the bed. 'I know what you must be thinking,' Muriel said. She took Alexander's shoes off. 'You're thinking, "Oh, now I see, this Muriel was just on the lookout for anybody in trousers." Aren't you.'

Macon didn't answer. (He worried they'd wake Alexander.)

'I know what you're thinking!'

She tucked Alexander in. Turned off the light. They started back downstairs. 'But that's not the way it was; I swear it,' she said. 'Oh, of course since he was single the possibility did cross my mind. Who would I be kidding if I said it didn't? I'm all alone, raising a kid. Scrounging for money. Of course it crossed my mind!'

'Well, of course,' Macon said mildly.

'But it wasn't like she made it sound,' Muriel told him.

She clattered after him across the living room. When he sat on the couch she sat next to him, still in her coat. 'Are you going to stay?' she asked.

'If you're not too sleepy.'

Instead of answering, she tipped her head back against the couch. 'I meant are you giving up on me. I meant did you want to stop seeing me.'

'Why would I want to stop seeing you?'

'After how bad she made me look.'

'You didn't look bad.'

'Oh, no?'

When she was tired, her skin seemed to tighten over her bones. She pressed her fingertips to her eyelids.

'Last Christmas,' Macon said, 'was the first one we had without Ethan. It was very hard to get through.'

He often found himself talking with her about Ethan. It felt good to say his name out loud.

'We didn't know how to have a childless Christmas anymore,' he said. 'I thought, "Well, after all, we managed before we had him, didn't we?" But in fact I couldn't remember how. It seemed to me we'd *always* had him; it's so unthinkable once you've got children that they ever didn't exist. I've noticed: I look back to when I was a boy, and it seems to me that Ethan was somehow there even then; just not yet visible, or something. So anyway. I decided what I should do was get Sarah a whole flood of presents, and I went out to Hutzler's the day before Christmas and bought all this junk—closet organizers and such. And Sarah: She went to the other extreme. She didn't buy anything. So there we were, each of us feeling we'd done it all wrong, acted inappropriately, but also that the other had done wrong; I don't know. It was a terrible Christmas.'

He smoothed Muriel's hair off her forehead. 'This one was better,' he said.

She opened her eyes and studied him a moment. Then she slipped her hand in her pocket, came up with something and held it toward him—palming it, like a secret. 'For you,' she said.

'For me?'

'I'd like you to have it.'

It was a snapshot stolen from her family album: Muriel as a toddler, clambering out of a wading pool.

She meant, he supposed, to give him the best of her. And so she had. But the best of her was not that child's Shirley Temple hairdo. It was her fierceness—her spiky, pugnacious fierceness as she fought her way toward the camera with her chin set awry and her eyes bright slits of determination. He thanked her. He said he would keep it forever.

14

— You would have to say that he was living with her now. He began to spend all his time at her house, to contribute toward her rent and her groceries. He kept his shaving things in her bathroom and squeezed his clothes among the dresses in her closet. But there wasn't one particular point at which he made the shift. No, this was a matter of day by day. First there was that long Christmas vacation when Alexander was home alone; so why shouldn't Macon stay on with him once he'd spent the night there? And why not fetch his typewriter and work at the kitchen table? And then why not remain for supper, and after that for bed?

Though if you needed to put a date on it, you might say he truly moved in the afternoon he moved Edward in. He'd just got back from a business trip—an exhausting blitz of five southern cities, not one of which was any warmer than Baltimore—and he stopped by Rose's house to check the animals. The cat was fine, Rose said. (She had to speak above Edward's yelps; he was frantic with joy and relief.) The cat had probably not noticed Macon was missing. But Edward, well . . . 'He spends a lot of time sitting in the hall,' she said, 'staring at the door. He keeps his head cocked and he waits for you to come back.'

That did it. He brought Edward with him when he returned to Singleton Street.

'What do you think?' he asked Muriel. 'Could we keep him just a day or two? See if Alexander can take it, without any shots?'

'I can take it!' Alexander said. 'It's cats that get to me; not dogs.'

Muriel looked doubtful, but she said they could give it a try.

Meanwhile, Edward darted madly all over the house snuffling into corners and under furniture. Then he sat in front of Muriel and grinned up at her. He reminded Macon of a schoolboy with a crush on his teacher; all his fantasies were realized, here he was at last.

For the first few hours they tried to keep him in a separate part of the house, which of course was hopeless. He had to follow Macon wherever he went, and also he developed an immediate interest in Alexander. Lacking a ball, he kept dropping small objects at Alexander's feet and then stepping back to look expectantly into his face. 'He wants to play fetch,' Macon explained. Alexander picked up a matchbook and tossed it, angling his arm behind him in a prissy way. While Edward went tearing after it, Macon made a mental note to buy a ball first thing in the morning and teach Alexander how to throw.

Alexander watched TV and Edward snoozed on the couch beside him, curled like a little blond cashew nut with a squinty, blissful expression on his face. Alexander hugged him and buried his face in Edward's ruff. 'Watch it,' Macon told him. He had no idea what to do if Alexander started wheezing. But Alexander didn't wheeze. By bedtime he just had a stuffy nose, and he usually had that anyhow.

Macon liked to believe that Alexander didn't know he and Muriel slept together. 'Well, that's just plain ridiculous,' Muriel said. 'Where does he imagine you spend the night—on the living room couch?'

'Maybe,' he said. 'I'm sure he has some explanation. Or maybe he doesn't. All I'm saying is, we shouldn't hit him in the face with it. Let him think what he wants to think.'

So every morning, Macon rose and dressed before Alexander woke. He started fixing breakfast and then roused him. 'Seven o'clock! Time to get up! Go call your mother, will you?' In the past, he learned, Muriel had often stayed in bed while Alexander woke on his own and got ready for school. Sometimes he left the house while she was still asleep. Macon thought that was shocking. Now he made a full breakfast, and he insisted that Muriel sit at the table with them. Muriel claimed breakfast made her sick to her stomach. Alexander said it made him sick, too, but Macon said that was just too bad. 'Ninety-eight percent of all A students eat eggs in the morning,' he said (making it up as he went along). 'Ninety-nine percent drink milk.' He untied his apron and sat down. 'Are you listening, Alexander?'

'I'll throw up if I drink milk.'

'That's all in your head.'

'Tell him, Mama!'

'He throws up,' Muriel said gloomily. She sat hunched at the table in her long silk robe, resting her chin on one hand. 'It's something to do with enzymes,' she said. She yawned. Her hair, growing out of its permanent at last, hung down her back in even ripples like the crimps on a bobby pin.

Alexander walked to school with Buddy and Sissy Ebbetts, two tough-looking older children from across the street. Muriel either went back to bed or dressed and left for one or another of her jobs, depending on what day it was. Then Macon did the breakfast dishes and took Edward out. They didn't go far; it was much too cold. The few people they encountered walked rapidly, with jerky steps, like characters in a silent film. They knew Macon by sight now and would allow their eyes to flick over his face as they passed—a gesture like a nod—but they didn't speak. Edward ignored them. Other dogs could come up and sniff him and he wouldn't even break stride. Mr Marcusi, unloading crates outside Marcusi's Grocery, would pause to say, 'Well, hey there, stubby. Hey there, tub of lard.' Edward, smugly oblivious, marched on. 'Weirdest animal I ever saw,' Mr Marcusi called after Macon. 'Looks like something that was badly drawn.' Macon always laughed.

He was beginning to feel easier here. Singleton Street still unnerved him with its poverty and its ugliness, but it no longer seemed so dangerous. He saw that the hoodlums in front of the Cheery Moments Carry-Out were pathetically young and shabby—their lips chapped, their sparse whiskers ineptly shaved, an uncertain, unformed look around their eyes. He saw that once the men had gone off to work, the women emerged full of good intentions and swept their front walks, picked up the beer cans and potato chip bags, even rolled back their coat sleeves and scrubbed their stoops on the coldest days of the year. Children raced past like so many scraps of paper blowing in the wind—mittens mismatched, noses running—and some woman would brace herself on her broom to call, 'You there! I see you! Don't think I don't know you're skipping school!' For this street was always backsliding, Macon saw, always falling behind, but was caught just in time by these women with their carrying voices and their pushy jaws.

Returning to Muriel's house, he would warm himself with a cup of coffee. He would set his typewriter on the kitchen table and sit down with his notes and brochures. The window next to the table had large, cloudy panes that rattled whenever the wind blew. Something about the rattling sound reminded him of train travel. *The airport in Atlanta must have ten miles of corridors*, he typed, and then a gust shook the panes and he had an eerie sensation of movement, as if the cracked linoleum floor were skating out from under him.

He would telephone hotels, motels, Departments of Commerce, and his travel agent, arranging future trips. He would note these arrangements in the datebook that Julian gave him every Christmas—a Businessman's Press product, spiral-bound. In the back were various handy reference charts that he liked to thumb through. The birthstone for January was a garnet; for February, an amethyst. One square mile equaled 2.59 square kilometers. The proper gift for a first anniversary was paper. He would ponder these facts dreamily. It seemed to him that the world was full of equations; that there must be an answer for everything, if only you knew how to set forth the questions.

Then it was lunchtime, and he would put away his work and make himself a sandwich or heat a can of soup, let Edward have a quick run in the tiny backyard. After that he liked to putter around the house a bit. There was so much that needed fixing! And all of it somebody else's, not his concern, so he could approach it lightheartedly. He whistled while he probed the depth of a crack. He hummed as he toured the basement, shaking his head at the disarray. Upstairs he found a three-legged bureau leaning on a can of tomatoes, and he told Edward, 'Scandalous!' in a tone of satisfaction.

It occurred to him—as he oiled a hinge, as he tightened a doorknob—that the house reflected amazingly little of Muriel. She must have lived here six or seven years by now, but still the place had an air of transience. Her belongings seemed hastily placed, superimposed, not really much to do with her. This was a disappointment, for Macon was conscious while he worked of his intense curiosity about her inner workings. Sanding a drawer, he cast a guilty eye upon its contents but found only fringed shawls and yellowed net gloves from the forties—clues to other people's lives, not hers.

But what was it he wanted to know? She was an open book, would tell him anything—more than he felt comfortable with. Nor did she attempt to hide her true nature, which was certainly far from perfect. It emerged that she had a nasty temper, a shrewish tongue, and a tendency to fall into spells of self-disgust from which no one could rouse her for hours. She was inconsistent with Alexander to the point of pure craziness—one minute overprotective, the next minute callous and offhand. She was obviously intelligent, but she counteracted that with the most global case of superstition Macon had ever witnessed. Hardly a day passed when she didn't tell him some dream in exhaustive detail and then sift through it for omens. (A dream of white ships on a purple sea came true the very next morning, she claimed, when a door-to-door salesman showed up in a purple sweater patterned with little white boats. 'The very same purple! Same shape of ship!' Macon only wondered what kind of salesman would wear such clothing.) She believed in horoscopes and tarot cards and Ouija boards. Her magic number was seventeen. In a previous incarnation she'd been a fashion designer, and she swore she could recall at least one of her deaths. ('We think she's passed on,' they told the doctor as he entered, and the doctor unwound his muffler.) She was religious in a blurry, nondenominational way and had no doubt whatsoever that God was looking after her personally—ironic, it seemed to Macon, in view of how she'd had to fight for every little thing she wanted.

He knew all this and yet, finding a folded sheet of paper on the counter, he opened it and devoured her lurching scrawl as if she were a stranger. *Pretzels. Pantyhose. Dentist*, he read. *Pick up Mrs Arnold's laundry.*

No, not that. Not that.

Then it was three o'clock and Alexander was home from school, letting himself in with a key that he wore on a shoelace around his neck. 'Macon?' he'd call tentatively. 'Is that you out there?' He was scared of burglars. Macon said, 'It's me.' Edward leapt up and went running for his ball. 'How was your day?' Macon always asked.

'Oh, okay.'

But Macon had the feeling that school never went very well for Alexander. He came out of it with his face more pinched than ever, his glasses thick with fingerprints. He reminded Macon of a homework paper that had been erased and rewritten too many times. His clothes, on the other hand, were as neat as when he'd left in the morning. Oh, those clothes! Spotless polo shirts with a restrained brown pinstripe, matching brown trousers gathered bulkily around his waist with a heavy leather belt. Shiny brown shoes. Blinding white socks. Didn't he ever play? Didn't kids have recess anymore?

Macon gave him a snack: milk and cookies. (Alexander drank milk in the afternoons without complaint.) Then he helped him with his schoolwork. It was the simplest sort—arithmetic sums and reading questions. 'Why did Joe need the dime? Where was Joe's daddy?'

'Umm . . .' Alexander said. Blue veins pulsed in his temples.

He was not a stupid child but he was limited, Macon felt. Limited. Even his walk was constricted. Even his smile never dared to venture beyond two invisible boundaries in the center of his face. Not that he was smiling now. He was wrinkling his forehead, raising his eyes fearfully to Macon.

'Take your time,' Macon told him. 'There's no hurry.'

'But I can't! I don't know! I don't know!'

'You remember Joe,' Macon said patiently.

'I don't think I do!'

Sometimes Macon stuck with it, sometimes he simply dropped it. After all, Alexander had managed without him up till now, hadn't he? There was a peculiar kind of luxury here: Alexander was not his own child. Macon felt linked to him in all sorts of complicated ways, but not in that inseparable, inevitable way that he'd been linked to Ethan. He could still draw back from Alexander; he could still give up on him. 'Oh, well,' he could say, 'talk it over with your teacher tomorrow.' And then his thoughts could wander off again.

The difference was, he realized, that he was not held responsible here. It was a great relief to know that.

When Muriel came home she brought fresh air and bustle and excitement. 'Is it ever cold! Is it ever windy! Radio says three below zero tonight. Edward, down, this minute. Who wants lemon pie for dessert? Here's what happened: I had to go shopping for Mrs Quick. First I had to buy linens for her daughter who's getting married, then I had to take them back because they were all the wrong color, her daughter didn't want pastel but white and told her mother plain as day, she said . . . and then I had to pick up pastries for the bridesmaids' party and when Mrs Quick sees the lemon pie she says, "Oh, no, not lemon! Not that tacky lemon that always tastes like Kool-Aid!" I'm like, "Mrs Quick, you don't have any business telling me what is tacky. This is a fresh-baked, lemon meringue pie without a trace of artificial . . ." So anyway, to make a long story short, she said to take it home to my little boy. "Well, for your information I'm certain he can't eat it," I say. "Chances are he's allergic." But I took it.'

She ranged around the kitchen putting together a supper—BLTs, usually, and vegetables from a can. Sometimes things were not where she expected (Macon's doing—he couldn't resist reorganizing), but she adapted cheerfully. While the bacon sputtered in the skillet she usually phoned her mother and went over all she'd just told Macon and Alexander. 'But the daughter wanted white and . . . "Oh, not that tacky lemon pie!" she says . . .'

If Mrs Dugan couldn't come to the phone (which was often the case), Muriel talked to Claire instead. Evidently Claire was having troubles at home. 'Tell them!' Muriel counseled her. 'Just tell them! Tell them you won't stand for it.' Cradling the receiver against her shoulder, she opened a drawer and took out knives and forks. 'Why should they have to know every little thing you do? It doesn't *matter* that you're not up to anything, Claire. Tell them, "I'm seventeen years old and it's none of your affair anymore if I'm up to anything or not. I'm just about a grown woman," tell them.'

But later, if Mrs Dugan finally came to the phone, Muriel herself sounded like a child. 'Ma? What kept you? You can't say a couple of words to your daughter just because your favorite song is playing on the radio? "Lara's Theme" is more important than flesh and blood?'

Even after Muriel hung up, she seldom really focused on dinner. Her girlfriend might drop by and stay to watch them eat—a fat young woman named Bernice who worked for the Gas and Electric Company. Or neighbors would knock on the kitchen door and walk right in. 'Muriel, do you happen to have a coupon for support hose? Young and slim as *you* are, I know you wouldn't need it yourself.' 'Muriel, Saturday morning I got to go to the clinic for my teeth, any chance of you giving me a lift?' Muriel was an oddity on this street—a woman with a car of her own—and they knew by heart her elaborate arrangement with the boy who did her repairs. Sundays, when Dominick had the car all day, nobody troubled her; but as soon as Monday rolled around they'd be lining up with their requests. 'Doctor wants me to come in and show him my . . .' 'I promised I'd take my kids to the . . .'

If Muriel couldn't do it, they never thought to ask Macon instead. Macon was still an outsider; they shot him quick glances but pretended not to notice he was listening. Even Bernice was bashful with him, and she avoided using his name.

By the time the lottery number was announced on TV, everyone would have left. That was what mattered here, Macon had discovered: the television schedule. The news could be missed but the lottery drawing could not; nor could 'Evening Magazine' or any of the action shows that followed. Alexander watched these shows but Muriel didn't, although she claimed to. She sat on the couch in front of the set and talked, or painted her nails, or read some article or other. 'Look here! "How to Increase Your Bustline."'

'You don't want to increase your bustline,' Macon told her.

' "Thicker, More Luxurious Eyelashes in Just Sixty Days."'

'You don't want thicker eyelashes.'

He felt content with everything exactly the way it was. He seemed to be suspended, his life on hold.

And later, taking Edward for his final outing, he liked the feeling of the neighborhood at night. This far downtown the sky was too pale for stars; it was pearly and opaque. The buildings were muffled dark shapes. Faint sounds threaded out of them—music, rifle shots, the whinnying of horses. Macon looked up at Alexander's window and saw Muriel unfolding a blanket, as delicate and distinct as a silhouette cut from black paper.

*

One Wednesday there was a heavy snowstorm, starting in the morning and continuing through the day. Snow fell in clumps like white woolen mittens. It wiped out the dirty tatters of snow from earlier storms; it softened the street's harsh angles and hid the trash cans under cottony domes. Even the women who swept their stoops hourly could not keep pace with it, and toward evening they gave up and went inside. All night the city glowed lilac. It was absolutely silent.

The next morning, Macon woke late. Muriel's side of the bed was empty, but her radio was still playing. A tired-sounding announcer was reading out cancellations. Schools were closed, factories were closed, Meals on Wheels was not running. Macon was impressed by the number of activities that people had been planning for just this one day—the luncheons and lectures and protest meetings. What energy, what spirit! He felt almost proud, though he hadn't been going to attend any of these affairs himself.

Then he realized he was hearing voices downstairs. Alexander must be awake, and here he was, trapped in Muriel's bedroom.

He dressed stealthily, making sure the coast was clear before crossing the hall to the bathroom. He tried not to creak the floorboards as he descended the stairs. The living room was unnaturally bright, reflecting the snow outside. The couch was opened, a mass of sheets and blankets; Claire had slept over the last few nights. Macon followed the voices into the kitchen. He found Alexander eating pancakes, Claire at the stove making more, Muriel curled in her usual morning gloom above her coffee cup. Just inside the back door Bernice stood dripping snow, swathed in various enormous plaids. 'So anyhow,' Claire was telling Bernice, 'Ma says, "Claire, who was that boy you drove up with?" I said, "That was no boy, that was Josie Tapp with her new punk haircut," and Ma says, "Expect me to believe a cock-and-bull story like that!" So I say, "I've had enough of this! Grillings! Curfews! Suspicions!" And I leave and catch a bus down here.'

'They're just worried you'll turn out like Muriel did,' Bernice told her.

'But Josie Tapp! I mean God Almighty!'

There was a general shifting motion in Macon's direction. Claire said, 'Hey there, Macon. Want some pancakes?'

'Just a glass of milk, thanks.'

'They're nice and hot.'

'Macon thinks sugar on an empty stomach causes ulcers,' Muriel said. She wrapped both hands around her cup.

Bernice said, 'Well, *I'm* not saying no,' and she crossed the kitchen to pull out a chair. Her boots left pads of snow with each step. Edward toddled after her, licking them up. 'You and me ought to build a snowman,' Bernice told Alexander. 'Snow must be four feet deep out there.'

'Have the streets been cleared?' Macon asked.

'Are you kidding?'

'They couldn't even get through with the newspaper,' Alexander told him. 'Edward's about to lose his mind wondering where it's got to.'

'And there's cars abandoned all over the city. Radio says nobody's going anywhere at all.'

But Bernice had hardly spoken when Edward wheeled toward the back door and started barking. A figure loomed outside. 'Who's that?' Bernice asked.

Muriel tapped her foot at Edward. He lay down but kept on barking, and Macon opened the door. He found himself face to face with his brother Charles—unusually rugged-looking in a visored cap with earflaps. 'Charles?' Macon said. 'What are you doing here?'

Charles stepped in, bringing with him the fresh, expectant smell of new snow. Edward's yelps changed to welcoming whines. 'I came to pick you up,' Charles said. 'Couldn't reach you on the phone.'

'Pick me up for what?'

'Your neighbor Garner Bolt called and said pipes or something have burst in your house, water all over everything. I've been trying to get you since early morning but your line was always busy.'

'That was me,' Claire said, setting down a platter of pancakes. 'I took the receiver off the hook so my folks wouldn't call me up and nag me.'

'This is Muriel's sister, Claire,' Macon said, 'and that's Alexander and that's Bernice Tilghman. My brother Charles.'

Charles looked confused.

Come to think of it, this wasn't an easy group to sort out. Claire was her usual mingled self—rosebud bathrobe over faded jeans, fringed moccasin boots that laced to her knees. Bernice could have been a lumberjack. Alexander was neat and polished, while Muriel in her slinky silk robe was barely decent. Also, the kitchen was so small that there seemed to be more people than there actually were.

And Claire was waving her spatula, spangling the air with drops of grease. 'Pancakes?' she asked Charles. 'Orange juice? Coffee?'

'No, thank you,' Charles said. 'I really have to be—'

'I bet you want milk,' Muriel said. She got to her feet, fortunately remembering to clutch her robe together. 'I bet you don't want sugar on an empty stomach.'

'No, really I—'

'It won't be any trouble!' She was taking the carton from the refrigerator. 'How'd you get here, anyways?'

'I drove.'

'I thought the streets were blocked.'

'They weren't so bad,' Charles said, accepting a glass of milk. '*Finding* the place was the hard part.' He told Macon, 'I looked it up on the map but evidently I was mizzled.'

'Mizzled?' Muriel asked.

'He was misled,' Macon explained. 'What did Garner say, exactly, Charles?'

'He said he saw water running down the inside of your living room window. He looked in and saw the ceiling dripping. Could have been that way for weeks, he said; you know that cold spell we had over Christmas.'

'Doesn't sound good,' Macon said.

He went to the closet for his coat. When he came back, Muriel was saying, 'Now that you don't have an empty stomach, Charles, won't you try some of Claire's pancakes?'

'I've had half a dozen,' Bernice told him. 'They don't call me Big-Ass Bernice for nothing.'

Charles said, 'Uh, well—' and gave Macon a helpless look.

'We have to be going,' Macon told the others. 'Charles, are you parked in back?'

'No, in front. Then I went around back because I couldn't get the doorbell to work.'

There was a reserved, disapproving note in Charles's voice when he said this, but Macon just said airily, 'Oh, yes! Place is a wreck.' He led the way toward the front of the house. He felt like someone demonstrating how well he got on with the natives.

They pushed open the door with some difficulty and floundered down steps so deeply buried that both men more or less fell the length of them, trusting that they would be cushioned. The sunlight sparked and flashed. They waded toward the street, Macon's shoes quickly filling with snow—a refreshing sharpness that almost instantly turned painful.

'I guess we'd better take both cars,' he told Charles.

'How come?'

'Well, you don't want to have to drive all the way back down here.'

'But if we take just one, then one of us can drive and one can push if we get stuck.'

'Let's take mine, then.'

'But mine's already cleared and dug out.'

'But with mine I could drop you off home and save you the trip back down.'

'But that leaves my car stranded on Singleton Street.'

'We could get it to you after they plowed.'

'And *my* car has its engine warmed!' Charles said.

Was this how they had sounded, all these years? Macon gave a short laugh, but Charles waited intently for his answer. 'Fine, we'll take yours,' Macon told him. They climbed into Charles's VW.

It was true there were a lot of abandoned cars. They sat in no particular pattern, featureless white mounds turned this way and that, so the street resembled a river of drifting boats. Charles dodged expertly between them. He kept a slow, steady speed and talked about Rose's wedding. 'We told her April was too iffy. Better wait, we told her, if she's so set on an outdoor service. But Rose said no, she'll take her chances. She's sure the weather will be perfect.'

A snow-covered jeep in front of them, the only moving vehicle they'd yet encountered, suddenly slurred to one side. Charles passed it smoothly in a long, shallow arc. Mason said, 'Where will they live, anyhow?'

'Why, at Julian's, I suppose.'

'In a singles building?'

'No, he's got another place now, an apartment near the Belvedere.'

'I see,' Macon said. But he had trouble picturing Rose in an apartment—or anywhere, for that matter, if it wasn't her grandparents' house with its egg-and-dart moldings and heavily draped windows.

All through the city people were digging out—tunneling toward their parked cars, scraping off their windshields, shoveling sidewalks. There was something holidaylike about them; they waved to each other and called back and forth. One man, having cleared not only his walk but a section of the street as well, was doing a little soft-shoe dance on the wet concrete, and when Charles and Macon drove through he stopped to shout, 'What are you, crazy? Traveling around in this?'

'I must say you're remarkably calm in view of the situation,' Charles told Macon.

'What situation?'

'Your house, I mean. Water pouring through the ceiling for who knows how long.'

'Oh, that,' Macon said. Yes, at one time he'd have been very upset about that.

By now they were high on North Charles Street, which the plows had already cleared. Macon was struck by the spaciousness here—the buildings set far apart, wide lawns sloping between them. He had never noticed that before. He sat forward to gaze at the side streets. They were still completely white. And just a few blocks over, when Charles turned into Macon's neighborhood, they saw a young girl on skis.

His house looked the same as ever, though slightly dingy in comparison with the snow. They sat in the car a moment studying it, and then Macon said, 'Well, here goes, I guess,' and they climbed out. They could see where Garner Bolt had waded through the yard; they saw the scalloping of footprints where he'd stepped closer to peer in a window. But the sidewalk bore no tracks at all, and Macon found it difficult in his smooth-soled shoes.

The instant he unlocked the door, they heard the water. The living room was filled with a cool, steady, dripping sound, like a greenhouse after the plants have been sprayed. Charles, who was the first to enter, said, 'Oh, my God.' Macon stopped dead in the hallway behind him.

Apparently an upstairs pipe (in that cold little bathroom off Ethan's old room, Macon would bet) had frozen and burst, heaven only knew how long ago, and the water had run and run until it saturated the ceiling and started coming through the plaster. All over the room it was raining. Chunks of plaster had fallen on the furniture, turning it white and splotchy. The floorboards were mottled. The rug, when Macon stepped on it, squelched beneath his feet. He marveled at the thoroughness of the destruction; not a detail had been overlooked. Every ashtray was full of wet flakes and every magazine was sodden. There was a gray smell rising from the upholstery.

'What are you going to *do*?' Charles breathed.

Macon pulled himself together. 'Why, turn off the water main, of course,' he said.

'But your living room!'

Macon didn't answer. His living room was . . . appropriate, was what he wanted to say. Even more appropriate if it had been washed away entirely. (He imagined the house under twelve feet of water, uncannily clear, like a castle at the bottom of a goldfish bowl.)

He went down to the basement and shut off the valve, and then he checked the laundry sink. It was dry. Ordinarily he let the tap run all winter long, a slender stream to keep the pipes from freezing, but this year he hadn't thought of it and neither had his brothers, evidently, when they came to light the furnace.

'Oh, this is terrible, just terrible,' Charles was saying when Macon came back upstairs. But he was in the kitchen now, where there wasn't any problem. He was opening and shutting cabinet doors. 'Terrible. Terrible.'

Macon had no idea what he was going on about. He said, 'Just let me find my boots and we can leave.'

'Leave?'

He thought his boots must be in his closet. He went upstairs to the bedroom. Everything here was so dreary—the naked mattress with its body bag, the dusty mirror, the brittle yellow newspaper folded on the nightstand. He bent to root through the objects on the closet floor. There were his boots, all right, along with some wire hangers and a little booklet of some sort. *A Gardener's Diary, 1976.* He flipped through it. *First lawn-mowing of the spring*, Sarah had written in her compact script. *Forsythia still in bloom.* Macon closed the diary and smoothed the cover and laid it aside.

Boots in hand, he went back downstairs. Charles had returned to the living room; he was wringing out cushions. 'Never mind those,' Macon said. 'They'll just get wet again.'

'Will your insurance cover this?'

'I suppose so.'

'What would they call it? Flood damage? Weather damage?'

'I don't know. Let's get going.'

'You should phone our contractor, Macon. Remember the man who took care of our porch?'

'Nobody lives here anyhow,' Macon said.

Charles straightened, still holding a cushion. 'What's that supposed to mean?' he asked.

'Mean?'

'Are you saying you'll just let this stay?'

'Probably,' Macon told him.

'All soaked and ruined? Nothing done?'

'Oh, well,' Macon said, waving a hand. 'Come along, Charles.'

But Charles hung back, still gazing around the living room. 'Terrible. Even the curtains are dripping. Sarah will feel just terrible.'

'I doubt she'll give it a thought,' Macon said.

He paused on the porch to pull his boots on. They were old and stiff, the kind with metal clasps. He tucked his wet trouser cuffs inside them and then led the way to the street.

Once they were settled in the car, Charles didn't start the engine but sat there, key in hand, and looked soberly at Macon. 'I think it's time we had a talk,' he said.

'What about?'

'I'd like to know what you think you're up to with this Muriel person.'

'Is that what you call her? "This Muriel person"?'

'No one else will tell you,' Charles said. 'They say it's none of their business. But I can't just stand by and watch, Macon. I have to say what I think. How old are you—forty-two? Forty-three now? And she is . . . but more than that, she's not your type of woman.'

'You don't even know her!'

'I know her type.'

'I have to be getting home now, Charles.'

Charles looked down at his key. Then he started the car and pulled into the street, but he didn't drop the subject. 'She's some kind of symptom, Macon! You're not yourself these days and this Muriel person's a symptom. Everybody says so.'

'I'm more myself than I've been my whole life long,' Macon told him.

'What kind of remark is that? It doesn't even make sense!'

'And who is "everybody," anyway?'

'Why, Porter, Rose, me . . .'

'All such experts.'

'We're just worried for you, Macon.'

'Could we switch to some other topic?'

'I had to tell you what I thought,' Charles said.

'Well, fine. You've told me.'

But Charles didn't look satisfied.

The car wallowed back through the slush, with ribbons of bright water trickling down the windshield from the roof. Then out on the main road, it picked up speed. 'Hate to think what all that salt is doing to your underbody,' Macon said.

Charles said, 'I never told you this before, but it's my opinion sex is overrated.'

Macon looked at him.

'Oh, when I was in my teens I was as interested as anyone,' Charles said. 'I mean it occupied my thoughts for every waking moment and all that. But that was just the *idea* of sex, you know? Somehow, the real thing was less . . . I don't mean I'm opposed to it, but it's just not all I expected. For one thing, it's rather messy. And then the weather is such a problem.'

'Weather,' Macon said.

'When it's cold you hate to take your clothes off. When it's hot you're both so sticky. And in Baltimore, it does always seem to be either too cold or too hot.'

'Maybe you ought to consider a change of climate,' Macon said. He was beginning to enjoy himself. 'Do you suppose anyone's done a survey? City by city? Maybe the Businessman's Press could put out some sort of pamphlet.'

'And besides it often leads to children,' Charles said. 'I never really cared much for children. They strike me as disruptive.'

'Well, if that's why you brought this up, forget it,' Macon said. 'Muriel can't have any more.'

Charles gave a little cough. 'That's good to hear,' he said, 'but it's not why I brought it up. I believe what I was trying to say is, I just don't think sex is important enough to ruin your life for.'

'So? Who's ruining his life?'

'Macon, face it. She's not worth it.'

'How can you possibly know that?'

'Can you tell me one unique thing about her?' Charles asked. 'I mean one really special quality, Macon, not something sloppy like "She appreciates me" or "She listens . . ." '

She looks out hospital windows and imagines how the Martians would see us, Macon wanted to say. But Charles wouldn't understand that, so instead he said, 'I'm not such a bargain myself, in case you haven't noticed. I'm kind of, you could say, damaged merchandise. Somebody ought to warn *her* away from *me*, when you get right down to it.'

'That's not true. That's not true at all. As a matter of fact, I imagine her people are congratulating her on her catch.'

'Her catch!'

'Someone to support her. Anyone,' Charles said. 'She'd be lucky to find anyone. Why, she doesn't even speak proper English! She lives in that slummy house, she dresses like some kind of bag lady, she's got that little boy who appears to have hookworm or something—'

'Charles, just shut the hell up,' Macon said.

Charles closed his mouth.

They had reached Muriel's neighborhood by now. They were driving past the stationery factory with its tangled wire fence like old bedsprings. Charles took a wrong turn. 'Let's see, now,' he said, 'where do I . . .'

Macon didn't offer to help.

'Am I heading in the right direction? Or not. Somehow I don't seem to . . .'

They were two short blocks from Singleton Street, but Macon hoped Charles would drive in circles forever. 'Lots of luck,' he said, and he opened the door and hopped out.

'Macon?'

Macon waved and ducked down an alley.

Freedom! Sunlight glinting off blinding white drifts, and children riding sleds and TV trays. Cleared parking spaces guarded with lawn chairs. Throngs of hopeful boys with shovels. And then Muriel's house with its walk still deep in snow, its small rooms smelling of pancakes, its cozy mix of women lounging about in the kitchen. They were drinking cocoa now. Bernice was braiding Claire's hair. Alexander was painting a picture. Muriel kissed Macon hello and squealed at his cold cheeks. 'Come in and get warm! Have some cocoa! Look at Alexander's picture,' she said. 'Don't you love it? Isn't he something? He's a regular da Vinci.'

'Leonardo,' Macon said.

'What?'

'Not da Vinci. For God's sake. It's Leonardo,' he told her. Then he stamped upstairs to change out of his clammy trousers.

15

'I'm sorry I'm so fat,' Macon's seatmate said.

Macon said, 'Oh, er, ah—'

'I know I'm using more than my share of space,' the man told him. 'Do you think I'm not aware of that? Every trip I take, I have to ask the stewardess for a seatbelt extender. I have to balance my lunch on my knees because the tray can't unfold in front of me. Really I ought to purchase two seats but I'm not a wealthy man. I ought to purchase two tickets and not spread all over my fellow passengers.'

'Oh, you're not spreading all over me,' Macon said.

This was because he was very nearly sitting in the aisle, with his knees jutting out to the side so that every passing stewardess ruffled the pages of *Miss MacIntosh*. But he couldn't help feeling touched by the man's great, shiny, despairing face, which was as round as a baby's. 'Name's Lucas Loomis,' the man said, holding out a hand. When Macon shook it, he was reminded of risen bread dough.

'Macon Leary,' Macon told him.

'The stupid thing is,' Lucas Loomis said, 'I travel for a living.'

'Do you.'

'I demonstrate software to computer stores. I'm sitting in an airplane seat six days out of seven sometimes.'

'Well, none of us finds them all that roomy,' Macon said.

'What do you do, Mr Leary?'

'I write guidebooks,' Macon said.

'Is that so? What kind?'

'Oh, guides for businessmen. People just like you, I guess.'

'*Accidental Tourist*,' Mr Loomis said instantly.

'Why, yes.'

'Really? Am I right? Well, what do you know,' Mr Loomis said. 'Look at this.' He took hold of his own lapels, which sat so far in front of him that his arms seemed too short to reach them. 'Gray suit,' he told Macon. 'Just what you recommend. Appropriate for all occasions.' He pointed to the bag at his feet. 'See my luggage? Carry-on. Change of underwear, clean shirt, packet of detergent powder.'

'Well, good,' Macon said. This had never happened to him before.

'You're my hero!' Mr Loomis told him. 'You've improved my trips a hundred percent. You're the one who told me about those springy items that turn into clotheslines.'

'Oh, well, you could have run across those in any drugstore,' Macon said.

'I've stopped relying on hotel laundries; I hardly need to venture into the streets anymore. I tell my wife, I say, you just ask her, I tell her often, I say, "Going with the *Accidental Tourist* is like going in a capsule, a cocoon. Don't forget to pack my *Accidental Tourist*!" I tell her.'

'Well, this is very nice to hear,' Macon said.

'Times I've flown clear to Oregon and hardly knew I'd left Baltimore.'

'Excellent.'

There was a pause.

'Although,' Macon said, 'lately I've been wondering.'

Mr Loomis had to turn his entire body to look at him, like someone encased in a hooded parka.

'I mean,' Macon said, 'I've been out along the West Coast. Updating my U.S. edition. And of course I've covered the West Coast before, Los Angeles and all that; Lord, yes, I knew the place as a child; but this was the first I'd seen of San Francisco. My publisher wanted me to add it in. Have you been to San Francisco?'

'That's where we just now got on the plane,' Mr Loomis reminded him.

'San Francisco is certainly, um, beautiful,' Macon said.

Mr Loomis thought that over.

'Well, so is Baltimore too, of course,' Macon said hastily. 'Oh, no place on earth like Baltimore! But San Francisco, well, I mean it struck me as, I don't know . . .'

'I was born and raised in Baltimore, myself,' Mr Loomis said. 'Wouldn't live anywhere else for the world.'

'No, of course not,' Macon said. 'I just meant—'

'Couldn't pay me to leave it.'

'No, me either.'

'You a Baltimore man?'

'Yes, certainly.'

'No place like it.'

'Certainly isn't,' Macon said.

But a picture came to his mind of San Francisco floating on mist like the Emerald City, viewed from one of those streets so high and steep that you really could hang your head over and hear the wind blow.

He'd left Baltimore on a sleety day with ice coating the airport runways, and he hadn't been gone all that long; but when he returned it was spring. The sun was shining and the trees were tipped with green. It was still fairly cool but he drove with his windows down. The breeze smelled exactly like Vouvray—flowery, with a hint of mothballs underneath.

On Singleton Street, crocuses were poking through the hard squares of dirt in front of basement windows. Rugs and bedspreads flapped in backyards. A whole cache of babies had surfaced. They cruised imperiously in their strollers, propelled by their mothers or by pairs of grandmothers. Old people sat out on the sidewalk in beach chairs and wheelchairs, and groups of men stood about on corners, their hands in their pockets and their posture elaborately casual—the unemployed, Macon imagined, emerging from the darkened living rooms where they'd spent the winter watching TV. He caught snatches of their conversation:

'What's going down, man?'

'Nothing much.'

'What you been up to?'

'Not a whole lot.'

He parked in front of Muriel's house, where Dominick Saddler was working on Muriel's car. The hood was open and Dominick was deep in its innards; all Macon saw was his jeans and his gigantic, ragged sneakers, a band of bare flesh showing above his cowhide belt. On either side of him stood the Butler twins, talking away a mile a minute. 'So she says to us we're grounded—'

'Can't go out with no one till Friday—'

'Takes away our fake i.d.'s—'

'Won't let us answer the phone—'

'We march upstairs and slam our bedroom door, like, just a little slam to let her know what we think of her—'

'And up she comes with a screwdriver and takes our door off its hinges!'

'Hmm,' Dominick said.

Macon rested his bag on the hood and peered down into the engine. 'Car acting up again?' he asked.

The Butler twins said, 'Hey there, Macon,' and Dominick straightened and wiped his forehead with the back of his hand. He was a dark, good-looking boy whose bulging muscles made Macon feel inadequate. 'Damn thing keeps stalling out,' he said.

'How'd Muriel get to work?'

'Had to take the bus.'

Macon was hoping to hear she'd stayed home.

He climbed the steps and unlocked the front door. Just inside, Edward greeted him, squeaking and doing back flips and trying to hold still long enough to be petted. Macon walked through the rest of the house. Clearly, everyone had left in a hurry. The sofa was opened out. (Claire must have had another fight with her folks.) The kitchen table was littered with dishes and no one had put the cream away. Macon did that. Then he took his bag upstairs. Muriel's bed was unmade and her robe was slung across a chair. There was a snarl of hair in the pin tray on her bureau. He picked it up between thumb and index finger and dropped it into the wastebasket. It occurred to him (not for the first time) that the world was divided sharply down the middle: Some lived careful lives and some lived careless lives, and everything that happened could be explained by the difference between them. But he could not have said, not in a million years, why he was so moved by the sight of Muriel's thin quilt trailing across the floor where she must have dragged it when she rose in the morning.

It wasn't quite time for Alexander to come home from school, so he thought he would walk the dog. He put Edward on his leash and let himself out the front door. When he passed the Butler twins again they said, 'Hey, there, Macon,' singsong as ever, while Dominick cursed and reached for a wrench.

The men standing on the corner were discussing a rumor of jobs in Texas. Someone's brother-in-law had found work there. Macon passed with his head lowered, feeling uncomfortably privileged. He skirted a welcome mat that had been scrubbed and set out to dry on the pavement. The women here took spring cleaning seriously, he saw. They shook their dust mops out of upstairs windows; they sat on their sills to polish the panes with crumpled sheets of newspapers. They staggered between houses with borrowed vacuum cleaners, rug machines, and gallon jugs of upholstery shampoo. Macon rounded the block and started home, having paused to let Edward pee against a maple sapling.

Just as he was approaching Singleton Street, whom should he see but Alexander scurrying up ahead. There was no mistaking that stiff little figure with the clumsy backpack. 'Wait!' Alexander was crying. 'Wait for me!' The Ebbetts children, some distance away, turned and called something back. Macon couldn't hear what they said but he knew the tone, all right—that high, mocking chant. 'Nyah-nyah-nyah-NYAH-nyah!' Alexander started running, stumbling over his own shoes. Behind him came another group, two older boys and a girl with red hair, and they began jeering too. Alexander wheeled and looked at them. His face was somehow smaller than usual. 'Go,' Macon told Edward, and he dropped the leash. Edward didn't need any urging. His ears had perked at the sound of Alexander's voice, and now he hurtled after him. The three older children scattered as he flew through them, barking. He drew up short in front of Alexander, and Alexander knelt to hug his neck.

When Macon arrived, he said, 'Are you all right?'

Alexander nodded and got to his feet.

'What was that all about?' Macon asked him.

Alexander said, 'Nothing.'

But when they started walking again, he slipped his hand into Macon's.

Those cool little fingers were so distinct, so particular, so full of character. Macon tightened his grip and felt a pleasant kind of sorrow sweeping through him. Oh, his life had regained all its old perils. He was forced to worry once again about nuclear war and the future of the planet. He often had the same secret, guilty thought that had come to him after Ethan was born: *From this time on I can never be completely happy.*

Not that he was before, of course.

Macon's U.S. edition was going to be five separate pamphlets now, divided geographically, slipcased together so you had to buy all five even if you needed only one. Macon thought this was immoral. He said so when Julian stopped by for the West Coast material. 'What's immoral about it?' Julian asked. He wasn't really paying attention; Macon could see that. He was filing mental notes on Muriel's household, no doubt the real purpose of this unannounced, unnecessary visit. Even though he'd already collected his material, he was wandering around the living room in an abstracted way, first examining a framed school photo of Alexander and then a beaded moccasin that Claire had left on the couch. It was Saturday and the others were in the kitchen, but Macon had no intention of letting Julian meet them.

'It's always immoral to force a person to buy something he doesn't want,' Macon said. 'If he only wants the Midwest, he shouldn't have to buy New England too, for heaven's sake.'

Julian said, 'Is that your friend I hear out there? Is it Muriel?'

'Yes, I suppose it is,' Macon said.

'Aren't you going to introduce us?'

'She's busy.'

'I'd really like to meet her.'

'Why? Hasn't Rose given you a full report?'

'Macon,' Julian said, 'I'm soon going to be a relative of yours.'

'Ah, God.'

'It's only natural I'm interested in knowing her.'

Macon said nothing.

'Besides,' Julian told him, 'I want to invite her to the wedding.'

'You do?'

'So can I talk to her?'

'Oh. Well. I guess so.'

Macon led the way to the kitchen. He felt he'd made a mistake—that having acted so thorny, he'd caused this meeting to seem more important than it was. But Julian, as it happened, was breezy and offhand. 'Hello, ladies,' he said.

They looked up—Muriel, Claire, and Bernice, seated around a sheaf of notebook paper. Macon reeled their names off rapidly but got stuck on Julian's. 'Julian, ah, Edge, my . . .'

'Future brother-in-law,' Julian said.

'My boss.'

'I've come to invite you to the wedding, Muriel. Also your little boy, if—where's your little boy?'

'He's out walking the dog,' Muriel said. 'But he's not too good in churches.'

'This'll be a garden wedding.'

'Well, maybe, then, I don't know . . .'

Muriel was wearing what she called her 'paratrooper look'—a coverall from Sunny's Surplus—and her hair was concealed beneath a wildly patterned silk turban. A ballpoint pen mark slashed across one cheekbone. 'We're entering this contest,' she told Julian. 'Write a country-music song and win a trip for two to Nashville.

We're working on it all together. We're going to call it "Happier Days." '

'Hasn't that already been written?'

'Oh, I hope not. You know how they always have these photographs of couples in magazines? "Mick Jagger and Bianca, in happier days." "Richard Burton and Liz Taylor, in——" '

'Yes, I get it.'

'So this man is talking about his ex-wife. "I knew her in another time and place . . ." '

She sang it right out, in her thin, scratchy voice that gave a sense of distance, like a used-up phonograph record:

> *When we kissed in the rain,*
> *When we shared every pain,*
> *When we both enjoyed happier days.*

'Very catchy,' Julian said, 'but I don't know about "shared every pain." '

'What's wrong with it?'

'I mean, in happier days they had pain?'

'He's right,' Bernice told Muriel.

'Rain, brain, drain,' Julian reflected. ' "When our lives were more sane," "When we used to raise Cain . . ." '

'Let it be, why don't you,' Macon told him.

' "When I hadn't met Jane," "When she didn't know Wayne . . ." '

'Wait!' Bernice said, scribbling furiously.

'I may have tapped some hidden talent here,' Julian told Macon.

'I'll see you to the door,' Macon said.

' "When our love had no stain," "When she wasn't inane . . ." ' Julian said, trailing Macon through the living room. 'Don't forget the wedding!' he called back. He told Macon, 'If she wins, you could cover Nashville free for your next U.S. edition.'

'I think she's planning on taking Bernice,' Macon told him.

' "When we guzzled champagne . . ." ' Julian mused.

'I'll be in touch,' Macon said, 'as soon as I start on the Canada guide.'

'Canada! Aren't you coming to the wedding?'

'Well, that too, of course,' Macon said, opening the door.

'Wait a minute, Macon. What's your hurry? Wait, I want to show you something.'

Julian set down the West Coast material to search his pockets. He pulled out a shiny, colored advertisement. 'Hawaii,' he said.

'Well, I certainly see no point in covering—'

'Not for you; for me! For our honeymoon. I'm taking Rose.'

'Oh, I see.'

'Look,' Julian said. He unfolded the ad. It turned out to be a map—one of those useless maps that Macon detested, with outsized, whimsical drawings of pineapples, palm trees, and hula dancers crowding the apple-green islands. 'I got this from The Travel People Incorporated. Have you heard of them? Are they reliable? They suggested a hotel over here on . . .' He drew a forefinger across the page, hunting down the hotel.

'I know nothing at all about Hawaii,' Macon said.

'Somewhere here . . .' Julian said. Then he gave up, perhaps just at that moment hearing what Macon had told him, and refolded the map. 'She may be exactly what you need,' he said.

'Pardon?'

'This Muriel person.'

'Why does everyone call her—'

'She's not so bad! I don't think your family understands how you're feeling.'

'No, they don't. They really don't,' Macon said. He was surprised that it was Julian, of all people, who saw that.

Although Julian's parting words were, ' "When we stuffed on chow mein . . ." '

Macon shut the door firmly behind him.

He decided to buy Alexander some different clothes. 'How would you like some blue jeans?' he asked. 'How would you like some work shirts? How would you like a cowboy belt with "Budweiser Beer" on the buckle?'

'You serious?'

'Would you wear that kind of thing?'

'Yes! I would! I promise!'

'Then let's go shopping.'

'Is Mama coming?'

'We'll surprise her.'

Alexander put on his spring jacket—a navy polyester blazer that Muriel had just paid a small fortune for. Macon didn't know if she would approve of jeans, which was why he'd waited till she was off buying curtains for a woman in Guilford.

The store he drove to was a Western-wear place where he used to take Ethan. It hadn't changed a bit. Its wooden floorboards creaked, its aisles smelled of leather and new denim. He steered Alexander to the boys' department, where he spun a rack of shirts. How many times had he done this before? It wasn't even painful. Only disorienting, in a way, to see that everything continued no matter what. The student jeans were still stacked according to waist and inseam. The horsey tie pins were still arrayed behind glass. Ethan was dead and gone but Macon was still holding up shirts and asking, 'This one? This one? This one?'

'What I'd really like is T-shirts,' Alexander said.

'T-shirts. Ah.'

'The kind with a sort of stretched-out neck. And jeans with raggedy bottoms.'

'Well, that you have to do for yourself,' Macon said. 'You have to break them in.'

'I don't want to look new.'

'Tell you what. Everything we buy, we'll wash about twenty times before you wear it.'

'But nothing *pre*washed,' Alexander said.

'No, no.'

'Only nerds wear prewashed.'

'Right.'

Alexander chose several T-shirts, purposely too big, along with an assortment of jeans because he wasn't sure of his size. Then he went off to try everything on. 'Shall I come with you?' Macon asked.

'I can do it myself.'

'Oh. All right.'

That was familiar, too.

Alexander disappeared into one of the stalls and Macon went on a tour of the men's department. He tried on a leather cowboy hat but took it off immediately. Then he went back to the stall. 'Alexander?'

'Huh?'

'How's it going?'

'Okay.'

In the space below the door, Macon saw Alexander's shoes and his trouser cuffs. Evidently he hadn't got around to putting on the jeans yet.

Someone said, 'Macon?'

He turned and found a woman in a trim blond pageboy, her wrap skirt printed with little blue whales. 'Yes,' he said.

'Laurel Canfield. Scott's mother, remember?'

'Of course,' Macon said, shaking her hand. Now he caught sight of Scott, who had been in Ethan's class at school—an unexpectedly tall, gawky boy lurking at his mother's elbow with an armload of athletic socks. 'Why, Scott. Nice to see you,' Macon said.

Scott flushed and said nothing. Laurel Canfield said, 'It's nice to see *you*. Are you doing your spring shopping?'

'Oh, well, ah—'

He looked toward the stall. Now Alexander's trousers were slumped around his ankles. 'I'm helping the son of a friend,' he explained.

'We've just been buying out the sock department.'

'Yes, I see you have.'

'Seems every other week I find Scott's run through his socks again; you know how they are at this age—'

She stopped herself. She looked horrified. She said, 'Or, rather . . .'

'Yes, certainly!' Macon said. 'Amazing, isn't it?' He felt so embarrassed for her that he was pleased, at first, to see another familiar face behind her. Then he realized whose it was. There stood his mother-in-law. 'Why!' he said. Was she still Mother Sidey? *Mrs* Sidey? Who, for God's sake?

Luckily, it turned out that Laurel Canfield knew her too. 'Paula Sidey,' she said. 'I haven't seen you since last year's Hunt Cup.'

'Yes, I've been away,' Mrs Sidey told her, and then she dropped her lids somewhat, as if drawing a curtain, before saying, 'Macon.'

'How are you?' Macon said.

She was flawlessly groomed, industriously tended—a blue-haired woman in tailored slacks and a turtleneck. He used to worry that Sarah would age the same way, develop the same brittle carapace, but now he found himself admiring Mrs Sidey's resolve. 'You're looking well,' he told her.

'Thank you,' she said, touching her hairdo. 'I suppose you're here for your spring wardrobe.'

'Oh, Macon's helping a friend!' Laurel Canfield caroled. She was so chirpy, all of a sudden, that Macon suspected she'd just now recalled Mrs Sidey's relationship to him. She looked toward Alexander's stall. Alexander was in his socks now. One sock rose and vanished, stepping into a flood of blue denim. 'Isn't shopping for boys so difficult?' she said.

'I wouldn't know,' Mrs Sidey said. 'I never had one. I'm here for the denim skirts.'

'Oh, the skirts, well, I notice they're offering a—'

'What friend are you helping to buy for?' Mrs Sidey asked Macon.

Macon didn't know what to tell her. He looked toward the stall. If only Alexander would just stay hidden forever, he thought. How to explain this scrawny little waif, this poor excuse of a child who could never hold a candle to the real child?

Contrary as always, Alexander chose that moment to step forth.

He wore an oversized T-shirt that slipped a bit off one shoulder, as if he'd just emerged from some rough-and-tumble game. His jeans were comfortably baggy. His face, Macon saw, had somehow filled out in the past few weeks without anybody's noticing; and his hair—which Macon had started cutting at home—had lost that shaved prickliness and grown thick and floppy.

'I look *wonderful*!' Alexander said.

Macon turned to the women and said, 'Actually, I find shopping for boys is a pleasure.'

16

— There is no sound more peaceful than rain on the roof, if you're safe asleep in someone else's house. Macon heard the soft pattering; he heard Muriel get up to close a window. She crossed his vision like the gleam of headlights crossing a ceiling, white and slim and watery in a large plain slip from Goodwill Industries. She shut the window and the stillness dropped over him and he went back to sleep.

But in the morning his first thought was, *Oh, no! Rain! On Rose's wedding day!*

He got up, careful not to wake Muriel, and looked out. The sky was bright but flat, the color of oyster shells—not a good sign. The scrawny little dogwood in back was dripping from every twig and bud. Next door, Mr Butler's ancient heap of scrap lumber had grown several shades darker.

Macon went downstairs, tiptoeing through the living room where Claire lay snoring in a tangle of blankets. He fixed a pot of coffee and then called Rose on the kitchen phone. She answered instantly, wide awake. 'Are you moving the wedding indoors?' he asked her.

'We've got too many guests to move it indoors.'

'Why? How many are coming?'

'Everyone we've ever known.'

'Good grief, Rose.'

'Never mind, it will clear.'

'But the grass is all wet!'

'Wear galoshes,' she told him. She hung up.

Since she'd met Julian she'd grown so airy, Macon thought. So flippant. Lacking in depth.

She was right about the weather, though. By afternoon there was a weak, pale sun. Muriel decided to wear the short-sleeved dress she'd planned on, but maybe with a shawl tossed over her shoulders. She wanted Alexander to put on a suit—he did have one, complete with waistcoat. He protested, though, and so did Macon. 'Jeans and a good white shirt. That's plenty,' Macon told her.

'Well, if you're sure.'

Lately, she'd been deferring to him about Alexander. She had finally given in on the question of sneakers and she'd stopped policing his diet. Contrary to her predictions, Alexander's arches did not fall flat and he was not overtaken by raging eczema. At worst, he suffered a mild skin rash now and then.

The wedding was set for three o'clock. Around two thirty they started out, proceeding self-consciously toward Macon's car. It was a Saturday and no one else in the neighborhood was so dressed up. Mr Butler was standing on a ladder with a hammer and a sack of nails. Rafe Daggett was taking his van apart. The Indian woman was hosing down a glowing threadbare carpet that she'd spread across the sidewalk, and then she turned off the water and lifted the hem of her sari and stamped around so the carpet radiated little bursts of droplets. Every passing car, it seemed, labored under a top-heavy burden of mattresses and patio furniture, reminding Macon of those ants who scuttle back to their nests with loads four times their own size.

'I think I'm supposed to be the best man,' Macon told Muriel after he'd started driving.

'You didn't mention that!'

'And Charles is giving her away.'

'It's a real wedding, then,' Muriel said. 'Not just two people standing up together.'

'That's what Rose said she wanted.'

'I wouldn't do it like that at all,' Muriel said. She glanced toward the rear and said, 'Alexander, quit kicking my seat. You're about to drive me crazy. No,' she said, facing forward, 'if I was to marry, know what I'd do? Never tell a soul. Act like I'd been married for years. Slip off somewheres to a justice of the peace and come back like nothing had happened and make out like I'd been married all along.'

'This is Rose's first time, though,' Macon told her.

'Yes, but even so, people can say, "It sure *took* you long enough." I can hear my mother now; that's what she'd say for certain. "Sure *took* you long enough. I thought you'd never get around to it," is what she'd say. If I was ever to marry.'

Macon braked for a traffic light.

'If I was ever to decide to marry,' Muriel said.

He glanced over at her and was struck by how pretty she looked, with the color high in her cheeks and the splashy shawl flung around her shoulders. Her spike-heeled shoes had narrow, shiny ankle straps. He never could figure out why ankle straps were so seductive.

The first person they saw when they arrived was Macon's mother. For some reason it hadn't occurred to Macon that Alicia would be invited to her daughter's wedding, and when she opened the front door it took him a second to place her. She was looking so different, for one thing. She had dyed her hair a dark tomato red. She wore a long white caftan trimmed with vibrant bands of satin, and when she reached up to hug him a whole culvert of metal bangles clattered and slid down her left arm. 'Macon, dear!' she said. She smelled of bruised gardenias. 'And who may this be?' she asked, peering past him.

'Oh, um, I'd like you to meet Muriel Pritchett. And Alexander, her son.'

'Really?'

A politely inquisitive look remained on her face. Evidently no one had filled her in. (Or else she hadn't bothered to listen.) 'Well, since I seem to be the maître d',' she said, 'I'll show you out back where the bride and groom are.'

'Rose is not in hiding?'

'No, she says she doesn't see the logic in missing her own wedding,' Alicia said, leading them toward the rear of the house. 'Muriel, have you known Macon long?'

'Oh, kind of.'

'He's very stuffy,' Alicia said confidingly. 'All my children are. They get it from the Leary side.'

'I think he's nice,' Muriel said.

'Oh, *nice*, yes. All very well and good,' Alicia said, throwing Macon a look he couldn't read. She had linked arms with Muriel; she was always so physical. The trim on her caftan nearly matched Muriel's shawl. Macon had a sudden appalling thought: Maybe in his middle age he was starting to choose his mother's style of person, as if concluding that Alicia—silly, vain, annoying woman—might have the right answers after all. But no. He put the thought away from him. And Muriel slipped free of Alicia's arm. 'Alexander? Coming?' she asked.

They stepped through the double doors of the sun porch. The backyard was full of pastels—Rose's old ladies in pale dresses, daffodils set everywhere in buckets, forsythia in full bloom along the alley. Dr Grauer, Rose's minister, stepped forward and shook Macon's hand. 'Aha! The best man,' he said, and behind him came Julian in black—not his color. His nose was peeling. It must be boating season again. He put a gold ring in Macon's palm and said, 'Like for you to have this.' For a moment Macon imagined he was really meant to *have* it. Then he said, 'Oh, yes, the ring,' and dropped it in his pocket.

'I can't believe I'm finally getting a son-in-law,' Alicia told Julian. 'All I've ever had is daughter-in-laws.'

'Daughters,' Macon said automatically.

'No, daughter-in-laws.'

'*Daughters*-in-law, Mother.'

'And didn't manage to keep them long, either,' Alicia said.

When Macon was small, he used to worry that his mother was teaching him the wrong names for things. 'They call this corduroy,' she'd said, buttoning his new coat, and he had thought, *But do they really?* Funny word, in fact, corduroy. Very suspicious. How could he be sure that other people weren't speaking a whole different language out there? He'd examined his mother distrustfully—her foolish fluff of curls and her flickery, unsteady eyes.

Now here came Porter's children, the three of them sticking close together; and behind them June, their mother. Wasn't it unusual to invite your brother's ex-wife to your wedding? Particularly when she was big as a barn with another man's baby. But she seemed to be enjoying herself. She pecked Macon on the cheek and cocked her head appraisingly at Muriel. 'Kids, this is Alexander,' Macon said. He was hoping against hope that they'd all just fall in together somehow and be friends, which of course didn't happen. Porter's children eyed Alexander sullenly and said nothing. Alexander knotted his fists in his pockets. June told Julian, 'Your bride is looking just radiant,' and Julian said, 'Yes, isn't she,' but when Macon located Rose he thought she looked tense and frayed, as most brides do if people would only admit it. She wore a white dress, mid-calf length but very simple, and a little puff of lace or net or something on her head. She was talking to their hardware man. And yes, there was the girl who cashed their checks at the Mercantile Bank, and over next to Charles was the family dentist. Macon thought of *Mary Poppins*—those late-night adventures he used to read to Ethan, where all the tradespeople showed up behaving nothing like their daytime selves.

'I'm not sure if there's been any research on this,' Charles was telling the dentist, 'but have you ever tried polishing your teeth with a T-shirt after flossing?'

'Er . . .'

'A plain cotton T-shirt. One hundred percent cotton. I think you're going to be impressed when I have my next checkup. See, my theory is—'

Muriel and June were discussing Caesareans. Julian was asking Alicia if she'd ever sailed the Intracoastal Waterway. Mrs Barrett was telling the mailman that Leary Metals used to make the handsomest stamped tin ceilings in Baltimore.

And Sarah was talking to Macon about the weather.

'Yes, I worried when it rained last night,' Macon said. Or he said something; something or other . . .

He was looking at Sarah. Really he was consuming her: her burnished curls and her round, sweet face, and the dusting of powder on the down along her jawline.

'How have you been, Macon?' she asked him.

'I've been all right.'

'Are you pleased about the wedding?'

'Well,' he said, 'I am if Rose is, I guess. Though I can't help feeling . . . well, Julian. You know.'

'Yes, I know. But there's more to him than you think. He might be a very good choice.'

When she stood in this kind of sunlight her eyes were so clear that it seemed you could see to the backs of them. He knew that from long ago. They might have been his own eyes; they were so familiar. He said, 'How have *you* been?'

'I've been fine.'

'Well. Good.'

'I know that you're living with someone,' she told him in a steady voice.

'Ah! Yes, actually I . . . yes. I am.'

She knew who it was, too, because she looked past him then at Muriel and Alexander. But all she said was, 'Rose told me when she invited me.'

He said, 'How about you?'

'Me?'

'Are you living with anyone?'

'Not really.'

Rose came over and touched their arms, which was unlike her. 'We're ready now,' she said. She told Macon, 'Sarah's my matron of honor, did I happen to mention that?'

'No, you didn't,' Macon said.

Then he and Sarah followed her to a spot beneath a tulip tree, where Julian and Dr Grauer were waiting. There was some kind of makeshift altar there—some little table or something covered with a cloth; Macon didn't pay much attention. He stood beside the minister and fingered the ring in his pocket. Sarah stood across from him, looking gravely into his face.

It all felt so natural.

17

Muriel said, 'I never told you this, but a while before I met you I was dating somebody else.'

'Oh? Who was that?' Macon asked.

'He was a customer at the Rapid-Eze Copy Center. He brought me his divorce papers to copy and we started having this conversation and ended up going out together. His divorce was awful. Really messy. His wife had been two-timing him. He said he didn't think he could ever trust a woman again. It was months before he would spend the night, even; he didn't like going to sleep when a woman was in the same room. But bit by bit I changed all that. He relaxed. He got to be a whole different man. Moved in with me and took over the bills, paid off all I still owed Alexander's doctor. We started talking about getting married. Then he met an airline stewardess and eloped with her within the week.'

'I see,' Macon said.

'It was like I had, you know, cured him, just so he could elope with another woman.'

'Well,' he said.

'You wouldn't do anything like that, would you, Macon?'

'Who, me?'

'Would you elope with someone else? Would you see someone else behind my back?'

'Oh, Muriel, of course not,' he told her.

'Would you leave me and go home to your wife?'

'What are you talking about?'

'Would you?'

'Don't be silly,' he said.

She cocked her head and considered him. Her eyes were alert and bright and knowing, like the eyes of some small animal.

It was a rainy Tuesday morning and Edward, who was squeamish about rain, insisted he didn't need to go out, but Macon took him anyway. While he was waiting in the backyard beneath his umbrella, he saw a young couple walking down the alley. They caught his attention because they walked so slowly, as if they didn't realize they were getting wet. The boy was tall and frail, in ragged jeans and a soft white shirt. The girl wore a flat straw hat with ribbons down the back and a longish, limp cotton dress. They swung hands, looking only at each other. They came upon a tricycle and they separated to walk around it; only instead of simply walking the girl did a little sort of dance step, spinning her skirt out, and the boy spun too and laughed and took her hand again.

Edward finally, finally peed, and Macon followed him back into the house. He set his umbrella in the kitchen sink and squatted to dry Edward off with an old beach towel. He rubbed briskly at first, and then more slowly. Then he stopped but remained on the floor, the towel bunched in his hands, the tin-can smell of wet dog rising all around him.

When he'd asked Sarah whether she was living with anyone, and Sarah had said, 'Not really,' what exactly had she meant by that?

The rain stopped and they put Edward on his leash and went out shopping. Muriel needed bedroom slippers with feathers on them. 'Red. High-heeled. Pointy-toed,' she said.

'Goodness. Whatever for?' Macon asked her.

'I want to clop around the house in them on Sunday mornings. Can't you just see it? I wish I smoked cigarettes. I wish Alexander wasn't allergic to smoke.'

Yes, he could see it, as a matter of fact. 'In your black-and-gold kimono,' he said.

'Exactly.'

'But I don't believe they sell those feathered slippers anymore.'

'In thrift shops they do.'

'Oh. Right.'

Lately, Macon had begun to like thrift shops himself. In the usual sea of plastic he had found, so far, a folding box-wood carpenter's rule, an ingenious wheeled cookie cutter that left no waste space between cookies, and a miniature brass level for Alexander's toolbox.

The air outside was warm and watery. Mrs Butler was propping up the squashed geraniums that flopped in the white-washed tire in her yard. Mrs Patel—out of her luminous sari for once, clumsy and unromantic in tight, bulgy Calvin Klein jeans—was sweeping the puddles off her front steps. And Mrs Saddler stood in front of the hardware store waiting for it to open. 'I don't guess you'd have seen Dominick,' she said to Muriel.

'Not lately.'

'Last night he never came home,' Mrs Saddler said. 'That boy just worries the daylights out of me. He's not what you would call bad,' she told Macon, 'but he's worrisome, know what I mean? When he's at home he's so much at home, those big noisy boots all over the place, but then when he's away he's so much away. You wouldn't believe how the house feels: just empty. Just echoing.'

'He'll be back,' Muriel said. 'Tonight's his turn to have the car.'

'Oh, and when he's out with the car it's worst of all,' Mrs Saddler said. 'Then every siren I hear, I wonder if it's Dommie. I know how he screeches round corners! I know those fast girls he goes out with!'

They left her still standing there, distractedly fingering her coin purse, although the hardware-store owner had unlocked his door by now and was cranking down his awnings.

Outside a shop called Re-Runs, they ordered Edward to stay. He obeyed, looking put upon, while they went in. Muriel sifted through stacks of curled, brittle shoes that had hardened into the shapes of other people's feet. She shucked off her own shoes and stepped into a pair of silver evening sandals. 'What do you think?' she asked Macon.

'I thought you were looking for slippers.'

'But what do you think of these?'

'I can live without them,' he said.

He was feeling bored because Re-Runs carried nothing but clothes.

Muriel abandoned the shoes and they went next door to Garage Sale Incorporated. Macon tried to invent a need for a rusty metal Rolodex file he found in a heap of tire chains. Could he use it for his guidebooks in some way? And make it tax-deductible. Muriel picked up a tan vinyl suitcase with rounded edges; it reminded Macon of a partly sucked caramel. 'Should I get this?' she asked.

'I thought you wanted slippers.'

'But for travel.'

'Since when do you travel?'

'I know where you're going next,' she said. She came closer to him, both hands clutching the suitcase handle. She looked like a very young girl at a bus stop, say, or out hitching a ride on the highway. 'I wanted to ask if I could come with you.'

'To Canada?'

'I mean the next place after that. France.'

He set down the Rolodex. (Mention of France always depressed him.)

'Julian *said*!' she reminded him. 'He said it's getting to be time to go to France again.'

'You know I can't afford to bring you.'

Muriel replaced the suitcase and they left the shop. 'But just this once,' she said, hurrying along beside him. 'It wouldn't cost much!'

Macon retrieved Edward's leash and motioned him up. 'It would cost a mint,' he said, 'not to mention that you'd have to miss work.'

'No, I wouldn't. I've quit.'

He looked over at her. 'Quit?'

'Well, at the Meow-Bow. Then things like George and the dog training I'll just rearrange; if I was to travel I could just—'

'You quit the Meow-Bow?'

'So what?'

He couldn't explain the sudden weight that fell on him.

'It's not like it really paid much,' Muriel said. 'And you do buy most of the groceries now and help me with the rent and all; it's not like I needed the money. Besides, it took so much time! Time I could spend with you and Alexander! Why, I was coming home nights literally dead with exhaustion, Macon.'

They passed Methylene's Beauty Salon, an insurance agency, a paint-stripping shop. Edward gave an interested glance at a large, jowly tomcat basking on the hood of a pickup.

'Figuratively,' Macon said.

'Huh?'

'You were *figuratively* dead with exhaustion. Jesus, Muriel, you're so imprecise. You're so sloppy. And how could you quit your job like that? How could you just assume like that? You never even warned me!'

'Oh, don't make such a big deal about it,' Muriel said.

They arrived at her favorite shop—a nameless little hole in the wall with a tumble of dusty hats in the window. Muriel started through the door but Macon stayed where he was. 'Aren't you coming in?' she asked him.

'I'll wait here.'

'But it's the place with all the gadgets!'

He said nothing. She sighed and disappeared.

Seeing her go was like shucking off a great, dragging burden.

He squatted to scratch behind Edward's ears, and then he rose and studied a sun-bleached election poster as if it held some fascinating coded message. Two black women passed him, pulling wire carts full of laundry. 'It was just as warm as this selfsame day I'm speaking to you but she wore a very very fur coat . . .'

'May-con.'

He turned toward the door of the shop.

'Oh, Maay-con!'

He saw a mitten, one of those children's mittens designed to look like a puppet. The palm was a red felt mouth that widened to squeak, 'Macon, *please* don't be angry with Muriel.'

Macon groaned.

'Come into this nice store with her,' the puppet urged.

'Muriel, I think Edward's getting restless now.'

'There's lots of things to buy here! Pliers and wrenches and T-squares . . . There's a silent hammer.'

'What?'

'A hammer that doesn't make a sound. You can pound in nails in the dead of night.'

'Listen—' Macon said.

'There's a magnifying glass all cracked and broken, and when you look at broken things through the lens you'd swear they'd turned whole again.'

'Really, Muriel.'

'I'm not Muriel! I'm Mitchell Mitten! Macon, don't you know Muriel can always take care of herself?' the puppet asked him. 'Don't you know she could find another job tomorrow, if she wanted? So come inside! Come along! There's a pocketknife here with its own whetstone blade.'

'Oh, for Lord's sake,' Macon said.

But he gave a grudging little laugh.

And went on inside.

Over the next few days she kept bringing up France again and again. She sent him an anonymous letter pasted together from magazine print: *Don't FoRget tO BUY plANe Ticket for MuRiel.* (And the telltale magazine—with little blocks clipped out of its pages—still lay on the kitchen table.) She asked him to get her her keys from her purse and when he opened her purse he found photographs, two slick colored squares on thin paper showing Muriel's eyes at half mast. Passport photos, plainly. She must have meant for him to see them; she was watching him so intently. But all he did was drop her keys in her palm without comment.

He had to admire her. Had he ever known such a fighter? He went grocery shopping with her unusually late one evening, and just as they were crossing a shadowed area a boy stepped forth from a doorway. 'Give over all what you have in your purse,' he told Muriel. Macon was caught off guard; the boy was hardly more than a child. He froze, hugging the sack of groceries. But Muriel said, 'The hell I will!' and swung her purse around by its strap and clipped the boy in the jaw. He lifted a hand to his face. 'You get on home this instant or you'll be sorry you were ever born,' Muriel told him. He slunk away, looking back at her with a puzzled expression.

When Macon had caught his breath again, he told Muriel she was a fool. 'He might have had a gun, for all you knew,' he said. 'Anything might have happened! Kids show less mercy than grown-ups; you can see that any day in the papers.'

'Well, it turned out fine, didn't it?' Muriel asked. 'What are you so mad at?'

He wasn't sure. He supposed he might be mad at himself. He had done nothing to protect her, nothing strong or chivalrous. He hadn't thought as fast as she had or thought at all, in fact. While Muriel . . . why, Muriel hadn't even seemed surprised. She might have strolled down that street expecting a neighbor here, a stray dog there, a holdup just beyond—all equally part of life. He felt awed by her, and diminished. Muriel just walked on, humming 'Great Speckled Bird' as if nothing particular had happened.

'I don't think Alexander's getting a proper education,' he said to her one evening.

'Oh, he's okay.'

'I asked him to figure what change they'd give back when we bought the milk today, and he didn't have the faintest idea. He didn't even know he'd have to subtract.'

'Well, he's only in second grade,' Muriel said.

'I think he ought to switch to a private school.'

'Private schools cost money.'

'So? I'll pay.'

She stopped flipping the bacon and looked over at him. 'What are you saying?' she asked.

'Pardon?'

'What are you saying, Macon? Are you saying you're committed?'

Macon cleared his throat. He said, 'Committed.'

'Alexander's got ten more years of school ahead of him. Are you saying you'll be around for all ten years?'

'Um . . .'

'I can't just put him in a school and take him out again with every passing whim of yours.'

He was silent.

'Just tell me this much,' she said. 'Do you picture us getting married sometime? I mean when your divorce comes through?'

He said, 'Oh, well, marriage, Muriel . . .'

'You don't, do you. You don't know *what* you want. One minute you like me and the next you don't. One minute you're ashamed to be seen with me and the next you think I'm the best thing that ever happened to you.'

He stared at her. He had never guessed that she read him so clearly.

'You think you can just drift along like this, day by day, no plans,' she said. 'Maybe tomorrow you'll be here, maybe you won't. Maybe you'll just go on back to Sarah. Oh yes! I saw you at Rose's wedding. Don't think I didn't see how you and Sarah looked at each other.'

Macon said, 'All I'm saying is—'

'All *I'm* saying,' Muriel told him, 'is take care what you promise my son. Don't go making him promises you don't intend to keep.'

'But I just want him to learn to subtract!' he said.

She didn't answer, and so the last word rang in the air for moments afterward. Subtract. A flat, sharp, empty sound that dampened Macon's spirits.

At supper she was too quiet; even Alexander was quiet, and excused himself the minute he'd finished his BLT. Macon, though, hung around the kitchen. Muriel was running a sinkful of water. He said, 'Shall I dry?' Without any sort of warning, she whirled and flung a wet sponge in his face. Macon said, 'Muriel?'

'Just get out!' she shouted, tears spiking her lashes, and she turned away again and plunged her hands into water so hot that it steamed. Macon retreated. He went into the living room where Alexander was watching TV, and Alexander moved over on the couch to give him space. He didn't say anything, but Macon could tell he'd heard from the way he tensed at each clatter in the kitchen. After a while the clatters died down. Macon and Alexander looked at each other. There was a silence; a single murmuring voice. Macon rose and returned to the kitchen, walking more quietly than usual and keeping a weather eye out, the way a cat creeps back after it's been dumped from someone's lap.

Muriel was talking on the phone with her mother. Her voice was gay and chirpy but just a shade thicker than usual, as if she were recovering from a cold. 'So anyhow,' she said, 'I ask what kind of trouble her dog is giving her and the lady's like, "Oh, no trouble," so I ask her, "Well, what's his problem, then?" and the lady's like, "No real problem." I say, "Ma'am. You must have called me here for some reason." She says, "Oh. Well. That." She says, "Actually," she says, "I was wondering about when he makes." I say, "Makes?"

She says, "Yes, when he makes number one. He makes like little girl dogs do, he doesn't lift his leg." I say to her, "Now let me see if I've got this straight. You have called me here to teach your dog to lift his leg when he tinkles." '

Her free hand kept flying out while she talked, as if she imagined her mother could see her. Macon came up behind her and put his arms around her, and she leaned back against him. 'Oh, there's never a dull moment, I tell you,' she said into the phone.

That night he dreamed he was traveling in a foreign country, only it seemed to be a medley of all the countries he'd ever been to and even some he hadn't. The sterile vast spaces of Charles de Gaulle airport chittered with those tiny birds he'd seen inside the terminal at Brussels; and when he stepped outdoors he was in Julian's green map of Hawaii with native dancers, oversized, swaying near the dots that marked various tourist attractions. Meanwhile his own voice, neutral and monotonous, murmured steadily: *In Germany the commercial traveler must be punctual for all appointments, in Switzerland he should be five minutes early, in Italy delays of several hours are not uncommon . . .*

He woke. It was pitch dark, but through the open window he heard distant laughter, a strain of music, faint cheers as if some sort of game were going on. He squinted at the clock radio: three thirty. Who would be playing a game at this hour? And on this street—this worn, sad street where nothing went right for anyone, where the men had dead-end jobs or none at all and the women were running to fat and the children were turning out badly. But another cheer went up, and someone sang a line from a song. Macon found himself smiling. He turned toward Muriel and closed his eyes; he slept dreamlessly the rest of the night.

The mailman rang the doorbell and presented a long, tube-shaped package addressed to Macon. 'What's this?' Macon asked. He returned to the living room, frowning down at the label. Muriel was reading a paperback book called *Beauty Tips from the Stars*. She glanced up and said, 'Why not open it and find out.'

'Oh? Is this some of your doing?'

She only turned a page.

Another plea for the France trip, he supposed. He pulled off the tape on one end and shook the package till a cylinder of glossy paper slid out. When he unrolled it, he found a full-color photo of two puppies in a basket, with DR MACK'S PET-VITES above it and a calendar for January below it.

'I don't understand,' he said to Muriel.

She turned another page.

'Why would you send me a calendar for a year that's half gone?'

'Maybe there's something written on it,' she told him.

He flipped through February, March, April. Nothing there. May. Then June: a scribble of red ink across a Saturday. '*Wedding*,' he read out. 'Wedding? Whose wedding?'

'Ours?' she asked him.

'Oh, Muriel . . .'

'You'll be separated a year then, Macon. You'll be able to get your divorce.'

'But, Muriel—'

'I always did want to have a June wedding.'

'Muriel, please, I'm not ready for this! I don't think I ever will be. I mean I don't think marriage ought to be as common as it is; I really believe it ought to be the exception to the rule; oh, perfect couples could marry, maybe, but who's a perfect couple?'

'You and Sarah, I suppose,' Muriel said.

The name brought Sarah's calm face, round as a daisy.

'No, no . . .' he said weakly.

'You're so selfish!' Muriel shouted. 'You're so self-centered! You've got all these fancy reasons for never doing a single thing I want!'

Then she flung down her book and ran upstairs.

Macon heard the cautious, mouselike sounds of Alexander as he tiptoed around the kitchen fixing himself a snack.

Muriel's sister Claire arrived on the doorstep with a suitcase spilling clothes and her eyes pink with tears. 'I'm never speaking to Ma again,' she told them. She pushed past them into the house. 'You want to know what happened? Well, I've been dating this guy, see: Claude McEwen. Only I didn't let on to Ma, you know how she's scared I'll turn out like Muriel did, and so last night when he came for me I jumped into his car and she happened to catch sight of me from the window, noticed he had a bumper sticker reading EDGEWOOD. That's because he used to go to a high school called Edgewood Prep in Delaware, but Ma thought it was Edgewood Arsenal and therefore he must be an Army man. So anyhow, this morning I get up and there she is fit to be tied, says, "I know what you've been up to! Out all hours last night with the General!" and

I say, "Who? The what?" but there's never any stopping her once she gets started. She tells me I'm grounded for life and can't ever see the General again or she'll have him hauled up for court-martial and all his stars ripped off his uniform, so quick as a wink I pack up my clothes . . .'

Macon, listening absently while Edward sighed at his feet, had a sudden view of his life as rich and full and astonishing. He would have liked to show it off to someone. He wanted to sweep out an arm and say, 'See?'

But the person he would have liked to show it to was Sarah.

Rose and Julian were back from their honeymoon; they were giving a family supper and Macon and Muriel were invited. Macon bought a bottle of very good wine as a hostess gift. He set the bottle on the counter, and Muriel came along and said, 'What's this?'

'It's wine for Rose and Julian.'

'Thirty-six dollars and ninety-nine cents!' she said, examining the sticker.

'Yes, well, it's French.'

'I didn't know a wine *could* cost thirty-six ninety-nine.'

'I figured since, you know, this'll be our first visit to their apartment . . .'

'You sure do think a lot of your family,' Muriel said.

'Yes, of course.'

'You never bought *me* any wine.'

'I didn't know you wanted any; you told me it makes your teeth feel rough.'

She didn't argue with that.

Later that day he happened to notice that the bottle had been moved. And was opened. And was half emptied. The cork lay beside it, still impaled on the corkscrew. A cloudy little juice glass gave off the smell of grapes. Macon called, 'Muriel?'

'What,' she answered from the living room.

He went to the living room doorway. She was watching a ball game with Alexander. He said, 'Muriel, have you been drinking that wine I bought?'

'Yes.'

He said, 'Why, Muriel?'

'Oh, I just had this irresistible urge to try it out,' she said.

Then she looked at him with slitted eyes, tilting her chin. He felt she was challenging him to take some action, but he said nothing. He picked up his car keys and went out to buy another bottle.

Macon felt shy about attending this dinner, as if Rose had turned into a stranger. He took longer than usual dressing, unable to decide between two shirts, and Muriel seemed to be having some trouble too. She kept putting on outfits and taking them off; brightly colored fabrics began to mount on the bed and on the floor all around it. 'Oh, Lord, I wish I was just a totally nother person,' she sighed. Macon, concentrating on tying his tie, said nothing. Her baby photo grinned out at him from the frame of the mirror. He happened to notice the date on the border: AUG 60. Nineteen sixty.

When Muriel was two years old, Macon and Sarah were already engaged to be married.

Downstairs, Dominick Saddler was sitting on the couch with Alexander. 'Now this here is your paste wax,' he was saying. He held up a can. 'You never want to polish a car with anything but paste wax. And here we have a diaper. Diapers make real good rags because they don't shed hardly no lint. I generally buy a dozen at a time from Sears and Roebuck. And chamois skins: well, you know chamois skins. So what you do is, you get yourself these here supplies and a case of good beer and a girl, and you head on out to Loch Raven. Then you park in the sun and you take off your shirt and you and the girl start to polishing. Ain't no sweeter way that I know of to use up a spring afternoon.'

Dominick's version of a bedtime story, Macon supposed. He was baby-sitting tonight. (The Butler twins had dates, and Claire was out with the General. As everybody referred to him now.) In payment, Muriel's car would be Dominick's to use for a week; mere money would never have persuaded him. He slouched next to Alexander with the diaper spread over one knee, muscles bulging under a T-shirt that read WEEKEND WARRIOR. A Greek sailor cap was tipped back on his head with a Judas Priest button pinned above the visor. Alexander looked enthralled.

Muriel came tapping down the stairs; she arrived craning her neck to see if her slip showed. 'Is this outfit okay?' she asked Macon.

'It's very nice,' he said, which was true, although it was also totally unlike her. Evidently, she had decided to take Rose for her model. She had pulled her hair back in a low bun and she wore a slim gray dress with shoulder pads. Only her spike-heeled sandals seemed her own; probably she didn't possess any shoes so sensible as Rose's schoolgirl flats. 'I want you to tell me if there's anything not right,' she said to Macon. 'Anything you think is tacky.'

'Not a thing,' Macon assured her.

She kissed Alexander, leaving a dark red mark on his cheek. She made one last survey in the mirror beside the front door, meanwhile calling, 'Don't let him stay up too late, now, Dommie; don't let him watch anything scary on TV—'

Macon said, '*Muriel.*'

'I look like the wrath of God.'

The Leary children had been raised to believe that when an invitation involved a meal, the guests should arrive exactly on time. Never mind that they often caught their hostess in curlers; they went on doing what they were taught. So Macon pressed the buzzer in the lobby at precisely six twenty-seven, and Porter and Charles joined them in front of the elevator. They both told Muriel it was nice to see her. Then they rode upward in a gloomy silence, eyes fixed on the numbers over the door. Charles carried a potted jade tree, Porter another bottle of wine.

'Isn't this exciting?' Muriel said. 'We're their first invited guests.'

'At home now we'd be watching the CBS Evening News,' Charles told her.

Muriel couldn't seem to think of any answer to that.

By six thirty sharp they were ringing the doorbell, standing in a hushed corridor carpeted in off-white. Rose opened the door and called, 'They're here!' and set her face lightly against each of theirs. She wore Grandmother Leary's lace-trimmed company apron and she smelled of lavender soap, the same as always.

But there was a strip of peeling sunburn across the bridge of her nose.

Julian, natty and casual in a navy turtleneck and white slacks (when it wasn't yet Memorial Day), fixed the drinks while Rose retreated to the kitchen. This was one of those ultra-modern apartments where the rooms all swam into each other, so they could see her flitting back and forth. Julian passed around snapshots of Hawaii. Either he had used inferior film or else Hawaii was a very different place from Baltimore, because some of the colors were wrong. The trees appeared to be blue. In most of the photos Rose stood in front of flower beds or flowering shrubs, wearing a white sleeveless dress Macon had never seen before, hugging her arms and smiling too broadly so that she looked older than she was. 'I tell Rose you'd think she went on our honeymoon by herself,' Julian said. 'I'm the one who took the pictures because Rose never did learn how to work my camera.'

'She didn't?' Macon asked.

'It was one of those German models with all the buttons.'

'She couldn't figure out the buttons?'

'I tell her, "People will think I wasn't even there." '

'Why, Rose could have taken that camera apart and put it together twice over,' Macon said.

'No, this was one of those German models with—'

'It wasn't very logically constructed,' Rose called from the kitchen.

'Ah,' Macon said, sitting back.

She entered the room with a tray and placed it on the glass coffee table. Then she knelt and began to spread pâté on little crackers. There was some change in the way she moved, Macon noticed. She was more graceful, but also more self-conscious. She offered the pâté first to Muriel, then to each of her brothers, last to Julian. 'In Hawaii I started learning to sail,' she said. She pronounced the two *i*'s in 'Hawaii' separately; Macon thought it sounded affected. 'Now I'm going to practice out on the Bay.'

'She's trying to find her sea legs,' Julian said. 'She tends to feel motion-sick.'

Macon bit into his cracker. The pâté was something familiar. It was rough in texture but delicate in taste; there was a kind of melting flavor that he believed came from adding a great amount of butter. The recipe was Sarah's. He sat very still, not chewing. He was flooded by a subtle blend of tarragon and cream and home.

'Oh, I know just what you're going through,' Muriel said to Rose. 'All I have to do is look at a boat and I get nauseous.'

Macon swallowed and gazed down at the carpet between his feet. He waited for someone to correct her, but nobody did. That was even worse.

In bed she said, 'You wouldn't ever leave me, would you? Would you ever think of leaving me? You won't be like the others, will you? Will you promise not to leave me?'

'Yes, yes,' he said, floating in and out of dreams.

'You do take me seriously, don't you? Don't you?'

'Oh, Muriel, for pity's sake . . .' he said.

But later, when she turned in her sleep and moved away from him, his feet followed hers of their own accord to the other side of the bed.

18

Macon was sitting in a hotel room in Winnipeg, Manitoba, when the phone rang. Actually it took him a second to realize it was the phone. He happened to be having a very good time with a mysterious object he'd just discovered—an ivory-painted metal cylinder affixed to the wall above the bed. He'd never noticed such a thing before, although he'd stayed in this hotel on two previous trips. When he touched the cylinder to see what it was, it rotated, disappearing into the wall, while from within the wall a light bulb swung out already lit. At the same moment, the phone rang. Macon experienced an instant of confusion during which he imagined it was the cylinder that was ringing. Then he saw the telephone on the nightstand. Still he was confused. No one had his number, so far as he knew.

He picked up the receiver and said, 'Yes?'

'Macon.'

His heart lurched. He said, 'Sarah?'

'Have I caught you at a bad time?'

'No, no . . . How did you know where I was?'

'Well, Julian thought you'd be in either Toronto or Winnipeg by now,' she said, 'so I looked in your last guidebook, and I knew the hotels where you discussed night noises were the ones where you stayed yourself, so . . .'

'Is anything wrong?' he asked.

'No, I just needed a favor. Would it be all right with you if I moved back into our house?'

'Um—'

'Just as a place to stay,' she said hastily. 'Just for a little while. My lease runs out at the end of the month and I can't find a new apartment.'

'But the house is a mess,' he told her.

'Oh, I'll take care of that.'

'No, I mean something happened to it over the winter, pipes burst or something, ceiling came down—'

'Yes, I know.'

'You do?'

'Your brothers told me.'

'My brothers?'

'I went to ask them your whereabouts when they wouldn't answer their phone. And Rose said she'd been over to the house herself and—'

'You went to Rose's, too?'

'No, Rose was at your brothers'.'

'Oh.'

'She's living there for a while.'

'I see,' he said. Then he said, 'She's what?'

'Well, June has had her baby,' Sarah said, 'so she asked Porter to keep the children a while.'

'But what does that have to do with Rose?' he said. 'Does Rose imagine Porter can't open a tin of soup for them? And how come June sent them away?'

'Oh, you know June, she always was kind of a birdbrain.'

She sounded like her old self, when she said that. Up till now there'd been something careful about her voice, something wary and ready to retreat, but now a certain chuckly, confiding quality emerged. Macon leaned back against his pillow.

'She told the children she needs time to bond,' Sarah said.

'Time to what?'

'She and her husband need to bond with the baby.'

'Good grief,' Macon said.

'When Rose heard that, she told Porter she was coming home. Anyhow she didn't think the boys were eating right, Porter and Charles; and also there's a crack in the side of the house and she wanted to get it patched before it spreads.'

'What kind of crack?' Macon asked.

'Some little crack in the masonry; I don't know. When the rain comes from a certain direction water seeps in above the kitchen ceiling, Rose says, and Porter and Charles were planning to fix it but they couldn't agree on the best way to do it.'

Macon slipped out of his shoes and hoisted his feet up onto the bed. He said, 'So is Julian living alone now, or what?'

'Yes, but she brings him casseroles,' Sarah said. Then she said, 'Have you thought about it, Macon?'

His heart gave another lurch. He said, 'Have I thought about what?'

'About my using the house.'

'Oh. Well. It's fine with me, but I don't believe you realize the extent of the damage.'

'But we'd have to fix that anyway, if we were to sell it. So here's what I was thinking: I could pay for the repairs myself—anything the insurance doesn't cover—with what I'd ordinarily use for rent. Does that seem fair to you?'

'Yes, of course,' Macon said.

'And maybe I'll get someone to clean the upholstery,' she said.

'Yes.'

'And the rugs.'

'Yes.'

After all these years, he knew when she was leading up to something. He recognized that distracted tone that meant she was bracing herself for what she really wanted to say.

'Incidentally,' she said, 'the papers came through from the lawyer.'

'Ah.'

'The final arrangements. You know. Things I have to sign.'

'Yes.'

'It was kind of a shock.'

He said nothing.

'I mean of course I knew they were coming; it's been nearly a year; in fact he called ahead and told me they were coming, but when I saw them in black and white they just seemed so brisk. They didn't take into account the feelings of the thing. I guess I wasn't expecting that.'

Macon had a sense of some danger approaching, something he couldn't handle. He said, 'Ah! Yes! Certainly! That seems a natural reaction. So anyway, good luck with the house, Sarah.'

He hung up quickly.

His seatmate on the flight to Edmonton was a woman who was scared of flying. He knew that before the plane had left the ground, before he'd looked in her direction. He was gazing out the window, keeping to himself as usual, and he heard her swallowing repeatedly. She kept tightening and releasing her grasp on the armrests and he could feel that, too. Finally he turned to see who this was. A pair of pouched eyes met his. A very old, baggy woman in a flowered dress was staring at him intently, had perhaps been willing him to turn. 'Do you think this plane is safe,' she said flatly, not exactly asking.

'It's perfectly safe,' he told her.

'Then why have all these signs about. Oxygen. Life vests. Emergency exits. They're clearly expecting the worst.'

'That's just federal regulations,' Macon said.

Then he started thinking about the word 'federal.' In Canada, would it apply? He frowned at the seat ahead of him, considering. Finally he said, '*Government* regulations.' When he checked the old woman's expression to see if this made any better sense to her, he discovered that she must have been staring at him all this time. Her face lunged toward him, gray and desperate. He began to worry about her. 'Would you like a glass of sherry?' he asked.

'They don't give us sherry till we're airborne. By then it's much too late.'

'Just a minute,' he said.

He bent to unzip his bag, and from his shaving kit he took a plastic travel flask. This was something he always packed, in case of sleepless nights. He had never used it, though—not because he'd never had a sleepless night but because he'd gone on saving it for some occasion even worse than whatever the current one was, something that never quite arrived. Like his other emergency supplies (the matchbook-sized sewing kit, the tiny white Lomotil tablet), this flask was being hoarded for the *real* emergency. In fact, its metal lid had grown rusty inside, as he discovered when he unscrewed it. 'I'm afraid this may have . . . turned a bit, or whatever sherry does,' he told the old woman. She didn't answer but continued staring into his eyes. He poured the sherry into the lid, which was meant to double as a cup. Meanwhile the plane gave a creak and started moving down the runway. The old woman drank off the sherry and handed him the cup. He understood that she was not returning it for good. He refilled it. She drank that more slowly and then let her head tip back against her seat.

'Better?' he asked her.

'My name is Mrs Daniel Bunn,' she told him.

He thought it was her way of saying she was herself again— her formal, dignified self. 'How do you do,' he said. 'I'm Macon Leary.'

'I know it's foolish, Mr Leary,' she said, 'but a drink does give the illusion one is doing something to cope, does it not.'

'Absolutely,' Macon said.

He wasn't convinced, though, that she was coping all that well. As the plane gathered speed, her free hand tightened on the armrest. Her other hand—the one closest to him, clutching the cup—grew white around the nails. All at once the cup popped up in the air, squeezed out of her grip. Macon caught it nimbly and said, 'Whoa there!' and screwed it onto the flask. Then he replaced the flask in his bag. 'Once we're off the ground—' he said.

But a glance at her face stopped him. She was swallowing again. The plane was beginning to rise now—the nose was lifting off— and she was pressed back against her seat. She seemed flattened. 'Mrs Bunn?' Macon said. He was scared she was having a heart attack.

Instead of answering, she turned toward him and crumpled onto his shoulder. He put an arm around her. 'Never mind,' he said. 'Goodness. You'll be all right. Never mind.'

The plane continued slanting backward. When the landing gear retracted (groaning), Macon felt the shudder through Mrs Bunn's body. Her hair smelled like freshly ironed tea cloths. Her back was large and boneless, a mounded shape like the back of a whale.

He was impressed that someone so old still wanted so fiercely to live.

Then the plane leveled off and she pulled herself together — straightening and drawing away from him, brushing at the teardrops that lay in the folds beneath her eyes. She was full of folds, wide and plain and sagging, but valiantly wore two pearl buttons in her long, spongy earlobes and maintained a coat of brave red lipstick on a mouth so wrinkled that it didn't even have a clear outline.

He asked, 'Are you all right?'

'Yes, and I apologize a thousand times,' she said. And she patted the brooch at her throat.

When the drink cart came he ordered her another sherry, which he insisted on paying for, and he ordered one for himself as well, even though he didn't plan to drink it. He thought it might be needed for Mrs Bunn. He was right, as things turned out, because their flight was unusually rough. The seatbelt sign stayed lit the whole way, and the plane bounced and grated as if rolling over gravel. Every now and then it dropped sharply and Mrs Bunn winced, but she went on taking tiny sips of sherry. 'This is nothing,' Macon told her. 'I've been in much worse than this.' He told her how to give with the bumps. 'It's like traveling on a boat,' he said. 'Or on wheels, on roller skates. You keep your knees loose. You bend. Do you understand what I'm saying? You go along with it. You ride it out.'

Mrs Bunn said she'd certainly try.

Not only was the air unsteady, but also little things kept going wrong inside the plane. The drink cart raced away from the stewardess every time she let go of it. Mrs Bunn's tray fell into her lap twice without warning. At each new mishap Macon laughed and said, 'Ah, me,' and shook his head. 'Oh, not again,' he said. Mrs Bunn's eyes remained fixed on his face, as if Macon were her only hope. Once there was a bang and she jumped; the door to the cockpit had flung itself open for no good reason. 'What? What?' she said, but Macon pointed out that now she could see for herself how unconcerned the pilot was. They were close enough to the front so she could even hear what the pilot was talking about; he was shouting some question to the copilot, asking why any ten-year-old girl with half a grain of sense would wear a metal nightbrace in a sauna room. 'You call that a worried man?' Macon asked Mrs Bunn. 'You think a man about to bail out of his plane would be discussing orthodontia?'

'Bail out!' Mrs Bunn said. 'Oh, my, I never thought of that!'

Macon laughed again.

He was reminded of a trip he'd taken alone as a boy, touring colleges. Heady with his new independence, he had lied to the man sitting next to him and said he came from Kenya, where his father led safaris. In the same way he was lying now, presenting himself to Mrs Bunn as this merry, tolerant person.

But after they had landed (with Mrs Bunn hardly flinching, bolstered by all those sherries), and she had gone off with her grown daughter, a very small child ran headlong into Macon's kneecap. This child was followed by another and another, all more or less the same size—some kind of nursery school, Macon supposed, visiting the airport on a field trip—and each child, as if powerless to veer from the course the first had set, careened off Macon's knees and said, 'Oops!' The call ran down the line like little bird cries—'Oops!' 'Oops!' 'Oops!'—while behind the children, a harassed-looking woman clapped a hand to her cheek. 'Sorry,' she said to Macon, and he said, 'No harm done.'

Only later, when he passed a mirror and noticed the grin on his face, did he realize that, in fact, he might not have been lying to Mrs Bunn after all.

'The plumber says it won't be hard to fix,' Sarah told him. 'He says it *looks* bad but really just one pipe is cracked.'

'Well, good,' Macon said.

He was not as surprised this time by her call, of course, but he did feel there was something disconcerting about it—standing in an Edmonton hotel room on a weekday afternoon, listening to Sarah's voice at the other end of the line.

'I went over there this morning and straightened up a little,' she said. 'Everything's so disorganized.'

'Disorganized?'

'Why are some of the sheets sewn in half? And the popcorn popper's in the bedroom. Were you eating popcorn in the bedroom?'

'I guess I must have been,' he said.

He was near an open window, and he could look out upon a strangely beautiful landscape: an expanse of mathematical flatness, with straight-edged buildings rising in the distance like a child's toy blocks on a rug. It was difficult, in these surroundings, to remember why he'd had a popcorn popper in the bedroom.

'So how's the weather there?' Sarah asked.

'Kind of gray.'

'Here it's sunny. Sunny and humid.'

'Well, it's certainly not humid here,' he told her. 'The air's so dry that rain disappears before it hits the ground.'

'Really? Then how can you tell it's raining?'

'You can see it above the plains,' he said. 'It looks like stripes that just fade away about halfway down from the sky.'

'I wish I were there to watch it with you,' Sarah said.

Macon swallowed.

Gazing out of the window, he all at once recalled Ethan as an infant. Ethan used to cry unless he was tightly wrapped in a blanket;

the pediatrician had explained that new babies have a fear of flying apart. Macon had not been able to imagine that at the time, but now he had no trouble. He could picture himself separating, falling into pieces, his head floating away with terrifying swiftness in the eerie green air of Alberta.

In Vancouver she asked if the rain vanished there as well. 'No,' he said.

'No?'

'No, it rains in Vancouver.'

It was raining this minute—a gentle night rain. He could hear it but not see it, except for the cone of illuminated drops spilling beneath a street lamp just outside his hotel room. You could almost suppose it was the lamp itself that was raining.

'Well, I've moved back into the house,' she said. 'Mostly I just stay upstairs. The cat and I: We camp in the bedroom. Creep downstairs for meals.'

'What cat is that?' he asked.

'Helen.'

'Oh, yes.'

'I went and picked her up at Rose's. I needed company. You wouldn't believe how lonely it is.'

Yes, he would believe it, he could have said. But didn't.

So here they were in their same old positions, he could have said: He had won her attention only by withdrawing. He wasn't surprised when she said, 'Macon? Do you . . . What's her name? The person you live with?'

'Muriel,' he said.

Which she knew before she asked, he suspected.

'Do you plan on staying with Muriel forever?'

'I really couldn't say,' he said.

He was noticing how oddly the name hung in this starchy, old-fashioned hotel room. Muriel. Such a peculiar sound. So unfamiliar, suddenly.

On the flight back, his seatmate was an attractive young woman in a tailored suit. She spread the contents of her briefcase on her folding tray, and she riffled through computer printout sheets with her perfectly manicured hands. Then she asked Macon if he had a pen she might borrow. This struck him as amusing—her true colors shining out from beneath her businesslike exterior. However, his only pen was a fountain pen that he didn't like lending, so he said no. She seemed relieved; she cheerfully repacked all she'd taken from her briefcase. 'I could have sworn I swiped a ballpoint from my last hotel,' she said, 'but maybe that was the one before this one; you know how they all run together in your mind.'

'You must do a lot of traveling,' Macon said politely.

'Do I! Some mornings when I wake up I have to check my hotel stationery just to find out what city I'm in.'

'That's terrible.'

'Oh, I like it,' she said, bending to slip her briefcase under her seat. 'It's the only time I can relax anymore. When I come home I'm all nervous, can't sit still. I prefer to be a . . . moving target, you could say.'

Macon thought of something he'd once read about heroin: how it's not a pleasure, really, but it so completely alters the users' body chemistry that they're forced to go on once they've started.

He turned down drinks and dinner, and so did his seatmate; she rolled her suit jacket expertly into a pillow and went to sleep. Macon got out *Miss MacIntosh* and stared at a single page for a while. The top line began with *brows bristling, her hair streaked with white*. He studied the words so long that he almost wondered if they *were* words; the whole English language seemed chunky and brittle. 'Ladies and gentlemen,' the loudspeaker said, 'we will be starting our descent . . .' and the word 'descent' struck him as an invention, some new euphemism concocted by the airlines.

After they landed in Baltimore, he took a shuttle bus to the parking lot and retrieved his car. It was late evening here and the sky was pale and radiant above the city. As he drove he continued to see the words from *Miss MacIntosh*. He continued to hear the stewardess's gliding voice: *complimentary beverages* and *the captain has asked us* and *trays in an upright position*. He considered switching on the radio but he didn't know what station it was set to. Maybe it was Muriel's country music station. This possibility made him feel weary; he felt he wouldn't have the strength to press the buttons, and so he drove in silence.

He came to Singleton Street and flicked his signal on but didn't turn. After a while the signal clicked off on its own. He rode on through the city, up Charles Street, into his old neighborhood. He parked and cut the engine and sat looking at the house. The downstairs windows were dark. The upstairs windows were softly glowing. Evidently, he had come home.

19

— Macon and Sarah needed to buy a new couch. They set aside a Saturday for it—actually just half a Saturday, because Sarah had a class to attend in the afternoon. At breakfast, she flipped through an interior decorating book so they could get a head start on their decision. 'I'm beginning to think along the lines of something flowered,' she told Macon. 'We've never had a flowered couch before. Or would that be too frilly?'

'Well, I don't know. I wonder about winter,' Macon said.

'Winter?'

'I mean right now in the middle of June a flowered couch looks fine, but it might seem out of place in December.'

'So you prefer something in a solid,' Sarah said.

'Well, I don't know.'

'Or maybe stripes.'

'I'm not sure.'

'I know you don't like plaids.'

'No.'

'How do you feel about tweeds?'

'Tweeds,' Macon said, considering.

Sarah handed over the book and started loading the dishwasher.

Macon studied pictures of angular modern couches, cozy chintz-covered couches, and period reproduction couches covered in complex fabrics. He took the book to the living room and squinted at the spot where the couch would be sitting. The old one, which had turned out to be too waterlogged to salvage, had been carted away, along with both armchairs. Now there was just a long blank wall, with the freshly plastered ceiling glaring above it. Macon observed that a room without furniture had a utilitarian feeling, as if it were merely a container. Or a vehicle. Yes, a vehicle: He had a sense of himself speeding through the universe as he stood there.

While Sarah got dressed, Macon took the dog out. It was a warm, golden morning. Neighbors were trimming their grass and weeding their flower beds. They nodded as Macon walked past. He had not been back long enough for them to feel at ease yet; there was something a little too formal about their greetings. Or maybe he was imagining that. He made an effort to remind them of how many years he had lived here: 'I've always liked those tulips of yours!' and 'Still got that nice hand mower, I see!' Edward marched beside him with a busybody waggle of his hind end.

In movies and such, people who made important changes in their lives accomplished them and were done with it. They walked out and never returned; or they married and lived happily ever after. In real life, things weren't so clean-cut. Macon, for instance, had had to go down to Muriel's and retrieve this dog, once he'd decided to move back home. He had had to collect his clothing and pack up his typewriter while Muriel watched in silence with her accusing, reproaching eyes. Then there were all kinds of other belongings that he discovered too late he'd forgotten—clothes that had been in the wash at the time, and his favorite dictionary, and the extra-large pottery mug he liked to drink his coffee from. But of course he couldn't go back for them. He had to abandon them—messy, trailing strings of himself cluttering his leavetaking.

By the time he and Edward returned from their outing, Sarah was waiting in the front yard. She wore a yellow dress that made her tan glow; she looked very pretty. 'I was just wondering about the azaleas,' she told Macon. 'Weren't we supposed to feed them in the spring?'

'Well, probably,' Macon said, 'but they seem all right to me.'

'In April, I think,' she said. 'Or maybe May. No one was here to do it.'

Macon veered away from that. He preferred to pretend that their lives had been going on as usual. 'Never mind, Rose has whole sacks of fertilizer,' he said. 'We'll pick up some from her while we're out.'

'No one was here to seed the lawn, either.'

'The lawn looks fine,' he said, more forcefully than he'd meant to.

They shut Edward in the house and climbed into Macon's car. Sarah had brought along a newspaper because there were several furniture ads. 'Modern Homewares,' she read off. 'But that's all the way down on Pratt Street.'

'Might as well give it a try,' Macon said. Pratt was one of the few streets he knew how to find.

After they left their neighborhood, with its trees arching overhead, the car grew hotter and Macon rolled his window down. Sarah lifted her face to the sunlight. 'Be a good day to go to the pool,' she said.

'Well, if we have time. I was thinking of asking you to lunch.'

'Oh, where?'

'Anywhere you like. Your choice.'

'Aren't you nice,' she said.

Macon drove past two unshaven men talking on a corner. Sarah locked her door. Macon thought of what the men would be saying: 'What's coming down, man?' 'Not all that much.'

The sidewalks grew more crowded. Women lugged string-handled shopping bags, an old man dragged a grocery cart, and a girl in a faded dress leaned her head against a bus stop sign.

At Modern Homewares, huge paper banners covered the plate glass windows. SPECIAL FOR FATHER'S DAY! they read. Sarah hadn't mentioned that this was a Father's Day sale. Macon made a point of mentioning it himself, to show it didn't bother him. Taking her arm as they entered, he said, 'Isn't that typical. Father's Day! They'll capitalize on anything.'

Sarah looked away from him and said, 'All they seem to have is beds.'

'I suppose it began with reclining chairs,' Macon said. 'A Barcalounger for Dad, and next thing you know it's a whole dinette set.'

'Could we see your couches,' Sarah told a salesman firmly.

The couches were all of the straight-backed, Danish sort, which was fine with Macon. He didn't really care. Sarah said, 'What do you think? Legs? Or flush with the floor.'

'It's all the same to me,' he said. He sat down heavily on something covered in leather.

Sarah chose a long, low couch that opened into a queen-sized bed. 'Macon? What do you say?' she asked. 'Do you like what you're sitting on better?'

'No, no,' he said.

'Well, what do you think of this one?'

'It's fine.'

'Don't you have any opinion?'

'I just gave you my opinion, Sarah.'

Sarah sighed and asked the salesman if he offered same-day delivery.

They'd been so efficient about picking out the couch that time remained for other errands as well. First they drove to Hutzler's and bought queen-sized sheets. Then they checked the furniture department for armchairs; there was a Father's Day sale there, too. 'Maybe we're on a roll,' Sarah told Macon. But they weren't as lucky with the armchairs; nothing looked just right. Not to Macon, at least. He gave up trying and stood watching a kiddie show on a row of television sets.

After Hutzler's they went to get fertilizer from Rose, but Macon braked on the way and said, 'Wait! There's my bank.' It had come upon him unexpectedly—the branch where he rented a safe deposit box. 'I need my passport for the France trip,' he told Sarah. 'Might as well pick it up while I'm here.'

Sarah said she'd just wait in the car.

He had to stand in line; two elderly women were ahead of him. They were checking out their jewels for Saturday night, he liked to imagine. Or clipping their coupons—whatever coupons were. While he stood there he kept feeling the presence of someone behind him. For some reason he didn't want to turn and find out who it was. He just kept staring ahead, every now and then glancing at his watch in a businesslike way. This person breathed very gently and smelled like flowers—bitter, real-life flowers, not the kind in perfume bottles. But when he finally squared his shoulders and looked around, he found only another stranger waiting for her jewels.

It wasn't true that Muriel had watched in silence as he packed. Actually, she had spoken. She had said, 'Macon? Are you really doing this? Do you mean to tell me you can just use a person up and then move on? You think I'm some kind of . . . bottle of something you don't have any further need for? Is that how you see me, Macon?'

His turn for the vault had arrived, and he followed a girl in a miniskirt across a carpeted area, into the windowless cubicle lined with drawers. 'I won't need to take my box to the other room,' he told the girl. 'I just want to get one thing.'

She gave him his card to sign and accepted his key. After she had unlocked his box she stood back, scrutinizing her nails, while he rummaged through various papers for his passport. Then he turned to tell her he was finished, but all at once he was so moved by her tact in looking elsewhere, by the delicacy that people could come up with on their own (for surely it wouldn't have been written into the bank's instructions) . . . Well, he must be going soft in the head.

It was the weather or something; it was the season or something; he had not been sleeping well. He said, 'Thank you very much,' and took back his key and left.

At his grandfather's house, Rose was out front pruning the hedge. Her gardening smock was an enormous gray workshirt inherited from Charles. When she saw their car pull up she straightened and waved. Then she went on pruning while they consulted her about fertilizers. 'For azaleas and what else do you have, andromeda, acid-loving plants . . .' she mused.

Sarah said, 'Where are the children today?'

'Children?'

'Your nephew and nieces.'

'Oh, they went home to their mother.'

Sarah said, 'I just assumed, since you hadn't moved back with Julian . . .'

'Well, not yet, of course,' Rose said.

Macon, anxious to guard her privacy, murmured, 'No, of course not,' practically at the same moment, but Sarah said, 'Why? What's keeping you?'

'Oh, Sarah, you wouldn't believe what a state I found the boys in when I came back here,' Rose said. 'They were living in their pajamas so as not to have too much laundry. They were eating gorp for their suppers.'

'I'm not even going to ask what gorp is,' Sarah said.

'It's a mixture of wheat germ and nuts and dried—'

'But what about your apartment, Rose? What about Julian?'

'Oh, you know, I kept losing that apartment every time I turned around,' Rose said vaguely. 'I'd head one block east to the grocery store and then turn west to get back again and I'd always be wrong; always. The apartment building would have worked over to the east somehow; *I* don't know how.'

There was a silence. Finally Macon said, 'Well, if you could get us some of that fertilizer, Rose . . .'

'Certainly,' she said. And she went off to the toolshed.

They had lunch at the Old Bay Restaurant—Sarah's idea. Macon said, 'Are you sure?' and Sarah said, 'Why wouldn't I be?'

'But you always tell me it's boring,' Macon said.

'There are worse things than boring, I've decided.'

He didn't think that was much of a recommendation, but he went along with it.

The restaurant was full, even though it was barely noon, and they had to wait a few minutes to be seated. Macon stood by the hostess's podium trying to adjust to the dimness. He surveyed the other diners and found something odd about them. They were not the usual Old Bay crowd—middle-aged, one face much like the next—but an assortment of particular and unusual individuals. He saw a priest offering a toast to a woman in a tennis dress, and a smartly suited woman with a young man in an orange gauze robe, and two cheerful schoolgirls loading all their potato chips onto the plate of a small boy. From where he stood Macon couldn't hear what any of these people were saying; he had to guess. 'Maybe the woman wants to join a convent,' he told Sarah, 'and the priest is trying to discourage her.'

'Pardon?'

'He's pointing out that sorting her husband's socks can be

equally whatever-he'd-call-it, equally holy. And the young man in gauze, well . . .'

'The young man in gauze is Ashley Demming,' Sarah said. 'You know Ashley. Peter and Lindy Demming's son. My, he's aged poor Lindy twenty years in the last six months, hasn't he? I don't think they're ever going to get over this.'

'Ah, well,' Macon said.

Then they were shown to a table.

Sarah ordered something called a White Lady and Macon ordered a sherry. With their meal they had a bottle of wine. Macon wasn't used to drinking in the daytime; he grew a little muzzy. So did Sarah, evidently, for she drifted off in the middle of a sentence about upholstery fabrics. She touched his hand, which was lying on the tablecloth. 'We ought to do this more often,' she said.

'Yes, we ought to.'

'You know what I missed most when we were separated? The little, habitual things. The Saturday errands. Going to Eddie's for coffee beans. Even things that used to seem tiresome, like the way you'd take forever in the hardware store.'

When he folded her hand into a fist it was round, like a bird. It had no sharp angles.

'I'm not sure if you know this,' she said, 'but for a while I was seeing another man.'

'Well, fine; whatever; eat your salad,' he told her.

'No, I want to say it, Macon. He was just getting over the death of his wife, and I was getting over things too so of course . . . Well, we started out very slowly, we started as friends, but then he began talking about getting married someday. After we'd given ourselves some time, he meant. In fact I think he really loved me. He took it hard when I told him you'd moved back.'

She looked straight at Macon when she said that, her eyes a sudden blue flash. He nodded.

'But there were these things I had trouble with,' she said. 'I mean good things; qualities I'd always wished for. He was a very dashing driver, for instance. Not unsafe; just dashing. At first, I liked that. Then bit by bit it began to feel wrong. "Double-check your rearview mirror!" I wanted to tell him. "Fasten your seatbelt! Inch past stop signs the way my husband does!" He never examined a restaurant bill before he paid it—shoot, he didn't even take his credit card receipt when he walked away from a table—and I thought of all the times I sat stewing while you totted up every little item. I thought, "Why do I miss that? It's perverse!"'

Like 'eck cetera,' Macon thought.

Like Muriel saying, 'eck cetera.' And Macon wincing.

And the emptiness now, the thinness, when he heard it pronounced correctly.

He stroked the dimpled peaks that were Sarah's knuckles.

'Macon, I think that after a certain age people just don't have a choice,' Sarah said. 'You're who I'm with. It's too late for me to change. I've used up too much of my life now.'

You mean to tell me you can just use a person up and then move on? Muriel had asked.

Evidently so, was the answer. For even if he had stayed with Muriel, then wouldn't Sarah have been left behind?

'After a certain age,' he told Sarah, 'it seems to me you can only choose what to lose.'

'What?' she said.

'I mean there's going to be something you have to give up, whichever way you cut it.'

'Well, of course,' she said.

He supposed she'd always known that.

They finished their meal but they didn't order coffee because they were running late. Sarah had her class; she was studying with a sculptor on Saturdays. Macon called for the bill and paid it, self-consciously totaling it first. Then they stepped out into the sunshine. 'What a pretty day,' Sarah said. 'It makes me want to play hooky.'

'Why don't you?' Macon asked. If she didn't go to class, he wouldn't have to work on his guidebook.

But she said, 'I can't disappoint Mr Armistead.'

They drove home, and she changed into a sweat suit and set off again. Macon carried in the fertilizer, which Rose had poured into a bucket. It was something shredded that had no smell—or only a harsh, chemical smell, nothing like the truckloads of manure the men used to bring for his grandmother's camellias. He set it on the pantry floor and then he took the dog out. Then he made himself a cup of coffee to clear his head. He drank it at the kitchen sink, staring into the yard. The cat rubbed against his ankles and purred. The clock over the stove ticked steadily. There was no other sound.

When the telephone rang, he was glad. He let it ring twice before he answered so as not to seem overeager. Then he picked up the receiver and said, 'Hello?'

'Mr Leary?'

'Yes!'

'This is Mrs Morton calling, at Merkle Appliance Store. Are you aware that the maintenance policy on your hot water heater expires at the end of the month?'

'No, I hadn't realized,' Macon said.

'You had a two-year policy at a cost of thirty-nine eighty-eight. Now to renew it for another two years the cost of course would be slightly higher since your hot water heater is older.'

'Well, that makes sense,' Macon said. 'Gosh! How old *is* that thing by now?'

'Let's see. You purchased it three years ago this July.'

'Well, I'd certainly like to keep the maintenance policy.'

'Wonderful. I'll send you a new contract then, Mr Leary, and thank you for—'

'And would that still include replacement of the tank?' Macon asked.

'Oh, yes. Every part is covered.'

'And they'd still do the yearly checkups.'

'Why, yes.'

'I've always liked that. A lot of the other stores don't offer it; I remember from when I was shopping around.'

'So I'll send you the contract, Mr—'

'But I would have to arrange for the checkup myself, as I recall.'

'Yes, the customer schedules the checkup.'

'Maybe I'll just schedule it now. Could I do that?'

'That's a whole different department, Mr Leary. I'll mail you out the contract and you can read all about it. Bye bye.'

She hung up.

Macon hung up too.

He thought a while.

He had an urge to go on talking; anyone would do. But he couldn't think what number to dial. Finally he called the time lady. She answered before the first ring was completed. (*She* had no worries about seeming overeager.) 'At the tone,' she said, 'the time will be one ... forty-nine. And ten seconds.' What a voice. So melodious, so well modulated. 'At the tone the time will be one ... forty-nine. And twenty seconds.'

He listened for over a minute, and then the call was cut off. The line clicked and the dial tone started. This made him feel rebuffed, although he knew he was being foolish. He bent to pat the cat. The cat allowed it briefly before walking away.

There was nothing to do but sit down at his typewriter.

He was behind schedule with this guidebook. Next week he was supposed to start on France, and he still hadn't finished the conclusion to the Canada book. He blamed it on the season. Who could sit alone indoors when everything outside was blooming? *Travelers should be forewarned*, he typed, but then he fell to admiring a spray of white azaleas that trembled on the ledge of his open window. A bee crawled among the blossoms, buzzing. He hadn't known the bees were out yet. Did Muriel know? Would she recall what a single bee could do to Alexander?

... *should be forewarned*, he read over, but his concentration was shot now.

She was so careless, so unthinking; how could he have put up with her? That unsanitary habit she had of licking her finger before she turned a magazine page; her tendency to use the word 'enormity' as if it referred to size. There wasn't a chance in this world that she'd remember about bee stings.

He reached for the phone on his desk and dialed her number. 'Muriel?'

'What,' she said flatly.

'This is Macon.'

'Yes, I know.'

He paused. He said, 'Um, it's bee season, Muriel.'

'So?'

'I wasn't sure you were aware. I mean summer just creeps up, *I* know how summer creeps up, and I was wondering if you'd thought about Alexander's shots.'

'Don't you believe I can manage that much for myself?' she screeched.

'Oh. Well.'

'What do you think I am, some sort of ninny? Don't you think I know the simplest dumbest thing?'

'Well, I wasn't sure, you see, that—'

'A fine one you are! Ditch that child without a word of farewell and then call me up on the telephone to see if I'm raising him right!'

'I just wanted to—'

'Criticize, criticize! Tell me Oodles of Noodles is not a balanced meal and then go off and desert him and then have the nerve to call me up and tell me I'm not a good mother!'

'No, wait, Muriel—'

'Dominick is dead,' she said.

'What?'

'Not that you would care. He died.'

Macon noticed how the sounds in the room had stopped. 'Dominick Saddler?' he asked.

'It was his night to take my car and he went to a party in Cockeysville and coming home he crashed into a guardrail.'

'Oh, no.'

'The girl he had with him didn't get so much as a scratch.'

'But Dominick . . .' Macon said, because he didn't believe it yet.

'But Dominick died instantly.'

'Oh, my Lord.'

He saw Dominick on the couch with Alexander, holding aloft a can of paste wax.

'Want to hear something awful? My car will be just fine,' Muriel said. 'Straighten the front end and it'll run good as ever.'

Macon rested his head in his hand.

'I have to go now and sit with Mrs Saddler in the funeral home,' she said.

'Is there something I can do?'

'No,' she said, and then, spitefully, 'How could *you* be any help?'

'I could stay with Alexander, maybe.'

'Alexander's got people of our own to stay with him,' she said.

The doorbell rang, and Edward started barking. Macon heard him in the front hall.

'Well, I'll say good-bye now,' Muriel said. 'Sounds like you have company.'

'Never mind that.'

'I'll let you get back to your *life*,' she said. 'So long.'

He kept the receiver to his ear a moment, but she had hung up.

He went out to the hall and tapped his foot at Edward. 'Down!' he said. Edward lay down, the hump on his back still bristling. Macon opened the door and found a boy with a clipboard.

'Modern Homewares,' the boy told him.

'Oh. The couch.'

While the couch was being unloaded, Macon shut Edward in the kitchen. Then he returned to the hall and watched the couch lumbering toward him, borne by the first boy and another, just slightly older, who had an eagle tattooed on his forearm. Macon thought of Dominick Saddler's muscular, corded arms grappling beneath the hood of Muriel's car. The first boy spat as he approached the house, but Macon saw how young and benign his face was. 'Aw, man,' the second one said, stumbling over the doorstep.

Macon said, 'That's all right,' and gave them each a five-dollar bill when they'd placed the couch where he directed.

After they'd gone he sat down on the couch, which still had some sort of cellophane covering. He rubbed his hands on his knees. Edward barked in the kitchen. Helen padded in softly, stopped still, eyed the couch, and continued through the room with an offended air. Macon went on sitting.

When Ethan died, the police had asked Macon to identify the body. But Sarah, they suggested, might prefer to wait outside. Yes, Sarah had said; she would. She had taken a seat on a molded beige chair in the hallway. Then she'd looked up at Macon and said, 'Can you do this?'

'Yes,' he'd told her, evenly. He had felt he was barely breathing; he was keeping himself very level, with most of the air emptied out of his lungs.

He had followed a man into a room. It was not as bad as it could have been because someone had folded a wad of toweling under the back of Ethan's head to hide the damage. Also it wasn't Ethan. Not the real Ethan. Odd how clear it suddenly became, once a person had died, that the body was the very least of him. This was simply an untenanted shell, although it bore a distant resemblance to Ethan— the same groove down the upper lip, same cowlick over the forehead. Macon had a sensation like pressing against a blank wall, willing with all his being something that could never happen: *Please, please come back inside.* But finally he said, 'Yes. That is my son.'

He'd returned to Sarah and given her a nod. Sarah had risen and put her arms around him. Later, when they were alone in their motel, she'd asked him what he had seen. 'Not really much of anything, sweetheart,' he had told her. She kept at him. Was Ethan . . . well, hurt-looking? Scared? He said, 'No, he was nothing.' He said, 'Let me get you some tea.'

'I don't want tea, I want to hear!' she'd said. 'What are you hiding?' He had the impression she was blaming him for something. Over the next few weeks it seemed she grew to hold him responsible, like a bearer of bad tidings—the only one who could say for a fact that Ethan had truly died. She made several references to Macon's chilliness, to his appalling calm that night in the hospital morgue. Twice she expressed some doubt as to whether, in fact, he was really capable of distinguishing Ethan from some similar boy. In fact, that may not have been Ethan at all. It may have been somebody else who had died. She should have ascertained for herself. She was the mother, after all; she knew her child far better; what did Macon know?

Macon said, 'Sarah. Listen. I will tell you as much as I can. He was very pale and still. You wouldn't believe how still. He didn't have any expression. His eyes were closed. There was nothing bloody or gruesome, just a sense of . . . futility. I mean I wondered what the purpose had been. His arms were down by his sides and I thought about last spring when he started lifting weights. I thought, "Is this what it comes to? Lift weights and take vitamins and build yourself up and then—nothing?"'

He hadn't been prepared for Sarah's response. 'So what are you saying?' she asked him. 'We die in the end, so why bother to live in the first place? Is that what you're saying?'

'No—' he said.

'It all comes down to a question of economy?' she asked.

'No, Sarah. Wait,' he had said.

Thinking back on that conversation now, he began to believe that people could, in fact, be used up—could use each other up, could be of no further help to each other and maybe even do harm to each other. He began to think that who you are when you're with somebody may matter more than whether you love her.

Lord knows how long he sat there.

Edward had been barking in the kitchen all this time, but now he went into a frenzy. Somebody must have knocked. Macon rose and went to the front of the house, where he found Julian standing on the porch with a file folder. 'Oh. It's you,' Macon said.

'What's all that barking I hear?'

'Don't worry, he's shut in the kitchen. Come on in.'

He held the screen door open and Julian stepped inside. 'Thought I'd bring you the material for Paris,' Julian said.

'I see,' Macon said. But he suspected he was really here for some other reason. Probably hoping to hurry the Canada book. 'Well, I was just this minute touching up my conclusion,' he said, leading the way to the living room. And then, hastily, 'Few details here and there I'm not entirely happy with; may be a little while yet . . .'

Julian didn't seem to be listening. He sat down on the cellophane that covered the couch. He tossed the folder aside and said, 'Have you seen Rose lately?'

'Yes, we were over there just this morning.'

'Do you think she's not coming back?'

Macon hadn't expected him to be so direct. In fact, Rose's situation had begun to look like one of those permanent irregularities that couples never refer to. 'Oh, well,' he told Julian, 'you know how it is. She's worried about the boys. They're eating glop or something.'

'Those are not boys, Macon. They're men in their forties.'

Macon stroked his chin.

'I'm afraid she's left me,' Julian said.

'Oh, now, you can't be sure of that.'

'And not even for a decent reason!' Julian said. 'Or for any reason. I mean our marriage was working out fine; that much I can swear to. But she'd worn herself a groove or something in that house of hers, and she couldn't help swerving back into it. At least, I can't think of any other explanation.'

'Well, it sounds about right,' Macon told him.

'I went to see her two days ago,' Julian said, 'but she was out. I was standing in the yard wondering where she'd got to when who should drive past but Rose in person, with her car stuffed full of old ladies. All the windows packed with these little old faces and feathered hats. I shouted after her, I said, "Rose! Wait!" but she didn't hear me and she drove on by. Then just at the last minute she caught sight of me, I guess, and she turned and stared, and I got the funniest feeling, like the car was driving *her*—like she was just gliding past helpless and couldn't do a thing but send me one long look before she disappeared.'

Macon said, 'Why don't you give her a job, Julian.'

'Job?'

'Why don't you show her that office of yours. That filing system you never get sorted, that secretary chewing her gum and forgetting whose appointment is when. Don't you think Rose could take all that in hand?'

'Well, sure, but—'

'Call her up and tell her your business is going to pieces. Ask if she could just come in and get things organized, get things under control. Put it that way. Use those words. *Get things under control*, tell her. Then sit back and wait.'

Julian thought that over.

'But of course, what do I know,' Macon said.

'No, you're right.'

'Now let's see your folder.'

'You're absolutely right,' Julian said.

'Look at this!' Macon said. He held up the topmost letter. 'Why do you bother me with this? *I just wanted to appraise you folks of a wonderful little hotel in* . . . A man who says he wants to "appraise" us, do you really suppose he'd know a good hotel when he saw one?'

'Macon,' Julian said.

'The whole damn language has been slaughtered,' Macon said.

'Macon, I know you feel I'm crass and brash.'

This took Macon a moment to answer, only partly because he first heard it as 'crash and brass.' 'Oh,' he said. 'Why, no, Julian, not at—'

'But I just want to say this, Macon. I care about that sister of yours more than anything else in the world. It's not just Rose, it's the whole way she lives, that house and those turkey dinners and those evening card games. And I care about you, too, Macon. Why, you're my best friend! At least, I hope so.'

'Oh, why, ah—' Macon said.

Julian rose and shook his hand, mangling all the bones inside, and clapped him on the shoulder and left.

Sarah came home at five thirty. She found Macon standing at the kitchen sink with yet another cup of coffee. 'Did the couch get here?' she asked him.

'All safe and sound.'

'Oh, good! Let's see it.'

She went into the living room, leaving tracks of gray dust that Macon supposed was clay or granite. There was dust in her hair, even. She squinted at the couch and said, 'What do you think?'

'Seems fine to me,' he said.

'Honestly, Macon. I don't know what's come over you; you used to be downright finicky.'

'It's fine, Sarah. It looks very nice.'

She stripped off the cellophane and stood back, arms full of crackling light. 'We ought to see how it opens out,' she said.

While she was stuffing the cellophane into the wastebasket, Macon pulled at the canvas strap that turned the couch into a bed. It made him think of Muriel's house. The strap's familiar graininess reminded him of all the times Muriel's sister had slept over, and when the mattress slid forth he saw the gleam of Claire's tangled golden hair.

'Maybe we should put on the sheets, now that we've got it open,' Sarah said. She brought the sack of linens from the front hall. With Macon positioned at the other side of the couch, she floated a sheet above the mattress and then bustled up and down, tucking it in. Macon helped, but he wasn't as fast as Sarah. The clay dust or whatever it was had worked itself into the seams of her knuckles, he saw. There was something appealing about her small, brown, creased hands against the white percale. He said, 'Let's give the bed a trial run.'

Sarah didn't understand at first. She looked up from unfolding the second sheet and said, 'Trial run?'

But she allowed him to take the sheet away and slip her sweat shirt over her head.

Making love to Sarah was comfortable and soothing. After all their years together, her body was so well known to him that he couldn't always tell the difference between what he was feeling and what she was feeling. But wasn't it sad that they hadn't the slightest uneasiness about anyone's walking in on them? They were so alone. He nestled his face in her warm, dusty neck and wondered if she shared that feeling as well—if she sensed all the empty air in the house. But he would never ask.

*

While Sarah took a shower, he shaved. They were supposed to go to Bob and Sue Carney's for supper. When he came out of the bathroom Sarah was standing in front of the bureau, screwing on little gold earrings. (She was the only woman Macon knew of who didn't have pierced ears.) He thought Renoir could have painted her: Sarah in her slip with her head cocked slightly, plump tanned arms upraised. 'I'm really not in the mood to go out,' she said.

'Me neither,' Macon said, opening his closet door.

'I'd be just as content to stay home with a book.'

He pulled a shirt off a hanger.

'Macon,' she said.

'Hmm.'

'You never asked me if I slept with anyone while we were separated.'

Macon paused, halfway into one sleeve.

'Don't you want to know?' she asked him.

'No,' he said.

He put on the shirt and buttoned the cuffs.

'I would think you'd wonder.'

'Well, I don't,' he said.

'The trouble with you is, Macon—'

It was astonishing, the instantaneous flare of anger he felt. 'Sarah,' he said, 'don't even start. By God, if that doesn't sum up every single thing that's wrong with being married. "The trouble with you is, Macon—" and, "I know you better than you know yourself, Macon—"'

'The trouble with you is,' she continued steadily, 'you think people should stay in their own sealed packages. You don't believe in opening up. You don't believe in trading back and forth.'

'I certainly don't,' Macon said, buttoning his shirt front.

'You know what you remind me of? That telegram Harpo Marx sent his brothers: *No message. Harpo.*'

That made him grin. Sarah said, 'You *would* think it was funny.'

'Well? Isn't it?'

'It isn't at all! It's sad! It's infuriating! It would be infuriating to go to your door and sign for that telegram and tear it open and find no message!'

He took a tie from the rack in his closet.

'For your information,' she said, 'I didn't sleep with anyone the whole entire time.'

He felt she'd won some kind of contest. He pretended he hadn't heard her.

Bob and Sue had invited just neighbors—the Bidwells and a new young couple Macon hadn't met before. Macon stuck mainly to the new couple because with them, he had no history. When they asked if he had children, he said, 'No.' He asked if they had any children.

'No,' Brad Frederick said.

'Ah.'

Brad's wife was in transit between girlhood and womanhood. She wore her stiff navy blue dress and large white shoes as if they belonged to her mother. Brad himself was still a boy. When they all went out back to watch the barbecue, Brad found a Frisbee in the bushes and flung it to little Delilah Carney. His white polo shirt pulled loose from his trousers. Dominick Saddler came to

Macon's mind like a deep, hard punch. He remembered how, after his grandfather died, the sight of any old person could make his eyes fill with tears. Lord, if he wasn't careful he could end up feeling sorry for the whole human race. 'Throw that thing here,' he said briskly to Delilah, and he set aside his sherry and held out a hand for the Frisbee. Before long they had a real game going—all the guests joining in except Brad's wife, who was still too close to childhood to risk getting stuck there on a visit back.

At supper, Sue Carney seated Macon at her right. She put a hand on his and said it was wonderful that he and Sarah had worked things out. 'Well, thank you,' Macon said. 'Gosh, you make a really good salad, Sue.'

'We all have our ups and downs,' she said. For a second, he thought she meant her salads weren't consistently successful. 'I'll be honest,' she told him, 'there've been times when I have wondered if Bob and I would make it. There's times I feel we're just hanging in there, you know what I mean? Times I say, "Hi, honey, how was your day?" but inside I'm feeling like a Gold Star mother.'

Macon turned the stem of his glass and tried to think what step he'd missed in her logic.

'Like someone who's suffered a loss in a war,' she said, 'and then forever afterward she has to go on supporting the war; she has to support it louder than anyone else, because otherwise she'd be admitting the loss was for no purpose.'

'Um . . .'

'But that's just a passing mood,' she said.

'Well, naturally,' Macon said.

*

He and Sarah walked home through air as heavy as water. It was eleven o'clock and the teenagers who had eleven o'clock curfews were just returning. These were the youngest ones, most of them too young to drive, and so they were chauffeured by grown-ups. They jumped out of cars shouting, 'See you! Thanks! Call me tomorrow, hear?' Keys jingled. Front doors blinked open and blinked shut again. The cars moved on.

Sarah's skirt had the same whispery sound as the Tuckers' lawn sprinkler, which was still revolving slowly in a patch of ivy.

When they reached the house, Macon let Edward out for one last run. He tried to get the cat to come in, but she stayed hunched on the kitchen window ledge glaring down at him, owlish and stubborn; so he let her be. He moved through the rooms turning off lights. By the time he came upstairs Sarah was already in bed, propped against the headboard with a glass of club soda. 'Have some,' she said, holding out the glass. But he said no, he was tired; and he undressed and slid under the covers.

The tinkling of Sarah's ice cubes took on some meaning in his mind. It seemed that with every tinkle, he fell deeper. Finally he opened a door and traveled down an aisle and stepped into the witness stand. They asked him the simplest of questions. 'What color were the wheels?' 'Who brought the bread?' 'Were the shutters closed or open?' He honestly couldn't remember. He tried but he couldn't remember. They took him to the scene of the crime, a winding road like something in a fairy tale. 'Tell us all you know,' they said. He didn't know a thing. By now it was clear from their faces that he wasn't merely a witness; they suspected him. So he racked his brain, but still he came up empty. 'You have to see my side of this!' he cried. 'I put it all out of my mind; I worked to put it out! Now I can't bring it back.'

'Not even to defend yourself?' they asked.

He opened his eyes. The room was dark, and Sarah breathed softly next to him. The clock radio said it was midnight. The midnight-curfew group was just returning. Hoots and laughter rang out, tires scraped a curb, and a fanbelt whinnied as someone struggled to park. Then gradually the neighborhood fell silent. It would stay that way, Macon knew, till time for the one-o'clock group. He would first hear faint strands of their music and then more laughter, car doors slamming, house doors slamming. Porch lights would switch off all along the street, gradually dimming the ceiling as he watched. In the end, he would be the only one left awake.

20

—— The plane to New York was a little bird of a thing, but the plane to Paris was a monster, more like a building. Inside, great crowds were cramming coats and bags into overhead compartments, stuffing suitcases under seats, arguing, calling for stewardesses. Babies were crying and mothers were snapping at children. Steerage could not have been worse than this, Macon felt.

He took his place next to a window and was joined almost immediately by an elderly couple speaking French. The man sat next to Macon and gave him a deep, unsmiling nod. Then he said something to his wife, who passed him a canvas bag. He unzipped it and sorted through its contents. Playing cards, an entire tin of Band-aids, a stapler, a hammer, a light bulb . . . Macon was fascinated. He kept sliding his eyes to the right to try and see more. When a wooden mousetrap tumbled out, he began to wonder if the man might be some sort of lunatic; but of course even a mousetrap could be explained, given a little thought. Yes, what he was witnessing, Macon decided, was just one answer to the traveler's eternal choice: Which was better? Take all you own, and struggle to carry it? Or travel light, and spend half your trip combing the shops for what you've left behind? Either way had its drawbacks.

He glanced up the aisle, where more passengers were arriving. A Japanese man festooned with cameras, a nun, a young girl in braids. A woman with a little red vanity kit, her hair a dark tent, her face a thin triangle.

Muriel.

First he felt a kind of flush sweep through him—that flood of warmth that comes when someone familiar steps forth from a mass of strangers. And then: *Oh, my God*, he thought, and he actually looked around for some means of escape.

She walked toward him in a graceful, picky way, watching her feet, and then when she was next to him she raised her eyes and he saw that she'd known all along he was there. She wore a white suit that turned her into one of those black-white-and-red women he used to admire on movie screens as a child.

'I'm going to France,' she told him.

'But you can't!' he said.

The French couple peered at him curiously, the wife sitting slightly forward so as to see him better.

More passengers arrived behind Muriel. They muttered and craned around her, trying to edge past. She stood in the aisle and said, 'I'm going to walk along the Seine.'

The wife made a little O with her mouth.

Then Muriel noticed the people behind her and moved on.

Macon wasn't even sure it was possible to walk along the Seine.

As soon as the aisle was cleared he half stood and peered over the back of his seat, but she had vanished. The French couple turned to him, eyes expectant. Macon settled down again.

Sarah would find out about this. She would just somehow know. She had always said he had no feelings and this would confirm it— that he could tell her good-bye so fondly and then fly off to Paris with Muriel.

Well, it was none of his doing and he'd be damned if he'd assume the blame.

By the time it was dark they were airborne, and some kind of order had emerged inside the plane. It was one of those flights as fully programmed as a day in kindergarten. Safety film, drinks, headphones, dinner, movie. Macon turned down all he was offered and studied Julian's file folder instead. Most of the material was ridiculous. Sam'n'Joe's Hotel, indeed! He wondered if Julian had made it up to tease him.

A woman passed wearing white and he glanced at her surreptitiously, but it was no one he knew.

Just before the end of the movie, he got out his shaving kit and went to use one of the lavatories near the rear. Unfortunately other people had had the same idea. Both doors were locked, and he was forced to wait in the aisle. He felt someone arrive at his side. He looked and there was Muriel.

He said, 'Muriel, what in—'

'You don't own this plane!' she told him.

Heads turned.

'And you don't own Paris, either,' she said.

She was standing very close to him, face to face. She gave off a scent that barely eluded him; it was not just her perfume, no, but her house; yes, that was it—the smell inside her closet, the tantalizing, unsettling smell of other people's belongings. Macon pressed his left temple. He said, 'I don't understand any of this. I don't see how you knew which flight to take, even.'

'I called your travel agent.'

'Becky? You called Becky? What must she have thought?'

'She thought I was your editorial assistant.'

'And how could you afford the fare?'

'Oh, some I borrowed from Bernice and then some from my sister, she had this money she earned at . . . and I did everything economy-style, I took a train to New York instead of a plane—'

'Well, *that* wasn't smart,' Macon said. 'It probably cost you the same, in the long run, or maybe even more.'

'No, what I did was—'

'But the point is, why, Muriel? Why are you doing this?'

She lifted her chin. (Her chin could get so sharp, sometimes.) 'Because I felt like it,' she said.

'You felt like spending five days alone in a Paris hotel? That's what it will be, Muriel.'

'You need to have me around,' she said.

'Need you!'

'You were falling to pieces before you had me.'

A latch clicked and a man stepped out of one of the lavatories. Macon stepped inside and locked the door quickly behind him.

He wished he could just vanish. If there had been a window, he believed he would have pried it open and jumped—not because he wanted to commit any act so definite as suicide but because he wanted to erase it all; oh, Lord, just go back and erase all the untidy, unthinking things he'd been responsible for in his life.

If she had read even a one of his guidebooks, she'd have known not to travel in white.

When he emerged, she was gone. He went back to his seat. The French couple drew in their knees to let him slide past; they were transfixed by the movie screen, where a blonde wearing nothing but a bath towel was pounding on a front door. Macon got out *Miss MacIntosh* just for something to pin his mind to. It didn't work, though. Words flowed across his vision in a thin, transparent stream, meaningless. He was conscious only of Muriel somewhere behind him. He felt wired to her. He caught himself wondering what she made of this—the darkened plane, the invisible ocean beneath her, the murmur of half-real voices all around her. When he turned off his reading light and shut his eyes, he imagined he could sense that she was still awake. It was a feeling in the air— something alert, tense, almost vibrating.

By morning he was resolved. He used a different lavatory, toward the front. For once he was glad to be in such a large crowd. When they landed he was almost the first one off, and he cleared Immigration quickly and darted through the airport. The airport was Charles de Gaulle, with its space-age pods of seats. Muriel would be thoroughly lost. He exchanged his money in haste. Muriel must still be at Baggage Claims. He knew she would carry lots of baggage.

There was no question of waiting for a bus. He hailed a cab and sped off, feeling wonderfully lightweight all of a sudden. The tangle of silvery highways struck him as actually pleasant. The city of Paris, when he entered, was as wide and pale and luminous as a cool gray stare, and he admired the haze that hung over it. His cab raced down misty boulevards, turned onto a cobbled street, lurched to a stop. Macon sifted through his envelopes of money.

Not till he was entering his hotel did he recall that his travel agent knew exactly where he was staying.

It wasn't a very luxurious hotel—a small brown place where mechanical things tended to go wrong, as Macon had discovered on past visits. This time, according to a sign in the lobby, one of the two elevators was not marching. The bellman led him into the other, then up to the third floor and down a carpeted corridor. He flung open a door, loudly exclaiming in French as if overcome by such magnificence. (A bed, a bureau, a chair, an antique TV.) Macon burrowed into one of his envelopes. 'Thank you,' he said, offering his tip.

Once he was alone, he unpacked and he hung up his suit coat. Then he went to the window. He stood looking out over the rooftops; the dust on the glass made them seem removed in time, part of some other age.

How would she manage alone in such an unaccustomed place?

He thought of the way she navigated a row of thrift shops—the way she cruised a street, deft and purposeful, greeting passersby by name. And the errands she took the neighbors on: chauffeuring

Mr Manion to the reflexologist who dissolved his kidney stones by massaging his toes; Mr Runkle to the astrologer who told him when he'd win the million-dollar lottery; Mrs Carpaccio to a certain tiny grocery near Johns Hopkins where the sausages hung from the ceiling like strips of flypaper. The places Muriel knew!

But she didn't know Paris. And she was entirely on her own. She didn't even have a credit card, probably carried very little money, might not have known to change what she did carry into francs. Might be wandering helpless, penniless, unable to speak a word of the language.

By the time he heard her knock, he was so relieved that he rushed to open the door.

'Your room is bigger than mine is,' she said. She walked past him to the window. 'I have a better view, though. Just think, we're really in Paris! The bus driver said it might rain but I told him *I* didn't care. Rain or shine, it's Paris.'

'How did you know what bus to take?' he asked her.

'I brought along your guidebook.'

She patted her pocket.

'Want to go to Chez Billy for breakfast?' she asked. 'That's what your book recommends.'

'No, I don't. I can't,' he said. 'You'd better leave, Muriel.'

'Oh. Okay,' she said. She left.

Sometimes she would do that. She'd press in till he felt trapped, then suddenly draw back. It was like a tug of war where the other person all at once drops the rope, Macon thought. You fall flat on the ground; you're so unprepared. You're so empty-feeling.

*

He decided to call Sarah. At home it was barely dawn, but it seemed important to get in touch with her. He went over to the phone on the bureau and picked up the receiver. It was dead. He pressed the button a few times. Typical. He dropped his key in his pocket and went down to the lobby.

The lobby telephone was housed in an ancient wooden booth, very genteel. There was a red leather bench to sit on. Macon hunched over and listened to the ringing at the other end, far away. 'Hello?' Sarah said.

'Sarah?'

'Who is this?'

'It's Macon.'

'Macon?'

She took a moment to absorb that. 'Macon, where are you?' she asked. 'What's the matter?'

'Nothing's the matter. I just felt like talking to you.'

'What? What time is it?'

'I know it's early and I'm sorry I woke you but I wanted to hear your voice.'

'There's some kind of static on the line,' she said.

'It's clear at this end.'

'You sound so thin.'

'That's because it's an overseas call,' he said. 'How's the weather there?'

'How's who?'

'The weather! Is it sunny?'

'I don't know. All the shades are down. I don't think it's even light yet.'

'Will you be gardening today?'

'What?'

'Gardening!'

'Well, I hadn't thought. It depends on whether it's sunny, I guess.'

'I wish I were there,' he said. 'I could help you.'

'You hate to garden!'

'Yes, but . . .'

'Macon, are you all right?'

'Yes, I'm fine,' he said.

'How was the flight over?'

'Oh, the flight, well, goodness! Well, I don't know; I guess I was so busy reading I didn't really notice,' he said.

'Reading?' she said. Then she said, 'Maybe you've got jet lag.'

'Yes, maybe I do,' he told her.

Fried eggs, scrambled eggs, poached eggs, omelets. He walked blindly down the sidewalk, scribbling in the margins of his guidebook. He did not go near Chez Billy. *It's puzzling*, he wrote, *how the French are so tender in preparing their food but so rough in serving it*. In the window of a restaurant, a black cat closed her eyes at him. She seemed to be gloating. She was so much at home, so sure of her place.

Displays of crushed velvet, scattered with solid gold chains and watches no thicker than poker chips. Women dressed as if for the stage: elaborate hairdos, brilliant makeup, strangely shaped trousers that had nothing to do with the human anatomy. Old ladies in little-girl ruffles and white tights and Mary Janes. Macon descended the steps to the Métro; he ostentatiously dropped his canceled ticket into a tiny receptacle marked PAPIERS. Then he turned to glare at all the others who flung their tickets on the floor, and as he turned he thought he saw Muriel, her white face glimmering in the crowd, but he must have been mistaken.

In the evening he returned to his hotel—footsore, leg muscles aching—and collapsed on his bed. Not two minutes later he heard a knock. He groaned and rose to open the door. Muriel stood there with her arms full of clothes. 'Look,' she said, pushing past him. 'See what-all I bought.' She dumped the clothes on the bed. She held them up one by one: a shiny black cape, a pair of brown jodhpurs, a bouffant red net evening dress sprinkled with different-sized disks of glass like the reflectors on bicycles. 'Have you lost your senses?' Macon asked. 'What must all this have cost?'

'Nothing! Or next to nothing,' she said. 'I found a place that's like the granddaddy of all garage sales. A whole city of garage sales! This French girl was telling me about it where I went to have my breakfast. I complimented her hat and she told me where she got it. I took a subway train to find it; your book's really helpful about the subways; and sure enough, there's everything there. Tools and gadgets too, Macon. Old car batteries, fuse boxes . . . and if you say something's too expensive, they'll bring the price down till it's cheap enough. I saw this leather coat I would have killed for but that never did get cheap enough; the man wanted thirty-five francs.'

'Thirty-five francs!' Macon said. 'I don't know how you could get any cheaper than that. Thirty-five francs is four dollars or so.'

'Oh, really? I thought francs and dollars were about the same.'

'Lord, no.'

'Well, then these things were *super* bargains,' Muriel said. 'Maybe I'll try again tomorrow.'

'But how will you get all this stuff on the plane?'

'Oh, I'll figure out some way. Now let me take it back to my room so we can go eat.'

He stiffened. He said, 'No, I can't.'

'What harm would it do to eat supper with me, Macon? I'm someone from home! You've run into me in Paris! Can't we have a bite together?'

When she put it that way, it seemed so simple.

They went to the Burger King on the Champs-Elysées; Macon wanted to recheck the place anyhow. He ordered two 'Woppaires.' 'Careful,' he warned Muriel, 'these are not the Whoppers you're used to. You'll want to scrape the extra pickle and onion off.' But Muriel, after trying hers, said she liked it the way it was. She sat next to him on a hard little seat and licked her fingers. Her shoulder touched his. He was amazed, all at once, that she really was here.

'Who's looking after Alexander?' he asked her.

'Oh, different people.'

'What different people? I hope you haven't just parked him, Muriel. You know how insecure a child that age can—'

'Relax. He's fine. Claire has him in the daytime and then Bernice comes in and cooks supper and any time Claire has a date with the General the twins will keep him or if the twins can't do it then the General says Alexander can . . .'

Singleton Street rose up in front of Macon's eyes, all its color and confusion.

After supper Muriel suggested they take a walk, but Macon said he was tired. He was exhausted, in fact. They returned to their hotel. In the elevator Muriel asked, 'Can I come to your room a while? My TV set only gets snow.'

'We'd better say good night,' he told her.

'Can't I just come in and keep you company?'

'No, Muriel.'

'We wouldn't have to *do* anything,' she said.

The elevator stopped at his floor. He said, 'Muriel. Don't you understand my position? I've been married to her forever. Longer than you've been alive, almost. I can't change now. Don't you see?'

She just stood in her corner of the elevator with her eyes on his face. All her makeup had worn off and she looked young and sad and defenseless.

'Good night,' he said.

He got out, and the elevator door slid shut.

He went to bed immediately but couldn't sleep after all, and ended up switching on the TV. They were showing an American western, dubbed. Rangy cowboys spoke a fluid, intricate French. Disaster followed disaster—tornadoes, Indians, droughts, stampedes. The hero stuck in there, though. Macon had long ago noticed that all adventure movies had the same moral: Perseverance pays. Just once he'd like to see a hero like himself—not a quitter, but a man who did face facts and give up gracefully when pushing onward was foolish.

He rose and switched the set off again. He tossed and turned a long time before he slept.

*

Large hotels, small hotels, dingy hotels with their wallpaper flaking, streamlined hotels with king-sized American beds and Formica-topped American bureaus. Dim café windows with the proprietors displayed like mannequins, clasping their hands behind their backs and rocking from heel to toe. *Don't fall for* prix fixe. *It's like a mother saying, 'Eat, eat'—all those courses forced on you . . .*

In the late afternoon Macon headed wearily back to his own hotel. He was crossing the final intersection when he saw Muriel up ahead. Her arms were full of parcels, her hair was flying out, and her spike-heeled shoes were clipping along. 'Muriel!' he called. She turned and he ran to catch up with her.

'Oh, Macon, I've had the nicest day,' she said. 'I met these people from Dijon and we ended up eating lunch together and they told me about . . . Here, can you take some of these? I think I overbought.'

He accepted several of her parcels—crumpled, used-looking bags stuffed with fabrics. He helped her carry them into the hotel and up to her room, which seemed even smaller than it was because of the piles of clothing everywhere. She dumped her burdens on the bed and said, 'Let me show you, now, where is it . . .'

'What's this?' Macon asked. He was referring to an oddly shaped soft drink bottle on the bureau.

'Oh, I found that in the fridge,' she said. 'They have this little fridge in the bathroom, Macon, and it's just full of soft drinks, and wine and liquor too.'

'Muriel, don't you know those cost an arm and a leg? They'll put it on your bill, don't you know that? Now, that fridge is called a mini-bar, and here's what you use it for: In the morning, when they wheel in the continental breakfast, they bring a pitcher of hot milk for some strange reason and you just take that pitcher and stick it in the mini-bar so later you can have a glass of milk. Otherwise, Lord knows how you'd get your calcium in this country. And don't eat the rolls; you know that, don't you? Don't start your day with carbohydrates, especially under the strain of travel. You're better off taking the trouble to go to some café for eggs.'

'Eggs, ugh,' Muriel said. She was stepping out of her skirt and trying on another—one she'd just bought, with long fringes at the hem. 'I *like* the rolls,' she said. 'And I like the soft drinks, too.'

'Well, I don't know how you can say that,' he said. He picked up the bottle. 'Just look at the brand name: Pschitt. If that's not the most suspicious-sounding . . . and there's another kind called Yukkie, Yukkery, something like that—'

'That's my favorite. I already finished those off,' Muriel said. She was pinning her hair on top of her head. 'Where we having dinner tonight?'

'Well, I don't know. I guess it's time to try someplace fancy.'

'Oh, goody!'

He moved what appeared to be an antique satin bedjacket and sat down to watch her put her lipstick on.

They went to a restaurant lit with candles, although it wasn't quite dark yet, and were seated next to a tall, curtained window. The only other customers were American—four American business types, plainly enjoying themselves over four large platters of snails. (Sometimes Macon wondered if there really was any call for his books.)

'Now, what do I want?' Muriel said, studying the menu. 'If I ask them what something is in English, do you think they'll be able to tell me?'

'Oh, you don't have to bother doing that,' Macon said. 'Just order Salade Niçoise.'

'Order what?'

'I thought you said you'd read my guide! Salade Niçoise. It's the one safe dish. I've been all through France eating nothing but, day in and day out.'

'Well, that sounds kind of monotonous,' Muriel said.

'No, no. Some places put green beans in it, some don't. And at least it's low-cholesterol, which is more than you can say for—'

'I think I'll just ask the waiter,' Muriel told him. She laid her menu aside. 'Do you suppose they call them French windows in France?'

'What? I wouldn't have the slightest idea,' he said. He looked toward the window, which was paned with deep, greenish glass. Outside, in an overgrown courtyard, a pitted stone cherub was cavorting in a fountain.

The waiter spoke more English than Macon had expected. He directed Muriel toward a cream of sorrel soup and a special kind of fish. Macon decided to go for the soup as well, rather than sit idle while Muriel had hers. 'There,' Muriel said. 'Wasn't he nice?'

'That was a rare exception,' Macon said.

She batted at the hem of her skirt. 'Durn fringe! I keep thinking something's crawling up my leg,' she said. 'Where you going tomorrow, Macon?'

'Out of Paris altogether. Tomorrow I start on the other cities.'

'You're leaving me here alone?'

'This is high-speed travel, Muriel. Not fun. I'm waking up at crack of dawn.'

'Take me anyway.'

'I can't.'

'I haven't been sleeping so good,' she said. 'I get bad dreams.'

'Well, then you certainly don't want to go gallivanting off to more new places.'

'Last night I dreamed about Dominick,' she said. She leaned toward him across the table, two spots of color high on her cheekbones. 'I dreamed he was mad at me.'

'Mad?'

'He wouldn't talk to me. Wouldn't look at me. Kept kicking something on the sidewalk. Turned out he was mad because I wouldn't let him use the car anymore. I said, "Dommie, you're dead. You *can't* use the car. I'd let you if I could, believe me."'

'Well, don't worry about it,' Macon said. 'It was just a travel dream.'

'I'm scared it means he's mad for real. Off wherever he's at.'

'He's not,' Macon told her. 'He wouldn't be mad.'

'I'm scared he is.'

'He's happy as a lark.'

'You really think so?'

'Sure! He's up there in some kind of motor heaven, polishing a car all his own. And it's always spring and the sun is always shining and there's always some blonde in a halter top to help him with the buffing.'

'You really think that might be true?' Muriel asked.

'Yes, I do,' he said. And the funny thing was that he did, just at that moment. He had a vivid image of Dominick in a sunlit meadow, a chamois skin in his hand and a big, pleased, cocky grin on his face.

She said at the end of the evening that she wished he would come to her room—couldn't he? to guard against bad dreams?—and he said no and told her good night. And then he felt how she drew at him, pulling deep strings from inside him, when the elevator creaked away with her.

In his sleep he conceived a plan to take her along tomorrow. What harm would it do? It was only a day trip. Over and over in his scattered, fitful sleep he picked up his phone and dialed her room. It was a surprise, when he woke in the morning, to find he hadn't invited her yet.

He sat up and reached for the phone and remembered only then—with the numb receiver pressed to his ear—that the phone was out of order and he'd forgotten to report it. He wondered if it were something he could repair himself, a cord unplugged or something. He rose and peered behind the bureau. He stooped to hunt for a jack of some kind.

And his back went out.

No doubt about it—that little twang! in a muscle to the left of his spine. The pain was so sharp it snagged his breath. Then it faded. Maybe it was gone for good. He straightened, a minimal movement. But it was enough to bring the pain zinging in again.

He lowered himself to the bed inch by inch. The hard part was getting his feet up, but he set his face and accomplished that too. Then he lay pondering what to do next.

Once he had had this happen and the pain had vanished in five minutes and not returned. It had been only a freaky thing like a foot cramp.

But then, once he'd stayed flat in bed for two weeks and crept around like a very old man for another month after that.

He lay rearranging his agenda in his mind. If he canceled one trip, postponed another . . . Yes, possibly what he'd planned for the next three days could be squeezed into two instead, if only he were able to get around by tomorrow.

He must have gone back to sleep. He didn't know for how long. He woke to a knock and thought it was breakfast, though he'd left instructions for none to be brought today. But then he heard Muriel. 'Macon? You in there?' She was hoping he hadn't left Paris yet; she was here to beg again to go with him. He knew that as clearly as if she'd announced it. He was grateful now for the spasm that gripped him as he turned away from her voice. Somehow that short sleep had cleared his head, and he saw that he'd come perilously close to falling in with her again. *Falling in*: That was the way he put it to himself. What luck that his back had stopped him. Another minute—another few seconds—and he might have been lost.

He dropped into sleep so suddenly that he didn't even hear her walk away.

When he woke again it was much later, he felt, although he didn't want to go through the contortions necessary to look at his watch. A wheeled cart was passing his room and he heard voices—hotel employees, probably—laughing in the corridor. They must be so comfortable here; they must all know each other so well. There was a knock on his door, then a jingle of keys. A small, pale chambermaid poked her face in and said, '*Pardon, monsieur.*' She started to retreat but then stopped and asked him something in French, and he gestured toward his back and winced. 'Ah,' she said, entering, and she said something else very rapidly. (She would be telling him about *her* back.) He said, 'If you could just help me up, please,' for he had decided he had no choice but to go call Julian. She seemed to understand what he meant and came over to the bed. He turned onto his stomach and then struggled up on one arm—the only way he could manage to rise without excruciating pain. The chambermaid took his other arm and braced herself beneath his weight as he stood. She was much shorter than he, and pretty in a fragile, meek way. He was conscious of his unshaven face and his rumpled pajamas. 'My jacket,' he told her, and they proceeded haltingly to the chair where his suit jacket hung. She draped it around his shoulders. Then he said, 'Downstairs? To the telephone?' She looked over at the phone on the bureau, but he made a negative movement with the flat of his hand—a gesture that cost him. He grimaced. She clucked her tongue and led him out into the corridor.

Walking was not particularly difficult; he felt hardly a twinge. But the elevator jerked agonizingly and there was no way he could predict it. The chambermaid uttered soft sounds of sympathy. When they arrived in the lobby she led him to the telephone booth and started to seat him, but he said, 'No, no, standing's easier.

Thanks.' She backed out and left him there. He saw her talking to the clerk at the desk, shaking her head in pity; the clerk shook his head, too.

Macon worried Julian wouldn't be in his office yet, and he didn't know his home number. But the phone was answered on the very first ring. 'Businessman's Press.' A woman's voice, confusingly familiar, threading beneath the hiss of long distance.

'Um—' he said. 'This is Macon Leary. To whom am I—'

'Oh, Macon.'

'Rose?'

'Yes, it's me.'

'What are *you* doing there?'

'I work here now.'

'Oh, I see.'

'I'm putting things in order. You wouldn't believe the state this place is in.'

'Rose, my back has gone out on me,' Macon said.

'Oh, no, of all times! Are you still in Paris?'

'Yes, but I was just about to start my day trips and there are all these plans I have to change—appointments, travel reservations— and no telephone in my room. So I was wondering if Julian could do it from his end. Maybe he could get the reservations from Becky and—'

'I'll take care of it myself,' Rose said. 'Don't you bother with a thing.'

'I don't know when I'm going to get to the other cities, tell him. I don't have any idea when I'll be—'

'We'll work it out. Have you seen a doctor?'

'Doctors don't help. Just bed rest.'

'Well, rest then, Macon.'

He gave her the name of his hotel, and she repeated it briskly and then told him to get on back to bed.

When he emerged from the phone booth the chambermaid had a bellboy there to help him, and between the two of them he made it to his room without much trouble. They were very solicitous. They seemed anxious about leaving him alone, but he assured them he would be all right.

All that afternoon he lay in bed, rising twice to go to the bathroom and once to get some milk from the mini-bar. He wasn't really hungry. He watched the brown flowers on the wallpaper; he thought he had never known a hotel room so intimately. The side of the bureau next to the bed had a streak in the woodgrain that looked like a bony man in a hat.

At suppertime he took a small bottle of wine from the mini-bar and inched himself into the armchair to drink it. Even the motion of raising the bottle to his lips caused him pain, but he thought the wine would help him sleep. While he was sitting there the chambermaid knocked and let herself in. She asked him, evidently, whether he wanted anything to eat, but he thanked her and said no. She must have been on her way home; she carried a battered little pocketbook.

Later there was another knock, after he had dragged himself back to bed, and Muriel said, 'Macon? Macon?' He kept absolutely silent. She went away.

The air grew fuzzy and then dark. The man on the side of the bureau faded. Footsteps crossed the floor above him.

He had often wondered how many people died in hotels. The law of averages said some would, right? And some who had no close relatives—say one of his readers, a salesman without a family—well, what was done about such people? Was there some kind of potters' field for unknown travelers?

He could lie in only two positions—on his left side or on his back—and switching from one to the other meant waking up, consciously deciding to undertake the ordeal, plotting his strategy. Then he returned to a fretful semiconsciousness.

He dreamed he was seated on an airplane next to a woman dressed all in gray, a very narrow, starched, thin-lipped woman, and he tried to hold perfectly still because he sensed she disapproved of movement. It was a rule of hers; he knew that somehow. But he grew more and more uncomfortable, and so he decided to confront her. He said, 'Ma'am?' She turned her eyes on him, mild, mournful eyes under finely arched brows. 'Miss MacIntosh!' he said. He woke in a spasm of pain. He felt as if a tiny, cruel hand had snatched up part of his back and wrung it out.

When the waiter brought his breakfast in the morning, the chambermaid came along. She must keep grueling hours, Macon thought. But he was glad to see her. She and the waiter fussed over him, mixing his hot milk and coffee, and the waiter helped him into the bathroom while the chambermaid changed his sheets. He thanked them over and over; 'Merci,' he said, clumsily. He wished he knew the French for, 'I don't know why you're being so kind.' After they left he ate all of his rolls, which the chambermaid had thoughtfully buttered and spread with strawberry jam. Then he turned on the TV for company and got back in bed.

He was sorry about the TV when he heard the knock on the door, because he thought it was Muriel and she would hear. But it seemed early for Muriel to be awake. And then a key turned in the lock, and in walked Sarah.

He said, 'Sarah?'

She wore a beige suit, and she carried two pieces of matched luggage, and she brought a kind of breeze of efficiency with her. 'Now, everything's taken care of,' she told him. 'I'm going to make your day trips for you.' She set down her suitcases, kissed his forehead, and picked up a glass from his breakfast table. As she went off to the bathroom she said, 'We've rescheduled the other cities and I start on them tomorrow.'

'But how did you get here so soon?' he asked.

She came out of the bathroom; the glass was full of water. 'You have Rose to thank for that,' she said, switching off the TV. 'Rose is just a wizard. She's revamped that entire office. Here's a pill from Dr Levitt.'

'You know I don't take pills,' he said.

'This time you do,' she told him. She helped him rise up on one elbow. 'You're going to sleep as much as you can, so your back has a chance to heal. Swallow.'

The pill was tiny and very bitter. He could taste it even after he'd lain down again.

'Is the pain bad?' she asked him.

'Kind of.'

'How've you been getting your meals?'

'Well, breakfast comes anyway, of course. That's about it.'

'I'll ask about room service,' she told him, picking up the phone. 'Since I'll be gone so . . . What's the matter with the telephone?'

'It's dead.'

'I'll go tell the desk. Can I bring you anything while I'm out?'

'No, thank you.'

When she left, he almost wondered if he'd imagined her. Except that her suitcases sat next to his bed, sleek and creamy—the same ones she kept on the closet shelf at home.

He thought about Muriel, about what would happen if she were to knock now. Then he thought about two nights ago, or was it three, when she had strolled in with all her purchases. He wondered if she'd left any traces. A belt lost under the bed, a glass disk fallen off her cocktail dress? He began to worry about it seriously. It seemed to him almost inevitable; of course she'd left something. The only question was, what. And where.

Groaning, he rolled over and pushed himself upright. He struggled off the bed and then sagged to his knees to peer beneath it. There didn't seem to be anything there. He got to his feet and tilted over the armchair to feel around the edges of the cushion. Nothing there either. Actually she hadn't gone anywhere near the armchair, to his recollection; nor had she gone to the bureau, but even so he slid out the drawers one by one to make sure. His own belongings—just a handful—occupied one drawer. The others were empty, but the second one down had a sprinkling of pink face powder. It wasn't Muriel's, of course, but it looked like hers. He decided to get rid of it. He tottered into the bathroom, dampened a towel, and came back to swab the drawer clean. Then he saw that the towel had developed a large pink smear, as if a woman wearing too much makeup had wiped her face with it. He folded the towel so the smear was concealed and laid it in the back of the drawer. No, too incriminating. He took it out again and hid it beneath the armchair cushion. That didn't seem right either. Finally he went into the bathroom and washed the towel by hand, scrubbing it with a bar of soap till the spot was completely gone. The pain in his back was constant, and beads of sweat stood out on his forehead. At some point he decided he was acting very peculiar; in fact it must be the pill; and he dropped the wet towel in a heap on the floor and crawled back into bed. He fell asleep at once. It wasn't a normal sleep; it was a kind of burial.

He knew Sarah came in but he couldn't wake up to greet her. And he knew she left again. He heard someone knock, he heard lunch being brought, he heard the chambermaid whisper, '*Monsieur?*' He remained in his stupor. The pain was muffled but still present—just covered up, he thought; the pill worked like those inferior room sprays in advertisements, the ones that only mask offending odors. Then Sarah came back for the second time and he opened his eyes. She was standing over the bed with a glass of water. 'How do you feel?' she asked him.

'Okay,' he said.

'Here's your next pill.'

'Sarah, those things are deadly.'

'They help, don't they?'

'They knock me out,' he said. But he took the pill.

She sat down on the edge of the mattress, careful not to jar him. She still wore her suit and looked freshly groomed, although she must be bushed by now. 'Macon,' she said quietly.

'Hmm.'

'I saw that woman friend of yours.'

He tensed. His back seized up.

'She saw me, too,' she said. 'She seemed very surprised.'

'Sarah, this is not the way it looks,' he told her.

'What is it then, Macon? I'd like to hear.'

'She came over on her own. I didn't even know till just before the plane took off, I swear it! She followed me. I told her I didn't want her along. I told her it was no use.'

She kept looking at him. 'You didn't know till just before the plane took off,' she said.

'I swear it,' he said.

He wished he hadn't taken the pill. He felt he wasn't in full possession of his faculties.

'Do you believe me?' he asked her.

'Yes, I believe you,' she said, and then she got up and started uncovering his lunch dishes.

He spent the afternoon in another stupor, but he was aware of the chambermaid's checking on him twice, and he was almost fully awake when Sarah came in with a bag of groceries. 'I thought I'd make you supper myself,' she told him. 'Fresh fruit and things; you always complain you don't get enough fresh fruit when you travel.'

'That's very nice of you, Sarah.'

He worked himself around till he was half sitting, propped against a pillow. Sarah was unwrapping cheeses. 'The phone's fixed,' she said. 'You'll be able to call for your meals and all while

I'm out. Then I was thinking: After I've finished the trips, if your back is better, maybe we could do a little sightseeing on our own. Take some time for ourselves, since we're here. Visit a few museums and such.'

'Fine,' he said.

'Have a second honeymoon, sort of.'

'Wonderful.'

He watched her set the cheeses on a flattened paper bag. 'We'll change your plane ticket for a later date,' she said. 'You're reserved to leave tomorrow morning; no chance you could manage that. I left my own ticket open-ended. Julian said I should. Did I tell you where Julian is living?'

'No, where?'

'He's moved in with Rose and your brothers.'

'He's what?'

'I took Edward over to Rose's to stay while I was gone, and there was Julian. He sleeps in Rose's bedroom; he's started playing Vaccination every night after supper.'

'Well, I'll be damned,' Macon said.

'Have some cheese.'

He accepted a slice, changing position as little as possible.

'Funny, sometimes Rose reminds me of a flounder,' Sarah said. 'Not in looks, of course . . . She's lain on the ocean floor so long, one eye has moved to the other side of her head.'

He stopped chewing and stared at her. She was pouring two glasses of cloudy brown liquid. 'Apple cider,' she told him. 'I figured you shouldn't drink wine with those pills.'

'Oh. Right,' he said.

She passed him a glass. 'A toast to our second honeymoon,' she said.

'Our second honeymoon,' he echoed.

'Twenty-one more years together.'

'Twenty-one!' he said. It sounded like such a lot.

'Or would you say twenty.'

'No, it's twenty-one, all right. We were married in nineteen—'

'I mean because we skipped this past year.'

'Oh,' he said. 'No, it would still be twenty-one.'

'You think so?'

'I consider last year just another stage in our marriage,' he said. 'Don't worry: It's twenty-one.'

She clinked her glass against his.

Their main dish was a potted meat that she spread on French bread, and their dessert was fruit. She washed the fruit in the bathroom, returning with handfuls of peaches and strawberries; and meanwhile she kept up a cozy patter that made him feel he was home again. 'Did I mention we had a letter from the Averys? They might be passing through Baltimore later this summer. Oh, and the termite man came.'

'Ah.'

'He couldn't find anything wrong, he said.'

'Well, that's a relief.'

'And I've almost finished my sculpture and Mr Armistead says it's the best thing I've done.'

'Good for you,' Macon said.

'Oh,' she said, folding the last paper bag, 'I know you don't think my sculptures are important, but—'

'Who says I don't?' he asked.

'I know you think I'm just this middle-aged lady playing artist—'

'Who says?'

'Oh, I know what you think! You don't have to pretend with me.'

Macon started to slump against his pillow, but was brought up short by a muscle spasm.

She cut a peach into sections, and then she sat on the bed and passed him one of the sections. She said, 'Macon. Just tell me this. Was the little boy the attraction?'

'Huh?'

'Was the fact that she had a child what attracted you to that woman?'

He said, 'Sarah, I swear to you, I had no idea she was planning to follow me over here.'

'Yes, I realize that,' she said, 'but I was wondering about the child question.'

'What child question?'

'I was remembering the time you said we should have another baby.'

'Oh, well, that was just . . . I don't know what that was,' he said. He handed her back the peach; he wasn't hungry anymore.

'I was thinking maybe you were right,' Sarah said.

'What? No, Sarah; Lord, that was a terrible idea.'

'Oh, I know it's scary,' she told him. 'I admit I'd be scared to have another.'

'Exactly,' Macon said. 'We're too old.'

'No, I'm talking about the, you know, world we'd be bringing him into. So much evil and danger. I admit it: I'd be frantic any time we let him out on the street.'

Macon saw Singleton Street in his mind, small and distant like Julian's little green map of Hawaii and full of gaily drawn people scrubbing their stoops, tinkering with their cars, splashing under fire hydrants.

'Oh, well, you're right,' he said. 'Though really it's kind of . . . heartening, isn't it? How most human beings do try. How they try to be as responsible and kind as they can manage.'

'Are you saying yes, we can have a baby?' Sarah asked.

Macon swallowed. He said, 'Well, no. It seems to me we're past the time for that, Sarah.'

'So,' she said, 'her little boy wasn't the reason.'

'Look, it's over with. Can't we close the lid on it? I don't cross-examine *you*, do I?'

'But I don't have someone following me to Paris!' she said.

'And what if you did? Do you think I'd hold you to blame if someone just climbed on a plane without your knowing?'

'Before it left the ground,' she said.

'Pardon? Well, I should hope so!'

'Before it left the ground, you saw her. You could have walked up to her and said, "No. Get off. Go this minute. I want nothing more to do with you and I never want to see you again." '

'You think I own the airline, Sarah?'

'You could have stopped her if you'd really wanted,' Sarah said. 'You could have taken steps.'

And then she rose and began to clear away their supper.

*

She gave him his next pill, but he let it stay in his fist a while because he didn't want to risk moving. He lay with his eyes closed, listening to Sarah undress. She ran water in the bathroom, slipped the chain on the door, turned off the lights. When she got into bed it stabbed his back, even though she settled carefully, but he gave no sign. He heard her breathing soften almost at once. She must have been exhausted.

He reflected that he had not taken steps very often in his life, come to think of it. Really never. His marriage, his two jobs, his time with Muriel, his return to Sarah—all seemed to have simply befallen him. He couldn't think of a single major act he had managed of his own accord.

Was it too late now to begin?

Was there any way he could learn to do things differently?

He opened his hand and let the pill fall among the bedclothes. It was going to be a restless, uncomfortable night, but anything was better than floating off on that stupor again.

In the morning, he negotiated the journey out of bed and into the bathroom. He shaved and dressed, spending long minutes on each task. Creeping around laboriously, he packed his bag. The heaviest thing he packed was *Miss MacIntosh, My Darling*, and after thinking that over a while, he took it out again and set it on the bureau.

Sarah said, 'Macon?'

'Sarah. I'm glad you're awake,' he said.

'What are you doing?'

'I'm packing to leave.'

She sat up. Her face was creased down one side.

'But what about your back?' she asked. 'And I've got all those appointments! And we were going to take a second honeymoon!'

'Sweetheart,' he said. He lowered himself cautiously till he was sitting on the bed. He picked up her hand. It stayed lifeless while she watched his face.

'You're going back to that woman,' she said.

'Yes, I am,' he said.

'Why, Macon?'

'I just decided, Sarah. I thought about it most of last night. It wasn't easy. It's not the easy way out, believe me.'

She sat staring at him. She wore no expression.

'Well, I don't want to miss the plane,' he said.

He inched to a standing position and hobbled into the bathroom for his shaving kit.

'You know what this is? It's all due to that pill!' Sarah called after him. 'You said yourself it knocks you out!'

'I didn't take the pill.'

There was a silence.

She said, 'Macon? Are you just trying to get even with me for the time I left you?'

He returned with the shaving kit and said, 'No, sweetheart.'

'I suppose you realize what your life is going to be like,' she said. She climbed out of bed. She stood next to him in her nightgown, hugging her bare arms. 'You'll be one of those mismatched couples no one invites to parties. No one will know what to make of you. People will wonder whenever they meet you, "My God, what does he see in her? Why choose someone so inappropriate? It's grotesque, how does he put up with her?" And her friends will no doubt be asking the same about you.'

'That's probably true,' Macon said. He felt a mild stirring of interest; he saw now how such couples evolved. They were not, as he'd always supposed, the result of some ludicrous lack of perception, but had come together for reasons that the rest of the world would never guess.

He zipped his overnight bag.

'I'm sorry, Sarah. I didn't want to decide this,' he said.

He put his arm around her painfully, and after a pause she let her head rest against his shoulder. It struck him that even this moment was just another stage in their marriage. There would probably be still other stages in their thirtieth year, fortieth year—forever, no matter what separate paths they chose to travel.

He didn't take the elevator; he felt he couldn't bear the willy-nilliness of it. He went down the stairs instead. He managed the front door by backing through it, stiffly.

Out on the street he found the usual bustle of a weekday morning—shopgirls hurrying past, men with briefcases. No taxis in sight. He set off for the next block, where his chances were better. Walking was fairly easy but carrying his bag was torture. Lightweight though it was, it twisted his back out of line. He tried it in his left hand, then his right. And after all, what was inside it? Pajamas, a change of underwear, emergency supplies he never used . . . He stepped over to a building, a bank or office building with a low stone curb running around its base. He set the bag on the curb and hurried on.

Up ahead he saw a taxi with a boy just stepping out of it, but he discovered too late that hailing it was going to be a problem. Raising either arm was impossible. So he was forced to run in an absurd, scuttling fashion while shouting bits of French he'd never said aloud before: '*Attendez! Attendez, monsieur!*'

The taxi was already moving off and the boy was just slipping his wallet back into his jeans, but then he looked up and saw Macon. He acted fast; he spun and called out something and the taxi braked. '*Merci beaucoup*,' Macon panted, and the boy, who had a sweet, pure face and shaggy yellow hair, opened the taxi door for him and gently assisted him in. 'Oof!' Macon said, seized by a spasm. The boy shut the door and then, to Macon's surprise, lifted a hand in a formal good-bye. The taxi moved off. Macon told the driver where he was going and sank back into his seat. He patted his inside pocket, checking passport, plane ticket. He unfolded his handkerchief and wiped his forehead.

Evidently his sense of direction had failed him, as usual. The driver was making a U-turn, heading back where Macon had just come from. They passed the boy once again. He had a jaunty, stiff-legged way of walking that seemed familiar.

If Ethan hadn't died, Macon thought, wouldn't he have grown into such a person?

He would have turned to give the boy another look, except that he couldn't manage the movement.

The taxi bounced over the cobblestones. The driver whistled a tune between his teeth. Macon found that bracing himself on one arm protected his back somewhat from the jolts. Every now and then, though, a pothole caught him off guard.

And if dead people aged, wouldn't it be a comfort? To think of Ethan growing up in heaven—fourteen years old now instead of twelve—eased the grief a little. Oh, it was their immunity to time that made the dead so heartbreaking. (Look at the husband who dies young, the wife aging on without him; how sad to imagine the husband coming back to find her so changed.) Macon gazed out the cab window, considering the notion in his mind. He felt a kind of inner rush, a racing forward. The real adventure, he thought, is the flow of time; it's as much adventure as anyone could wish. And if he pictured Ethan still part of that flow—in some other place, however unreachable—he believed he might be able to bear it after all.

The taxi passed Macon's hotel—brown and tidy, strangely homelike. A man was just emerging with a small anxious dog on his arm. And there on the curb stood Muriel, surrounded by suitcases and string-handled shopping bags and cardboard cartons overflowing with red velvet. She was frantically waving down taxis—first one ahead, then Macon's own. '*Arrêtez!*' Macon cried to the driver. The taxi lurched to a halt. A sudden flash of sunlight hit the windshield, and spangles flew across the glass. The spangles were old water spots, or maybe the markings of leaves, but for a moment Macon thought they were something else. They were so bright and festive, for a moment he thought they were confetti.